AND THE DEAD SHALL RISE

AND THE DEAD SHALL RISE

A NOVEL BY

M. FREDERIC JENNINGS

Donnalnk Publications, L.L.C. 2015
Registered offices: 129 Daisy Hill, Carthage, NC 28327, United States
(888) 564-7741 (office) | (703) 373-9552 (fax)
www.donnaink.com

Donnalnk Publications, L.L.C. Editors: Mr. Quante Bryan, Mr. Philip Bartholomew, Ms. Shelby Catalano; ZenCon an Art of Zen Consultancy Interior Layout and Cover Designer, Ms. Dana Queen.

Synopsis: "Can Udo sent back to Earth in his, perfected superhuman heavenly form, make it to his family before the King of Evil does? More importantly, are there much greater prizes at stake? It soon becomes apparent God and Jesus are in on this project too. Although the quake was an extinction level event . . . can a remnant of humans survive and possibly carry on?" . . . from the back cover.

PUBLISHER'S NOTE

12 11 10 9 8 7 6 5 4 3 2 1

THE LIBRARY OF CONGRESS HAS CATALOGUED THIS TITLE AS FOLLOWS:

Library of Congress Cataloging-in-Publication Data

Jennings, M. Frederic – Author, 2015.

And the Dead Shall Rise, M. Frederic Jennings

338 p. cm.

ISBN – 13 – 978-1-939425-61-4 (alk. paper); 978-1-939425-62-1 (alk. digital)

[1) Literature-Fiction, 2) Horror-Fiction, 3) Fantasy-Fiction, 4) Dark-Fiction, 5) Monster-Fiction, 6) Speculative-Fiction, 7) Thriller-Fiction, 8) Religious-Fiction, 9) Revelation-Fiction, 10) Visceral-Fiction; 11) Armaggedon-Fiction, 12) California Authors-Fiction, 13) United States-Authors].

TABLE OF CONTENTS

TABLE OF CONTENTS

FOREWORD

So there I was, sitting at my laptop, while also watching the latest episode of The Walking Dead on TV, trying to figure out what to write my latest novel about. I needed something real catchy, I'd been thinking more and more. I was having just the worst time getting published. My batting average in the literary league was a big fat zero, but all I needed was just one hit. I grabbed the rosin rag and rubbed it on the handle of my bat.

I'd taken my swings before. One publisher had even taken me halfway through their back and forth editing process before completely folding as both a publisher and a company. R.I.P. I guess. Not too much sympathy from here. I've died several times too on the treacherous road to professional authordom, including that one they had just inflicted me with right then. So R.I.P. and pass the rum, maybe more like it.

But then trying again, which has always been a strong suit of mine. Not that I never give up. But if I really want something , and then even too have God on my side—the genesis of which you can read about on the back cover—well, since then it's been almost impossible to stop writing. Ever since the Holy Spirit came and got me, my imagination has been a nonstop movie making machine. Although unfortunately, it would seem, the movies ending up either too strange or stupid or gory or religious or whatever, and like I said:

A big fat zero.

So there I was. And so were the zombies. And I don't know if you've ever watched that show, "The Walking Dead," but they've taken the genre to a whole new level. The production, the acting and the storytelling is, in my opinion, par excellence, or however you spell that French stuff. But the point being, there I was trying to decide what to write my next novel about, taking in that great show, when . . . BINGO!

Zombies!

They sure are catchy these days, I couldn't help but realize. They even have a hit TV show! So zombies then, I figured and dumped a whole basketful of them into the movie making machine in my mind. But of course then too, and as usual these days, Jesus and Satan and their angels and demons jumped in too, followed by some monsters and even some humans as well. You can read what followed in the rest of this book if you want. Hopefully you'll find it as entertaining as the show, "The Walking Dead." I know without that show I probably never would have written this book, and hopefully too, just like that show, my book will, 'catch,' on, and my quest for professional authordom can come to a happy conclusion.

Thank you for all your help,

The author.

ACKNOWLEDGEMENT

When you are at the stage of your career that I am, unless you are really lucky, acknowledgments of those who assisted you in the creation of your novel may be few and far between. But at least and of course I have to thank my wife. If for nothing more, and she does so much, but in aid to my writing she has always allowed me the necessary space to do so. Meaning really of course the time spent behind a laptop and not doing things with her that it takes to write a book. That much space, which is actually quite a lot. I'm sure behind every writer whoever gets to do it enough to become successful, there is a helpmate. An indispensable life partner, in this case my wife, who understands when the writer goes away they'll come back sooner or later, and hopefully with a good story to tell, and sell, all about where they've been. Here's to that day hopefully coming soon, my darling. I love you.

DEDICATION

For my Father. A writer of great beauty and truth, and in whose honor and name I will persevere until I am the same.

AND THE DEAD SHALL RISE

EPIGRAPH

"The world is filled with dead people."

A not-so-eminent geologist.

PROLOGUE

God created our world as a ball of roiling water, filled it with more life than imaginable, ordered it and then had to watch its unspeakable corruption. So he turned it all back into a ball of roiling water and tried again, only to achieve the same result. Why not then, one could suppose He might figure, give it such a shaking as to destroy all superficial structure and almost all life?

So He tried that this time, and what would happen He was perfectly content to wonder with his feet up in warm slippers and just beyond them all of it happening as if on a huge flat-screen television. He dipped his large hand into the even larger bowl of popcorn right next to Him.

He ate with a slight smile.

As usual, He had a plan.

Or, maybe make that, Plan B.

CHAPTER I

ULTIMATE POWER SESSION

The lettering on the door read, Universal Laboratories Inc. Behind it, in the seemingly walless room, two beings were visibly present. One of them of average height, medium to strong build, long hair and closely trimmed beard, looking as well to be of Middle Eastern descent and dressed neatly in shirt and tie, dark slacks and dress shoes under a freshly pressed lab coat. The other was notice-ably larger, probably stronger, though that might be hard to assuredly ascertain as this one wore a goldentoned, decontamination suit complete with head covering.

"Dad? Is that get up really necessary?"

"Yes. You know it would be fatal for the precious things to be so near to me in their current form without this suit on."

"Oh . . . yes. I suppose. And I can hear you fine. It obviously won't hamper our communication in any way."

"Which I would like to continue with if we could."

"Of course, father." The young man ever so slightly bowed to his father.

The room was mostly dark, except for that portion shared by the two beings which was spotlighted somehow. As the two walked casually along, a newly and very strategically lighted section of the ever growing laboratory was soon displayed. It held head-high, chromium racks, sporting row after row of test tubes, larger than normal at about a foot in length. Each glass cylinder held a liquid that looked like colored light. The unusually beautiful fluid swirled and continually changed color inside. It was almost kaleidoscopic. The racks stretched far back into the darkness, further than the eye could see.

"They are beautiful," the deep and strong voice from inside the decon suit said. The voice of the father. "And they are yours, I am assuming."

"Yes. Well . . . some of them. Judgment yet to come. All will be revealed and, of course, I will be as merciful as I can."

"Yes. Your mercy is monumental. If it were up to me . . ."

"And where's the fun in that."

"Fun?"

"Heaven would be an even lonelier place without mercy, and you know it, father."

"Which is why I made you," the father mumbled while gently returning one of the colorful tubes to its spot on the rack.

"What was that, father?"

"Nothing," He answered.

The two continued on. The tubes returned into hiding in the darkness and next the entire area they headed into lit up with life. For all intents and purposes, they now seemed to be standing on an exquisitely carved, all marble patio and parapet overlooking a beautiful and lushly vegetated valley below. It was filled with more marble structures, buildings, and even amphitheaters of varying size and shape. All of it was connected by pristine walkways and adorned by all manner of gorgeous flowers, bushes and trees.

The most striking thing to be seen, however, were the people populating the area. They were perfect and beautiful, muscularly toned bodies evident beneath toga style garments. Even more noticeable was how they were flying from point A to point B with incredible ease. They seemed to just have to run and hop and off they went, up, up and away.

"And, speaking of which, the numbers here at home are drastically low. What are the latest calculations?"

"Twelve percent. Give or take," the young man in the lab coat read off of a computerized tablet device. "And, though they all greatly love us, which was what it was all about in the first place, that number is just unacceptable. Un . . . ac . . . ceptable."

The paradise-like environment succumbed next to the darkness and the two continued on across more blue tiles. The decon suited one spoke again. "So you want to initiate, 'Operation . . .' what do you call it again?"

"Shake it up!" the young man answered with audible enthusiasm, as if he were singing the opening line to a popular rock song. The whole time he had held an air of barely contained joy and excitement. "Operation Shake It Up!"

"Of course, my advisors will fill me in on the details soon enough. But you go ahead and sell it, son. I want to hear it from you first, of course."

"H.S.," the young man said up toward the still invisible ceiling as if talking to someone there.

Suddenly this newest area of the lab lighted up again, just more dimly now. In the area with a slightly lighter darkness just ahead of the two of them, as if approaching from the distance in the back of a very large room, a planet approached. At first it was about the size of a volleyball. It grew gradually as it came nearer. Soon it was easily discernable to be an amazingly detailed and realistic version of the Earth. It hung, and again for all intents and purposes, served as a rotating reality in midair right before the two beings. It was now about the size of a small car.

The three dimensional, holographic creation bore no static interruption, nor the color loss or distortion manmade attempts at holograms seem to always have. Active weather systems even coursed around its wide equatorial plane and were one to look close enough cities and their occupants, waves breaking on stony or sandy shores, snow or rain falling, fog forming, traffic coursing, or any other exact detail of that which was actually happening on planet Earth would have been observable.

"First, and suddenly . . ." the Middle Eastern young man began narrating, looking solemn for the first time. "On October twenty-first, at or near three a.m., an earthquake of incredible magnitude and duration will crack and tear and completely rearrange our once greatest creation." As if on cue the Earth model did exactly as he said, shaking with terrific tremor all throughout.

Next, a new and even more interesting capability of the presentation made itself apparent as sections of the globe became more easily visible at much greater magnification in 50" screens, that might have been attached to TVs in our world, but here needed no means of creating an image and hung invisibly somehow, just curved glass panels suspended in thin air and bordering the planet, three on each side in a stacked fashion.

"The sum total of which will be the nearly complete extinction of our children," the lab suited one continued. "The destruction of everything they have built, as well as topographical restructuring of their home planet on a monumental scale."

Again, only this time more closely on the six screens, the earthquake and its immediate aftereffects, were displayed in scene after scene. Also again, all of it appearing pretty much as described by the young man. "Unfortunate. In fact tragic. But it has to happen, one way or the other. 'No one there gets out alive,' as I believe one of their spokesman put it." The father mused. "But knowing you my son, I'm sure their deaths will be merciful."

"To all who deserve mercy, mercy will be given," the young man answered, for the first time also reflecting seriousness in both tone and manner. He thought for a moment, then resumed. "Father, for our purposes the humans can be grouped in four classes. First are those who came to know me while alive, my dedicated and obedient servants, who, of course, are also those, who if they have not already ascended to us in perfected form, soon will be.

"Second are those, like the souls we just examined, who were unable to do that in their earthly life, and their lives exhibit this as well. They are basically decent and good, and judgment may yet find them deserving of a heavenly home with us."

The elder one shifted his large frame nervously about. "Once again my son, you are pushing the boundaries."

"Well, perhaps from these . . . that number which you find unacceptable may be brought up to an acceptable level. Especially after "Operation Shake It Up.""

"All right . . . all right. I think I see where this is headed. But go ahead and finish."

"Well, then there are the other two types of humans who have time and time again turned to him."

"Oh . . . him."

"Yes . . . him. And though I will make certain to destroy them all in this operation, at least in their earthly form, their spirits will still be trapped, awaiting his return."

"Yes. They wait and wait. So sad. Trying to delay their judgment."

"The fourth type," the young man immediately resumed with, not wanting to let his father dwell on the always disappointing and frustrating topic of the damned. "The fourth and final type are those survivors of the operation, a very few handpicked and located in a select area, all made necessary by the parameters of the operation, which will be rigorously enforced, both by my own actions, and his."

"If he only knew how much he actually helps us . . ."

"Then he'd really be angry."

"Yes. Well. So all right then. This little operation of yours begins to intrigue me. You have always been so creative my son. Tell me more. Tell me more," the now and apparently highly interested, decon suited one said and placed a large hand on his son's shoulder.

As the two continued their discussion, the Holy Spirit continued to assist with many more incredible and wonderful instructional aides like those already exhibited. Outside the laboratory door, which once outside of it was all that could be seen of the facility, a door seemingly to nowhere suspended in space, but still flashes of light and the excited exclamations of the two super beings inside could be heard.

Beyond and surrounding all that, space stretched out cold and star flecked, while not all that farther below, relatively speaking at least, a worldwide lightning and thunder storm of unprecedented proportion encircled planet Earth. Like an electric blanket all wet, it pumped the old globe with more energy than it could ever possibly be expected to handle, as well as electrically obliterating every plane in the air, grounding all flights locally and internationally. This emergency measure would be enforced for 24 hours per International Air protocol in the event of cataclysmic acts of God.

Exactly.

As things usually happened in the heavenly realms, they had commenced without haste, or waste. *Operation Shake It Up* was entering preliminary stages.

CHAPTER II

THE STAGE

The first most noticeable things to appear right after the planet killing quake were the spirits, or ghosts, if you like, seeping out through the cracks, fissures, gullies, canyons and caves. They then floated up to join those who were already out and hovering wraith-like over the land.

Their faces—the only humanoid aspect of the otherwise amorphous but vaguely human-sized apparitions—confirmed the lost, confused and frightened state their quickly flitting about also belied. As of yet, they had not been able to, "go into the light."

All of them were, of course, invisible to the human eye. But they weren't invisible, unfortunately for them, to the eyes of the super-humans, the fallen angels who until then had been trapped far underground but now had been unleashed by the quake as well. The ever ready and able-bodied servants of their leader who was arguably the second most powerful spiritual force in the universe, otherwise known as Lucifer—were more than any eye, human or otherwise could number. They blackened the sky like a huge flock of carrion, with their high horned, big black winged bodies, twice the size of most men.

Also like carnivorous bird of prey, they flew low over the land, swooping down to devour lost souls with their great, fang-filled maws; unable then to not scream with the delight the exercise brought to them. Even their calls were reminiscent of crows, but huge and mad ones, a laugh sometimes audible beneath their low toned and sky grating peal. Finishing off then their first mission for their dark lord, they delivered the spirits intact and whole to the metallic mountains he had already made to store them in. That is, until such a time as they may be used later.

The next most notable beings to enter the scene were the living again dead ones, the zombies, as they are more commonly called. They dug and climbed their way up out of the ground however they could, wherever the quake had killed them.

They'd been revived in the earliest stages of decomposition by and to serve their master, the same as the demons, yeah him, in a manner yet to be more fully exhibited. For now, they simply followed that most basic human drive, the one to consume and survive, to eat and to live in their own sick and twisted way.

Finally, at least for now, and perhaps most importantly—which was what had started all the trouble in the first place were the living and somehow still surviving humans. Having found their way back to conscious breath, motion and sensual intake, and in a fairly localized geographical area where they had to be for reasons soon to be discussed, they continued their own struggle to survive.

CHAPTER III

THE GOOD

Udo Henkman was thinking probably for sure he was dead. Either that or something real close to it. Because all of a sudden there was just blackness and silence everywhere. It was as if someone had turned out all the lights, and that someone also then being the last one out of the building.

Then too it even felt as if the building must be buried deep underground. It was so completely quiet. Like time had stopped completely still. What the heck time is it, by the way, he had to wonder. He felt as if he'd been asleep forever. Could he even move? He realized then he couldn't tell. He couldn't feel anything either.

So, in review . . .

Total blackness . . . complete silence . . . deep underground . . .

Asleep forever . . . yeah, most likely . . .

Dead.

Dead dead and buried beneath, deeply in the deepest of the deep.

It was weird though, Udo realized then, it was weird how he still had mental awareness somehow. He still seemed able to think. Or at least he thought he could think. So that meant he was thinking, right? Because otherwise how had he been able to figure out he was dead? So that was good news anyway. Thinking was important! Thank goodness he could do that much, at least.

Except for when he tried to remember anything and nothing came to him. He couldn't remember *anything* from before, from when he must have still been alive. Even when he tried really hard, all that came to him was the sudden and shock-like explosion of an incredibly bright flash of light. This had happened at the same moment as the sudden and all encompassing concussion from the huge and body wide impact that not only knocked the crap out of him, but knocked him out too. Which of course then also knocked the life out of him as well. Or must have. Since he was dead like he was.

But that was it. That was all he could remember. So he busied his thinking instead with wondering about what he was now. Was he just a consciousness floating around somewhere? A consciousness floating around in the middle of a big bunch of . . . nothingness?

The deceased appliance repairman might have puzzled over these matters a bit longer, but then the review started. Of course, he'd heard of all that before . . . how one's life would flash before their very eyes when they died. A *life* review, they called it, he remembered. And sure enough, here came his. Luckily, and although he probably didn't even have any eyes anymore—being dead like he was—he could still see it, just stating up all around him. It was as if it was playing in his mind, or in his consciousness he presumed. Since probably he was something like that now, a disembodied consciousness. He'd heard of that too.

So, in fact then, the review seemed to be happening all around him. It was like a 3D movie – one he was right in the middle of. He could see himself in the review. Like . . . right there . . . and right there . . . and . . .

Although for some crazy reason the review had started at the end of Udo's life, instead of the beginning. The first thing he saw—which now he was remembering for the first time too—was the momentary glimpse he'd gotten of the massive front end of the delivery truck hitting him like a moving wall of colored metal. Then there was a bright flash; *so that was it! That was what had killed me,* Udo realized.

The movie of his life then jumped a little further back in time. It showed a young girl and how she'd darted out into traffic. It next displayed how Udo then rushed to grab her arm and flung her back toward the sidewalk where he and his wife, with their own little girl, had been walking.

Oh yeah. I remember now, Udo thought. The little girl had been walking with her mother who was walking their dog too about ten feet in front of them. Then the little doggie broke in a run across the street, jerking its leash right out of the girl's hand. She, of course, then broke in a run to catch it.

Udo remembered then seeing the delivery truck headed toward the small child. He knew the truck was not slowing down, so he also realized just an instant later that he had to save her. Or die trying. Or maybe even worse, just watch her die.

A new thought came to Udo. *Had she made it okay? The little girl? Was she okay?* He hoped so. He remembered flinging her back as hard as he could and how it felt like maybe he'd hurt her arm. It seemed to have come out of the socket. It all happened so fast. Udo would have watched while he was living, of course, to see if the little girl had made it, but then he turned only just in time to see the truck already on him.

Thank heavens, Udo then realized, that this memory was edited somehow it seemed. The dying itself and any associated fear and all else that must have happened during and after the truck hit him would have undoubtedly been very unpleasant to go through, he could only figure. Gratefully he next noticed as he watched the review continue, he wasn't worrying about the little girl anymore. Everything else being shown from the remainder of his life was more than enough to worry about. Man, he thought to himself, *was I an idiot! And a pervert. And a goofball. And oh yeah, right there, an idiot again.*

The good, the bad, and the really really ugly . . . all of it came tumbling through a virtual 360 degree, surround video . . . Udo's different jobs, family events, various crises, fighting, hating and loving. The super movie continued to run, going further and further backward in time . . . back to when he was growing up, back to when he was dating, his irresponsible behavior as a teen, all of it. *What a goofball,* was all he could think.

However, and luckily too, there were little victories as well. The review covered all of it – every millisecond, or seemingly so.

Overall though, Udo was more than glad when it kept getting faster and faster as the review kept on. It was sort of like how an old home movie on a big reel might act as it rewound. The film reels will always speed up as the amount of film left on the reel continues to lessen and lessen and the reel gets lighter and lighter. So too was the life review running like that until finally Udo was just a baby, sleeping most the time away . . . then crying, nursing and sleeping some more.

Best of all was when it was completely over and he wasn't born yet. Then Udo was finally free of all he'd ever done and been. The guilt, anguish, frustration and lack of fulfillment . . . all of it was gone now. It was as if the review emptied it all out him. He felt like someone . . . or maybe more accurately something . . . something brand new.

Then came a voice. A voice like that of a man, Udo could tell, but that was all he could tell. Although too the voice was very . . . calm. *Otherworldly. Was it? Shouldn't it be anyway,* he was thinking. *Since I'm dead. It must be. It has to be . . .*

"Hey," the voice said. "Nap time's over. Come on sleepy head. Time to get ready to go."

Sleepy head!?

At first Udo was a little offended. But come to think of it he was feeling a little sleepy at that. So he wanted to say, No! No thanks. I'll just rest here some more. It's all right. Better this way. I'm glad it's all over. And you're right, I am sleepy. I don't wanna go anywhere. And go where?

But then Udo realized as he tried that he couldn't talk. It seemed to be something beyond the capabilities of a mere consciousness. Or so he could only figure. Which pretty much sucked. But then he realized he didn't have to talk as the voice seemed to be hearing his thoughts and answered his mental question without prodding.

"Time to go home to heaven . . ." it said, then added, "and that doesn't suck."

Oh. Yeah. Okay. Of course. Udo felt happy at first too, though guarded for some reason as well. Almost like it was too good to be true. But it made sense. He'd been a really good Christian after all. Eventually that is, once he grew up. And then, after saving that little girl's life like he did, which he was thinking now he must have since he was going to heaven and all.

But then something else came to mind, or to his consciousness as it were . . . which maybe too was why his happiness was not coming so easy. Because they were so important to him. And what about them?

Before we go, can I just ask about them? About my wife? My son? My daughter? He made himself mentally ask, hoping the voice would pick up on it.

The voice said nothing in response, but soon he could see them . . . his wife and kids. Pretty much like in the review. But this sure hadn't been in the review. It couldn't have been. Because he'd already been dead when this happened.

Now he was watching his funeral. Or what would have had to pass for one, because money had always been an issue with them. A fancy funeral would have been so expensive. So he'd told his wife all he'd really would want was to be cremated and have his ashes thrown off "their pier . . . Sandy Point Pier." It was the same pier where they'd met, he and his wife. They'd met in the amusement park at the end of the pier, on the huge rounded out portion of what was now a historical structure. The whole pier, that is.

And there they were. He could see them ... her and the children and each of them taking a handful of gray, chalky dust from a small cardboard box before throwing it high up and over the old wooden planked railings just beyond the benches where they'd met. Luckily, the sea wind was blowing away from them.

The three little dust clouds wafted out and down before dissipating into the misty waves.

Suddenly, there was a shift in Udo's point-of-view. Now he was watching things as if he was in the ashes, floating and then sinking, down into the darkness of the deep. Before he knew it, everything was gone and again . . . it all became the darkness. The darkness, in fact, that he was in right now.

Oh! I get it! So that's how I got here! That's why it's so dark, Udo realized. He quickly got back on topic. *But how are they now? My family,* he questioned out into the . . . nothingness or whatever, hoping the voice would hear once more and answer him again.

"That is all I can show you for now," the voice answered, coolly but ever-so-calmly.

But . . . but that was nothing! And why even show me that? Udo countered.

"For something more important. My main function. To reorient you."

Reorient? But . . .

"Which will then make it easier to reanimate you."

Re- what? Reorient . . . yeah sure. I get that. But reanimate? Isn't that?

The voice laughed quietly, but not maliciously, more kind than that. Then kindness came too with the clarification. "You have to know what you are first, in order to become something new."

Reanimation began.

Which then made Udo forget all about everything else, including his loved ones. All of a sudden he was able to feel something again. *Wow,* he would have exclaimed if he could. Compared to the complete void he'd been in all this time, it was not only exhilarating and exciting, but downright mind blowing!

Even though at first all he could feel was sand. But compared to nothingness its grinding grittiness had never felt better. Soon, however, he could feel water as well, which after only another moment completely replaced the grittiness with its cool smoothness as he then seemed to be floating up off the sand. *Ahhh,* how exquisite that was! To feel motion again, also in contrast to nothingness.

Then and even better, the current's gentle motion started carrying him to and fro. All of which got Udo thinking, and thinking more clearly. Suddenly he was thinking more fully, as if the motion and registering it in his consciousness was kick starting other segments of his mind, which then also got him considering other things as well.

Like who was this voice, he couldn't help but wonder. Was it God? He was supposed to get to see God wasn't he? He remembered that now. He remembered believing in Jesus and expecting to see Him when he died. In heaven. Or wherever. Wasn't that supposed to happen? To be absent from the body is to be present with the Lord, they'd told him. He remembered that phrase particularly, and probably right now because he was. Absent from the body, that is. That was even in the Bible, and then thinking about that stirred memories of how cool and good it would be to be with Jesus. So maybe pretty soon, Udo really hoped. Maybe right after this reanimation stuff he'd get to be with Jesus.

Which he was going to ask the voice about but then he remembered what it had said earlier. The part about how he would be going to heaven now. So then would come his visit with Jesus. *Yes. All right . . . all right . . .*

Udo rested his mind then. With a thought as wonderful as one of seeing Jesus, he could. Soon the reanimation process resumed , however, and his rest rather abruptly ended. Suddenly things had gotten very serious.

An explosion of sparkling energy about the size of someone's head was the first step of actual physical restructuring. Then as the process continued, it was probably a good thing a mirror wasn't positioned nearby. If Udo could have seen himself, it undoubtedly would have been rather shocking to observe.

Like a pair of eyeballs—his new ocular orbs—floating in space on either side of his disembodied brain would be shocking. Especially as it all was somehow stabilized approximately a foot off the ground.

Then even more shocking to see would have been how the floating eyeballs started moving, rotating from side to side as Udo took in his surroundings. After a moment or two of this he could tell that he had washed up on a beach somewhere.

But not just any beach. He knew this beach. Which made sense. If his ashes had been thrown off Sandy Point Pier then this was probably Sandy Point Beach. *Oh yeah, now I am really thinking good. Well, sort of. Baby steps,* Udo concluded.

Not that it mattered, however, as then and all of a sudden the next freaky thing started happening. It was the freakiest thing yet even as the ashes he'd been burned down into started reforming into his body. Which was then made even more spectacularly weird by how the miniscule particles were twinkling and glowing as they came together in a body-sized cloud all around him. The luminescent molecules swirled there for a moment, coming together, becoming more solid. Then they sparked a little brighter before zipping down right into the middle of where his new body was starting to form.

The first major component of which was Udo's skeleton. White molecules dropped down out of the colorful cloud and came together, creating his new frame bone by bone. The immediately calcified segments formed rapidly. They started with his spine as the vertebrae lined up like blocks and attached to the base, a freshly formed pelvis. The also newly formed skull importantly encased the aforementioned brain. Then came the ribcage, the thigh bones down low, shoulders up high, collarbone and then the extremities taking shape last.

Then just as a guess—because Udo had never seen a live skeleton before, of course—but as he gave his new bones a good looking over he felt they seemed a little thicker. They were also maybe even harder than normal human ones might be too.

"Yes. They are stouter and stronger than normal human bones," the voice told him. "Because they are perfect. The body you will be given now will be perfect. It will be composed of the same molecules as your old one, but now the molecules have been restructured, as will be the rest of your body into a perfected version."

Wow, Udo thought again and made a fist with one of his new but still all-bone hands. He knocked against his hard skull with still only eyeballs in it. His wife had always called him a blockhead. Now, well . . . now maybe she was finally right. The voice had a different take though, thank goodness. It kept right on going in its explanatory monologue as if ignoring his antics.

"Because only that which is perfect can be allowed into heaven. Your soul is perfect through the saving grace of your Lord Jesus. But now your body will be too. And both must be so in order to even come near to God, who is of course the essence of perfection and can therefore have nothing imperfect in His presence."

Huh?

The voice laughed. "Don't worry, good servant. Just enjoy the show . . . and the ride soon to follow."

Which said show in its next act exhibited the formation and arrangement of all the cartilage and ligaments needed to hold "them bones" together. The strings and straps, shiny too and off white to pink in color, formed across his joints while others grew right out of some of the bone ends—the tendons—and all of them magically fed, just like the bones had been, by streaming molecules shooting down from the surrounding and still glowing mist.

Attaching next to the freshly formed tendons came bloody red molecules that grew by strands and sheets into muscles. Now he was really filling in. He was even starting to look like one of those see-through plastic models, Udo was thinking. Especially when after that the multicolored inner organs formed and on top of them the big, pink lungs fluttered to life and he could feel himself breathing again.

"Ahhhh . . . God does that feel good," he shouted out, because it really did, to breathe again, and better yet to take in the cool ocean air he knew from before, from when he lived here.

He'd surprised himself though when he'd heard his own voice again after being silent for so long. It sounded funny. Sort of hollowlike. So he felt up at his ears and his mouth but then quickly drew his still just bone and muscle fingers away after feeling mostly just slimy and still exposed ear organs and at his mouth teeth, a tongue and more slimy muscles. Yuck, was all he could think. But ob-viously though his nerves were forming now. At least in his fingers.

"Please don't move until the process is completed," the voice told him, sound-ng stern.

Udo started to speak again, wanting to ask the voice how much longer, want-ing to tell it too how painful things were getting, now that he had nerves after all. But somehow he seemed to be able to handle the pain, and before he could speak the voice cut him off again anyway.

"Please don't speak either. And in answer to your question, the process is almost completed. We are only seconds away. I should probably also inform you, so as to make it all the more bearable, that in your perfected form you will be surprised what you are capable of. Like handling the pain you should be experiencing. Your much improved mind easily and rapidly compartmentalizes the pain impulses that should be excruciating. You will also have supernatural physical capabilities. Because in heaven you will need them."

Oh wow, Udo couldn't help but think one more time, partly because he could feel it. He could feel the supernatural power coursing through him. But also, now he could see too what he could only think of as a supernatural physique forming below his amazed gaze as the flesh was filling in, almost as if being spray painted on.

Then, *wow*, one more time, and then, almost like *I'm Mr. Universe or some-thing. I can't wait to show Ivy*, who was his wife. *Can I move yet?* Udo finally thought out then too.

The voice didn't answer, though. It didn't have to. Because then Udo's body started to lift, but mostly just the upper portion, as if he were being raised up on a tilting laboratory table, reminding him humorously of how the Frankenstein monster first got up after being brought to life in that famous movie. Except there was no table. Some sort of invisible powers were at work, holding him in a state of paralysis too, until once he was completely vertical and freed he fell to his feet then staggered forward for the first time in perfected form.

"Wow," he actually said this time, assuming it was okay now, now that he was fully formed, and this time saying wow because it felt so awesome to be using a body again. Especially one so perfect.

Which he could tell as he stretched out his well-muscled limbs, then sprung surprisingly high in the air just by flexing in the knees and jumping straight up.

"Wow," he couldn't help but say again after landing surprisingly lightly too. He'd had to have gotten about six feet of air, and almost effortlessly.

Udo wondered about something else and just took off running up the beach in the firm moist sand. He was really getting going strong, feeling the amazing power in his new legs, looking from side to side with a wide smile lifting his lips. Man, was he moving! Pump . . . pump . . . pump . . . pump . . . his legs were going like the pistons of some crazy runaway engine. *How fast?* Seemed like 60 . . . 70 miles an hour.

After just a ways he pulled up. He did so, partly afraid he might run into something. He'd got going so fast his eyes were watering and everything around him was blurry. But he slowed also because along the way the one thing he'd been able to make out was a big line of black up ahead jutting out long into the water. The pier, he realized. *Sandy Point Pier.*

He laughed some then too while he slowed, because it felt so good, and plus too because he knew he'd just sprinted probably a quarter of a mile but wasn't the least bit winded. *How cool was that!* So he laughed some more as he pulled up all the way and then flexed the muscles of his legs which were pumped and big and just getting warmed up.

But the pier. Yeah, the pier! That was what was the best of all. *Sandy Point Pier* where he'd met his wife. Where his ashes had been thrown off. So yes. Of course. It all made sense now. That was why he'd come up out of the darkness here. This was where his ashes had been all along. He'd never even really left. He'd always been here. Sandy Point Beach and the good old pier too.

Although old might have been an understatement, Udo then remembered too. It had been there as long as he'd had been alive, and even further back too. It had been built in like the twenties or something, he seemed to remember. Sandy Point Beach without its pier wouldn't have been Sandy Point Beach.

The old local landmark was a pretty big pier too, extra wide and including the aforementioned and very large, rounded portion at its end that supported a small carnival, which was how he'd met his wife there. As was to be expected, the old seaworn structure was a main attraction in the otherwise sleepy seaside town that Sandy Point Beach was. All the kids, eight to eighteen, flocked there regu-larly, at times outnumbering even the gulls and pigeons decorating the old wood structure as well.

But something was wrong with it all now, Udo realized as he neared the familiar landmark one more time. Something had happened to the place since he'd been gone, and from the looks of it, the pier's main attraction days were long over. The section supporting the carnival looked dangerously slanted and anyone going there today would have to hold on for dear life just to keep from sliding into the sea. Well, not really, but something cataclysmic had certainly rocked the old girl.

The Ferris Wheel, that back in Udo's day had brightly sign-posted the place for miles around, now looked more than ready to roll right off into the ocean. But worst of all, and something Udo didn't notice until he got a little closer was that a large center section of the boardwalk portion leading out to the carnival had collapsed altogether.

Then something else couldn't escape his currently not-so-keen attention, which considering what he'd recently been through was certainly understandable, even though his mental faculties had supposedly been improved. But just then it had finally sunk in. *Where are all the people?*

Normally, back in his day, most of the time the pier would be crowded, and on the weekends packed. *And where were all the people up and down the beach too?* There was not a soul in sight. *What was going on? How long had he been dead? And had the rest of the world died too since then?*

Now somewhat dazed, Udo continued on, and turning his attention away from the pier another interesting development caught his eye. *What the heck?* There hadn't been a jetty there before! But now huge black and gray boulders jutted up and trailed smaller and smaller into the sea about a quarter mile further down the beach.

Had some sort of horrible cataclysm created the jetty? While at the same time knocking the crud out the pier? And maybe what? Killed all the people too? Or maybe they'd all evacuated? Or-

Another, even greater concern then derailed that train of thought. *What about his family? Should he just go and look for them?* He knew they only lived a couple miles away. That is, if they were even still around.

"Ivy," Udo partly said and partly yelled as he started to run again. "Joannie . . . Jason," and by then he was totally yelling, and of course these were the names of his children.

Although this time instead of running just along the beach, he cut up away from the ocean at an angle. He knew at the top of the sand's rise the beach met up with a waist-high, concrete wall. A concrete boardwalk was on the other side of it, and after that a grassy park area. Then Udo would come to the parking lots, which let out onto Sandy Point Beach Boulevard.

From there he knew exactly where to go, which turns to take. Just head up SPB Boulevard as they used to call it, wait until it turned into Sandy Point

Parkway, then left on Mission, right on Harbor, then another right on his old street, Griffith way. And as fast as he could run now, he also was thinking, I can probably get there in just a few minutes. It was only maybe five miles in total at the most.

A funny thing happened then, though. As he was building up a good head of speed and nearing the beach's crest and the accompanying wall just ahead . . . his feet came off the ground. At first he just kept running, but could tell, of course, he was now treading air and rising up and up. Then, it hit him. He was . . . flying?

Udo looked down. Fear strained his perfect features. *"Hey. HEY!"* he yelled, fear creeping too into his voice as now he was starting to get up there pretty high. Like higher than on top of his two story house even, he could tell, and that was about as high as he usually ever went.

He looked down once, then quickly shut his eyes. He tried again, figuring he had to. But what he saw now was not good. Now, what before had just been tears of anxiety became also tears of sadness and grief. His once upon a time hometown—as far as he could tell as it rapidly diminished in size beneath him—appeared to be a bombed out ruin.

"Hey!" he yelled frantically up into the sky. "What the heck's going on? What's happened to everything? And what am I supposed to do now?"

"It's all right," came the voice again and this time sounding like more than just a comment. The words had the tone of a command. Like a parent hushing its crying child. Which was a good thing because Udo, at the present time, was close to becoming the world's biggest crybaby.

But then, just as the voice had promised, everything was all right. Or at least it felt that way, as far as Udo was concerned. Waves of happiness and joy were washing over him, and better yet, coming with those inner sensations were beautiful clouds of different colors wafting around him too as he continued to ascend up and up.

"You remember what I said about heaven, right?" the voice asked.

"Ahahahahahaaaaa," Udo laughed out loud through a huge smile. "Yes . . . Yesss!"

He wasn't so worried about his family anymore. He wasn't worried about anything. He was too busy enjoying the ever increasing tidal waves of God's perfect love that kept washing over him as he rose higher and higher into the sky.

Soon and up ahead he could also see an image forming from a cloud, which certainly looked like his God. Jesus' smiling bearded face was located above His outstretched, white robed arms.

Udo flew happily into them.

CHAPTER IV

THE BAD

"Dude! That is sooo brutal," the teenager said and sat back on the rather tat-tered couch. "Where did you get her from?" He passed the marijuana joint to another teenager seated next to him.

They were both probably eighteen or nineteen years old, and other than their different facial features and hair colors—although both coifs were identically gelled and spiked, but one blonde and the other black—the two young men were practically identical. They wore similar, dirty and darkly colored, graphically adorned t-shirts, similar somewhat greasy pants—khaki on one, and denim on the other—slightly grimy sneakers, and tattoos on all visible skin, up to and including their necks.

"Over at that stupid fuc_in' junior college," the one with dark hair answered and let slip a stoned giggle.

"In the new parking structure. We took the van . . . night classes got out—"

"And there's always a few stragglers," a third, rather large and semi-obese one said as he came into the room.

He wore remarkably similar attire too, substituting though a sleeveless sweatshirt also graphically adorned like the others t-shirts were, and like theirs too, skulls were a major theme. A thin crescent of his hairy belly showed at the sweatshirt's lower hem. The bit of tummy shook as he laughed with his friends. They then also traded high fives and the pot smoke clouded up and out around them.

"I'll bet you thought of that Mike. Man, you are too fu__in' smart."

"Oh yeah. I got lots of other plans too," the chubby one said and smiled an evil grin.

"His I.Q. is like 180 or something," the dark haired one said then, his voice high from holding in a hit.

"No way . . ."

"Like 154 . . . 155," the big one corrected his friend. "I forget . . . too much dope." He then let out a hit too and they all laughed some more. He plopped down onto the sofa and passed the joint along.

The subject of their previous conversation, the, "her," first referred to was a young woman in the bedroom just off the small living room the three of them shared.

How could they not talk about her, the bedroom's open door in fact straight across from the sofa they all sat on now? It was almost as if they were watching a show, and that show being her as she lay naked and sprawled with her arms and legs wide out, tied at the wrists and ankles to the corners of a small, metal-framed, twin-sized bed.

Then to make it an even better show, the bed had been purposely positioned in the center of the bedroom straight across from the doorway they all currently looked through.

The unfortunate flesh of the lead actress in this adhoc, one woman show was pale in contrast to some darkly dirty splotches marking her here and there, as well as the bruising and small amounts of blood that crowned each of her tethered joints. The wire they'd used for the bindings had cut into her young, soft and especially sensitive flesh in those areas, and even though painfully wounded, she still struggled and the somewhat rusty bed frame squeaked and rattled in response.

"Sounds like time for some more lemon juice."

"You want more lemon juice bit_? Huh?"

"Lemon juice?" the latest arrival asked.

"Yeah. Stings like hell. On the cuts. Stops them from squirming," the chubby one said.

"Makes them squeal too."

"Oh yeah." They all snickered at that.

"Fuc_in' cun_ was making so much racket when we first got back. After she came to again. The sound of the ocean out here hides all that though. Plus the waves are really breaking tonight."

"Hey . . . how about that wicked thunderstorm last night. Man . . . that was awesome. That would have covered up any noise she could make."

"Oh yeah, but that's what's so awesome about this place. It's always real noisy, right by the cliffs like we are. Plus we're way down past all those tourist traps and apartments. Nice and secluded. We can get away with anything out here . . . and have!"

"Yeah. And my stupid old Grandma in the main house is deaf as a board."

They all shared some more laughter, then the newcomer had another idea. "Hey! Why don't you just cut her up good? Or take a finger. That'll get her to obey. I'll do it!" he enthusiastically volunteered.

"She might pass out then and . . . and then the sex wouldn't be as good. We've both had her. She's hottt! Now it's your turn, dude!"

The big one and the first one on the sofa looked at each other around the newcomer in the middle and shared snide laughter over their little joke. "Tight," the big one added and passed the joint along.

"Yeah. And just look at those ti_s, man . . ."

The later arrival stood to look across. "Nice ones . . . big," he commented.

The woman's only article of clothing was the blue bandana tied tight for a gag across her mouth. Another bandana was wadded up and filled her oral cavity. It was a darker color though, possibly just because her saliva had thoroughly saturated it.

"Yeah. Silicone. Or whatever. Firm . . ."

"Wow," the standing one added and started toward her. He grabbed hard at his crotch. "But then I get to do a finger, right?"

"Yeah. Then we'll have some real fun. And hey! Did you do a line yet?"

"Oh yeah," the soon to be rapist enthused, but just as he was turning back toward the coffee table in front of the sofa, and the drugs thereon, an incredibly intense jolting knocked him off his feet.

With his falling he couldn't see anything for a moment, but then as he got his bearings again, lying on the still rocking floor, through the falling plaster and boards and dust, for just a second he could also see the young woman on the bed. The floor beneath her buckled and then opened up and swallowed her. The bed was like a Jello shooter going down at happy hour.

Right away the young man tried to turn to where he remembered the front door being, thinking, *if I can just get out of here!* But then he felt the floor give way beneath him. All the way . . . just gone. Then all he could feel was falling and the dark nothingness that swallowed him next.

Even scarier was how falling kept happening and happening. It even speeded up too until eventually the young man was treated to a couple teeth jarring bounces, a scraping that ripped half his face off. Soon to follow came a merciful knockout thud.

His two friends fared similarly well. They never left the couch and somehow it even carried them down through the darkness of their own long fall.

Which at first was okay with them. They were really buzzed and it all felt like an amusement park ride. The sofa bucked and bounced and swayed and shook and when they finally realized they should maybe get up, before they could the whole thing folded up on itself. With them still in it. A sadistic-pervo-creep and sofa sandwich. Then in that form they continued to plunge.

They were soon followed by the rest of the house in bits and pieces, until further inside the Earth's now highly mobile crust they were soon smashed, squished and/or suffocated.

They weren't buried alive however. None of them were. They were all quite dead. And in the deep, dark sleep of that state none of them noticed they weren't being allowed to, 'Rest in Peace' as the saying goes. Neither could they feel the strange, sort of reverse gravitational pull that seemed to be slowly but relentlessly drawing them up out of their just recently discovered, unresting places.

With the advent of the next day, just as the sun was rising, so would they. But unlike the buttercups and pansies, or the creatures great and small, life would not be the mysterious and magnificent force fueling their frames as they once again strode the earth. A very different energy, one nearly and almost entirely the opposite of that would draw them up and on their way. Not that which their creator, the Lord of light, imbued all his marvelous creations with, but that which his eternal enemy, the rebellious and fallen Lord of darkness had somehow managed to conjure up.

Something, some mystical elixir that if not giving life to his newly stolen brigades of dead servants, at least gave them an existence hollowly similar. An existence that might finally help the great corrupter accomplish his greatest goal.

CHAPTER V

THE REMNANT

Ivy Henkman wished she was dead, for maybe like the millionth time today. But since she wasn't, she grabbed the vodka bottle out of the freezer, took a big pull and slammed the freezer door shut.

She took her bottle with her into the recklessly decorated and shabbily furnished living room. There she let herself fall into a worn old sofa sitting before a big, somewhat spotty picture window looking out onto a middle class, trending toward lower class neighborhood.

Two recessions and a foreclosure crisis had not been kind to the block the Henkman family had always called home. Luckily though, thick and dark curtains came across the window most of the way on each side, hiding the not-so-great outdoors. One side hung a little crooked however, having been pulled off some of its hooks up top. Small shafts of light cut into the otherwise darkly lighted room, making the inside difficult to discern as well, and that was lucky too, as far as Ivy was concerned.

"*Ah hell,*" she had to say then though and quickly bury her face in the crook of her arm. Plopping into the old sofa like she had created quite a little cloud of dust. The particles flickered like little stars where the light hit them and once their number dwindled sufficiently Ivy came up for air. She managed not to sneeze and swiped away the air just before her nose, then took another drink.

The dust was to be expected after all. She didn't bother with cleaning too much anymore. Sometimes she could get up a little gumption and do a thing or two. Make the beds maybe. Wash a few dishes. But then it would be time for a drink, and the drink would then wash all that gumption somewhere far, far away.

Although back when she'd been doing the crystal meth . . . heck . . . back then she could do a couple fat lines and clean the whole darn house. Just thinking about that damn stuff now, though, brought first a subconscious scowl to her lips, then that followed by the vodka bottle again to try and wash that away too.

Frickin' crystal meth. She'd had a real love/hate relationship with that crap. Used to love to do it, but now she hated to even remember that she ever did. Because of what had eventually happened.

She got up the remote, clicked on the TV and took another good, big drink. She found a channel with young people yelling and fighting and settled for that. She didn't know it most likely, or wouldn't admit it, but it was good to watch that sort of thing so she didn't feel like the most worthless human being in existence. *Hell, look at them!*

But yeah, the crystal had been okay for a while. After another while though, whenever she did it and got all cranked up she kept seeing Udo everywhere. Which was obviously because she couldn't ever sleep anymore. Which was the biggest problem with crystal meth. Sleep deprivation and visual hallucinations, as the doctor on TV had put it. That crap had gotten just too weird, was how she put it. And either way then, Ivy just stopped.

Especially after the last time when she'd chopped up some really nice and fluffy rails and was getting ready to get at them with her little, gold-plated tooter and then-

RIGHT HERE! Her mind screamed at her now. *RIGHT HERE ON THIS DAMN SOFA AND LEANING OVER THIS DAMN COFFEE TABLE!* There he was! Her Udo. With his eyeball hanging out and the bloody goo dripping down onto her nice lines of meth.

But even worse, scenes like that had been happening more and more often as her druggy career wound down. All of a sudden, he would be there, her deceased husband, but not looking normal, which would be scary enough. But it was all even scarier because now he always looked like the last time she'd ever seen him, hit by that damn delivery truck and his arms and legs all busted up and his skull half-smashed in and that damn eyeball hanging out.

All over town even too. Wherever she went when she was tweaking: at the liquor store in the beer cooler standing there kind of blue but smiling . . . at the gas station leaning on pump number three while she was filling up on number two . . . even in the ladies room at Burger World where she was going to hit her tooter real quick, but there he was, leaning on the sink with that damn eyeball hanging out, his skull caved in, the blood red against his graying skin and his arms and legs bending funny ways.

But then that last time right here in her own living room. The blood was so real looking, and then it was even still there after the rest of the hallucination went away. The red stuff got all mixed in with the off-white powder even after she violently and disgustedly smeared it all around on the coffee table top and mixed in some of her tears with it too.

So none of that crap anymore for her.

No thanks.

Once she stopped doing the crystal, Udo stopped showing up. *Thank God,* was all she could think. *Thank God for something anyway.*

Which was really the reason why she started all the drinking and meth anyway. God, that is. She *had* been a Christian, but after what happened to her husband . . . taken away from her and her children that needed him so much. If . . . and now as far as Ivy was concerned that was a mighty big if . . . but if there was a God, or Jesus or whatever, she sure didn't want anything to do with him. Not after that. Except maybe to hate Him.

But so what better way to get back at Him than to waste the rest of her life with booze and drugs, or even just the booze again now like she was. At least the booze never made her see Udo all dead like that. Not yet anyway. But it sure helped numb the pain. And what if the place looked like hell! Like she cared anymore. At least it was paid off.

Screw you if you don't like it, was how she always thought of things these days. Screw you, was pretty much her response in most situations.

"Is this Mrs. Ivy Henkman," a bill collector might say through the phone if she hadn't adequately screened the call. And since she could tell it was one of them, she'd just come right out with it.

"Screw you!" And click.

Even if it was Udo's parents calling it was the same thing, "Screw you Helga," or "Screw you, Hans." Because she knew they hated her after she'd sold the appliance store and repair service that they'd passed on to Udo. They hated her for selling it because his dad had wanted to try and run it again after Udo died. But she'd just wanted the cash. *So screw you, Hans and Helga, screw you too,* Ivy Henkman thought and with an evil looking half-smile put another dent in the vodka bottle's contents.

The front door swung open and the small girl standing there turned and yelled back out at the bright and sunny, afternoon world. "You shut up, Marisa Jernegan or I'll tell my brother and he'll kill you!" In a huff she then turned and came in, slamming the door shut behind her.

"That's my baby," Ivy said over at her eight-year-old daughter as she stomped past on her way toward her room. "Come sit with mommy and watch some TV, Joannie honey."

The girl turned and regarded her half-sloshed mom, who even just then was taking another swig. Joannie Henkman, still in a huff, put her little hands on her little hips.

"Mommy. I'm not going to have to cook dinner again am I?"

"Can you just make yourself a sandwich, sweetie? Mommy's not hungry . . ."

The little girl turned and put her back to the sofa as if to sit next to her mother but instead only shrugged her backpack from her shoulders and the full book bag took a seat instead.

"Well, I suppose," the precocious young thing said and bobbed her head.

With the bobbing her hair lifted and fell lightly. The just enough light in the room gave glints of gold there since her hair, though silky straight, was otherwise like Udo's, colored like shafts of wheat. Several strands stuck to her tan forehead, trapped in the light perspiration she'd created walking home from school. "But I've got quite a bit of homework too, Mommy. So please, please don't make any messes for me to clean up."

"I won't honey. And look. Mommy's last drink for now." Ivy tipped the vodka bottle back and drained it. She set it on the end table bordering the sofa on that side, but it fell since she'd only got half its circular bottom on the table.

"Mother!" the little girl chided at Ivy and picked up the bottle. "I will put *this* in the recycle bin." As promised she did just that, tromping off this time into the kitchen.

"Mommy's sweet little angel," Ivy cooed and lay back on the sofa.

Joannie proudly completed her task. She had, after all, set up the twin plastic waste cans next to the back door. That was her, "Recycling Center," and she hoped it would get her an A in her class.

When she got back to the living room, she saw her mother asleep already and took the light blanket off the back of a nearby and equally tattered easy chair. She draped it lightly over her mommy's legs. Mommy was just in her robe and slippers and at least looked a little better with her legs covered, Joannie figured.

The little girl stopped then and thought for a moment. She got her back pack on again and started up the stairs for her room. She would do a little Geography first, then eat something, and if her mommy was awake by then she'd make her something to eat too. Her brother Jason could fend for himself.

He probably wouldn't be in until late anyway. She hoped he wouldn't get in trouble again but knew he might. He was fifteen and even got kicked out of junior high for getting into too many fights. He even got sent to Juvenile Hall and now was in a special continuation school for bad kids. He was a good brother to her though and never hurt or did anything bad to her or mom. She just wished he could treat others that way too.

So since her big brother probably wouldn't be home until late, Ivy made a mental note to lock all the doors soon too. As soon as it got dark. But then thinking about being safe like that made her think of her daddy too. She shut those thoughts out though and made herself think about geography instead. She knew if she thought about her dad she would be too sad and it would hurt and she would just mope and not get any homework done, or anything else for that matter.

And, she had so much to do.

So much to do.

Like just then she remembered too that tomorrow probably the check would come from the government and she would have to make sure her mom got to the bank with it to cash it before she got too drunk. *But how would she, accomplish that?*

Joannie Henkman put her amazingly smart and disciplined nine-year-old mind on it.

Okay.

Yes.

That should work.

If there wasn't any booze in the house—and tonight she would make sure that her mother had no other money by taking it from her purse if she had to and returning it later—then her mom would have to cash the check to get some more booze with. Then Joannie could get some of the money to get groceries with when she got home from school. And if mommy was too drunk to take her to the store, Mr. Arwenson would help. He was a real nice old man that lived the next block over.

Then they could make it okay. With food at home to make for her and her mommy they would be okay. She could take care of mommy. She liked taking care of things. It made her feel good and good was the best way to feel. So she would do that. *Yes.* That was what she would do, she figured and started laying out her books in order for tonight's homework on her bed.

Jason Henkman wished everyone else was dead. Everyone except maybe his mom and his kid sister. They were okay. And maybe Griner too. Griner was okay. Griner was showing him the ropes. Helping him go pro, as Griner liked to call it. But everyone else. Go die mother___ker, was a phrase he liked to use. And he really meant it too.

"Now. Give it to me again, J.D," Griner said at Jason. The older but definitely bigger and stronger man sat behind the wheel of the also older, dark sedan the two shared the front seat of. The death sled, as Jason liked to call Griner's car, because of its low and mostly black appearance, was parked in the shadows up and across the street from Easy Eight Liquor in Westfall Heights, the poorer section, or ghetto, if you like, of Sandy Point Beach.

But since Sandy Point Beach wasn't a very big city, Westfall Heights wasn't a very big ghetto. Just five or six blocks of run down housing and a couple more of assorted shops created and maintained to cater to the low income residents nearby: a Quickie Cash, a couple pawn shops, a small market, head shop, porn shop, and more than a few places out of business whose boarded up storefronts were acting as canvas for graffiti artists.

"I let you go in first . . ." Jason started reciting, thinking and remembering at the same time what Griner had told him. "while I wait outside and keep watch. You'll make sure first that there aren't any other customers, but if there are, you'll just get some booze and come back out. Then we wait until the customers leave and go back in."

Jason paused and rolled his eyes up to read some more off his brain. His speech became more deliberate as well. "And if there aren't any customers when you first go in, you'll call me on my cell, pretending I'm someone you're picking up beer for, but that'll be my signal to come in."

The young, but big for his age, fifteen-year-old paused for a deep breath. Just talking about this stuff was making him nervous. But he had to go through with it. No. He *wanted* to go through with it. Nothing else in his stupid life was working out. Nothing. Once he hit Junior High it was just a matter of time. That was when things really started going bad. Especially after his dad died. That was when he started having, "anger problems," as the counselors liked to call it.

Because in Junior High the older kids always picked on the younger ones, and unlike the other kids his age, Jason didn't just sit there and take it. He got pissed off. Like really pissed off. Uncontrollably. He'd see red and just go ape on them and then there really would be red. Red blood on their faces and some too on his fists. Then worse case, he'd get his butt kicked. He was getting pretty good at fighting though, and usually it was the other way around.

Then in Juvie, which was where they soon sent him, it just got worse. More fights. Until certain, "staff members," just tried to beat the anger out of him. Which of course only made it even more worse. The anger, that is.

Then he met Griner at a, "Scared Straight," session, and the old con slipped Jason his number. Which was also why Griner called him J.D., short for juvenile delinquent, and Jason loved that. He was proud to be a juvenile delinquent. And was going to be even prouder when Griner turned him into a first rate hold-up man. This liquor store heist was just a warmup. Pretty soon Griner said they'd even try taking down a bank or two. Get serious.

"Then what," Griner questioned his young protégé further, and from the sounds of it the con had two ways of talking, quietly growling or downright roaring. Jason came back to the present to respond.

"We take 'em down. I hang back near the door, but pretend like I'm shopping. Until I hear you break out the sawed off and pump in a round.

"Then I whip out the nine, train it on the cashier, and if anyone else comes in I tell 'em to get on the floor or I'll blow their f_ckin' brains out. Then I wait and watch the cashier while you head out with the take."

"And watch the back of the store too," Griner cut in with, growling a little louder. "Lotsa guys get capped by someone strapped and hiding in the back. My dope on this joint is that it's a family op. And the guy that owns it only gots girls. Just be on your toes though. You never know."

"Aaight," Jason answered.

"And don't talk like that," Griner roared once more, even louder, mad at how Jake had answered like a black guy would, because, "I'm gonna introduce you to some guys pretty soon . . . and if you talk like that around them their liable to beat you senseless," the holdup man explained. "But you need their connection. We both do! In case we get sent up. In lockup the guys they know there can keep you alive. And you gotta remember, that can happen! One thing leads to another . . . somebody gets shot . . . your lookin' at five to ten . . . or more!"

Griner looked down and his jaw muscles danced. They even then seemed to jump start his vocal chords as he looked back up. "But not tonight! Right?" the older lawbreaker roared one last time, part in encouragement and part in warning.

To add emphasis the con also put his big hand onto Jason's shoulder and grabbed hard. He shot fire with his eyes at the young man too from beneath his bushy red brows. His chin looked carved out of pale rock resting solid under even more bushy red hair filling his big mustache. Later, on his way into the store, he would add a black ball cap pulled low over his eyes and his disguise would be complete. After the job the mustache would get shaved off, the ball cap would come off, and along too with most of his hair that at the moment hung to his shirt collar like a dirty, red and gray skirt.

"You got it bro. I am so on this," Jason enthused, even though he was still nervous, but the young man had learned quickly to model after his mentor and so he shot back his own, though somewhat smaller, fire out of his eyes. Then he pulled on a cap of his own too and like his partner got out of the car with purpose.

Jason let Griner go first across the street, then watched as the now almost completely nondescript man deftly tucked away his shortened shotgun inside his knee-length, black raincoat.

For himself, Jason reached around and slipped his 9 mm. pistol into his pants waistband at the small of his back. Then he resettled his own jacket, also black, but a more simple nylon windbreaker type, to hide the piece.

Not that their secrecy was totally necessary. As far as Jason could tell there was no one else out. It was after midnight and all the other businesses in the area were closed. And even though the liquor store was brightly signed and lighted against the dark, no customers could be seen coming or going from there either. But like Griner had said, you do things right, first time and every time.

Which Jason then remembered his next thing to do right was get across the street, because Griner had just ducked into the liquor store. Its door chime rang shrill but quiet in the even quieter night. Dogs barked somewhere, probably a block away, but that was about it.

On the other side of the street, Jason jump-stepped over the high curb and took position in the shadows against the wall about ten feet down from the store's already open door. A vato-filled sedan boom boomed up the street and Jason turned away from the road quickly just in case, hiding all that was really visible of himself, his face. The car passed without incident and Jason leaned back again, mostly just trying to look cool, but as before, not that anyone was watching.

Griner had gone over this stuff with him all day. They'd even gone out in the boonies and he'd gotten to empty seven clips learning how to shoot the nine. Which he loved the most. The shooting. It was a cool feeling of power, squeezing one off and watching whatever he aimed at get blasted.

Well, sometimes he hit his target, and at least more so after a while. Griner himself even said he seemed to have a natural shooting eye. Towards the end he almost couldn't miss. From up to about fifteen yards away anyway, which was usually good enough, Griner also told him.

So just then as a cat scuttled across the street, Jason pulled the pistol quick from behind his back and sighted up on it.

"Get on the floor motherf___er," he hissed and let a couple imaginary shots fly at the fleeing feline. "BAM . . . BAM!"

Thinking he might have been a little too loud he looked around real quick, then slipped the pistol back into hiding. He pulled his cell phone out and took a look at it. Yeah, it was on and working, so he put it back into his coat pocket where he could get at it quick. He looked up then just in time to watch the cat he hadn't shot go past the liquor store door and disappear around the corner right after it.

Man, his mom would kill him if he ever shot a cat, he realized then as well. And his sister would too. Which was all kind of academic anyway. Pretty soon he might have to say goodbye to them. Like forever. His mom he might not miss so much. She was toasted all the time these days anyway. It was almost like she already wasn't there. So what's to miss . . .

But his little sister, she he would miss. Although too, he had to admit, as hard as it was, she'd be better off without him around. Some role model he turned out to be. Not that she needed one. Luckily. She was something else. She'd be fine. He would really miss her though. But he just couldn't risk getting her caught up in any of this. He could be a wanted man pretty soon.

He liked the sound of that. Wanted Man. Wanted . . . Dead or Alive. Then the cell phone rang quiet in his coat pocket and Jason swallowed hard.

It rang again and he got it out. He knew what it was all about of course, but he answered like it was a real call, as per the plan.

"Yeah," he said, sounding tense.

"Hey Gino," he heard Griner slur into the other end, acting drunk, also per their plan. "I'm up at the liquor store but I forgot what you wanted. What kinda beer?"

Jason didn't say anything. He wasn't supposed to. But like he was supposed to do he just listened to Griner do his little play and started heading for the store's front door.

"What my man," Griner continued. "Bud? You want that horse pi__?!"

Jason hung up on Griner's self-induced laughter. His part of the telephone play was over. Then he ducked inside the store just in time to hear Griner end his part as well.

"All right. Don't let the cards get cold," the old con finished with and pocketed his phone, but then continued talking to himself while continuing toward the back of the store. "Bud . . . horsep__s. . ." he mumbled as he looked for the brand.

Jason hid a smile as he strolled up the first row of items in the store, pretending to be shopping. He picked up some nail clippers, a comb, then while inspecting them at eye level he also glanced toward the cashier.

Luckily, the dark haired and portly foreigner working there was mostly just watching Griner, who from the sounds of it was just then grabbing his beer out of the reefer box at the back of the store.

Jason headed the same way, but nonchalantly and purposely not looking toward Griner. He had strict instructions not to. What he could do though was keep going until he had an angle on both the cashier, and just like Griner had also instructed, on the back of the store.

As he scanned the rear area of the medium sized liquor store he noticed a doorway sized opening where a wall of bottles topped by three rows of ball caps ended. That was the spot he needed to watch. Anybody else who might be anywhere within the building would have to be back there. Otherwise he would have seen them.

After the opening, a wall of tobacco products: cigarettes, cigars, snuff and chewing tobacco started, made the back corner, changed to just cigarettes, then continued up and formed the back wall behind the cashier.

"You got your buddywieser, I see," the cashier said with a heavy accent and a mostly phony smile. Griner slammed the twelve-pack onto the counter top near the cash register.

"Yeah. And gimme a small bottle of Jack too will ya," Griner growled.

As the cashier turned and reached for the bottle, the holdup man smoothly and silently slipped the sawed off from his coat.

Oh boy. Here we go, Jason could almost hear himself think. He fought off the first feelings of paralyzing fear and got out the nine. He kept it down at his side though, worried that it might shake a lot if he brought it up at the moment.

The sound of Griner pumping in a shell got the cashier's attention real quick. "What is the meaning of this," he squealed after turning back to see the shotgun's big round barrel staring at him.

"It means gimme all your cash," and yeah, really a growl this time. Griner followed the terrified foreigner rock steady, holding his aim on the man's head, who in turn kept his quivering gaze on Griner. And the gun.

"Come on . . . come on," the ex-con yelled. "Open up!" In frustration he angrily tapped the register with the gun's barrel. The cashier did his best to obey, but slowly and with noticeably trembling hands.

"CHACHING," the register chimed open, but then its operator just stepped back and held up his hands which were now shaking even more.

"What the . . . COME ON!" Griner yelled. "Gimme the dough. Bag it up!" He plopped a plain, black gym bag on the counter, zipper open, then roughly shoved it toward the cashier. It scooted clear across the counter and fell at the man's feet. "Come on . . . pick it up!"

Griner gave up on the cashier momentarily, just long enough to yell over at Jason, "You watchin' the back, kid?"

"Yuh yeah," Jason told him and did look over again toward the back. At the same time, like he had been, he brought his gun up in a two handed grip chest high. He'd realized if he kept moving it like that, up and down from chest high, then lowering it, then back to chest high again and then aiming first at the cashier and then at the opening in back, getting serious about it all too, like he really might have to shoot any moment, then the shaking in his hands went away. After another moment he was feeling pretty brave. "I got it man," he yell-ed.

Meanwhile the cashier had finally seemed to work up the courage to at least pick up the bag and as Griner watched him he also all of a sudden noticed a small black foot switch not far from where the bag had just been on the floor.

"You sonofa-" he lowly growled this time, then screamed again. "Get back! Get over there!"

Griner waved the cashier away from the switch, shooing him with his wea-pon toward the back of the store. The frightened proprietor scuttled in the indicated direction along the wall. "J.D.!" he also yelled out for his partner.

Griner went to work on the register himself then, grabbing out the removable plastic cash tray with his left hand and slamming it hard onto the counter. Change erupted out of it and clattered all over the place. But he let all that go and went straight for the bills, grabbing up all he could and shoving them into his pockets. He reached back too into the now vacated drawer for the few bigger bills that had been slipped under the tray. "Come on kid, let's blow this craphole!"

"Hey," Jason shouted back, but not at his friend and partner. He was turn-ed and facing the back opening where another dark haired man, but this one younger and with long hair in a ponytail had a pistol of his own pointed right at Griner.

Without another word or even thought, Jason just squeezed the trigger and though he didn't seem to hit the second liquor store employee, at least his shot blasted into and scattered several items hanging on the back wall not far above his intended target's head. All of which at least made the guy duck so fast that he fell over backwards and shot his own gun up into the ceiling.

In the meantime up front, while Griner's attention was taken away from the cashier, the portly middle-easterner had managed to get a small, snub-nosed revolver he had hidden under the counter and even with his hands still shaking he also managed to put a small caliber slug in, or rather *through*, Griner's left upper arm.

The hardened gun user was only phased, however, but also knocked a little sideways by the bullet's blow. And then too, just like if someone punched him, he was mostly just really pissed. So he swung the shotgun quickly back and up and blasted a round into his attacker's generous midsection. With another growl for emphasis.

The cashier's broad paunch, held tight in an off-yellow, sweat stained dress shirt erupted in a bloody blowout. At the same time the force of the twelve-gauge's blast knocked both him against the wall and the gun from his hand before he crumpled to the floor.

"Araam!" his coworker and apparently friend screamed from the back. He was on his feet again and working his way toward the register but after hearing him yell up, Jason stopped him cold again with several more errant shots blasting into the wall above his head. An excited and obviously vindictive spew of Arabic curses was all the man then dared put out from his newest hiding place somewhere near the floor and still at the back of the store.

Jason made his way over to Griner and the two scuttled backwards toward the front door. All the while they watched the back as they did, weapons at the ready, but the second defender still just laid low, staying out of things for the moment.

"Holy shi_," Jason could only mutter, seeing his partner's blood-soaked wound. He had gotten close to Griner to help, but the older man shunned his assistance.

"I'm all right. We just gotta get outta here. What's the street look like?"

Jason leaned into the store's door and pushed it open just enough to sneak a peek into the darkness outside. Per the plan he'd pulled it shut as he came in. The clerk had been too busy watching Griner to say anything.

"Still quiet. I don't see nobody." Jason knew his voice sounded nervous and he was emotionally torn between hating that fact and like Griner had said, just wanting to get the hell outta there.

"Let's move then," Griner got in between hard breaths and the two darkly clad robbers took one last look toward the back, then slipped almost invisibly into the night.

They made their way quickly across the wide boulevard, Jason jogging with long, loping strides, his pistol still in his hand swinging low. Griner moved at the same pace, holding the sawed-off in similar fashion on his left while his other hand came across and squeezed hard around his wound.

"You drive," he hissed through the pain once they got to the car. He kept going around to the passenger side, jerked open the door and fell in.

"Oh yeah...yeah sure," Jason managed through heavy breaths of his own and slid in behind the wheel.

They'd practiced this too while they were out in the boonies earlier that day. Jason had driven before once on a joy ride with his friends in a car they'd stolen, but Griner made sure he could handle the sled, making the kid take it fast on some of the dirt roads up in the hills outside of town.

Good thing the old man thinks of everything, Jason mused real quickly before snatching up the keys from under the seat. That was another detail the old man had planned, that the keys would be left there. Jason, also as practiced, got the car quickly started.

The old man. Yeah . . . the old man. Jason would call Griner that when Griner called him the kid, even though Griner was only forty eight, which the old man always reminded him of, but then admitted, yeah, for a convict that is pretty frickin' old.

"You gonna be okay?" he asked over at the old man now. He had snuck a peak at Griner who'd gone quiet in the car's darkness next to him. They'd also disabled the sled's interior lights, but in the dim, green glow of the instruments the blood from the wound was a shiny highlight on the body sized shadow that was all the young man could make out.

"Yeah. I guess. Whatever," the old man hissed. "Bullet went clean through . . . I think. Need to get a pressure dressing on it though. Just get going, kid. Better head for your place. Plan B. You know the way there better than I do. And like you said before, it's safe, right?"

"Yeah . . . yeah. My mom'll be passed out drunk and my sister could sleep through an earthquake."

Jason put the sled in gear, made sure not to squeal the tires as he pulled away, lit up its lights only after they'd gotten a half a block away, driving under control like Griner had told him to. Luckily he was tall for his age and at 5'10" had no trouble reaching the pedals.

"Maybe we got something for your arm too at my house," Jason volunteered, feeling better and more relaxed now that they were getting away.

"Forget it. I got it," Griner said and reached up to flick on the dome light, then slipped out of his coat. "Ahhh," he had to howl quietly as he did. He kept moving though, knowing he had to, until the long coat was all the way off.

His upper left arm, including the sleeve of the black t-shirt he had on was covered in blood. Some flowed down his side as well. Jason watched him, glancing that way as he drove. He had to smile too because just like he'd just been thinking, Griner had thought of that too, pulling a first aid kit from under the car's passenger seat.

"Man, you always think of everything," Jason even said and allowed himself a little laugh while Griner started wrapping his arm tight in white bandage. Just prior to that with several hisses of pain he'd crammed a tube of cotton into the wound. A car coming their way caught Jason's eye. "Oh oh. Looks like-"

"What," Griner asked as he finished wrapping the whole roll of bandage material around his arm and then got some tape on top of that.

"Cops," Jason told him with all the nervousness suddenly back in his voice. All the while too he couldn't take his eyes off the patrol car as it sped past them going the other way, lights strobing and no doubt headed for the scene of their crime.

"Shiiii__," Griner hissed and looked back intently at the cop car too. He was relieved though, as was Jason, to then see that it kept going.

"Aw hell. Here comes another one."

"Crap."

The second car sped past as well, but then almost immediately its brake lights ignited in the death sled's rear window and this second car came to a swerving stop before ripping a quick U-turn. It came up on them slowly but surely after that.

"Take the next right, but only at the last second," Griner tersely instructed. "Then cut the lights but make sure you can see well enough to stay on the road. If not, turn 'em back on. Just keep taking turns then. As many as you can. But keep heading in the general direction toward your house if you can too."

Finished with the driving directions, Griner got out his shotgun and slipped in a shell to take the place of the one he'd put in the cashier at the liquor store. He set that gun aside then though. "Gimme that nine and roll down the window behind you," he ordered at the kid.

Jason dug the pistol out from behind his back and passed it over. Griner crawled into the back seat and then across until he had his right arm and the nine out the window behind Jason. He squeezed off several rounds at the pursuing vehicle before the kid took another turn hard.

Griner held on and watched, got ready to take some more shots, but then as the police car took the same turn it lost control and slammed into the side of a warehouse on the corner.

"Yeah!" Jason cheered and hit the gas.

"Wow. I never thought . . ." Griner let out and sighed with relief. He plopped against the back seat.

"And hey! I know where to go! I mean, I know where we are. We're on Redondo and all I gotta do is take this over to Harbor and then across the parkway and we're home free!"

"All right, kid. You guys got any booze?"

"Are you kidding? My mom's a lush, remember?"

Thank God, Griner could only think. And not just about the booze. But about the way this whole thing had ended up. And not that he was religious or anything, but if that hadn't been a miracle just then . . . the way that cop car lost it like that . . . frickin' God blessed miracle.

"What honey," Ivy Henkman groggily said up at her daughter. Joannie was standing by the side of her bed and rather pestily shaking her shoulder. Before the shaking the girl had told her something, but through the cobwebs of slumber it had all sounded like gibberish.

"Honey . . . honey! You can stop. I'm awake." Joannie kept right on shaking though until Ivy helped by moving her daughter's little hand away.

Somehow she did it gently, using all of her natural benevolence to tame her what otherwise would have been a hung-over and surly, more violent reaction. Even in a state like that, with her nightly drunk half worn off, her head throbbing and her nerves feeling like they were about to crawl right out through her skin, she still couldn't get mad at her sweet little girl. Well . . .

"Jason came home with some man and his arm is all bloody and they both have guns and the police are outside," Joannie reported again and this time even more rapidly.

"What . . . what?" Ivy could only manage as she swung her legs out of bed and then just sat there rubbing her temples.

Come to think of it though, she realized, what was that sound she was hearing? It was beating against her brain. Oh . . . was it . . . helicopters? She was thinking for sure it was that wop wop wop sound they made, and real close too. Like right overhead. So yeah. That made sense. A police helicopter. Especially since like Joannie was saying, Jason came home with some man and his arm was all bloody and they had guns and now the police were outside---

"WHAT?! What did you say," she screamed and even grabbed her little daughter by the shoulders. So much for not getting mad.

All of which might have frightened most little girls but Joannie was used to her mom's drug and or booze induced, moody eruptions. "I told you mommy. Jason came home with a man and his arm-"

The little girl didn't get a chance to finish this time though. Her mother grabbed her by the lower arm and pulled her across the room, stopping at the small upstairs landing across from her bedroom to peek carefully out its medium-sized window that looked out onto the front yard and the street. The light coming in through its frayed curtain though was so bright Ivy Henkman had to not only squint but then also brought her arm up to help shield her vision.

"Oh my God," she uttered as she maneuvered her gaze until she could see enough to confirm her worst fears.

As far as she could tell there were at least three or four police cars strategically positioned in front of the house: one in the driveway, another in the front yard, and just beyond the sidewalk two more were pulled up at the curb? Adding to all of their spot-lights shining on her house was one moving across it all, shooting down from the aforementioned helicopter up above. And man, just like she'd noticed before, was that thing loud!

Which in part helped fuel the energy that suddenly filled her frame, because mostly the noise just really pissed her off. How dare they drive her headache to pounding levels with their noise and searing lights! And sure Jason probably did something really stupid, but was all this really necessary? And hadn't she heard them say on the news that all flights would be grounded tonight because of that freak lightning storm last night? Figures though. Cops always do whatever they want.

"Jason!" she yelled and dragged little Joannie down the stairs with her. Luckily the girls little legs took them quickly enough to keep her on her feet. "Jason. What in the hell?!"

"Mom, get down," her boy yelled hard back at her.

From where she stood at the bottom of the stairs Ivy could see that Joannie hadn't been exaggerating. Jason really did have a gun, as did this other man along with his bloody arm and both of them sitting on the floor with their backs against the sofa, the same sofa Ivy had laid on that afternoon positioned just below the big window that looked out onto the neighborhood.

And just like before too, the off kilter curtains were keeping the living room mostly dark but lighted again too by bright shafts shining through like small polygonal spots where the curtains didn't quite cover in a few places.

"Seriously mom!" Jason continued. "I told you to tell her to stay in bed, Joannie! Both of you should have! But since you're here just go down into the basement or something. Yeah. Go down there. But get down! And crawl there. The cops are liable to blow your heads off!"

"Oh Jason. Jason Jason Jason," Ivy chided her son and let herself collapse right where she had ended up, a few feet to the left of the stairwell, against the back living room wall. She lazily slid down until she was sitting on the floor, using said wall for a back rest. "Come on Joannie honey. Sit down here with Mommy. It'll all be all right once your brother turns himself in. Which is what you are going to do, right Jason!" she yelled at the end.

"Mom! You don't get it. We just got here. We're still trying to figure out what happened . . . and what we're gonna do next."

"Like you have a choice," Ivy half slurred, some of her drunk returning. "Baby, crawl over to the TV stand and get mommy's bottle. You know where it is."

The little girl quickly crawled across the living room floor to the dark wooden stand beneath the big screen TV in the far corner. A little door in its center swung easily open and the girl reached in.

"Oh God," Jason groaned. "Even now? Really?"

"Especially now. May be my last chance." Ivy thanked her daughter, cracked open the large bottle she just retrieved and took a good swig of its amber liquid contents.

"The chopper must have picked us up after that patrol car crashed . . . followed us home and radioed our location," Griner recited, his growl a little quieter now. Both he and Jason sat stiff backed with their weapons held against their chests. A splotch of shiny black had welled on the carpet below Griner's left arm and the once mostly white bandage was now mostly red.

"This is the Police. We know you're in there and we know you're armed. Open the door and throw your weapons out. Then come out with your hands up. You will not be harmed if you're unarmed," a bullhorn powered voice blasted in through the open living room windows hidden behind the curtains. The helicopter's wopping still played over it all as well.

"What's to argue with there fellas," Ivy piped up and took another swig. "I don't know about your friend there, Jason, but all they'll probably do to you is toss your worthless butt back into juvie for another six months. Big frickin' deal." She followed all that with another swig.

Griner smiled. "Your mom's okay. And she's right, too. We'll throw out the guns and then I'll go out first. In case they're trigger happy." He struggled to his feet and got against the wall leading to the front door.

"No way, old man," Jason objected. "If you go . . . I go right behind you . . . or we go together." He quickly took a spot on the wall right next to Griner.

Griner started to object right back, but then Ivy staggered up and put her own two cents in. "I'llllll go. And when I get out there I'll explain it's just my boy and some old stickup man already half bled to death . . ."

Of course the two criminals, the old and the new, started to decline the offer, but then none of them got the chance to be a hero. Not yet.

Because all of a sudden the shaking started and it got so strong, so fast and lasted so long all any of them, man, woman, teenager and child could do was run for the nearby basement stairs—which seemed like their only out. Actually, Jason quickly scooped up and carried his mother while Joannie just as quickly grabbed Griner's index finger. They all dove into the subterranean darkness just as the brightly lighted world filled with police cars and helicopters caved in all around them.

CHAPTER VI

FREE AT LAST

As mentioned, the beast was freed in the quake too. Yes, him: leader of the fallen. Or had that been the original reason for the quake, to release the long held nemesis of all living things? He liked to think so. Maybe even he caused it as he came up, busting out of his solid rock cell forever inescapable until suddenly its obsidian boulder door deep within the earth's mantle broke open.

Of course, more rumbling followed as he dug his way up and up. So strong and hardened were his claw like hands that the remaining rocks and boulders bounced off and gave way to his relentless advance like Styrofoam fake ones would. Anything else in his way melted or moved aside as he also used forceful blasts of his super-heated, flame-filled breath to continue carving his way up. Up and out.

Finally, he broke through and unfurled his great wings. They were black and leathery like a bat's. Only the bat would have had to be the size of house like he was, twenty feet tall and hugely muscled and generally humanoid in shape. Even his head mostly humanoid too, but greatly horned. There were ten of them in all, sweeping back like thick tails of blackened hair, but were really harder than rock. Although also then like hair again in how they curved up at their ends around his overly thick neck in a ten-pointed crown.

A bigger crown than normal though, needed to adorn his bigger than normal, darkly red head. It was mostly bigger in the forehead and cranial areas where the final two horns grew extra-long and curved straight up. Below all of that the most cruelly and malevolently featured face ever created was carved as if by a sculpture's awl in living stone.

So out and now airborne and flying fast and high as only he could . . . the demon king scanned the land below. He soon realized that no, not even *he* could have caused an earthquake capable of destruction this immense.

The planet's entire surface lay in rubble. Great methane fueled flames spewed toxic smoke clouds the size of cities into the air thousands of feet high. On top of that or rather below all that, whole, state-sized areas of upturned real estate were shrouded in a darkness that grew darker and darker by the minute as flames kept burning and smoke kept rising.

But there too and mixed in with all of it was a smoke of a little different hue, or maybe as one might call them, segments of smoke. Living, or maybe make that *dying*, humanized segments.

Wispy ghostlike entities, spirits in fact, hovered about here and there. They were those that were his and were waiting for him to take them home.

Which he would do. Sort of. He would be taking them somewhere. Or rather, and how ironic was this, the king of evil sardonically realized then, they would be taking him. That is, once he gathered them all up.

Although even then he knew his many minions were busily at work, doing said gathering . . . the other fallen who would have either been set free by the great temblor like him, or he would soon set them free. They would all be with him sooner or later. He and his many would take all of them if they could.

Not much else to do now anyway, the Father of Murder, also had to forlornly realize. Not much living to be done down there anymore, or maybe make that *killing*. No more humans to play with, to spiritually influence, which was all he and his helpers could do before, locked up like they were.

How much fun they could have had with them now . . . set free like they were. But alas, there was virtually no one left to play with.

Or so it seemed. But just in case there were survivors, on and on the dragonesque demon thing searched, flying more speedily, intensifying his efforts. He zigged and zagged across whole countries, or where they should have been, Scythia, Persis, Media, Arabia, Issedones, which was how he had known them before. Before things went bad. Before He showed up, *the Holy Lord Son of God and all that blah blah blah.* Then yeah. Him to worry about too, always chaining him up . . .

Say bye bye to those old chains now, Satan rejoiced and turned some tight barrel rolls before resuming his search.

But it seemed no use. They were all gone. Not just the people but all the countries and their continents too, even the new ones. The China, the Japan, those lovely little island nations . . . the Russia, the Germany, the France and Great Britain too. They were all gone. Oceans now ruled where land once did and vice versa. Whole continents covered by water and others looking like they exploded. *And all of Africa gone too!?* Arghhh, the demon king wanted to scream up to the heavens.

Of course he knew what it all meant. He knew the prophecy. He knew he was meant to be trapped here in this hell the Earth had become. Him and all those souls given over to him, stuck in this fiery, cavernous construct. He knew all about God's plan for him.

But he had a plan too. He'd been busy over the eons, trapped like he was but loose among the minds of all the humans. Some of them so smart too. *And so evil. The witches. The Voodoo Priestesses . . . ahhh . . . the beautiful priestesses . . . the most delicious and sweet seductresses he had practically ever known.*

Together they had made it, concocted a potion for just such a time as this. It would trap the souls of those just recently dead inside their still dead bodies, driving them on in a mad form of half-life. Better yet, they would now serve him. Once infected they would also spread the disease to their victims. So more and more souls then left behind for him too, or more accurately captured, yes, captured, captured by him. The great corrupter.

Then the souls would be his to use, as many as he could get, to fuel his . . .

He made himself not think about the wonderful way he planned to use the souls. He didn't want you-know-who finding out and ruining it all. Oh sure, most of the time God knew about everything as far as the humans knew. He had ways to hide things, though, from the supposedly omniscient one. How else would he have gotten away with so much of what he had?

So now, however, to complete all this work he had to find the survivors. Only from those could he get new souls. Fresher, more powerful ones. He had to find where people remained, the freshest meat. If any even did.

On and on he flew, fervently seeking the remaining masses from North Pole to South, but nothing. Eventually he made his way west until . . . *yes . . . yes . . . there! There they were.* He could sense them somewhere down there and swooped in lower for visual confirmation.

Yes. Yes. Some still alive here, many recent dead left behind too. The dead he could use as well, he knew. They would be a big part of his plan. He couldn't wait to--

Oh yes, the dark one realized then too. It made sense they were here in so many numbers, both the living and the dead.

It all made sense, he realized, because as he zoomed in on them he also figured out where he was. Even as changed as everything was, the weather remained so accommodating here. The sun's warming rays broke through because no toxic clouds were here. The land always so fertile. Especially upturned as it was now. The fruited plain . . .

Probably He, the almighty one, had saved, "This land," because they had actually believed in Him in this land. And, they had loved Him. Many of them, at least. It was even written into their culture. "One nation under God. In God we trust. God bless . . . America."

Which then too of course was why *he*, being exactly the anti of Him, hated them so much and corrupted as many as he could here.

Especially, where the flying king of the demons was coming now, this southwest corner that had become the epicenter of sin. Sin city, they'd even so happily referred to one of their habitation centers in the area. If they only knew.

But not just that one. Others too. All the cities were so deliciously packed with easy pickings, as the humans used to say. His spirit had been very active here over the years. And they had all wanted it so bad. Maybe it was the sun . . . . so warm on their sweet little bodies tirelessly being perfected. And, the fun . . . fun in the sun, fun in the sun. The happiest place on earth. City of Angels. Home to the stars . . .

So no wonder it was all ending up here. Probably also, however, because of the lay lines. The vortices. This had always been where everything was headed. The latest and the greatest. *Tomorrow land*, as that one human had called it in his amusement park erected here. Of course here. Copied and duplicated and spreading out from here, but starting here first.

And then just a little north the Silicon Valley too, and the computer age growing out from there. The computers which had just about become everything. But starting here with those few fellows in their garages. Because the lay lines and vortices of spiritual power converged here. And had those been what kept this area from being destroyed now? Most likely.

Either way it was just as well. He loved it here too. *What God was up to, who knew? Who cared?* Satan was just happy to be free and in the flesh again, so to speak. And the weather just so gorgeous. Sunny Southern California. Ahhhhhh . . .

Although at the moment he knew there was a change in the weather coming. Courtesy of himself. Just a little afternoon shower. He got some altitude and began the dispersal of his new potion. His revivification potion. They would receive it as a disease, and think of it that way down there, but he knew its true origin. He'd made it, or like so many time before in human history with the many diseases, arranged for its creation. So many wonderful diseases he'd given them over the eons, the king of evil warmly reflected and gloated.

This time again he'd found all the right ingredients: select minerals and chemicals, certain herbs, animal parts, and human parts too. An ancient recipe. One he and the beautiful voodoo priestesses had come up with. Then all of it washed down with almost more water than even his large organs could hold.

Finally too, all of that mixed and married in the special way only his aforementioned organs could and then showered over the land like a yellow rain. Yellow because even in God's immortal creations their urine was that color too.

"All you need are souls," the flying beast even sang then in a parody of the old Beatles song as he oh so happily showered the land below. "All you need are souls . . . souls . . . souls are all you need . . ."

CHAPTER VII

RIDE OR DIE

The spiritual essence of God descended into the pasture as invisibly as it usually would: light puffs of wind rustling around taller tufts of grass. A little extra glisten on the sun's shiny face. An extra sharp freshness in the warm spring air hinting at His sudden return and everywhere all at once presence.

Or, and if there had been any humans present, a sudden lightening of mood, inexplicable joy or maybe even a strengthening of determination to overcome a current, personal challenge might have belied His coming too. But in this pasture, at least in this back portion thereof, where the head high, white and thick picketed fence met at a distant corner (distant even from the nearest outbuildings) only a lone horse roamed.

Not alone for much longer though, as then the Holy Spirit became visible, and in a form the horse would hopefully find non-threatening . . . if not downright pleasing. That was of paramount importance. The horse needed to be calm and receptive. God had a special and very important message for him. About a very special mission.

So at the moment His celestial eminence more closely resembled a ranch hand, complete with the odor of animals and hard work and just a little bit saddle sore and bowlegged to boot. All in the name of authenticity.

The horse was fooled too, or seemed to be. The big strong animal waited patiently, albeit at the same time warily watching the Lord's lanky approach. Jesus' pointed toe boots scuffed gently across the grass and hard dirt. A well-worn cowboy hat hemmed in his dark, shoulder length hair.

"Yes . . . yes, my sweet beast . . . fine and beautiful . . . yes you are . . . of my loveliest," the Lord cooed while also gently stroking the animal's strong neck with his left hand. The creature's generous musculature, so readily visible throughout its large and almost entirely black frame, twitched shyly beneath his touch. With his other hand Jesus let the horse nuzzle a fresh cut quarter of big red apple, then engulf it.

Next came the real business at hand and rancher Jesus pressed close to deliver his message in a still, small voice. The exquisitely streamline, mammalian running machine listened, pawed at the earth, then drew back from the Lord and suddenly pranced around Him in a tight circle. All the while too the horse's nostrils flared as it gruntingly snorted in air, tilted its head first to one side then the other, and next the prancing turned into a controlled gallop as the circle around the Lord widened.

Jesus smiled and watched the horse run, marveling at its magnificence, and stepping back toward the fence to give the great beast plenty of room. "That's right baby," the Lord of the universe shouted too. "Let it out. The time has come. The time has come to run. Run my beauty. Run like the wiiinnnd . . ."

The great shining and black blur of ever-increasing mass came like a streak straight for the Lord. A still smiling Jesus ducked just as the airborne equine leapt harder and higher than it ever had. Possibly harder and higher than any horse ever had. The stallion easily cleared both the crouching creator of all things and the fence just behind him.

"Yeeeee Hawww," Jesus yelled after standing back up and turning to watch the stallion run. The wonderful animal made two long sprints back and forth before Him, but now free on the other side of the high fence.

On its third trip back the horse pulled up and stopped where Jesus had been standing, but now only His hat rested atop one of the fence posts. The freshly frothed galloper nuzzled the old tan sombrero for just a moment before turning and running hard and long into the setting sun.

Kellen Andrews took a breath, a long, deep one. Mostly just so she could tell she was still alive. Otherwise she would have never believed it. That she was still alive, that is.

Because it had felt like the whole world had caved in and then flipped over. Although half of that had happened as if in a dream, because she'd been rather deeply asleep. She realized right away, however, it was all very real when finally she was fully awake and could see that her bed had sunk straight down and now lay at the bottom of the ten foot deep hole her bedroom had become.

Even more amazing was how there she was now, still laying comfortably in bed after only having had to kick a not too heavy floor lamp from across her legs. That and brush some dust from her face. Then not breathe for a moment after roughly casting away her dust covered bedspread and sheet.

Her bed really was still sitting in almost exactly the same position as it always did . . . only now ten feet lower. And luckily, oh so luckily, all the chunks of ceiling and roof, the heavier pieces of furniture in her room (a big chest of drawers and her desk, computer and stereo) all piled to either side of her bed. Talk about a miracle.

Which Kellen knew she'd be needing more of. Miracles, that is. Because she was still stuck down there, and from the looks of things it wasn't much better above. All the light to be had was showering down through the new skylight up above (well, really it looked like the whole roof was gone) affording her a lovely view of the partially moonlit, starry night sky.

The power was obviously out. And then even more distressing was the lone voice of a male child wailing from up in the house somewhere.

"Kellen . . . Kellllennnn," her little brother, as she thought of him, wailed out both in distress and in-between quiet sobs. Evidently, thank God, he'd survived as well, from the sounds of it.

"It's okay Aaron," she hollered back and carefully got up on the bed, first to her knees, and then once she'd satisfied herself that the whole thing was stable enough, she stood on the mattress next. "Are you hurt?" she yelled up next, angling her head and voice toward where she thought she'd heard Aaron calling out from . . . *it seemed he was up there off to her right.*

"Scared . . . I'm really scared . . . what happened?"

"I don't know honey. Just a big earthquake I guess. Really big! But are you okay? Are you hurt, hon?"

"No . . . I'm okay. I made a boo boo though in the bed. I'm sorry." The young boy fought back tears.

"That's okay honey," Kellen reassured him and forced down the chuckle that the obvious irony of his dismay at such a trivial matter couldn't help but cause. Although it broke her heart too, thinking of her eight-year-old little brother up there in wet PJs and scared out of his wits.

Not that he was really her little brother; she'd just always thought of him like that. Kellen's real father had worked for Mr. Andrews, Aaron's father, here on his horse ranch as far back as she could remember.

Mr. Andrews was such a good guy, though, that when both of Kellen's parents were killed in an automobile accident, he and Mrs. Andrews went ahead and adopted the twelve-year-old that Kellen was back then. She'd been so grateful, of course, and since they'd always treated her as one of their own ever since, she even took their surname.

Not that any of that mattered anymore, the now fifteen-year-old Kellen realized. She hadn't had a chance to check the news, obviously, but her gut was telling her the vacationing Andrews would be a long time in coming home from their Mediterranean cruise. This was no ordinary earthquake. Even after being asleep for the first part of it, Kellen remembered it still seemed to last forever. It shook like nothing she'd ever felt before.

So it'd probably be just her and little Aaron, for now at least, the young lady knew. And she damn well better figure out how to get up there to him, whether he was her real little brother or not. Maybe . . . .

"Aaron," Kellen called up. "Can you walk over toward my voice? Can you come over to the edge of the hole I'm in? Where my bedroom used to be? Be careful! But can you get through to here? Does the floor look sturdy? Is there a clear path?"

"It's very dirty," he answered timidly, still sounding very scared. "There's stuff all over the place."

Kellen again fought off the urge to laugh. She also didn't bother to explain what she'd really said. That she'd said *sturdy*, not *dirty*. Poor little guy probably didn't even know what it meant anyway. "Just stay put honey . . . I'll come to you," she decided to leave it at. Although how, she wasn't really sure.

Her impromptu *Plan A* had been to maybe guide Aaron to find something to throw down to her to help her climb out, but it sounded just too dangerous up there. *Plan B?* She stood there and took a moment while also taking a look around.

It really did look like about ten feet, maybe twelve up to the top. Worse yet, it was all bare wall, and plus too the bare floor that rose up before her now, like a wall.

So that was what had happened! The whole room had been jolted backwards and sideways and then just dropped, leaving her bed settled on the back wall of the shoebox shaped room which was now its bottom. The front wall it shared with the rest of the house had been ripped right off and was now the hole at the top. So . . .

Then she saw it. One of the two by fours making up the inner frame of the wall jutted out over the edge of the hole in a three foot plank. *Would it be strong enough though?* Hopefully it was still well anchored to the rest of the wall's frame. But what could she use to get up there?

Of course she'd heard stories before about people tying their sheets together to make a rope, but . . .

Oh yeah!

A rope!

Of course!

But could she get to it? And was it still even there? She thought hard back to the last time she'd used it. It had been what? A couple months ago? Yeah. Had to be. Just before the Junior Riders and Ropers competition. She'd practiced for hours tying and cinching that rope over and over. Then seated across the room and back over her shoulder she'd lassoed her bedposts over and over again. Just for practice of course, with plenty of real roping and riding later, barrel after barrel after barrel outside.

But the real point being, as far as she could remember, she'd left the lasso in the back of her closet, which now would be . . . *Yeah! Right over there.*

She rummaged down into it, practically standing on top of all the stuff that now lay piled across the bottom of the dugout-like structure her closet had become. *Oh gosh . . . that old outfit too . . . and the shoes and boots . . . how many pairs did she have? And yeah . . . there it was . . . still tied even too . . . ready to go . . . yeah . . . yeah!*

Then, since she was in her closet like that, Kellen also dug out some good jeans, one of her favorite flannel shirts and the leather vest adorned with her many award patches. And oh yeah, she figured then too, her most comfortable pair of boots.

Ready to go, she pretty much figured, before one more thing caught her eye. Her Marlin, lever action .22 rifle. She kept it in her closet just in case. It was good for keeping coyotes away. Whenever she heard them yelping in the night out back she'd fire a couple scare rounds. She wished no creature of God's ill will but when those damn Devil dogs had torn the throat out of her contest ready, beautiful little black wool lamb, she'd been shooting them away every chance she'd had since.

So she grabbed up the gun too. She dipped her head and one arm through the sling to rest it across her back. She looked up again to the beam jutting out above and readied the lariat.

The rope looped over the board after only about a half dozen tries. She was a little rusty and somewhat stressed—Aaron kept hollering out her name and each time it was like a ball of anxiety exploding in her gut. She'd just wanted to yell at him to shut up, he wasn't helping, but instead through clenched teeth she reassured him, she was coming, be a brave little scout.

Up top the rope cinched good and tight. It was just long enough. A couple hard tugs seemed to indicate the board was pretty darn strong too. All she had to do now was flash back to last year in PE when they'd all had to shimmy up a rope in gym class. She was one of the few girls who could make it to the top and those prissier girls had made fun of her.

Then word had gone from them to their boyfriends and one of them, Jason LaRue had made fun of her. How come she looked mostly like a boy? How come she was just as strong as and taller than most the boys too, and never wore makeup and them jeans and cowboy boots all the time? Was she a cowgirl or maybe a cowboy? Or maybe one of them sex changers, was she one of them?

Everybody laughed and Kellen lost it. She remembered hitting and hitting at Jason LaRue and then even knocking him to the ground before she got pulled off. The vice principal handled it from there.

Thinking about all that made her mad enough again now to get up the rope strong and quick. Hand over hand with some angry grunting and before she knew it she had the two by four in hand. She even had enough energy left over for kicking a leg across the edge of the wall. She then swung herself over it to fall on the surface of some debris a few feet below.

"Holy shi_," she let out between labored breaths and sat back for just a second. She didn't like to cuss like that, but sometimes she couldn't help it.

"Kellen! Is that you?" little Aaron called out. He must have only seen a flash of her coming out and over that edge of the wall. It was pretty dark up here too.

"It's me honey. I'm coming. Don't worry. I'm coming in a minute. Let me-" She'd cut herself off because as she stood up and looked around she realized getting to him wasn't going to be as easy as promised. The whole house had been flattened and all the materials it was made of lay scattered around. There was no sign of the floor anywhere. But . . . then she saw it, little Aaron's room remained relatively intact somehow. One wall was half knocked out but the other three were intact. The boy's bedroom stood there like a little shack all unto itself. In its doorway stood the little boy.

"I'm glad it's not winter," he said. ". . . these bajama bottoms are cold. Can you help me get my pants on Kellen?"

"Of course, honey. I'm coming. Be patient though. I have to be careful." Which she was doing by keeping both hands on the wall edges bordering the hole she'd just come out of as she shimmied around it. She was afraid one of the many wall sections or even the pieces of roof lying about might conceal another hole like her room had become and she didn't want to fall through. In a situation like this—and she could only assume things were really, really bad: no sirens, no lights, everything completely and eerily silent—falling through and breaking a leg could be fatal, both for her and Aaron.

With care she finally made it all the way around the edge of the hole— almost hypnotized by the strange image of her bed at the bottom of it. Now she was only about ten feet away from Aaron. Unfortunately, the entire distance was covered by several more layers of debris.

The little boy, who still stood by his bedroom's doorway quietly sniveling, took a couple quick but furtive steps Kellen's way.

"No, honey! No," she shouted at him and he stepped back quickly. "Just wait . . . we have to be careful. There could be more holes."

"Okay, but hurry . . . hurrrrry, okay?"

Kellen told him again to just hold on and thought about telling him too how he needed to be brave because things might be pretty bad, but then she thought better of it. One thing at a time, she decided, and told him instead everything was going to be okay. Even though she was far from sure about that.

To prove it, though, she started across, kicking away the sections of fallen wall and their accompanying boards that lay in her path. If by doing this she could then see solid floor beneath her, she'd step onto it and move forward.

Nearly there, only a few more feet away from the boy, she kicked and kicked at a big five foot by five foot section of wall still between them but it wouldn't budge. Which was weird. All the others had moved pretty easy.

She waited and looked it over a little more and though there was a smaller section of wall laying on it just outside Aaron's door, and a jumble of boards and roof tiles were all around, it still should have scooted pretty easy. *Why . . .*

Stabilizing her feet, Kellen bent down and tried picking up the piece. She gripped it along the nearest edge and pulled up hard. *What the-*

The slab lifted a few inches, but then an incredible whooshing sound whooped and whistled from below. In an instant the chunk of wall got sucked hard right straight back down. Almost like there was . . . *some big sucking hole under there?*

No. Kellen couldn't believe that. But who knew! Things had certainly been rearranged by that quake. And come to think of it, looking back at the section of wall she could see a slight bowing toward its center. She didn't dare walk across it, she knew. But there was no other way! The big piece of stucco and wood—and therefore the hole too if there really was one—blocked and took up all the area fronting little Aaron's bedroom door. He stood just beyond it, just inside the door's frame. He whined a little more and squeezed at his groin with both hands.

"It's okay, honey. I'm coming. Just have to figure out . . ."

Oh. Yeah. Maybe. Maybe if she walked just along the edge of the section. Should be strongest there. And hopefully too mostly supported by some of the two-by-fours. *And the floor. So . . .*

She got up on the edge and with her two booted feet started heel to toe walking, holding both arms out, and the coiled lariat in her right. Now she also noticed for the first time, that heat seemed to be coming up from below.

Halfway across she just went for it and took the last few feet in two normal sized strides then added a sideways one, which landed her almost on top of little Aaron.

"Whoa," she even said and had to hug the little boy to her legs hard so as not to knock him over. He hugged her back even harder.

Oh oh, she had to stop and think then too. She sniffed at the air. And sure, she could smell that slightly acrid, urine odor from Aaron's PJ bottoms. But also there was something else in the air.

Gas?

She'd heard of that before with earthquakes, how gas lines could rupture. Which then the risk of fire and explosion was very high. *But this smell . . . was it? Yeah, it smelled like sulfur too. Either way . . .*

"Come on, buddy. We need to get you dressed. Quick. And then go find help. Okay?" She turned the little boy around and started back into his room with him.

"Can I wear my new football uniform?"

Kellen had a small laugh and after thinking about it had to tell him, "No buddy. Probably not." Then she thought of something. "You can wear your helmet though. How's that. But let's just get your high tops, some jeans, maybe a long sleeve sweatshirt. That'll be better, okay?"

"Okay . . ."

Kellen stopped a moment in the middle of the little boy's bedroom to get her bearings. It was amazing how well the room had come through it all. Things were jumbled, of course. The furniture had been knocked around. His roof was gone and one corner up toward the roofline had been knocked out somehow, but there . . . there was a bunch of his clothes piled up in a corner near his bed which sat at an odd angle now but was at least upright. She got the little boy over there and got to work getting him dressed.

They did it quickly too, like she had said, and then Kellen took little Aaron by the hand to get him out of there. He had his football helmet on and was ready for anything. The junior sized but otherwise almost NFL regulation grade head gear was mostly white with blue lightning bolts on it. And besides protection, Kellen realized also that at least it might make him easier to keep an eye on too.

Either way, together the little football player and the cowgirl hip hopped over the corner of the slab covered hole, and just as Kellen had helped Aaron over the last bit of broken wall separating the inside of the house from the outside, with an even louder whoop and a whoosh the hole blew open.

"Stay down, Aaron," Kellen yelled to the boy, then rolled over the last bit of wall too. She came up in a defensive, one-knee stance close to the wall just in case and the boy hugged hard to her raised leg. She might have also just headed out at a run with the boy then, except a quick check had showed her that now, post-earthquake, this end of the house, which used to give way to a back yard patio area and then the first few acres of the ranch's rear portion was now blocked by big boulders jutting up. Behind these was what looked like a big, impassable mountainside shrouded in the night. No use heading that way.

Besides which too, when the hole blew and the odor of sulfur grew, she knew there wasn't any gas leak. More like a hell leak, she was thinking, albeit semi-humorously, but this she had to see so she carefully peeked over the edge of the broken wall they were hiding behind.

Of particular interest was how once the piece of wall blew off the hole a reddish glow filled the room due to the similarly colored light being cast up and out from within. Maybe it really was connected to hell, the young woman couldn't help but consider after seeing that. Well . . . not really, she didn't really believe that, but it sure was something she'd never seen before.

But since no demons were coming out right away, nor anything else too interesting, she turned and sat down with her back against the waist high piece of wall. Aaron imitated her. The little boy also squinted out from his helmet at the boulders only a few feet away.

"What happened to the back yard?" he couldn't help but ask.

"I guess it was that earthquake," Kellen answered, but at the same time noticed that at least a narrow trail fronted the boulders, hopefully providing a way out to somewhere.

"I never seen an earthquake do that!"

"This was a special one, honey."

They waited there a few moments longer while Kellen decided they'd better go ahead and try the trail. Hopefully it would-

She'd cut her thought train off all of a sudden because she'd heard something just then, something strange and something real close. It sounded like people, but ones that were maybe retarded or something. And evil. Worse yet, it sounded like they were men and they were right behind the piece of wall her and Aaron were leaning against. Like they had come out of that hole. But that couldn't be, could it?

After quietly telling Aaron to stay down, she slowly rose along their little barricade until she could see them. There were two, and though the crimson backlighting of the still dimly glowing hole made it hard to make out their features, she could now tell they were males for sure. Age unknown though. They were moving kind of funny too, also like mentally retarded people might, or like those that had that muscle disease she couldn't think of the name for. Or like . . . but no . . . those were only in the movies. Either way she knew her and Aaron better get going.

But which way? The little trail lead both left and right along the wall of boulders. And both ways also just lead into darkness.

"Come on, buddy. We gotta go."

"But I hear someone."

"Yeah. That's the problem. I don't think they're good someone's. Come on." She took Aaron's little hand and started in a duck walk away from the wall. Aaron started in right behind her, but at his height he didn't have to duck walk to stay hidden.

At the trail and turning left—she'd done a real quick eenie meenie minie moe—with more than a little alarm she heard the strange ones at the hole noticeably increase their vocalizations. Or in other words, their guttural moaning had turned to excited growling.

"Come on," she more urgently hissed at Aaron because now the boy had turned back in response to their noise.

"They sound like monsters . . ." The boy sounded both frightened and mystified.

"Yeah, so we better get going. Give me Spaceman Spike." Spaceman Spike was the cartoon space ship shaped flashlight Kellen had grabbed in Aaron's room and stuffed into his pocket. Aaron fished it out.

"Go Spaceman Spike," Aaron cheered quietly. "He'll lead us to safety . . ."

"Here." She quickly grabbed the light away from the boy. He'd been flying the little thing as if they were having a happy day at the park. Kellen regretted her hastiness, but apologies would have to wait.

They were a good twenty feet up the trail now, but in her turning to take the light she couldn't help but notice against the red glow that the . . . monsters? Err, whatever or whoever they were, they too were getting on the trail now. And it looked like there were even three of them now as well.

"We have to hurry," she told the boy and strengthened her grip on his hand. She clicked the flashlight on and it's fairly bright, LED beam gave them a good ten feet to see in front of themselves. The trail was easily visible, but also still only lead to darkness ahead.

They bravely made their way, though, and looking off to her left Kellen could see far enough to tell that the rest of the house had fared no better than the part they'd just left. In fact, a major portion . . . right there, where she remembered their spacious kitchen used to be along with the dining and oh oh, was all else she could think then.

Because now she could see the whole back portion of the house had crumbled. It lay in a great pile almost the size of a small normal house, which made sense. The second story bedrooms had been here too, and the house overall was really big. But the problem was that now it all lay in a one story high mound, blocking their exit.

"Hold on, buddy," Kellen said as the boy bumped into the back of her legs. "Okay . . . okay . . ."

She nervously shone the light here and there all around while she tried to think of something. The path ahead of them was definitely blocked. And on one side the boulders were still way too steep and impassable. On the other the wreckage of the Andrew's residence showed no safe passage either. Although possibly . . .

Then Kellen turned and could see there'd be no time for thinking about it too much anymore. The weirdoes . . . as she suddenly found herself thinking of their three pursuers . . . it looked like they were rapidly coming up on her and the boy. She knew what she had to do.

"Here. Aaron. Hold the light for me. Come on." She tried to sound as calm as she could, but was far from it. Apparently, the lawlessness a crisis like this could cause had already started. "Yeah. There. Like that. Shine it on those people we saw before. I think they're coming after us."

"Why . . . why would they?" The boy took the light, obviously scared.

"Doesn't matter. Don't worry, okay? I'm going to stop them. Just shine the light right on them. Straight ahead. That's good."

The light wavered up and down and from side to side, but generally and adequately illuminated the area directly ahead of them. The pursuers weren't in full view yet, but could easily be heard coming. They were still making their sick moaning and groaning sounds and now too Kellen could hear a rough scooting noise. Evidently they didn't like to pick up their feet either.

"That's good, Aaron. Real good. Be brave. Just like Spaceman Spike would be." Kellen said all this as calmly as possible, all the while also smoothly and quickly—obviously with much practice—brought the rifle around from her back to bear on the upcoming, potential targets.

And sure, it was only a .22, she knew. But also, she reminded herself, a .22 caliber round could be particularly effective as a head shot. The bullet was small enough to enter the skull fairly easily. Then once there, after cutting its way through the brain it usually would not have enough power to exit. It would, however, have enough to ricochet around in the skull for a while, turning the target's brain into Swiss cheese.

"I'll give you Swiss cheese," she then thought out loud before also shouting, "I got a gun. You better think twice. I'll shoot. I'll shoot-"

She was going to also say, ". . . to kill," but then as the first of the weirdoes came into the light, she was truly speechless. Good thing she kind of liked horror movies, and with the recent glut of zombie movies . . . well . . . otherwise it might have been too much to handle. Because if what she was seeing now wasn't a zombie, then there never would be one.

Which yeah, she then realized, there really wasn't supposed to be . . . but . . .

Kellen did a quick mental check.

No.

It isn't Halloween.

These aren't a bunch of drunk frat guys from the nearby junior college.

And either way, I've warned them I intend to to shoot, whoever or whatever they are.

So, she decided, what the heck. The way things were now it was pretty clear she couldn't get in trouble anyway. Which she always considered after having shot out that car window that one time. Accidentally.

Then the deal was totally sealed when she heard Aaron let out a frightened cry. Whoever they were or whatever the cost, they weren't getting to Aaron.

Kellen leveled off the rifle head high, sighted up on the lead weirdo and squeezed one off.

As she'd been trained, she immediately cocked the lever and only held off sighting up on the next pursuer long enough to watch the one she'd just shot stagger forward and then nose dive about thirty feet in front of them.

"Kellen," Aaron cried out and swung quickly around behind her legs.

Everything went dark before them. Kellen quickly reached down and took the flashlight—it was one of the few things she could see because of its bright beam still on but shooting off to the side now. She regripped the rifle's barrel, now with the light held in the same hand and shining out along it from there.

She could then see that luckily one of the two remaining attackers had tripped and fallen over their leader . . . the one she'd just shot who lay still on the ground. Now the other two seemed uncertain of what to do. They were almost pathetic to watch, stumbling and bumbling around. *I'll be damned,* Kellen was thinking, *if they didn't look just like those zombies on TV. But why? Or more importantly, how? And could they really be? Really?*

Just another good reason to shoot them in the head, she realized then too. Wasn't that how they always killed them in the movies? And one thing was for sure, whoever, or whatever these guys were, they definitely needed killing.

Especially when they finally started to get their bearings again and seemed to sight up on the light Kellen still held trained on them. They drooled like dogs, Kellen repugnantly noticed. She rapidly let loose with five or six more shots, all aimed in the general area of their lolling heads. Most of the shots appeared to find the mark. The zombies' heads suddenly bobbed back hard with the impact of the rounds.

Kellen kept her aim on the two more fallen fellows and watched them quiver before coming to rest. Blood was pooling slowly under their heads now, just as it had for the first one.

"Come on, kiddo. I think we're okay now," Kellen whispered at Aaron. She shone the light on him, making a quick check. All he seemed able to do was look up at her with big eyes and shake. "Oh now . . . it's okay, hon. Here. I'll carry you. We gotta get going. Come on up . . ."

The tall and strong cowgirl shouldered her rifle again. She hefted the boy up and held him seated across her left arm. Good thing he was light. His parents had been forever trying to get him to eat more. In her right hand, Kellen carried the flashlight and aimed its beam across their path.

"Don't look down, Aaron. You just keep looking behind us, Okay?" Kellen was so glad when he answered.

"Okay," he said weakly.

She was afraid he'd gone into shock. Which was also why she wanted him to only look back into the darkness. Especially since she was just then having to shine the light ahead of them onto the dead zombie guys so as to avoid slipping on the blood puddles still filling out on the hard soil around them.

She and Aaron were backtracking now, which they continued doing until they got back to the red hole, then after a quick check just kept going in the opposite direction. There was no other way.

Halfway up the trail (the same one of course, but this time leading away from the house) and still bordered by boulders on their left now, they soon made their way out through some more big rocks, up a rise and then down into an area which appeared relatively unchanged and familiar.

For at least fifty yards or so, the grass graced front lawn of the Andrew's large ranch house was still intact. It even still sloped down to the winding, semiprivate road that ran out to the state highway less than a mile away.

From there though, where before the view had previously opened up in scope and distance to hint at the great San Moreno Valley and the nearby town of Earnston, now the ranch house looked out across a deep canyon. On the other side of that, the biggest fire Kellen had ever seen blazed.

"Holy . . ." Kellen couldn't help but utter as she let Aaron down. Her arm was getting tired, and besides, it looked pretty safe anyway. *Weird, what with a brand new canyon in the front yard, but safe.* And because of said canyon, safe from the fire as well, for the time being.

Because *what a fire!* Kellen realized, taking the entire scope of the big blaze in. Not that she hadn't seen her fair share of fires. Earnston and the other medium sized cities which made up Riverview County, one of Southern California's largest and most rural, were frequently threatened by brush fires.

But she'd never seen anything like this before. The flames stretched from end-to-end across what she knew was the Eastern horizon. She knew too from experience that just the fact that she could the flames from so far away meant they had to be huge. Their unearthly long red line separated the darkness of the land from the darkness of the night sky. And that was it. *Omigod*, Kellen then noticed as well. Half the night's stars, the eastern half, were missing as well, no doubt blocked by all the smoke the fire had produced. "Where'd everything go?" Aaron asked, which Kellen was glad to hear. He sounded stronger. ". . . the town . . ."

They always called Earnston, '. . . town.' As in, 'Are we going to town?' or 'Gotta go to town for groceries.' When one lived on a ranch out in the country it was like that. It was a half-hour trip just to get to town so you didn't get to go too often.

Either way there was no use going that way now. 'The town,' and probably the rest of the entire state was gone now from the looks of it.

"Do you think mommy and daddy are okay?" was Aaron's next question and the one Kellen had not wanted to hear or try to answer. She had to say something, though, and lowered to one knee before the boy to try and respond.

"Well . . . it looks like that big earthquake we had really messed things up around here. But you know what? Mom and dad are half-way around the world. Plus they're on a big, big cruise ship. I think they're probably okay." Kellen had a hold of the boy by both shoulders, looking deep into his eyes, hoping to assure him of the truth in her words. "Okay?" she repeated.

She'd said that because Little Aaron *sure* didn't look okay; his eyes, which hadn't had a dry moment since she'd first found him, were still brimming with tears. Trails of their predecessors lined his dust coated cheeks. Beneath that his dry lips quivered.

"Ohhhh honey," Kellen said consolingly. "We'll be okay. You'll see."

She took the boy in the biggest hug she could muster. He let loose with a good cry and Kellen held on and rubbed his little back. "You go ahead and cry little buddy. It's okay to cry sometimes and this sure is one of them."

In all honesty, Kellen felt like crying too. The harsh reality of the way things were now was really starting to sink in. So she let herself sit down on the soft grass and still cradling the boy she closed her eyes. For some reason then the dream she'd had just before the earthquake, a memory somewhat jostled out of the cobwebs of her mind by her choice of the term, '. . . little buddy,' or so she figured, started replaying in her mind.

The dream had featured a Gilligan's Island motif, where that same phrase had frequently graced the skipper's lips when he chatted with his, '. . . little buddy,' Gilligan. Although from there on, Kellen wished the characters of that once-upon-a-time favorite show of hers had been in the dream, instead of her. It was not a good dream.

In it Kellen found herself on a cruise ship, and as she walked about on it, along its wide, deck-like walkways, noticing how eerily empty the whole big boat was, she noticed too that she was dressed like Mary Anne from the show. Like an island survivor complete with handmade straw hat and those cute little sneakers she always wore.

But where was everybody? And the S.S Minnow, this ship was not. *But was it the ship Jack and Irene were on?* That's what she called Mr. and Mrs. Andrews when the kid wasn't around.

Unfortunately, the way dreams can, especially bad ones like this, it was telling her this was indeed their ship. She just knew somehow. And the way bad dreams can too, it was telling her they were in trouble. And that she needed to get to them. A feeling of impending disaster filled the air.

"*Jack . . . hey . . . guys . . . mom . . . dad . . . Irene,*" she excitedly yelled as she ran from gangway to gangway, up the stairs and down, but no sign of them could be seen. *No sign of anyone!*

Eventually, her frantic search lead her to the uppermost level of the large vessel and she ended up looking out over the railing at the vast and dark sea. A low rumble grew in the distance and just as she was wondering what the heck it could be she noticed a large wave stretching completely across her entire line of ocean view. That was what was causing the rumble.

Which she could tell because the rumbling grew in volume and intensity as the wave grew in size and approached. Worse yet, as it did, it was also sucking in all the water between the ship and itself. *This must be a tidal wave, a tsunami, she was thinking in the dream. Don't they come after a big earthquake?*

Oh God, the dream made her think. She had to find them! She had to find her mom and dad, even if just to say . . .

No.

No way.

Suddenly though she knew they were there. She turned and saw them standing just across the deck against the opposite side's railing. Ah, it was breaking her heart. They looked so cute, dressed to the nine's, arm-in-arm. They smiled sweetly as they looked her way. They both waved.

"Goodbye honey . . ."

"Bye dear . . ."

"We love you . . ."

"Take good care of Aaron and please make sure you both get to the island."

Questions wanted to explode from Kellen's head, but she knew there would be no time to get the answers. The dream wasn't going to let her.

Just as Jack and Irene had finished giving her the message they did, the ship rolled first so deep and far her way that her parents were almost directly overhead. Then in the next instant, everything flipped and she was flying over them, watching them still smiling and waving down below while she was hurled high and away out over the ocean.

Then with her own eyes, or just in her mind—because dreams could do that too—she watched the big ship completely capsize as the enormous wave consumed it like a giant sea monster in one big gulp.

Kellen splashed in herself then and because of how far she'd flown she went deep. Once she could, she swam up and up through the dark waters. It seemed to take forever. She knew she wouldn't make it to the top. She could feel herself drowning. She could feel herself dying. She had to make it though. Like Jack and Irene had said and like the dream was telling her, she had to make it for Aaron. No matter what it took. She had to-

Finally, she found the surface. She breathed in deep. Her lungs burned. It was a very detailed dream. Like one of those dreams that means something. She could tell that much. Which was why then, even after the dream was over, after the terror of being lost with nothing but big, black ocean all around her had woke her up, she still felt like she was swimming and her legs were rhythmically churning up her bedclothes. The words came thinly from her dry, still half-asleep lips.

"Find the island . . . find the . . . island," She'd paused that second time before saying it again because she was fully awake and had to wonder what the heck was she talking about.

But she hadn't forgotten, the words or the dream. Even now as she hugged Aaron and looked out on the completely different world it had all become, she uttered the words one more time.

". . . find the island . . ."

"Huh? What . . . what did you say Kellen?" Aaron was done crying and during Kellen's reminiscing had slipped out of her grasp. He looked at her and sniffled.

She stood and took him by the hand.

"Oh nothing . . . nothing." But she knew it wasn't nothing. Maybe . . . if they could get to the coast. It was kind of the last way to go anyway.

She turned to look back across the torn down house in the direction she knew was west. Often they would barbecue out back and watch the sunset that way. No more though. Now just rocks and hills rose there and behind them real mountains going for miles. But in about eighty of those miles the coast would have to put an end to all that, she knew. They'd been that way before, had several family outings going to the beach. The Andrews even had a vacation house in Sandy Point Beach. Hopefully it would still be there. Maybe not the house, but at least the beach. Now just to get there.

At least there seemed to be a way, she just then noticed, a small trail cutting up into the hills. That'd be a start, and like she was realizing, it was pretty much their only option.

"I'm thirsty, Kellen."

"Yeah . . . yeah . . . we better . . . you wait here though. Okay? Just wait."

She set the boy on a nearby rock so he could look out at the silent night. It was so quiet she knew it was safe.

"Okay. I got Spaceman Spike anyway." The little boy zoomed the spaceship around and around. She was glad to see he was doing better, but one thing else, she realized then too.

"Don't shine the light, okay kiddo. We need to save the battery."

"Oh . . . okay." Spaceman Spike went to dark mode, but still kept orbiting planet Aaron.

Kellen made her way back into the house. She could see where the red hole was, still sending up its glow across a few broken down walls over by Aaron's room. Which meant the pantry would be . . . there . . . and there was the stuff, or some of it at least that had been in the coat closet.

And yeah . . . yeah . . . there were the book bags. They had three of them. Two were hers and one was Aaron's for school. *Yeah. These will work.*

She took them to where the busted up and scattered contents of the pantry spread out across the wreckage. The water bottles winked like gems of pure crystal in the darkness. She gathered them up like the treasure she knew they would soon be, storing them in the book bags. She packed in too the few boxes of crackers she could find and, oh cool! A whole box of power bars. She stuffed it all into the book bags and started back out.

They would need the water and crackers and power bars for their trip to the coast. They'd have to hike it for starters, then hopefully catch a ride maybe. From the looks of it she had to figure none of the horses had survived. *Or would they be on the other side of the mountains that now rose up where the back acreage and their stables and pastures had been?* They'd have to head that way anyway. *So just get the boy now and . . .*

She was almost back out front when she heard it. The beautiful sound of a horse's whinny and nostril clearing snort. She hurried out through the remnants of the front door and there he was, standing right before the boy, half invisible in the darkness that was the same color as his coat. He was shinier, though, and when he shifted his weight and pawed twice at the ground like he always did, his muscles winked and rolled like ghosts in shadows. Which was his name too.

"Shadow," she said and ran to him, dropping the well-packed bags. She hugged his huge neck hard and cried into his warm, smooth skin. "Shadow . . . Shadow . . ."

"He just came up. Right outta nowhere," Aaron told her and couldn't hide the happiness in his voice either. She just kept hugging the horse and knew, she just knew everything would be all right now. They could both ride the big breeder stallion. All the way to the coast. And if only Shadow could swim, all the way to this supposed, ". . . island," too. But either way she just knew. She knew everything would be all right now.

CHAPTER VIII

GOOD ENOUGH TOO

Good thing he'd grabbed the shotgun right away. This was looking like it was going to be quite some battle.

It'd been more than tricky enough setting the helicopter down on the roof of the hospital as unevenly collapsed as the upper stories of the building were. But he had to. He'd been running away and hiding long enough. Time to get back in the fight, he was thinking. He was a police officer after all. Time to start acting like one again. Even if it probably would be the last time.

After he'd been called in on that possible hostage situation with the two armed robbery suspects in that house over on Griffith way, just in time to light the place up before it disappeared like the rest of the world had in an earthquake to end all earthquakes, right away he'd flown the bird back to base, per emergency protocol.

But the base was gone too. Hard to believe, but he wasn't blind. The entire, almost new police complex, which took up a whole city block, was pretty much subterranean now.

Gone.

Although he could see as he flew directly over, at the bottom of a very deep and cavernous hole where the parking and vehicle storage facility used to be, a few sets of some of the vehicle's emergency lights were strobing. *But man, are they way down there*, the officer could also tell.

That was about it. No other signs of activity or life. There were no radio transmissions either. Except that one trucker who radioed him over the CB that he had in the chopper just for kicks. But then suddenly that went dead too, with whoever was using it probably dead as well.

Even more ominous, except for those strobers in the hole, no lights at all were on anywhere else. Well, there were the fires. And luckily the moon was mostly full too. So at least he could see those strange things roaming the streets that he could only reluctantly surmise were actual, real life zombies. Mostly because they were killing and eating people. All over the place. Which was also hard to believe, but still, he wasn't blind. And either way, there was nowhere safe to set down near the station, that was for sure.

But at least he'd known about the secondary fueling station at Highpoint Park. It was in the hills, up and out of town. Once he got there, he could see that almost miraculously it had survived the quake. He landed there. He took all of his weapons with him into the brick walled pump house centermost in the station's lot.

Then, since he knew the bird was safe inside the high, razor wire topped fence surrounding the station, he'd slept a solid eight hours, dead tired like he was. He'd gotten aloft again the next day.

But now this, what appeared to be two survivors stranded on the aforementioned rooftop of Sandy Point Bay Memorial Hospital with some of those zombie things trying to get at them. At least four or five of the rickety walking creatures had somehow managed to make it up there too, which couldn't have been easy, getting through the collapsed stories below.

Which then also made Lieutenant John Hernandez, the Sandy Point Beach Police officer piloting the helicopter wonder, how had the two hospital employees gotten up there as well? Didn't matter, was his quick answer. He was just gonna make sure they got down again okay.

At least he could tell going in they were a rather large male dressed in light blue scrubs and a female. She appeared to be a diminutive woman with a whole bunch of really dark black hair fashioned in a thick pony tail, so apparent against her white physician's coat. All of which he knew marked them as an E.R. doctor and one of the lesser employees, probably a nurse or escort. He knew this from his own trips to the hospital earlier in his career. Often, he and other beat cops had to go to Sandy Point Bay E.R. with injured suspects.

Either way, he had to get down there. These were the only survivors he'd gotten this close to. But now, as mentioned, landing on the roof was going to be quite a challenge. On any other day it might have been relatively easy. It was a good-sized, flat surface. There were no wires within the landing zone. The only obstruction was the little outbuilding where the stairs let out onto the roof.

However now, because of the also mentioned tilted angle of the roof—*hey, Lieutenant Hernandez realized, that sure might help.* At the roof's edge, probably for safety and probably too in accordance with city codes, a four foot high, eighteen inch thick concrete retaining wall arose. If he could set down relatively close to it, even if the chopper's skids started to slide, which was a major con-cern . . .

Ah, what the hell, Officer John finally figured and started lining up for the landing. *There wasn't anything else left to live for anyway.* Still no radio transmissions. No TV. And from his view up high in the bird after making a scouting run, there was hardly much of anything left for miles and miles around. *So like he was saying, what the hell?* Which was really what the whole world, or at least this part of it, was starting to resemble.

The police officer pilot started his final descent. He even angled the skids to what he thought would be a comparable incline to that of the roof to avoid any extra jarring with the landing. Everything seemed to be going well, so he glanced over at the survivors whose own little drama was taking place three quarters of the way across the roof.

The big man in the blue scrubs had just finished setting the little woman doctor on the outbuilding's roof and was trying to draw off the attackers, scooting away across the other way while yelling and waving his arms.

"Good job, fella," Officer Hernandez let out through tight lips as he quickly scanned his surroundings one last time while working the pedals and stick just right to set the police chopper down.

"*All right,*" he added at first, feeling like the landing was successful. But then the sliding started.

Looking to his left he could see the retaining wall coming up quick. With emergent speed he ripped free of his harness and lunged across to the passenger's seat and held on. He knew it could now all boil down to a battle of weight distribution so he drew up his legs too.

As the helicopter hit, the bulletproof Plexiglas door cracked. Then the bird rocked hard over that way even further and the policeman pilot couldn't help but let an equally emergent prayer slip past his lips.

A prayer apparently answered though, as in the next moment the chopper rocked back and set hard but upright there at the roof's edge. Officer Hernandez righted himself and grabbed the shotgun before scrambling out of the cockpit.

This, as originally mentioned, was a good thing. Grabbing the shotgun, that is. Because one of the zombies had decided the raucously landing helicopter was worthy of closer investigation. A particularly large zombie at that, a male, also dressed in hospital scrubs, but his a light green color, albeit substantially stained blood red and grime gray at the moment.

What was even stranger though was how then the recently . . . *retired? Laid off?* Or whatever you call it when the whole world is mostly destroyed . . . but the retired or whatever policeman caught himself halfway through the no longer necessary command, "Stop! Police! Hold it right—" before then just shaking his head and rolling his eyes and letting go with an initial round from his pump action shotgun.

He apparently had forgotten in his haste to go for the head shot(or maybe he didn't know zombie lore too well)but with the six shot round he'd used, and since it impacted high left chest, he'd just killed a zombie by the only other method possible than complete brain damage. Complete heart damage.

The blast not only knocked the big walking dead guy reeling, but also ripped most of his heart out.

The officer quickly racked in another round and surveyed the scene.

Two more zombies were attacking the big hospital worker, and though he had knocked one of them down, it had gotten right back up. Or actually the thing was crawling now and the two creatures seemed to be going high-low on the hospital worker. It was probably only a matter of time. Unfortunately, the big guy had no weapon.

While at least for her part, the lady doctor seemed safe for the moment. Scared, but safe. These real life zombies were just as inept at climbing as the ones Officer Hernandez remembered from the movies. They just kept scrambling at and reaching up toward the probably six foot high or so roof of the outbuilding on which the woman shakily stood, near its middle.

"Oh Jarrod," she quietly begged of no one in particular while watching her coworker doing his best in his battle for life and death. Then she looked over at the landed policeman and yelled his way. "Help him! Help him first . . . please . . ."

That sounded like the best idea to Officer Hernandez too. He'd have to hurry though. He broke in a run for the outbuilding.

The attackers were already too close, however, for the scatter-gun. Collateral damage, a type the trained policeman was definitely supposed to avoid, had become too likely. So he slung the shotgun fast across his back and pulled out his nine.

Since these zombies were so intent on their prey—which was a bad sign, but helpful in this case—they didn't even notice him until he had the barrel of the gun against the back of the nearest one's head. He squeezed the trigger.

The round blew zombie blood and brains all over the big hospital worker's baby blue scrub top, and even onto his neck and face. At first Officer Hernandez couldn't tell if the poor guy had suffered any wounds of his own or not. But after he put the next nine millimeter round through the other zombie's head and that one went down too, it left only himself and their intended victim standing and then he could tell. The hospital worker fell into his arms and the police officer gently laid him down.

Underneath the blood and brain splatter, a fresh, mouth-sized wound gurgled new blood high on the hospital worker's chest. Also his right arm laid limp near his waist, seeping blood onto his shirt. The second zombie obviously had been using it for a chew toy.

It was too bad too that the doctor wasn't closer by. If she could have seen her coworker from a closer perspective she probably would have recognized, and felt the fallen man's head even to confirm, that he already had a rapidly increasing fever. Not that anything could have been done about it. Except that she may have recognized it as an early symptom of the zombie virus, if she were aware of such a thing, and then simply fled the scene.

The new victim's fever also escaped the officer's attention, who needed to turn said attention elsewhere anyway. The two remaining zombies trying to get to the lady doctor were apparently at least a little smarter than their cinematic counterparts. One of them even had his back against the wall of the outbuilding in the classic, "boosting up," pose. His smaller partner had not only then managed to step up into his stirrup held hands, but had also gotten his second step onto the taller one's shoulder. Then just a boosted step later he scrambled up onto the same little roof the lady doctor still cowered on.

Officer Hernandez stuck with the nine and sprinted like hell her way. As he closed he noticed how the taller zombie still held his boosting pose and seemed frozen that way, except for his head which had followed his partner's ascent with google eyes. The stock-still creature seemed thoroughly impressed and overjoyed at what had to have been the most coordinated act of his still young, undead existence. He veritably basked in the glow of zombie accomplishment.

As a result, the sprinting policeman decided what the heck . . . he was already there anyway and he just kept sprinting before placing his next step high and up into the zombie's hands still in place for boosting.

With adrenal glands no doubt on high, he just kept going. He placed his next running step onto the big dead guy's shoulder and vaulted beyond and above onto the roof himself. Only then did the boosting zombie finally lose his grin and look back down, dead man grim now.

But of course by then it was too late. He couldn't get up on the outbuilding's small roof by himself. There was no one left to boost him. But he *was* tall enough to watch that damn policeman who had just used his masterpiece pose to follow his friend up onto the roof where the pretty lady waited to be eaten. And worse yet, he was also unfortunately more than tall enough to watch as the cop then came up quickly behind his friend, who was by then almost to the lady, but then *Blammo!* The poor zombie's cold and lifeless heart dropped as his friend and partner went to his knees with half his head gone.

The pretty lady really started freaking out then, but the policeman calmed her down. Then he looked back at the zombie and saw that he was still standing there watching them, so he decided to help her down on the opposite end of the small roof. The zombie started their way.

Officer Hernandez couldn't believe what he'd just done. Which he kind of figured was why he couldn't stop smiling like an idiot as he lowered Dr. Ichikawa—as her nametag read—down from the roof. Although he knew as well it was probably also due to the fact that she was a steaming hottie.

Or maybe more accurately, *pretty cute for a doctor*, he was thinking as he quickly followed her down. "Come on," he then told her. "We better get airborne. I think there's more of those . . . *things* . . . not too far behind."

"But Jarrod . . . Jarrod," the doctor cried and broke in a run for her fallen coworker.

Officer Hernandez started to follow, then thought of something and turned back. Where had that other zombie gotten off to? No sign of him in sight. Was he hiding behind the outbuilding? Oh well. Gotta get the doctor and go.

"He didn't look so good doc," he tried at her, coming up as she knelt over her not-quite-dead friend and coworker. "He—"

The police officer had to cut himself off then because all of a sudden the doctor's friend came back to . . . life? *Whoa!* Then a little too much as next the big guy swept the little lady out of the way like a toy doll with a swipe of his arm. Officer Hernandez drew down on the new monster as it slowly got to its feet.

"No . . . no," Dr. Ichikawa begged, then tried, "Jarrod," again.

Jarrod, now much paler, a greenish gray sort of pale, red-eyed and growling, turned toward her.

"Run . . . run, doc. I'm not me anymore . . ." he groaned out between growls. "Run!"

Officer Hernandez was weighing the facts, his aim still held on the new zombie's head a mere fifteen feet away. Then he was just about ready to let him have it too, but the doctor pleaded for her friend once more. "No . . . please . . ."

So instead the policeman started a tactical retreat, angling towards the doctor, until suddenly the big zombified hospital worker started to charge him. The officer took aim again and his finger started to squeeze.

"Look out! Behind you," the doc said this time.

Officer Hernandez turned just in time to see now where the good old boosting zombie had been hiding. Or more accurately, *wasn't* hiding anymore. He was charging right for the policeman and closing fast. So fast, the young officer knew no way could he get his pistol around in time. And since he knew the other big guy was headed his way too, and not wanting to then become a zombie, raw meat sandwich, he dropped and rolled quickly to the side.

The two extra-large zombies he'd managed to evade collided like football players with a big, meaty thud. Then from where Officer Hernandez had ended up after rolling away, it sounded like a fight between two wild animals. Even though he knew it would be quite something to watch, he hurried over to the doctor and grabbed her up.

He got her on board the bird, despite her still wanting to help Jarrod. She was in denial, maybe some shock too, the young officer could only figure. She'd gone along with him okay, but kept looking back and calling out her friend's name. She finally quit once they were airborne, and especially after, while they still watched intently what he was doing, Jarrod managed to rip the other zombie's head off and hold it aloft. He even waved the bloody trophy at the helicopter as it ascended up and away. Obviously, he didn't need their help anymore.

Inside the chopper, the doctor now could only sit and weep while Officer Hernandez busied himself with the mechanics of flying. At first he'd warmly reflected about getting a last good deed done, but then hearing the doctor's grief washed all that away.

In the end his police training kicked in. He knew it was good for her to cry, and he gently told the doctor the same thing.

"I know," she wailed back at him. "But what the hell is going on?" She collapsed into crying again.

He put a consoling hand on her leg and tried to explain, from what he could tell, and she reciprocated with what she knew. All the while the helicopter continued on toward Highpoint Park refueling station, lost in a world turned inside out, but not lost to Officer John Hernandez.

CHAPTER IX

EXCEPT FOR BECAUSE OF THIS

Udo liked this a lot more than being dead. His new, perfect body rose up and up into the clouds higher and higher, then even beyond and above them. Also above them and coming up was a beautiful and verdant valley high in the mountains surrounded by lush hillsides. Udo banked to bring himself right to it. There was Jesus in a field of flowers waving him in. *What was not to like?*

Although there was one thing, or maybe more like three things, that weren't quite to his liking: his wife and kids. And how they weren't here. Here he was in heaven, and they were nowhere to be found. He'd looked like the dickens, until a neighbor had told him if they were here, he wouldn't have to look.

Udo was bummed, for a little while, but in heaven you just can't stay that way. Even if you try. But still . . .

One day Udo ran into old man Martinson and his wife Irmalene. And Pastor Jerry. And some other members of their church, but far from all of them. Pastor Jerry felt just horrible about that. As well as about his family too, he told Udo.

"They can still get in later, right?" Udo had to ask his ex-pastor, who now up here in heaven had been relegated to a staff position.

Heaven's church featured Jesus as pastor and services commenced every evening in any of the outdoor auditoriums. First under a gorgeous sunset. Then under the beautiful star-filled skies.

Udo didn't have to go every night, though. He could skip if he was on a star tour or in a historical reenactment production where he could be whoever he wanted to be at any point in history with the whole thing feeling like he was really there. Or performing any of the other incredibly fun and interesting activities around. Udo had just scratched the surface of that whole 'joy and wonders' thing. Or so he'd heard from others anyway.

And besides too, if you missed a message you could always get it somewhere else later. There were auditoriums in every neighborhood. And, the neighborhoods were all made of mansions of course. Sermons ran round robin in the beautiful outdoor amphitheaters. And since one could fly it was no problem getting anywhere and catching up. Best of all was how somehow Jesus was always preaching at all of them too. All at once. Omnipresent, as advertised.

"You missed message number 278, didn't you, Udo," Pastor Jerry came back with and strongly squeezed his former parishioner's shoulder. Pastor Jerry had a perfect body now too, and both men were built like Roman gladiators and looked the part too, but on vacation. If gladiators wore white togas on their days off, that is.

At least their attire went well with the Acropolis-style environment of open, restaurant and shop-filled squares and Greek-styled, marble walled, and columned buildings. These were surrounded and accented by beautiful and bountiful nature, including exotic flora and fauna and all manner of wonderful creatures tame and friendly.

"Oh . . . yeah. I must have," Udo confessed. "278, you say? I'll try and get it this evening. I mean . . . I'll find it. I love how they're all numbered, and all you have to do is take the cloud ride with the same number and poof, they drop you down in those wonderfully comfortable seats."

Udo looked down a moment, and then back up before continuing. "But . . . could you just give me the skinny, pastor. Err, I mean, brother . . . Jerry. You know . . . the abridged version. You were always real good at that in our church. I just need to know what's up. I mean, aren't they ever going to get here?" Udo had to fight back the tears.

Of course his former pastor could sense the young man's consternation. The situation was not new to the church leader. He looked deeply into Udo's eyes.

"Let me just tell you this, brother." Jerry's voice was full of reassurance. "You know we can do all things through Him. Am I right?"

Udo looked up. "Yuh . . . yuh . . . yes," he managed to stammer.

"Maybe even . . . well," the ex-church leader started in with, but then stopped. "I better . . . better let Him explain."

"But it could take a week to see Him. You know the demand," Udo almost whined and immediately felt silly for having sounded so desperate. Desperation was so out-of-place up there, what with everything so readily available. And time had become irrelevant there too. Everything being forever had a way of doing that. Except for because of this: this whole big mess with Udo's family not getting into heaven. Forever wasn't going to be too fun without them.

"Here," Jerry said and solemnly slipped a golden pendant and chain from his neck. The pendant was an old style key. Embedded in its circular head was a brilliant blue stone. The ex-pastor held it out draped across both hands in front of Udo's already bedazzled eyes. "This will get you an immediate audience with Him. All staff members have them. We are instructed only to use them or loan them out in emergencies. I think your case is one, and I think He will agree."

Udo continued to look at the key, and before he even touched it, he could feel its power pulling him in. His eyes felt like metal drawn to the blue stone as if it were magnetic, even as he reached for the dazzling piece of jewelry. Then as the somewhat heavy piece fell into his eager palm, the azure essence surrounded him and took him in.

Before he knew it, forming within the blueness all around him now was a dimly lit lounge, likewise entirely permeated by the same soothing color.

First to fully form before him was a wall about ten feet away, slightly convex. Udo let his head loll from side to side—about the only motion he seemed capable of in his new and current state of blissful and extreme relaxation—and soon discovered why the convex shape was needed. Mounted along it, without gap, were medium sized television screens, one after another after another, side-to-side and up and down as far as the eye could see in all directions.

A door of some sort opened behind him, sounding pneumatic and Star Trekkian. Udo didn't turn to look. He knew who it had to be. He could feel the change in the air, at first extremely awe inspiring, but then soothing, even more than the light. The undeniable source of these feelings took a seat next to him on the highly lush sofa they would have to share. There were no other seats. Udo just sat back and got ready to enjoy the show. He could tell that was what he was supposed to do, and then realized too that in fact he was totally incapable of doing anything else anyway.

Ask Him about my family. Ask Him about my family, Udo kept reminding himself, knowing if he didn't he might get lost in the Lord's intoxicating presence and forget about everything. Forget about it all.

After just a bit, though, Udo got at least somewhat used to hanging out with Jesus in the observation room. The buzz wore off a little, but it still felt eerily similar to one time when he was in high school and he and his friends tried marijuana brownies while watching late-night horror movies. Just like then, time had lost all meaning now too,(without the THC)and also like then he suddenly found himself grinning like a fool and totally digging the wild, cartoon images he was seeing on the TV screens.

But even more reminiscent was how also he was totally understanding everything in newly revealed levels of truth and meaning. *Maybe the Lord has pot smoke piping in through the vents,* Udo was thinking. *Maybe—*

"Oh goodness, no," Jesus said into Udo's mind, or so it seemed. As if he had headphones on or something, but Udo didn't. He even felt up around his ears just in case. "Hopefully it doesn't bother you like this," the Lord, or his voice, continued. "But I'm just more used to conversing telepathically."

"Oh . . . sure. Whatever you say . . . my lordship . . . or Jesus sir. Ummmmm . . . how—"

"Jesus is good. Or Lord. Just don't call me dude. I hate that. Thank goodness that is going out of style. For a while there . . ."

"Oh . . . yeah . . . I bet," Udo said, or as he then realized, thought. Somehow he just sort of naturally started communicating telepathically too. Which was probably for the best. He almost felt too relaxed to even talk.

"I know what brings you here," the Lord informed Udo, who for his part was still just grinning. He didn't want to be rude, but he couldn't help but stare at his savior who sat there in an immaculate, shiningly white, silk smoking jacket over a royal blue ascot. Below the robe-like top, His crossed legs shimmered in the sleek lines of the also silk; also white pajama bottoms. His right foot bounced lightly in its elevated perch at the end of His upper leg in the crossed style they rested in, crossed the way a man does when sitting on a sofa. On the foot, just as with the other one below of course, he wore a tan colored, suede leather slipper lined in velvet the same color as the ascot.

All of which was quite striking. But what had really caught Udo's eye and rendered him unable to look away was how the Lord's hair, both facial and cranial, was entirely silver-white. And also how his eyes glowed the same color as the ascot and the slipper linings. He had brilliantly blue embers in his strong as ever face, and he was tanned too, or more or less dark skinned with features belying middle-eastern descent.

"I would apologize for such opulent attire, but I really am retired you see. As I said once before when I left your world. It is finished. And now it really, really is."

The Lord smiled at his small joke and put a large, also tan hand gently on Udo's knee.

Which actually was Udo's nearest body part to the Lord, because also like in that marijuana induced incident of his youth . . . Udo was slouched almost impossibly low in the sofa. "But I am always willing to go back to work for any of my true servants, such as you my boy."

Jesus, who in stark contrast to Udo sat bolt upright, yet as mentioned with legs leisurely crossed, extended his other hand. In it he held a shining silver, remote control device. He used the device and with one click changed the cartoon images on the trillion or so televisions to real-life, news-like scenarios.

Udo sat up blinking. He tried to take in as many of the unlimited screens as he could, but soon they all just blended together. Scene after scene of really just ordinary people doing ordinary things, but it was weird. In his mind it was like he was watching the whole world at once. The overall effect was mind blowing. "Whoaaa," he couldn't help but exclaim.

Jesus had to smile at that one, but then continued. "The room we are in now was used mostly in the past and throughout all of what you would consider the 'historical' past, to observe, make decisions and then issue corresponding commands to my staff to intercede in the lives of my people to carry out, as I'm sure you've heard it called . . . 'my plan.'

"Each of these television screens shows every moment in the life of every individual ever created. And because of my special powers and properties, as well as the special properties of this room—and in fact the entire spiritual realm—I was able to monitor them all. My spiritual agents, just as I can, could then travel back and forth in time to implement my commands.

"This was possible because each TV, as my children so quaintly call them, has a forward and a reverse. And the life story inside each one is recorded as if on tape, err now how do they say . . . a disc. Yes a disc. Remember . . . I know the beginning from the end. Because it's all on tape . . . or disc, that is.

"So maybe now you can understand my current penchant for much more leisurely activities."

Udo shared his own small laugh with the Lord on that one. *Don't forget to ask Him about my family . . . don't forget—*

"

Yes, yes, my good servant," the Lord thought out to reassure Udo. At the same time He rose from the sofa before continuing. His movements were so fluid and effortless. Udo couldn't help but marvel at his graceful mannerisms.

"We can help them," the Lord pontificated, and something in His tone told Udo that Jesus was, as scary as it was to consider, all of a sudden really pissed. "Don't worry. We can save them because luckily I decided not to destroy this room as I did most of your world, and all those in it who fell from, and could not find their way back into my good graces. Believe, repent and obey! Believe, repent and obey! How hard is that?"

Then as the Lord spread out His arms, on each of the TV screens fanning out forever behind Him scenes of incredible cataclysm devolved into nothing but fire burning. Fire after fire after fire filled every one and then Udo noticed too that even Jesus' eyes had ignited in fire.

The newer resident of heaven quickly looked away and felt in that moment he would rather never see something like that again. In fact, he even realized, he'd rather be blind than have to see his Lord's anger like that again. That was scary!

But then love fell like a big blanket over him and Udo looked back up. With relief he saw that the Lord's eyes were blue once more, not glowing red any longer. Although sadly they were also rimmed with tears. Funny thing too, now his beard and hair were blacker than black.

"I'm sorry, my son, but anger is almost always born out of fear and failure, and I'm afraid I failed my children so horribly. So many were lost. So many . . ."

For a moment it appeared the Lord couldn't continue. He'd turned and looked away. But then He turned right back and fixed Udo firm with his gaze. A blue fire burned there now. "But how about . . . how about we see if we can't get at least a few of them back."

CHAPTER X

BORN AGAIN DEAD

They'd all died in rather close proximity—our three miscreants whose rape, torture and murder of their defenseless and naked kidnap victim was so rudely interrupted by a massive, earth opening quake. Likewise they were all born again dead in the same area, raising up from the dirt and rock. They took their first steps, their baby zombie steps across the flattened yet thoroughly avulsed parcel of land where their little granny flat hang out had once rested.

Similar to that which they did while alive, they gradually drifted together to stand and lightly jostle each other before mumbling and even growling into one another's greatly deteriorated faces. All of which somehow seemed to at least bring them to a consensus about which way to go in their new life's journey. In unison, or at least unidirectionally, off up the newly redesigned coastline just south of Sandy Point Beach, they started off on their shuffling way.

Another common factor that they had agreed upon was the one thing all zombies are known for, the desire to consume human flesh. Hunger gnawed at their internal organs, made all the worse because that was exactly what they desired, to find someone else's internal organs to feast on!

That was about it for now. They just wanted to eat. Their revivified minds didn't seem to have room for much else. They couldn't really remember anything of their pasts. Least of all the massive temblor, which had sent them to their deaths. They were unaware, or more accurately put, could have cared less, about how massively their world had been rearranged while they were briefly dead. They just hoped to find food somewhere in it all, starting with the street they'd just stumbled upon which was mostly composed of jagging and jutting, zigging and zagging slabs of upturned asphalt and concrete. And all that leading away from separate piles of shattered shafts of wood and more slabs collapsed and laying against each other at odd angles. Houses. Instinctively they seemed to know to search in these for food, which they did in a haphazard and somewhat feeble fashion.

There was nothing there, though. Several dead bodies, but those not the least bit enticing to our brave three. So they simply lumbered on, crawling and climbing when the terrain necessitated, or otherwise somewhat uncoordinatedly loping and lunging in the direction their senses and any other scanty remnants of memory told them to go to find their food.

Their hunger, of course, grew and grew. They moaned as they loped along. They drooled too, the excess saliva such a hunger had to create filling their slack jawed mouths, and without concern for their appearance, the shiny rivulets flowed forth and dangled from their lower jaws incessantly before reaching a final destination, redecorating their tattered shirt fronts. Only occasionally did they suck back the spit strings when they closed their mouths to take a strong whiff of the air, hoping to smell where people might be.

Another interesting personality trait of the wandering undead soon became apparent in their rather clannish personal practices of socialization. Or at least these three, friends as they still seemed to be, definitely exhibited said behavior.

An early example of this appeared as they approached a pair of zombies who seemed to be feasting on an elderly couple they'd apparently rooted out of a semi-demolished hovel nearby. Upon arrival to this scene, our intrepid band of three fought quite savagely with the other two, eventually beating them back. Then they settled in for a shared banquet of what remained of the older couple.

After that, other game had been quite hard to find. One time they did hear someone yelling for help deep within the crumbled shell of what looked to be a once-upon-a-time home. But luckily for the trapped survivor, the zombified threesome, even with their incredible, desperate energy and their maniacal strength, still were unable to clear the largest sections of rubble in their way.

Not for lack of trying. They seemed to be learning and intensifying their efforts. They had even screamed while they worked. One had also lost a finger. All had probably pulled a muscle or two. A caged pitbull in a butcher shop had nothing on these boys in a situation like that, with food so fetchingly close but entirely inaccessible. It was the worst thing a zombie could endure. But the boys had endured with the only added effect being a slight increase in their maniacal mindset, if that were possible.

And since, as one might suspect, the elderly couple they *had* gotten to eat were rather withered and without much meat on their old bones (they would have hardly even qualified as appetizers in a decent restaurant) the zombie boys were getting pretty hungry again. They moaned and drooled and continued on.

Eventually they made their way to the more populated stretches of the beachfront where parking lots and more shops and diners and some small apartment buildings started erupting in their path. The three hurried in, hoping these new environs held something better than the slim pickings they'd come across so far.

But this area had also suffered horribly under the catastrophic effects of the quake. Worse yet, it was starting to look like (not that our living dead friends could tell however) that the entire area had either been abandoned or evacuated for the most part.

Large structure fires burned in numbers of two or three per city block, no doubt fueled—or at least ignited—by the aforementioned natural gas leaks the shifting of the earth's surface naturally caused. And with fuel for the fires as ample as it was, buildings and homes just kindling now, how could it not all burn. The zombies then even got to see (though whether or not it really registered with them) just how the fires most likely got lit. A strong breeze lifted embers from the already burning fires high into the sky before also then carrying the little, almost living sparks further up the coast.

Sandy Point Beach was an older community too, with mostly older and somewhat stately, homes. Or at least, they had been. Stately had been destroyed in great quake worldwide. Part of the point probably. The first was now last and the last first and all of it mish mashed together and burning, as per some interpretations of Bible prophecy.

Not that the zombies cared about that much either, one can easily assume. All they knew was that all too little remained in the living human flesh aisle at the local grocery store. Which really was sort of how they perceived the whole world now really. A giant supermarket, but one ransacked and lacking in product.

Suddenly, however, and in keeping with the same metaphor, though the zombies wouldn't have been able to appreciate it, a voice drifted down from above, much like one in a supermarket might from speakers in the ceiling. Apparently there was a special in the meat department on freshly caught human. Or at least that was the gist of the message each of the zombies received directly into their minds.

As to be expected, as soon as they understood this magic transmission, they followed it toward the source as best as they could. They traveled along broken road after broken road, then also around a huge canyon into which the 305 and 71 freeways merged before disappearing into its seemingly bottomless blackness. Past that they continued up out of the seaside city into the hills. Then they saw it.

There, over the first ridge of said hills and across into a particularly wide valley paved with new plains of upturned soil and rock that they somehow still had the energy to lope and drool across, our intrepid zombie friends fell in line with about a thousand more of their kind headed the same direction. Directly ahead protruded a new mountain.

It was not too large but certainly magnificent to behold. It seemed made of metallic rock and was volcanic as well. In keeping with the apparent artificiality of the whole thing, its lava flowed gently, controlled somehow but burning brightly red and cutting away everything in its path.

Stranger still, big metal discs, which upon closer inspection could more accurately be seen to be composed of what had to be molten metal, like big, swimming-pool-sized, pancake shaped blobs of freshly melted solder, floated atop more streams of lava flowing out and away from the mountain.

Onto these silver ships, zombie after zombie stumbled and jumped after waiting streamside by one or another of the lava rivers flowing down on all sides. The meat seekers milled in a giant mass at the base of the metal mountain. The show was just starting, though, one could soon tell, as the living dead suddenly turned surfers understandably had trouble. The molten material seemed to help them, however, sticking their feet in place and bouncing their butts back up as need be. The real show then taking place, a strange but somehow rhythmic zombie bouncing boat ride, only needing calliope music to complete. They rode that way in shining silver flotillas composed of groups of twelve to fifteen zombies on five or six molten blobs.

Once they returned their way back to the base of the mountain (apparently part of a self-contained transport system) the lava streams then passed through the walls of the mountain into, just as the zombies hoped, the meat department.

A second half of the transport system could also be discerned with further inspection. Interlaced in the network of lava streams a dozen or so could be seen—were several that carried zombies away from the mountain as well.

For now, however, our three friends and the line they were in was headed for whatever waited inside the mountain. After branching and entering through more than one cave entrance low in the mountain's side, the horde of undead would next go through certain rituals and procedures. Then more perfected and improved, they would wait for their turn to ride the hell river to their satanic assignments.

The zombie was very glad to be part of *the one* now. A part of *him*: a part of the Master. That was all he or any of them needed. The master and his orders to follow, which would be easy. Especially now, because of how he'd taken them all in and fused his great mind with theirs, making them a part of him and then also making them a part of the one. Them and him together.

As the one they would accomplish great things, do much, and rule the new world. The master had promised.

And of course too they would also need lots to eat. This was another good thing about being with the master. The master liked to have them eat people. Or at least a little eating and then killing and infecting some too.

This helped bring new ones to him too. New members of the one. They must bring everyone into the one, the master ordered, and they would see that this was done. Their master loved them and must be obeyed.

In fact, just tonight the master showed them how much he loved them by feeding them all the captives he'd strung up in the big cavern inside the mountain. What a feast it had been. The fresh caught humans were all hanging and squirming and screaming from hooks through their heels. You could smell the blood and meat everywhere. Which was exciting enough, but then he slowly lowered them down and the feeding frenzy began. The zombie thought his dead heart would burst with it all.

But it didn't, and then he got a hold of one of the hanging meat people and found out like some of the others had that you could bite at their necks and pull real hard until their heads came off and since they'd been hanging upside down for so long the blood would come gushing and cover them head to toe. Then after they finished with the head they could reach right up into what was left and get some organs too. It was the most wonderful experience a young zombie could have.

There would be plenty more, the master promised too. So how wonderful, they could only think and they were all so happy and ready to serve him, him who gave them purpose and sustenance and a new home forever.

Then just to make sure, the spiders came down. Which was frightening at first because there were so many and they were crawling all over them. But then once they'd crawled in through their ears and eaten their way into their minds, then their minds were fused with the master's. They could just tell then everything would be all right. Everything was perfect, and they were all one.

Even better was how he could tell he knew more now than he had before. Ever since coming back to life like they had he'd felt so stupid. And he couldn't remember anything from before. All he could think about was hunting and feeding. That is, until he was called here to the great mountain.

Now he knew much more. Now he knew he had been serving the master all his life. That was what he remembered now. The master had helped him remember.

He remembered when he was younger and how his parents fought. Then one of them killed the other and then himself or herself too. He didn't know if his father killed his mother or vice versa. He just remembered lots of blood and that in the end they both were dead. Then he was sent to the place where the bad things started happening.

But that too was when the master came and made him bad too so he could survive. The master made it so it felt good to hurt people, which he had to do because they wanted to hurt him. That was how it worked in his world back then. The master ruled in that world too. He just hadn't known it until now.

So then, and ever since then too, the master was always there. He'd always been there for him. He'd always been there for his friends Jeff and Ronny too. Which was another wonderful thing the master had done. He gave them back their names. Him and Jeff and Ronny. Not many in the one had that privilege. But they were getting it because they had always served the master so well.

Back in the world of before . . . the world of burglaries . . . stealing cars . . . stealing whatever they could . . . robberies . . . assaults . . . and then the murders. That was when they'd reached full fruit, as the master had put it. It was all for him really anyway. All for the master. He knew that now.

Also for their good service they would get to stay together, him and his friends. Although they couldn't talk or sit on the sofa and do drugs and watch TV anymore—like there was any TV anymore anyway, and as for drugs who knew about those either . . .

The big, chubby zombie Mike was lost for a moment then in his delightful little reverie of evil, until the one took over and swept him up, swept them all up because now it was time to go out again. Out to hunt and kill and eat. Serve the master! Serve the master and make the one greater and greater!

They were all thinking that now, all the zombies. Like a cheer it rang in their heads as they started out. Once more they got back onto the silver discs which caught their feet and carried them back up into the world.

Which, of course, was so much fun too, riding on the rivers of lava up through the caves and tunnels?

Jeff and Ronny were enjoying it too, Mike could tell. They were laughing and smiling with their awful and ugly faces, just like he had a zombie face. But it was okay. This was how the master wanted them to look. They were beautiful in his eyes. For him they would hunt . . . and kill . . . and eat . . . soon . . . soon they would again. Once they got back up into the world . . . the world that would soon be theirs . . . forever.

As for himself, their master Satan, he watched and watched from within the highest point, or peak, of the artificial mountain. He stood in an observation or collection facility, housed inside the peak like a round, one story building stuck there. Out the rounded windows he watched most deliciously as the spirits and souls of those so beautifully slain below rose up into his little facility for processing and storage. The wispy white things even passed by ever-so-closely through the glasslike and circular, center portion within the observation room making up the lowest section of the seemingly magnetic edifice.

"Good work, gentleman," he then said to the technician and designer seated at instrument panels just in front of him. He stood right behind them, for the moment looking not much unlike a human, and in fact one painfully reminiscent of the international playboy type adorning liquor labels in the nineteen sixties. His purposeful transformation also came complete with silk smoking jacket and ascot, tight goatee neatly trimmed and devilishly dark. Devilishly, for obvious reasons.

The lab coated technician and rather flamboyantly attired designer didn't bother turning around to graciously accept the proffered compliment of their work. Not because it wasn't well deserved. They had designed and supervised the construction of the entire mountain, as well as with the other half dozen or so now dotting the coast. So compliments were certainly due, they both knew.

They didn't turn around, however, because they were both frozen in fear, and a little busy using the instruments and monitors before them. They were watching and managing what happened to said spirits coming up through the intake tube.

From there the souls would be separated out from the spirt bodies. Then, in the next room, the souls would in turn be stored in tubes almost identical to those used at Universal Laboratories, also very colorful and kept on rack after rack after rack.

"I hate to brag," young raconteur Satan went on while they worked. "But my plans, as you two have so brilliantly put them into action, of course with the help of me and my many minions, are playing out quite well. The most important aspect of which is this soul collection process. We've pretty much covered all the bases, as the humans like to say. All of them will be mine . . . errrr . . . ours.

Almost theatrically then, the bonvivant version of the tricky old Devil rubbed his hands together while moving close to the hardened glass tube the spirits floated through. His eyes sparkled with kaleidoscopic light. "And just wait 'till you see what we are going to do with them."

CHAPTER XI

LEARNING TO FLY, LEARNING TO DIE

Udo was on it! I mean, how super cool, was all he could think. Super cool that he would get the chance to be with his family again and maybe even bring them back to heaven with him. Although, it wouldn't be easy, the Lord had promised. *I mean, zombies! Really? Hundreds of them! Possibly even thousands. And other surprises too? So it was really cool, but . . . zombies! And what did He mean by surprises?*

"Kinda like end times," the Lord then further explained. Now Udo could only hear His voice though, like through loud speakers. After being in the lounge where the TVs stretched out forever, Jesus had shown him to a door that lead into the huge, all-white room he was in now. The Lord hadn't followed him in though and now was communicating with him from somewhere else, as mentioned, via speakers . . . somewhere.

"Although, who knows?" the creator of all things continued. "You know what I mean? Like a thief in the night and all that. So maybe not too. Maybe it's not the end yet. We'll see. Always remember, I work in mysterious ways. Like maybe you noticed."

Before Udo could answer and say yes, I had actually, what with cancer and aids and terrorists and war and everybody dying anyway and after one gets old enough to figure that out isn't it fun living with a death sentence over your head. And I could go on, he was thinking, but . . .

But then he would have had to apologize to the Lord. He was just feeling a little bitter. Because of what was going on with his family and all.

All of which not even coming up, however, as then and suddenly Udo was under attack by some of those aforementioned zombies. Although they were really only automated synthozombies, the Lord had already also explained, which made this part of his training somewhat like a video game. Except it was 3D and they were life-size and otherwise totally real.

Also very real was the environment suddenly all around too. The all-white room had somehow become an exact replica of the area where Udo had lived and worked, Sandy Point Beach, or what was left of it, the shattered ruins.

While also, just as the Lord had promised, they were hidden somewhere in this fake world too. His family. In fact, in the same place they had survived in, in the real world. And, just like in the real world too, they would survive a little while longer. Hopefully long enough for Udo to get the chance to get to them first before anything else did. So he could rescue them.

There was one catch. In the simulationhe would also experiencereal pain and death if he failed. Otherwise the training would be incomplete, the Lord felt. Without a realistic deterrent to failure. Or in other words, if the zombies or one of the other surprises got to him first, he would very realistically feel their violent fury and the resultant death they could cause.

But at least, because of his perfected body he now had a big advantage over them, the Lord had further explained and Udo breathed again. The walking dead were really just as vulnerable to wounding and damage as they had been when they were alive. With the caveat that one had to either remove their heart or grievously wound their brain to permanently stop them. But otherwise they were no faster or stronger than normal humans. More tenacious, fearless and psychotic maybe, which could make them a little stronger, but that was about it.

While Udo, on the other hand, had bones almost as hard as rock. And with an also perfect musculature and nervous system and synapses, his speed and strength in both action and thought were far superior, especially as compared to the rotting systems of reanimated corpses.

But they do have superior numbers, Jesus finished His introductory lesson with. And if they outnumbered him enough to overwhelm him; well, just don't let that happen, was the bottom line.

And, then it was, "Game on!"

In the next instant then, as already mentioned, Udo was learning firsthand about the 'superior numbers.' Three of the ghoulish creatures were coming at him from different angles and closing fast.

Udo had used the first few moments of the simulation, before their approach, to try and get his bearings. It hadn't helped much, though. The old hometown was just too torn up, *and* torn down. His quick scan of the surroundings hadn't revealed much he was at all familiar with.

But then in the last second he saw it looming up high. Somehow a major portion of the Liberty Tower, a central section of the old town hall, was still standing. Its brick ensconced stair-well-wide shaft of cement body still lead up to where its big bell used to toll, but would toll no more. That part of it had fallen off. If he could just get there though, and get up into its highest portion, Udo figured then he could see how to navigate his way home.

Hopefully.

And hopefully too they would be there.

His family.

The zombie's noise brought his attention back to earth quickly. Two of them were off to his right and scuffling their heavy footed way in his direction from the shadows of the nearby shell of a building. The third rounded the corner of some head-high rubble to his left.

"Remember. Try to remove either their head or their heart," the voice of the Lord said from somewhere again. "I know I told you a serious head wound will suffice, and it will, but if you remove their head and heart we can . . . well . . . I'll show you that later I guess. Just try to do that if you can."

Udo took a quick second to look at his empty hands. "Don't worry. You are mightily and well-made," the Lord continued. "And as I've already told you, with your perfected body, and it's equally perfected systems you will be capable of so much more than in your previous existence. Your hands themselves are weapons now, very hard, and with the velocity, you will be able to generate, well . . . you'll do fine . . . just fine."

Although fine was the last thing Udo was feeling at the moment. The zombies were close now, and of course he had never been close to a zombie before. He'd never been close enough to see their bones showing through their gray-green flesh in several places. Nor had he witnessed their bloodshot and psychotic stares above slack jawed, drooling mouths filled with jagged, blood-stained teeth. And then to the groaning and moaning as they got even closer. Finally, the growling. Television and the theatre just didn't do them justice. And, oh yeah . . . the smell.

"Amazingly realistic reproductions, don't you think?" the Lord cheerily added, as if zombies were no big deal, and then, "Go!" he yelled.

So Udo did just that, doing the first thing he could think of to do in a fight. He hit the closest zombie with a hard right square in the middle of its ugly face.

However, when Udo's fist became buried in the creature's cranium—boy, he really was strong now—in effect trapping that arm there, he was almost bitten in the throat by the second attacker who came up rapidly on the other side.

Just in time, he managed to bring up his free hand, the left one and wedged it like a thick china plate–an appropriate metaphor considering his hand's current constitution–in between the zombie's chompers and all the hungry people eater could do was shatter his half-rotten teeth on it.

"They will usually go for the throat like that," the Lord chimed in. "And not just because it's one of the few places you are still vulnerable. They don't know that. They just sense the blood there so near to the surface. Remember, though, as I said, take note: you *are* vulnerable there."

Take note, yeah right, Udo had to sarcastically think, not really able to write anything down at the moment, his hands as literally full as they were. Although for the next few seconds at least he did seem to have matters—and again forgive the pun—well in hand.

The first attacker was impaled on his right fist still stuck in its skull and could only quiver and spasm. The other one was still chomping on his left, karate-chop-shaped extremity and kept doing just that, mindlessly chomping and chomping.

All of which made it easy for Udo to figure out which zombie needed his more immediate attention. The chomping one, and along those same lines he also spied the slab of solid brick wall just behind this zombie's head.

With his newly enhanced strength and speed, he simply extended his still flattened hand there in the attacker's mouth until it slammed the thing's head with incredible force against the aforementioned brick wall.

The force of which would have not only flattened the back of any normal human skull, but would have killed them instantly as well. All it seemed to do to the zombie was get him to stop chewing for a moment, while also making his eyes roll up into his head.

Soon, however, they returned their red eyed focus onto Udo's throat. Remembering what the Lord had told him about his throat being one of his weaknesses, Udo reacted with extreme energy. He rapidly repeated the zombie head slamming maneuver again and again until his flattened hand that had been between the zombie's upper and lower jaw completed its resultant course and severed the zombie's head along the same plane.

The living dead thing, now just a dead, dead thing, could only collapse and gurgle blood. It gurgled stinky black blood from its mostly just mucous membrane and throat hole upper surface. The other half of its head rolled to the side like a discarded snack bowl with the snack being that of gray matter in blood sauce.

One down, one to go. Err, well, and then here was that other one coming up on Udo's left now, but at least this third attacker was showing more than a little reluctance after witnessing Udo's--and again, please forgive the pun—handiwork.

This third then slowed down even more when Udo next turned his attention on the poor undead fellow still quivering at the end of his extended right arm and fist. The deliberateness of Udo's next movements as he slowly rose said appendage until the quivering one's chest was right at his eye level, froze the third zombie dead in his tracks.

"Yes. Yes," the Lord's voice came in again, almost cooing. "Looks like you're a real natural at this, my boy. Only your first two kills and you are already so wisely deciding to explore both methods of extinction for these bothersome creatures. One by removal of the brain . . . and this . . ."

Udo barely heard his master, though. He really was a natural at this. In that moment his concentration on the chest of his next victim was so intense, all he could hear was the beating of the heart it held inside. Apparently, his hearing was perfected too, allowing him to hear the heart even from a foot or so away. Just as the Lord had also suggested, Udo did indeed plan on arranging this 'bothersome creature's' extinction by extracting the currently rather noisy organ.

. . . *bada, bada, bada, bada*, it was beating and as Udo continued to listen deeper and deeper he knew, he just knew that somehow he could tell exactly where the target organ was. *Right . . . there!*

After shaping his hand claw-like he shoved it hard into the monster's chest, felt around for a moment or two, and then ripped it back out, bloody and full of the creature's cardiac muscle now. He held up his new prize and watched the liberated blood-pumper take its last few beats while at the same time noticing that the body it once belonged to finally stopped shaking.

"By Jove! I think he's got it," the Lord joked in voice over. "One more to go though . . . for now."

The last zombie standing, already somewhat reticent, as mentioned, now just flat out turned and ran. The poor frightened fellow disappeared as quickly as he could around the corner of rubble he'd first come out from behind. Once Udo got around the same corner there was no sign of the fleeing thing.

Udo listened intently, and then also sniffed hard at the air. *The creature went that way,* his mind told him, but just as he started off in that direction, he thought of something else. He scanned the immediate area for a loftier lookout. Then he thought of it.

"Hey . . . can I? I mean, you said before that I could do it on Earth too," he questioned the air, or really, Jesus hidden somewhere up in it.

"It will be harder to fly on Earth. And as this simulation is of Earth . . . and very realistic , , , But there's no time like the present, I suppose," the Lord's voice came back with.

"But how? In heaven it just happens. But now I can tell . . ."

"Just think about doing it. Picture yourself doing it in your mind. Then just run and jump and throw your weight that way. Do the same while you're up there. Throw your weight and angle your body where you want to go. Didn't you ever dream about flying?"

"Uhm, well, now that you mention it. I think I did?!"

"Do it like that! Like you did in your dreams!"

"Oh," Udo answered, thought about it, and then took off, at first running several steps, then jumping, and there he went.

"Whoa . . . whoa . . . whoa," he had to shout. He also wheeled his arms about while he tried to get both his bearings and his balance. This wasn't like that first time when he was taken up to heaven. This time *he* was in control. Well, sort of in control.

After a few stressful seconds, he finally managed to obtain and then maintain a horizontal, forward gliding position. Like the Lord had said . . . just as in his dreams he had to hold his arms straight out at each side to stay that way. "*He . . . hey . . . Hey! I'm doing it. I'm doing it!*"

"I knew you could. Try it out a little, might as well get some practice in, before—" The Lord's voice trailed off.

"Huh?" Udo could only wonder out loud. "Before what?"

Then the 'what' hit when, even though he hadn't altered anything he was doing, his flying started becoming increasingly erratic. The ground below was starting to spin too. "Whoa . . . whoa!" he yelled this time because he'd lost all equilibrium and was plunging toward the ground. He felt suddenly light headed too. It was all he could do to brace for the hard landing coming up quick.

Like going through a roof hard, the roof of a formerly fast food joint, which slowed him down some. Still, though, he then slammed down onto a pile of tables and booths, which filled one of eatery's corners. *Crash . . . crunch . . . bam!*

"Udo? Udo, my boy? Are you okay?" the Lord's concerned inquiry came from the dark recesses inside the half-collapsed burger palace, sounding as if it were coming over the place's obviously destroyed speaker system. "Udo?"

Udo couldn't answer. It was all he could do just to hold on to consciousness. He picked himself up and staggered to the busted open and half-sideways, double glass doors leading out of the mostly demolished rat trap that used to be a restaurant.

"Such a fall would have killed a normal human. And at least you'll heal very quickly. I'm sensing a broken arm, some broken ribs, a mild concussion," the Lord informed Udo as he emerged into the sunlight. Now His voice seemed to be coming down from the sky itself again. ". . . and that's the good news."

"The . . . good . . . news," Udo could only weakly mutter, and indeed he was very gingerly holding his left arm close to his side. His breaths came shallow and painful too. And talk about a headache. Things were still spinning just a bit as well. He felt so weak. It was like he had a—

". . . fever. Yes," the Lord's voice came in with. "Do you remember when you had your hand in that zombie's mouth? Even though you made quick work of him and your bite wounds were very superficial and healed quickly, they were more than adequate to deliver his disease into your system."

Udo wanted to respond, ask him what disease, but he was far too weak. He could only go to one knee. Luckily, there was a nearby half-wall for him to lean against. And luckily too, Jesus continued with his explanation.

"In order to create his undead warriors, the enemy had to infect those who had recently died in the earthquake with a potion, a potion he created that causes a disease. He is the father of all disease you know. This one; however, is even more special to him and he recently developed it. It not only reanimates the recently dead, but when they bite others who are still living, within minutes the disease spreads throughout their victim's systems. The resultant fever is always fatal. And worse yet, these dead soon rise again and become new members of his legions.

"So, I am very sorry this has to happen, Udo. However, my boy, we need our training to be very effective. And believe me, after you go through what you are about to go through, you won't make this mistake again."

Oh great, Udo could only manage in thought form now as a group of four or five zombies who must have been waiting right outside the burger joint were on him almost instantaneously. He did, though, somehow manage to strike out and knock a couple of them reeling away. The others climbed on top of him like voracious animals, though, and soon overwhelmed him. All he could take in was their conjoined growling and flashes of their violent aggression whirling about him. Unfortunately then also he could feel the moments of contact created by their attack.

The biting hurt worst. The biting and the tearing. Because even though his bones were very hard and his flesh was thicker than normal, it still could be rent by a zombie's voracious attack. Under the resultant flood of pain, Udo could feel his consciousness waning again.

After that, the last thing he could feel was an electrifying pain of the greatest intensity ripping across his throat. In the rising tide of blackness, he heard the Lord's voice one more time.

"All right. Cut! Let's try again. We'll break for a bit and then roll again in thirty."

CHAPTER XII

FIRST DATE

The creatures emerged like crabs, driven by hunger and frantically skittering from between the rocks along the ocean's edge. They crawled out quickly in between wave-risen, tidal flows to feed, but, unlike the creeping crustaceans that always clamber back down into hiding when the water returns, these feeders came all the way up and out to stand and stay, and the returning water could only lick at their much longer and larger legs.

This most likely would be understandable (though quite shocking as well) to an observing passerby, especially since now the rocks along the coastline had been shoved out of the way by huge boulders. No wonder, they might then also figure, that the creatures coming up between them are much bigger too and humanoid even. Humanoid but not entirely human.

"What the hell are those things?" the smallest man of the passing group asked of the much larger one nearest him. The big man was shouldering one corner of a boat he and three others were carrying down to the water. The big man was muscular as well, his current activity highlighting this feature, especially since he wore only a tank top, board shorts, sockless sneakers and otherwise was only adorned by long and curly, golden locks crowning his very tan everywhere else appearance.

"I don't know. Hopefully not some more of those zombie things like we seen earlier. We'll know though, if they are," he commented, looking over his other shoulder toward the new jetty. Big continued to little as they loped along.

"Rebecca said the first group she was with this morning had been attacked by them, and she barely got away. Everyone else . . . munch, munch, munch.

"Hey Rebecca," he also then yelled over to the woman walking along the other side of the boat. Before she could respond the big man hollered out at his fellow carriers that they'd better pick up their pace.

That was the sum total of the group: The four bigger men shouldering the boat, the smaller man, and the woman named Rebecca. They'd come together earlier that day at the mostly demolished marina, which is to say, almost all of the boats were capsized and or sunk.

But the skiff had washed ashore, and since more new rock formations were now blocking the mouth of the marina, here they were with it. They'd decided this would be their best ticket to escape the madness nearly everywhere now. And everywhere too there was death. The whole world, or at least this part of it, seemingly had become a deathtrap. Maybe with a boat they could get to someplace better, run up the coast until hopefully they'd find . . . something . . . somewhere better.

For defensive purposes they'd also decided to make their dash in this current formation. Rebecca was to walk and watch along one side, with the aforementioned smaller man on the other side most open to attack. This part of the plan devised because though he was the smallest, he was carrying a handgun, the groups only ballistic weapon. Now, however, Rebecca ran around to the other side of the small caravan since the bigger man had beckoned like he had.

"I think we got some more of those frickin' walkin' dead things watching us from those boulders over there." As his hands were full, the big man could only nod hard toward the beings in the rocks.

The dark haired and tanned, thirty something, shapely lady scanned where he had indicated. "Oh sh_t! I think you're right. Come on . . . come on!" They all hurried even more.

The little fellow checked his pistol's cylinder one more time, then noticed he'd fallen behind and hurried to catch up. His big head of dark, curly hair bobbed as he ran through the deep sand.

They started covering ground pretty well then, but the ocean was still a good fifty yards away. Interestingly enough, this was also about the same distance the zombified marauders just coming down off the rocks were away from them. Luckily, though, as usual, the living dead could only seem to manage a sort of stumbling run, and as a result, at this point the race was a toss-up.

"Nathan . . . no . . . come on!" Rebecca yelled back, stopping and starting because she saw her little, curly haired friend with the gun mostly just stopping, heroically deciding to do so in order that he might hold off the attackers. "Arlo . . . Arlo . . . wait," she also then yelled ahead at the big, blonde-haired man.

"We can't wait," Arlo called back, while at the same time glancing two or three times in the same direction to figure out why she'd made her ardent request. After a few more steps he began to slow. "All right. Hey. Hey, you guys . . . hold on." The upside down boat-mobile with eight legs bounced to a slow stop. "All right. Set her down. Turn her over . . . on three! One, two, *three*," Arlo hollered and the four carriers worked together to get the skiff down and right side up.

While then the other three took advantage of the moment to get their wind and limber up their rather stiff shoulders, Arlo urgently reached into the craft's hull.

He pulled up hard on something stored there and seemed to have gotten whatever it was before staggering back from the boat. He quickly righted himself and walked off purposefully from the group with his new weapon, a long and polished, wooden oar. He took a couple quick, practice swings with it as he headed toward Nathan, who was already taking shaky aim at the advancing enemy.

"You guys keep going," Arlo shouted back at the remaining boat haulers. "There are still three more oars in there. You'll be fine. I gotta help Nathan. If we make it, we'll catch up. You guys go though. Go!" He had yelled all this at the top of his lungs, yet his words were almost lost in the nearby rising and falling roar of the surf.

"But—" the one who'd been shouldering opposite Arlo yelled back. With open arms he indicated the empty slot Arlo was leaving them to somehow now fill.

"Rebecca can row. Don't worry about it. Just drag the damn thing! You're on the wet sand now. You can do it. Get going! Get that damn thing in the water!"

"Arlo?" Rebecca called out. She was halfway between the boat and the big man and seemed to be trying to work up the courage to help fight off the zombies too.

"No! You go with them. They need you to row. And you'll just get hurt. This won't be an easy fight. Go!"

A strange silence fell over everything then. The air got thick too, and blinkingly all present lifted their eyes toward the sky. A low rumble grew there and then the blue gray nature bonnet even seemed to change color slightly, a pinkish tint bleeding through.

Other than that, no one moved, poised in the moment like they were, poised and then almost even frozen. The only sound to be heard was a tearing roar like that of rolling thunder, but no storm was near at this time.

As the sound's volume increased, its source nearing, it then brought to the mind of more than one present that possibly, hopefully a fighter jet was coursing in to give cover fire, or maybe even to take the evil walking dead out with a hellfire missile or two.

But then and much to the chagrin of all, the source of the sound was not their weaponized salvation. It was only something too swift to be seen, flying down from the heavens, and they all watched as the yellow-white streak of light ended with a soft and small explosion in the sand right in the middle of them all.

Zombie Mike was starting to wonder if their underground ride would ever end. Not because it wasn't fun. He enjoyed the strange scenery. The tunnels which the rivers of lava had made and flowed through showed all different kinds of colorful rock and new substances in their walls. Plus the dips and turns while riding the silver disc were really scary but fun too. Like a ride in . . . in one of them places . . . those places he couldn't think of the name for at the moment. Those places where people also ate too much food and wasted all their money trying to win stupid prizes.

It was a bummer though too, Mike also noticed right off, how all Jeff and Ronnie seemed to be able to do was look confused and agitated, especially when the disc took them on a particularly sharp turn. He knew why, though. The master had told Mike right off that he was different than his friends. He was smarter, and so when they all became zombies, Mike was able to keep more of his memories, and could think better too.

So then, as the master had also informed Mike, he was to be their team leader, with their team being him and Jeff and Ronnie. Well, one thing was for sure. Both Jeff and Ronnie definitely needed leading, as also could any others they might run into on the way. Mike had also been instructed to try and make his team bigger. That would give them more power and then they could do greater things. Mike liked the sound of that.

Eventually he could probably do all that. If he proved himself worthy; if he could survive that long, the master had finished explaining it all with. Of course he felt bad about his friends, he also told Mike. But that was just the way things were. He'd done all he could for them. If you got a complaint, go talk to God. Then the master laughed and laughed, but Mike didn't.

The big and chubby zombie stopped thinking about all that, however, when from the looks of things their journey was coming to an end. The disc had taken them up a rocky incline—albeit an underground one—that marked the end of this last tunnel they would travel through. The flat silver blob had left them on a large, equally flat-topped boulder. The silver stuff melted off then from around their feet and flowed down through the cracks and crevices back into the little lake of lava at the glowing red river's end just below.

Mike checked on his two charges and with a little concern noted how they simply seemed mostly enchanted with watching the shiny silver stuff flowing down and away beneath them. He growled their way to get their attention. Even he couldn't talk. No zombie could. But he could at least motion for them to follow him up the rocks where cracks of sunlight could be seen peeking through not far up along the wall of big boulders now before them. After the cracks of light the boulders then arched up and over their heads, becoming the roof of the tunnel. Light came through cracks there too, but Mike knew no way could they get through there. But right in front of them . . .

Mike started right in, grappling his way up the boulders just in front of where they'd been left. With more coordination than his friends had, he deftly made it to a level where a few more steps would put him outside.

He looked squinting into the light outside, then back and down at his friends. It was easy, he wanted to scream at them. And maybe then call them pussies too because they were hanging back, afraid to even step from the first boulder.

But it really had been easy, made that way by the dark lord his master, Mike knew. So they could make it . . . how about . . .

He growled back down at them, still able to see them from this spot so close to outside. That was how easy, he tried to yell at them again, but it only came out growls.

It was working, though. They finally got off the first boulder and had found the track leading up along the edge of the next one. But still they were scared. Then Mike thought of one more thing.

He turned a little more towards his friends. Just enough to then also mimic the act of eating, pretending he had a big meaty leg in his hands. He slurped and chewed and moaned with pleasure.

In the next instant he fervently pantomimed the act of going out the rest of the way. Then he did it again. They seemed to get the message and more bravely ascended. Mike turned back and squeezed out through the opening into the light of day.

The zombie team leader quickly scanned the surrounding area. There was no one within his field of vision, but he knew probably soon there would be. The master would not have lead them to this place unless there would be something to eat. He had told them all that in the great mountain, all the leaders. Their discs of silver would take them to places where they could find their first feeding to at least get them off to a good start. Then they would be on their own. Search and destroy, eat, and repeat.

So Mike knew to just wait here and—oh yes. Them. He had almost forgotten. How could he when, as he turned back to the rocks, there they were, or their hands at least, helplessly flailing out into the fresh air from between the boulders. To express his anger with his underlings, Mike helped pull them roughly through and out.

The master had warned him that they might act this way. For so many of the zombies, this new life would be frightening and disorienting. But their hunger would drive them on and with experience would come courage and new levels of understanding. They would learn fast like animals, his dark lord had also mentioned.

Hopefully, Mike was thinking, because he and his animals were about to try and catch prey again. The group carrying the boat had just come into view, and with a quick count, Mike could tell there were six of them. He liked the way they were traveling too, somewhat strung out in a line. Maybe if …

If the four carrying the boat, the zombie leader further strategized, and if they just kept going, they could then at least probably overpower the small one at the rear. He'd have to make Jeff and Ronnie understand that though. He'd—

Ah hell, Mike could only mentally exclaim then as his two partners were already scrambling down the rocks and falling into the sand. The two then quickly got to their feet and immediately started trudging hard through more of the beach's deep sand, of course having espied their next meal as well.

He'd have to get ahead of them, Mike knew. Make sure they didn't screw things up too bad. And since, as mentioned, he was a little more coordinated than they were, he was catching up.

Once he knew he was in earshot, Mike growled real hard and the two errant zombies stopped.

Then they started up again, turning back toward the people and their boat. Mike growled again and also hurried and got in front of them. He waved his arms like crazy. Then he pointed at each of them fervently before slapping his right hand hard against his chest. He did this again and growled some more as well and seeing the look of what he hoped was understanding on their faces, he turned and took the lead position in their assault.

At least now he could concentrate on catching up with their meal ticket. The hunger in his gut felt like a chainsaw trying to rip its way out. They had to get at least one of them. That would do. But if they didn't hurry . . .

The four with the boat had made it onto the harder, wet sand now. If they got the boat in the water and out to where he and his friends would have to swim after them, they would get away. *Zombies don't float too well and swimming was out of the question,* Mike knew. He really couldn't remember how, which meant Jeff and Ronnie for sure probably couldn't.

So then it was a good thing when the little man at the rear of the group turned around and started heading their way. If they could get to him quickly, and start eating him, then maybe the others would just run for the ocean. Then at least they could feast on this littlest one. His meat, though not a great amount, would keep them going.

Then things got even better when a woman seemed to be dropping back too, joining the smaller man. *More to eat,* Mike was thinking, and then had to admit too, wouldn't *it be much more fun ripping into the flesh of a woman? Ooohhhh. And wouldn't it be tastier too?*

But then as they were almost there, here came a much bigger man. He'd been one of the ones carrying the boat. Now he was carrying a long piece of wood, something he took out of the boat, something Mike couldn't think of the name for, but . . . well . . . *it was one of those things for making the boat go.* Either way, this guy would be trouble for sure, and Mike decided he would attack him while Jeff and Ronnie went for the smaller man and the—

Oh. Now the woman was heading back toward the boat where the three men still by it were dragging it even closer to the water. This was just as well. Jeff and Ronnie should be able to make pretty quick work of the little guy and then help him with the big guy, Mike figured. And even though Mike knew as a normal human being he wouldn't have stood a chance against a guy that big— especially with that board, or whatever you called it, for a weapon—but as a zombie, he would prevail. With the added advantage of being a psychotic cannibal driven by the strongest of instincts, well . . .

But now . . . what the hell was that?

All of a sudden the sky changed color and it seemed to get a little darker too. Then also something seemed to freeze them all in place just before a streak of light came shooting down with the sound of a big jet real close. Finally, whatever it was hit hard in the sand right in front of Jeff and Ronnie.

All that freezing stuff didn't last long though and soon the two lesser zombies resumed their charge on the smaller man. Mike made his move too. He cut between them and the big man who was heading over to help.

All those muscles sure would be delicious, Mike couldn't help but think. But he would have to work for them he knew. And if he could just get a bite in the big man at least, then the big man would become a part of *the one* too. The master had told them that was the most important thing of all. Get at least one bite, even if it kills you to do it.

So even though Mike knew he probably couldn't overpower the big man, he thought of a way to maybe trick him. Starting with really playing up the zombie limping, groaning and drooling thing, and appearing really uncoordinated too. All of which seemed to actually be working. The muscle bound man just stood there with his big wooden weapon at the ready and only watched as Mike managed a theatrical fall right at his feet. Very close to his feet. So close that his face, and particularly his mouth, ended up only inches away from the big man's large and tan—and deliciously sockless—ankle. Which only caused the big fellow to scoot back just a little, and he even laughed a little too.

Mike heard him laughing and knew he had him. All of which got the zombie leader so excited and filled with ravenous energy he sprang out with the speed of a viper, grabbing the aforementioned big and beefy ankle and getting his teeth into the sumptuous tower of flesh. He clentched them extra hard then too, sinking them in as deeply as he could. The juices seeped warmly across his lips. Mike was in heaven. Only for a second or so, though.

Then he felt a bone rattling KATHUNK as his victim, after howling out in pain and leaping back, then brought the big wooden weapon hard down across the back of Mike's neck and shoulders.

All Mike could do then was roll over and prepare to die. Well, if the big man was going to carry things far enough that is. Kill his brain or take his heart out, which wasn't really the young zombie's primary concern however. For starters he could tell for sure the big man was set to stove his head in at the very least with the big wooden thing. And judging by how much it had hurt getting hit with it the first time, Mike was not looking forward to this.

But then, just as the giant—which was what he looked like to Mike laying on his back like he was now—was about to bring down the wooden weapon with both hands, gun shots rang out and were soon followed by a scream that definitely sounded desperate.

So with desperation all his own, the big man stopped his assault on Mike and looked over quick to where the scream came from. He left then quickly too because, as Mike could then also see for himself, Jeff and Ronnie had overtaken the smaller man and were bloodily beginning their cannibalistic duties. Jeff was gnawing on an arm he'd managed to remove from the victim while Ronnie seemed to be trying for more vital organs in the victim's midsection. It was over for the smaller man, Mike could tell, who for his part could only lay there shaking in shock.

"Nathan," the big man yelled, his voice bouncing like the rest of him as he ran across the sand. Before he could reach the scene of feasting, he doubled over in pain and then dropped to his knees.

"Rebecca . . . no . . . come on," one of the men who'd remained with the boat was yelling now. They had almost gotten to the water when the woman left them and was now starting back to the battle. Hearing him call though, she begrudgingly turned back.

"No! You come on! We've got to help them. Grab one of the oars. Derrick and Justin can get the boat the rest the way into the water and then wait for us. Come on!" She started off again for the fight.

The man she'd beckoned fished another one of those big wooden things from the boat and followed her. The other two men moved to the leading edge of the boat and started tugging. Slowly the gigantic snail trail they'd been leaving since they'd hit the wet sand grew longer and longer as they got closer and closer to the surf.

Zombie Mike meanwhile had managed to get to his feet. He was headed toward the battle too. He saw how well Jeff and Ronnie were doing and was proud of them. But, what pleased him even more was how the big man who had attacked him was starting to succumb to the disease he'd infected him with. Now the battle would be theirs. Yes, he joyously thought to himself, as the big man rose to his feet again, only now so obviously part of the one.

"Nathan. Oh my God," the woman said as she got as close to her fallen friend as she could, about ten yards away. Luckily the zombies eating on him apparently hadn't noticed her arrival. She immediately bent over to vomit.

Mike couldn't help but smile. The master had told him it would be like this. That most humans would not be able to handle the mayhem and gore and violence that would be their zombie trademark. Even the man with his own big, wooden weapon who'd come up with the woman looked mostly just very scared. Especially now that his large friend, who was possibly the biggest and strongest zombie ever created, was heading straight for him.

Mike's smile grew, then became a delirious and drooling, moaning laugh as while he watched, Jeff and Ronnie, who'd already turned their first victim into picked over remnants were very hungrily heading for the woman now. He knew, just knew his first mission for the dark lord was going to be a smashing success now. And just wait until he met their newest member. He would be their greatest warrior yet. He—

But what was that? Oh . . . of course. In all the action he'd forgotten about that streak of light and the sky changing color and all that, Mike suddenly realized. Now, whatever it was that had landed in the sand was coming up to the surface.

Oh. Okay. It was a human. Or looked like a human. And he wearing one of those wet suit things shortened in the arms and legs too. He was also big and strong, Mike could see. Not quite as big as the other guy, but strong. His body looked . . . perfectly proportioned. Thinking about it, Mike realized then as well that this new being had to be strong, digging himself up like that from who knows how deep in the sand he was. He couldn't be a normal human. He . . .

Uh oh, was all Mike could think. Uh oh. Something wasn't right here.

Mike was smart enough to figure out that he himself and all who were part of the one came from under the ground. Yet this new . . . human, or whatever he was had come down from above. *From the sky. From?*

Oh yes, very bad. And worse yet, just as Jeff and Ronnie were almost on the woman, this new arriver ran over to them and faster than any human could, he . . . *oh yes, this was definitely no ordinary human.* He beheaded Jeff and Ronnie so quickly Mike couldn't even tell how it had happened. Now his two best friends and fellow servants of Satan lay dead on the sand, this time forever.

As can happen then, for zombies just as for humans, Mike's exhilaration was spun on its head and desperate, gut numbing fear flooded in and took its place. But at the same time he was hungry too. Should he stay or should he go? *Should he stay, and maybe get killed by this obviously very powerful being, but also maybe get some leftovers to eat? Or should he go while he knew he could most likely get away, but remain very hungry in the process?* For sure this new super being was going to be busy for at least a little bit. Long enough for him to get away, Mike knew. And besides, not only was the bigger man from the boat a zombie now, but also the second one from there who'd come over with his own big wooden weapon was newly part of the one as well. Together they could handle this new guy, super or not. Then he could eat. *And what might such a being as that taste like?* Zombie Mike could only wonder . . . and drool.

"No. You need to return to me," the immediately recognizable voice of his master rang in Mike's head. "Watch and listen though too. I want to see and hear what this new one does and says. But start your retreat."

Mike did exactly as instructed. He listened as hard as he could while slowly backing away from the scene where the new being was talking to the woman he'd just saved.

"Go . . . just go. The other two can row you to safety. Tell them to head for where the sun sets, and soon you will notice strong currents taking you to a safe place. An island out there. Go . . . go!" the being yelled. It seemed like everyone started yelling like that when they showed up, Mike semi-humorously realized.

The woman was a mess though and didn't seem to be going anywhere. She could only stay there bent over and hysterically cry and scream at the strange being. "But Arlo! What's wrong with him!? He looks—"

"Your friend is gone. The enemy has taken him. He is with them now. I will take care of him though. Set him free. You must run. Go. You will find safety in the boat."

The being turned then to face the two new zombies approaching. As he did, positioning himself between them and the woman, Mike got his first full frontal view of the . . . man . . . thing . . . or whatever it was. With this new view, all doubt as to whether it was just another human or not was completely dispelled.

Mostly because the being's body was just too perfect. And then there was the color of his skin. He was like a living statue. Mike could remember seeing those pictures of those famous statues in books and from the neck down at least this guy could be one of them come to life. His skin had the same almost too-white color, and like the statue's too, flawlessly toned and muscled throughout. Only the thing's light brown, shoulder length hair and seemingly golden toned eyes were at least somewhat alive and human looking.

All of which Mike could so easily discern, he was realizing, because obviously his master was enhancing his senses. Even though he was at least fifty yards away from the group and still heading back for the rocks, he could clearly hear, and now also see them as if he were right there.

Which there now the woman was finally showing signs of understanding what was going on and she somehow managed a struggling run back to the boat. Probably because she'd unfortunately had to witness the big man who'd been her friend start savagely attacking the statue man. And probably too because of the unearthly growl her old friend had also manufactured.

Either way she was gone, while the statue man, having faced off with the savagely growling ex-friend of hers, seemed to be letting the big fellow vent his rage while just somewhat lazily blocking the blows the large attacker brought repeatedly down on him with his big, wooden weapon. Soon, though, the club broke, no doubt cracking like kindling on the statue man's very hard-looking muscles.

The statue man stopped fooling around then. The new big zombie went for his throat and in a sudden whirl of what looked like martial arts mixed with professional wrestling the statue man somehow wrapped himself around the big man's head. Then just as quickly, he flung him to the ground and ended up sitting on his head. In the next instant, the statue man plunged his hand hard down into the new, big zombie guy's chest cavity and pulled his heart out. The zombie immediately started quivering like a fish flung too hard on a pier while the statue man held the blood red mass aloft, seemingly just to make sure it was what it was, then he got up off his vanquished foe.

Mike didn't want to see anymore, but he couldn't turn away. The master had a firm grip on him. He was hungry too, especially after seeing that heart. But . . .

Oh. The master particularly wanted to see this, a new message told Mike. He would be fed well later, his lord Satan also assured him. But just watch, and listen, a little longer.

So then . . . *and oh* . . . this was making Mike even hungrier. Now the statue man was somewhat reluctantly eating the heart he'd withdrawn from the big zombie. *Oh . . . it looked so juicy.* The statue man didn't like it though and he kept asking up into the sky if he really had to do this and what about the disease?

So the statue man knew about the disease, Mike realized. *Was he immune?* But then he heard him say into the sky that no, he had no sores in his mouth, and then he checked his statue-like arms and hands and said no again. Then he started in on the heart once more, chewing and chewing and soon enough he'd forced the whole thing down. He bent over then for a moment, seemingly to fight off the urge to throw it all up, and then stood back up.

Both Mike and he then turned their attention on the last zombie. Mike hoped the statue man was thinking the other new one was the last zombie. Either way, he let himself slip deeper into the boulders until only his head remained visible, and that barely.

He could still watch though as then this *alleged* last zombie, who was understandably very scared, staggered back and got ready to run away. Just as he did however, the statue man took off after him. In only a second or two the perfect being caught up to the fleeing party, grabbed him by the hair and pulled his head back hard.

But then, unlike what might have happened if anyone else had done this, the new zombie's head got pulled clean off. And again the statue man had accomplished this faster than Mike could really discern how he'd managed it all. Something having to do with a hard twist and a karate style chop to the neck though, the chubby zombie-in-hiding thought he'd seen.

Now could he go, Mike pleaded of his master?

No, his lord informed him, because now was to come the most important part. Which as far as Mike could tell involved the statue guy gathering up the four zombie heads he'd taken and arranging them in a loose circle. He then dropped to his knees in the middle of them and started praying.

After just a moment, shafts of multi-colored light started shooting up from each of the decapitated heads. Another moment later, the statue being lifted his arms up, threw his head back and a similar but slightly smaller beam shot up out of his thrown open mouth.

Oh my God. Did you see that!? Mike somewhat anxiously thought as he descended completely again through the boulders of the jetty and into the darkness. His master had finally released him and also informed him to return the same way he'd come. Another silver disc would be coming for him there soon. So he continued down further until he came to the glowing, red lava riverside and the flat boulder where they'd disembarked before and waited.

Outside and almost out to sea now, the three survivors, the last two men and the woman, rowed into the setting sun. The statue-like being stood almost that still, like a statue, watching them make their way.

CHAPTER XIII

LIVE LONG AND PERSPIRE

"We better change that dressing," Ivy Henkman told Griner. He didn't argue. He was looking pretty pale, but his rocklike expression didn't change. He just looked steady at Ivy and nodded. "Here," she added and held out the half-full bottle of whiskey she'd been nursing ever since the earthquake. "It's gonna hurt. I guess. I ain't a nurse. But I think it might. So maybe you better."

Griner seemed not to hear her offer of the booze as he intently looked over his saturated bandage and prepared the area best he could for the change. He pulled up his sleeve on that side and positioned his upper arm for easy access.

He'd agreed to let Ms. Henkman have at it because he felt so weak and tired. He would have done it himself, but he really didn't care anymore and was just going to skip it. That's how tired he was. She'd insisted though. An infection was something they *had* to prevent if they could, she'd said. So he'd said okay. But he really didn't care either way. From the looks of things there wasn't really much left to live for anyway. Especially, after what they'd seen today.

But at least they'd made it through the day, their first one since the quake. Now they were seated opposite each other on folding chairs near a shelf on which a small camping lantern gave them the best light they could get with no juice down there in their basement bungalow.

Ivy kept talking as she got together what she needed for the procedure. "We're just all real lucky my husband stocked up on all this stuff down here. Crazy nut. That's what we used to call him. He had a sense though. Something might happen, he used to say.

"Except no booze, dammit. He forgot the most important thing! But here."

She held the bottle out at Griner again.

"That's all right. I been shot before. Even got gut shot once. Talk about pain." Griner's words came wrapped in that low growl of his. "I appreciate it. But you take it. And make it last. You better. Keep those DTs away." He gently pushed the bottle back at her. "And I'm glad your husband stocked up on all this stuff too," he added. "We could hold out for weeks down here. Just might have to. Or it'll be safer anyway, staying down here. After seeing those . . . things."

Ivy slapped on some medical grade gloves and looked at Griner. He held his arm out, and she started in with some shiny silver scissors, cutting the bloody gauze off and away. She worked stiff-lipped, her jaw muscles twitching. She didn't want to speak of the 'things' Griner had mentioned.

Around her the large, dirt-floored cellar and all the stuff previously mentioned could be seen filling the wooden planked shelves lining the six and a half foot high, cement block walls. Gallon jugs of drinking water, can after can of fruit and milk and even canned meat, cases of crackers, several more first-aid kits, boxes of batteries of different sizes, some small portable radios, a hodge podge collection of flashlights, small camping lanterns and more and all of it prearranged and stored in their own little areas.

Filling the middle sections of the underground room were four cots equidistantly spaced and now adorned with the also stored pillows and blankets. Two of the cots cradled sleeping Henkman children nestled within. Against a rear wall a usually locked close, but now open gun case held a hunting shotgun; twin .22 caliber rifles and boxes of rounds set in a far corner. Griner's sawed off laid on and marked his cot.

Possibly most important of all was underneath the stairs that angled up the nearest wall toward the house. Inside the triangular nook created there was a curtained off porta potty with a generous supply of toilet paper.

Per the loose rules of the shelter, the contents of said porta-potty were to be immediately dumped through either one of the two, 1 by 2 foot, ground level window/vents at the top of each of the two opposite walls that formed this corner of the house's foundation where the basement was nested.

Through these small window's and their thickly wired, mesh screens that Udo had hinged to open inward—and heavy duty hinges and latches at that—the outside world from a ground squirrel's point of view could be seen. Just beneath the windows on the outside, large holes for said waste had been dug in the yard, posthole style cavities a good six to eight feet deep.

Unfortunately for Ivy Henkman, but understandable because of her drinking habits . . . she'd been the first one to use the cellar's makeshift commode earlier that day. Unfortunate, because as she was emptying the potty's bucket down the spout-like slide leading from the little window, she'd noticed beyond it something was moving outside.

"Hey . . . hey," she'd yelled and quickly set the bucket down. She'd then looked back out but could only see what looked like fleeing shadows, maybe coming closer, but acting too like they were hiding as they did, which was easy to do what with the big old oak tree having fallen down in the middle of the yard and debris piled head high all over the place too.

But hadn't they heard her yell? They needed help! This was no time to be playing hide-and-go-seek!

So she'd yelled again, this time more directly out through the little window. But still no response came.

"What? Somebody out there? Hopefully not the cops," Griner'd sardonically commented, coming to and slowly getting up from his cot. Out of reflex he'd quickly grabbed up his sawed off and approached the window warily.

Jason, who'd been trying to pry open the cellar's hatch-like door at the top of the stairs, entirely unsuccessfully, as there was apparently some very heavy debris resting on it, had come running down to see what was going on too. He got his pistol out as he did.

"Mom, what?" he'd excitedly asked.

"Mommy?" Joannie had asked too and started over, bringing the little teddy bear with her that Udo had put down there for her. He'd thought of just about everything, her daddy had.

"Stay back, little one," Griner'd then said. "Maybe you too," he'd added at Ivy. "Remember what we heard on the radio? Could be bad guys out there. Jason, you get the other side." The two armed men then took up positions on each side of the window.

Ivy had started to protest, but then when she *did* remember what they'd heard on the radio last night, she'd carefully backed away, taking the commode bucket with her.

Because what they'd heard on the radio last night after the earthquake—once they'd gotten to their feet, brushed themselves off, lighted some lanterns and made sure they were all relatively okay—was something that sounded like the infamous 'War of the Worlds' broadcast.

The DJ this time wasn't anyone as famous as Orson Welles, but he was the man at the mic of a powerful FM rock station that had barely survived the shaking up in Los Angeles, and as far as the survivors could tell, it was the only station that had. Then since Sandy Point Beach was only about eighty or so miles away, the station's signal could make it all the way down there. Kind of scratchy, but okay, and best at night.

Which last night it sure had been, Ivy remembered, the broadcast sounding like they were right there as the DJ went on and on trying to describe all of what he knew about what had happened. He described the incredible devastation, not a living soul in sight, and not even the rest of the city in sight either.

From the roof of their one story building, the DJ went on, where he'd managed to scramble during a break, all he could see to the east was La Cienega Boulevard disappearing down into a canyon. The newly formed natural wonder was so vast he couldn't even see all the way across. It looked bottomless too, as far as he could tell. The full moon was at least helping him see that much, he further related, and then also went off on a minute long tangent how full moons added to earthquake strength and frequency.

But he was thankful for said moon, the DJ also said, because of course all artificial lighting outside was down. Luckily their studio, being part of the Emergency Broadcast System, had backup generators, and well, this sure looked like an emergency.

But also outside and then to the West, the only other direction the DJ could see from his roofed perch, steam or possibly smoke looked to be escaping through more enormous crevasses leading to a new mountain where only the valley and all its traffic had stretched out before. Just large, dark rocks and ripped up earth could be seen there now.

Although then he had seen some people coming too, the DJ concluded his tale with. So maybe there was hope. Even though these survivors he'd seen approaching sure were a scruffy bunch, or seemed so at least in the moonlight. Pale looking too. Even stranger was how they seemed to crawl up right out of the crevices in the earth, climbing up and looking like . . . omigosh . . . was that what they were? Were they . . . illegal aliens!

Then the DJ played a siren sound effect followed by some canned laughter and even Griner and the Henkman's got a chuckle over that one. But it would be the last time they laughed for a while.

Because then as the DJ went on explaining how their newswire service was down, but before it died, a few messages had made it through telling pretty much the same story worldwide. And—wait a minute, the DJ cut in with. He also wanted to issue a disclaimer before he went any further, because he'd been up all night, and if things got weird it might only be him hallucinating, which he was only mentioning because he swore he could hear something just outside the studio. Was that somebody coming? He could hear feet, lots of feet shuffling his way.

Then after a moment it started to sound like the joke was over on his end too as the DJ began to stammer, "Uhh . . . okay . . . uhh . . . I don't think it's Halloween yet . . ." Then he forced some nervous laughter too, which might have been funny as well, except that the fear was unmistakable in his voice.

After that, his breathing became heavy and erratic. Then in another moment the microphone fell with a thud and his voice grew quietly distant. The sound of furniture moving and a guttural moaning and growling could then be heard.

"Noo . . . no . . . no," the DJ's voice could then be heard, still distant but yelling now. "What . . . what are you . . . oh my God . . . you can't . . . stop . . . no . . . please stop," and then just screaming.

Next, with the listener's imagination chock full of all the audio input necessary to almost see it happening, the panicked, helpless DJ was cornered by what sounded like several assailants savagely attacking him.

Worse yet, one could then also hear with startling clarity—because they seemed to have cornered him not far from the discarded microphone—the muffled cries and then spastic gasping followed by the meat tearing, the cartilage popping, the bone crunching and even the pleasured moaning and the blood slurping of the attackers. All of which made Ivy reach up rapidly to click the radio off.

Luckily, Joannie had earlier drifted off, and as her brother had already mentioned, she really could 'sleep through an earthquake,' or at least the aftermath, which then left just the adults staring at each other with widened irises.

Which was also why the next morning Ivy had backed away from the window and then just tossed the porta potty's bucket back in the general direction of their new but hopefully temporary restroom. Then from his side of the little window, Griner had stared hard across at Jason. "What?" Jason hissed his mentor's way.

Griner'd nodded at Jason to move back from the window and quietly growled, "Just cover me."

Jason stepped back slowly, all the while bringing the nine up to bear on the one by two foot opening through which the same but now unoccupied view could be seen. Still staying to the other side, Griner had also carefully moved closer and scanned the half of the outside view visible from his side. He held his gaze a little longer, then smoothly got to the wall and slid lower than the window. He duck walked across below it to the other side.

The sound of some of the debris shifting outside got both his and Jason's immediate attention. A scraping and then the hollow clapping of a board falling hard against other wood seemed quite loud in the sudden silence. A few feet back from the window, Jason adjusted his grip on his gun and blinked the sweat from his eyes while keeping a steady stare at the target zone. Griner slid slowly up the wall from this new side and was painstakingly peeling himself off of it to increase his purview of the outside world again, this time from this side.

Ivy sat on Joannie's cot with her little girl, one of her arms holding her tightly to her side, while the other covered the nine-year-old's downturned face.

Griner suddenly froze from the shoulders up, but his arms moved and while the right slowly lifted the shotgun, the left raised his other hand chest high where it then froze before flashing all five fingers out fan fashion as if to signal Jason to be ready for anything. Even that small but intense motion had sent painful impulses coursing from the old con's wound in the same shoulder, and he winced.

As if sensing a moment's weakness in its adversary, the prowling beast, or whatever it was in the yard, suddenly pounced for the small opening.

Luckily, the opening was too small for the zombie who was doing the pouncing. Try as he might to force more than just his horrifically torn, gouged, ripped and half-rotted face attached to its nearly hairless and equally wound riddled head through the miniscule aperture, he could not. He did, however, manage to lift said fearsome face toward the survivors and fixed each of them in rapid succession with his faded eyes while snapping and growling with his somehow rapacious though still human, jagged tooth-filled, slobbering and cut lipped mouth.

All of which froze the basement dwellers with fear if not downright shock. The stillness that followed may have even been dragged out longer as all inside realized that at least no way in hell was that thing getting in through that tiny window, *thank God.*

But that was just a brief respite in the horror, after which Jason, as he liked to do, let loose with a couple more rounds from his pistol. At least, though, and somehow since his previous live fire experience at the liquor store, the kid had gained a certain degree of accuracy. The first shot went high like his others, but the second impacted dead square center in the zombie's forehead. Then after a major expelling of blood coated, cerebral contents from the exit wound, the creature throbbed three times before stopping its movements altogether.

"I got him," Jason proudly exclaimed around some nervous laughter. "I got him."

The young gunslinger's stare still stuck there, even though he, 'got him,' as he carefully started up toward the creature, which now looked like a mounted trophy, albeit with a less-than-spectacular job of taxidermy.

"Wait," Griner growled. "Just wait." He dropped back to get a better angle on the window, zombie stuffed as it was or not. "From what we heard before on the radio, I'm thinking there's not gonna be just one."

"Mommy," little Joannie whimpered.

"It's okay, honey. Jason got him! And Mr. Griner's got a gun too. We'll be fine. They can't fit in anyway."

But Griner's suspicion's had then been confirmed as with incredible suddenness and power the zombie's head shook twice before being whisked back out through the window almost faster than the eye could see. Then all eyes had turned to the window trying to see what they soon wished they hadn't as pieces of the zombie were being flung this way and that by whatever had taken it. A sound came next as something also growled then even deeper than and more ferociously than Griner could. It was a lion-like growl, but at the same time tinged too with a shrieking trill that made it sound otherworldly.

Soon enough, however, they got a better look as next to cram it's cranium through the small window was said beast, with a hairless and scaly head resembling a lion's, but as mentioned, hairless and scaly, scaly like maybe that of a giant lizard. The eyes were serpentine too, closed mostly to slits under thick lids. It was almost as if, Griner would later reminisce, the thing was doing this for protection, as if it knew a blast from his shotgun was coming its way.

Which did come, and maybe the lids had in fact protected the strange creature's eyes, but some part of it had not been spared the gun's angry blast. The lion lizard beast pulled back out into the yard where the sound of its howling, squealing wail and the stomping thuds of what sounded like more than one pair of feet? Hooves? Or whatever the cryptic creature carried itself about on could be heard as well.

"Everybody back! Jason, get back," Griner hollered. "I'm gonna finish this damn . . . thing." The con got up to the window quick, right after pumping another round into the breach of his shotgun.

Jason, who had brought his nine up to bear on the window again, but had been too shocked to squeeze off a shot at the strange beast, followed Griner's advice and backed off, lowering his gun but staying ready with it held near his leg.

Maybe it was partly out of anger then, what with the grizzled holdup man having been recently shot by a fat liquor store clerk, shaken nearly to death in an earthquake, and now attacked by a couple monsters from weirdoville . . . maybe it was all that that made him do it. But then and partly too it was out of curiosity that Griner slowly brought his face up right in line with and close to the little window. He really did want to get a good look at what was out there. So he could fight it better, maybe see where to shoot it more effectively, maybe---

What he saw then, however, was too bizarre looking. Almost in shock, Griner's ability to get off another shot soon failed him. And then too the old saying came to his mind about curiosity killing the . . .

Because this thing sure could have done some killing. The strange head they'd all seen already. But even stranger was its scorpion-like body. And a giant one at that. Well, giant for a creature of that variety at least.

The crazy looking thing in total was maybe six to eight feet in length. The thunderous thumping they'd all heard was the creature scrambling angrily around in the front yard on its six, scorpion-like legs while also rubbing, or trying to at least, trying to rub the sting of Griner's shotgun blast out of its head with one of the two pincher adorned—also like a scorpion's—foremost appendages. Even its huge stinger wildly swung back and forth, stabbing with an additional thudding sound into the ground over and over again.

Adding to the horrible spectacle were grisly remnants of what looked like a couple more of the zombie guys torn apart and spread across the debris littering the yard as well. Most markedly of all that was a decapitated head sitting not far from the window looking right at Griner with unmoving wide open, albeit also faded, eyes.

Needless to say, even being a hardened ex-con like he was, Griner decided right then and there to just duck back in and slam the window's thick screened cover shut.

"Oh my God," Ivy Henkman said, mostly in reaction to the blood-drained and wide-eyed look on Griner's face. "What—" she could only add, while her little Joannie still just cried at her side and couldn't look up.

"Like what you saw . . . I don't know . . . things . . . those things," Griner had growled, but the faintest one yet, really just a gritty whisper. He stared straight ahead and made himself breathe.

"Like a . . . a zombie? Like the one I got? But what was that second thing?" Jason asked, obviously scared but holding his ground, still at the ready, his gun hands quivering ever so slightly however now.

"Some kind of wild dog or something, I guess. That's all I could see," Griner managed to lie, having recuperated just enough to make it believable. Then once they'd all regrouped near their cots, as far from both the windows as possible, in a whisper Griner more than heartily agreed when they'd all decided to lay low for a while, live off their ample stockpile of survival goods.

They'd decided too it would be a good idea not to try and breach the cellar door, which Jason told them felt impossible anyway. The whole house must have fallen on it.

The final two resolutions of the committee of four were that all communications from then on would take place only if totally necessary, and then carried out quietly.

In their final formal action, the little windows immediately got canvas curtains affixed with generous strips of duct tape, only to be peeled away for potty bucket emptying. Blackout conditions were in effect.

And so there they were, lying low, and quite literally now in their cots, as after finishing Griner's bandage change, Ivy Henkman tiptoed over to her daughter, kissed the little girl lightly on the forehead, then turned in herself.

Griner used a similar approach, getting over to Jason's cot and after using a small flashlight to check the gun the boy still held in his hand outside the covers—he carefully engaged its safety—then got back to his own cot. By the small camp light on the little table flanking his cot, the old holdup man started in reading the dog-eared paperback he'd selected from the stockpile they had of those down in the basement too.

Zombie Apocalypse, the book's title read. Couldn't hurt, Griner thought, although horror fiction had never been one of his favorite genres. Maybe he might pick up some good tips on killing zombies though, he was thinking. Could come in handy. *Especially since there seemed to be some hanging around for real now. Wasn't that a zombie they'd seen? Who could believe something like that, but . . . wasn't it? And besides, after seeing too that thing that then ate the . . . zombie, well, maybe they might have a giant scorpion/lion hybrid monster thing running around in the story too. And maybe they might also show me how to kill one of those.*

So he read.

But soon enough, due to his still weakened state most likely; he dropped down into a fitful sleep. And as to be expected, zombie filled dreams came too, nightmarish in that there were just too many to fight off. But wonderfully then an angel came who with strong arms lifted him up and carried him safely away.

He awoke with a start, and for a few seconds could remember the dream, but only long enough to think about how strange it was. His dreams never had happy endings like that. At least not that he could remember. Bad dreams were more normal for him. *And angels? That was totally a first too.*

Then, just as it had for everyone else in the basement, sleep took him once more. Outside, the world, though turned inside out now and crawling with things the likes of which it had never known before, at least kept spinning. There would be at least one more sunrise, sooner or later. Somewhere.

CHAPTER XIV

PERFECT MAN'S BEST FRIEND

After standing for a bit, Udo realized he actually felt pretty drained from battling the zombies. He laid back in the sand to finish watching the boat with the three survivors float off into the western horizon. Just like a tourist on vacation, he was thinking. *Sure, vacation in zombie hell maybe*, but he was that tired. Zombies or no zombies, he was kicking back.

In doing so, he could feel himself recharging already. The beauty of the beachside scene, and also knowing that without him the survivors would have been toast. The feeling of accomplishment that came with that. All of it was revitalizing both his body and his soul.

In his earlier life, he hadn't had much of a chance for heroics, except at the very end there. Even then, though, he hadn't had the chance to bask in the glow. He was now and it felt good.

It also felt good, as he further reflected, to realize too he'd done something really great by freeing the souls of those wandering dead ones. Albeit, as he also rather disgustedly remembered, in such a horrible and for himself, highly distasteful fashion. But to free their spiritual essence and send it to the Lord . . . *Yeah that was good. Worth it.*

It was fun too how he was getting messages from the Lord the way he was, like about the island being a safe place somewhere out there. And then too that the ocean's currents would take the survivor's boat right to it. All of which just came to him, almost like his own ideas, but he could just barely tell they weren't. That was fun too.

Which was a good thing because the Lord had told him it would be like this now . . . with ideas . . . ideas that would seem like his own, only they would be about something he didn't know already. That was all the Lord would be giving him anymore for now. That, and the happiness and joy that came with figuring out it was from Him.

"It is the way of human existence," the Lord had explained at the conclusion of Udo's training. "It's up to you to succeed or fail. Even though you are something more than human, what you will be doing will still be a part of the on-going human saga. Believe in me and my ability to help you and you will still hear from me. I'll communicate to you in thoughts and ideas and urges. Just don't be afraid to act on those urges. That is my greatest advice. Then I will reward you with success and the happiness it brings.

"Now get out of here, ya knucklehead!" the Lord finished with in a jocular outburst just as Udo realized that the creator of everything had also dropped back behind him. He next felt God's swift, yet somehow soft, but still incredibly powerful kick. Which at first sent the newly perfected human high and tumbling through the air . . . and then as he could make out one of the kingdom's great walls below, next he was over it and falling fast from heaven.

As he fell, at first he'd tried flying. But soon he reached speeds so fast it felt like his arms were going to be torn off if he didn't streamline, so he assumed a diver-like position and screamed through layers of space and atmosphere until before he knew it he did dive. He dove right into the sands of Sandy Point Beach.

Surprisingly, though, he seemed totally unharmed. The sand had actually felt very forgiving at first, but jarring when he was finally jostled to a quick stop. He knew he was buried though now. Buried deeply and totally constricted and in fear of soon suffocating so he quickly righted himself. He dug and turned and then burrowed. With his new perfected form and abilities he kept burrowing his way up like a human weasel until he erupted out through the surface.

It was a good thing too, which he'd then noticed for the first time (up in heaven just before Jesus kicked him out he'd had on a toga like usual) that now he had on a really strong and tight fitting wetsuit like thing. But so encased in rubber like that he'd just slipped right through the sand. Then the outfit had also made it easy to do all the fighting he'd had to do. Plus it looked pretty sharp in dark blue with yellow highlights.

Which he then admired some more, back in the present and still just lounging about. Hey, he then also noticed for the first time. His skin was this spooky white color now. *Maybe I should try and find some sun screen somewhere,* he was thinking. Although then after giving his oddly tinted skin a good pinch, showing him too how thick and durable it was now as well, he realized sun screen probably wouldn't be necessary.

So okay . . . okay, he let it all go with and slowly got up from his sandy spot of repose, stretched, and started to move again. *Back to work,* he made himself think, remembering too what it was all about after all. His wife and Joannie and Jason . . . out there . . . somewhere. He had to find them, along with freeing some zombie souls as well on the way . . . *yes* . . . that was good too, but now he was so close. He could feel his family near. He had to find them.

He turned and started back up the beach. He wasn't sure exactly where he was, what with the changes in the apocalyptic topography. Like this new jetty that seemed to have erupted right here. And he could sense something there, so he headed for it. Then he saw them.

Footprints.

They had come out of the rocks here, those zombie fellows, Udo could tell. He sniffed hard at the air and could smell something. He also then smelled his still zombie blood stained hands, and *oh yeah, that was them.*

Not wanting to delay the search for his family, but feeling impelled to do so, he followed the trail of zombie footprints instead. Maybe one would lead to the other, he figured, and went with the urge to search for zombie.

He'd been feeling that urge very strongly, Udo was starting to notice. To hunt and kill the zombies. As well as feeling that his family was safe for now somehow. *Hadn't the Lord said as much when he'd seen Him before? Back up there in heaven?*

Yes.

Oh. Is that you? Udo thought out, asking if it was Jesus talking to him.

No answer though. But then the voice said, Get your family but kill as many zombies as you can on the way.

Then it was over Udo could tell. It was like that too when He talked to you. You could tell when he was done.

Udo found the zombie tracks again and made his way to the new jetty. He jumped up onto one of the front most boulders like a big cat might. He looked at his legs and smiled. The boulder had to have been five or six feet tall too. He could get used to this, Udo was thinking.

He sniffed around some more, jumped to another boulder lower and to the right, then dipped his head into the stagnant air of an opening between two of the boulders that seemed to even open into some sort of cavern inside. There too he could smell their presence. *Had they . . . ?*

He continued further in, squeezing through the gap in the boulders with only a little more effort than the zombies had needed to go through the exact same spot. Wow, he could only think as he took in his new surroundings. He supposed that with the earthquake and everything . . .

But wow!

And no. This sort of thing couldn't have happened naturally. He'd heard of rivers of lava, but underground! And it seemed to go deeply back, back into a tunnel inside the jetty after lapping up here onto the shore in this small underground cavern part he was in now.

So yeah.

No. No way did this place just happen. It was too perfect, about six and a half feet of head room, a nice little beach area just below to walk on with firm, wet sand. Which then too was where Udo could see more zombie footprints leading away from the boulders next to him.

Then, *wait a minute*, he noticed next. Three sets of prints lead up to the boulders, while only one lead away back to the lava.

One got away.

One came back down through here to go back. But back where? Udo could only wonder. Was this tunnel . . . wait? It was almost as if the tunnel and the jetty had been specifically created for the purpose of transporting . . .

No . . .

But what if it was? Then if he could just follow it back to its source and . . .

He probably couldn't withstand swimming in lava. From the looks of it the glowing red river ran back along a small shore that shrunk and shrunk in size as it got ready to descend and enter a narrowing of the tunnel where walking along it would no longer be an option.

He followed the shore down that way as far as he could. Still no one to be seen, dead or alive. And man was it hot in here without the gaps in the boulders anymore to let the heat out. So where'd that other zombie go?

Udo's detective work was interrupted then as the ground started to shake, which of course was more than a little alarming, considering his current surroundings. At least, however, it was a steady rumble, not a jarring displacement of everything like an earthquake usually commenced with. Either way, Udo started a hasty retreat.

Which was just as well as all of a sudden the source of the rumbling revealed itself to be the rapid entry into the underground river cave of the biggest snake Udo, and probably anyone else on planet Earth had ever seen.

But how could a snake withstand that lava, Udo only had time to rapidly wonder as he dove for cover. Luckily he landed in a natural indentation in the boulder wall where two of the great stones protruded sharp corners out over his head. Looking up and pressing in with his back as far as he could against the boulders, he got his answer.

In the next instant the giant, all-white snake first showed Udo his blood red and strangely intelligent looking eyes, then opened its huge jaws to show off healthy red mucous membranes and gums holding giant white fangs. Then after snapping at him two or three times, the enormous reptile showed Udo how he'd survived the swim in the lava. During all the great viper's activity, remnant gobs of molten rock fell from the snake's sizeable scales in places, revealing small glints metal.

A metal snake! Udo could only shockingly realize, backing deeper into the boulder lined recess. He noticed too as he did that the big rocks seemed to move a little. There was no time to worry about that though as the big snake snapped a few more times his way.

He had to get out of there. Thick skin or no, that snake could probably snap him in half. Udo looked around hard. There were thin slits of light showing through above his head, and a few behind him too. Maybe . . .

Udo got his idea, maybe not the best one ever, but his only option as far as he could tell, after remembering how the boulder behind him had slipped a little when he'd been so fervently trying to keep out of reach of the big snake. Then remembering too how strong his legs were now . . .

He scooted across the rock surface beneath him until he got to the other corner of his little boulder bungalow. The snake seemed to be just watching him for a second, but Udo didn't watch back. He was too busy wedging himself in so he could press his back in hard against the boulder behind him, which he hoped would be one making up the wall of the tunnel itself.

Udo's huge thigh muscles flexed as he pushed with his back against the boulder behind him, using every ounce of his newfound strength until . . .

The big rock started to give way. Of course Udo also knew he was risking having the whole thing cave in on him, but as he'd already figured, it really was his only shot. He kept pushing. Funny, he then noticed too, that the snake wasn't attacking anymore. In fact it seemed to be backing away. Awful smart snake, Udo could tell, but just kept pushing.

Suddenly the big boulder shot out from behind Udo and the whole thing did cave in, but only partially onto him.

Luckily, with the great burst of strength he'd had to exert, Udo had not only dislodged the large boulder at his back in a rather ballistic fashion, kind of as planned, but he'd also then shot himself out right behind it. Only to be caught then, however, by another falling boulder which had landed hard and heavy across one of his legs.

"Aaarghhh," he yelled, and at first continued to struggle. Then he just laid back. It was immovable. Both his leg and the boulder lying across it. But at least he was mostly outside now. And the giant snake was gone. The rest of the jetty tunnel looked to have collapsed as well, either trapping the big snake under its huge rocks, or more likely, Udo knew, having seen the snake already retreating, sent it back to wherever it'd come from.

Udo continued to look for the huge creature that'd tried to eat him, but there was no sign of it. He'd be easy pickings now he could tell. He rested on his back on one of the lower boulders on this side of the still intact jetty. Mostly boulders were all he could see. That, and a decent view of the beach and ocean on this side too, but then more boulders.

Including, quite regrettably, a really big one, as mentioned, on top of his leg. The leg, which as far as he could tell, looked to be crushed, was also trapped. Just the slightest movement sent almost shock-inducing bolts of pain up through his body. Of course, in a normal human, the pain would have probably already sent them deeply into dark unconsciousness. But Udo's perfected neuronal capabilities were at least somewhat compartmentalizing the numerous pain impulses bombarding his brain.

But even though that helped and still made it possible for him to continue to attempt to move the great boulder from off his leg, even with his also highly improved strength, it was still no use. He'd tried grasping and pushing and pulling on every edge of the boulder he was laying on. But nothing.. He looked up into the somewhat faded sky. Maybe he should pray, he was thinking. But didn't the Lord say it was up to him? Didn't he say—?

Uh oh.

Oh no.

Not more of them already.

But it had to be.

Only *they* could make that obnoxious moaning, groaning and growling sound the special way they could. *Oh great.* Well. Maybe he could fight them off laying down. But probably not. Not all of them, and it sounded like there were at least a few.

Yeah, Udo could tell after managing to raise up to a seated position. Four zombies lopingly trudged their way across the beach toward him. He struggled futilely one last time and tried to get ready for them, but soon realized there was no way to further ready himself.

Get ready to die ugly, he was thinking once the zombies got up to the jetty and he was able to look right into their ugly faces. Their glazed and psycho looking eyes ravenously trained on him like he was a steak dinner or whatever was just a little too creepy.

Worse yet then was how the whole ordeal was getting dragged out because the zombies couldn't seem to figure out how to get up onto the big boulders. They were like stupid animals, Udo realized and he might have even felt sorry for them, except he knew that soon they would be eating him alive.

They continued to struggle, three of them just hopelessly and with no results at all, pressing their chests against some of the first level boulders in the jetty's side, the ones that were a whole level lower than the one Udo was stuck on. They flailed their arms against the slick surfaces of the rocks, evidently unable to find either a handhold or a foothold.

But then, and even further to his chagrin, Udo noticed the fourth member of their group, possibly a smarter zombie, maybe even a leader, working his way further down the shelf of big rocks until he found a pathway of smaller rocks, which let him make it up onto the top-most boulders of the jetty. Then even worse, he began steadily progressing along the hillock's spine until he was at most only fifty feet away and closing fast. The final act, or near to that, Udo realized, then came as there went the others . . . quickly falling in behind their leader. Within moments a whole cavalcade of drooling death was headed Udo's way.

Perhaps if they kept coming spaced apart like they were, Udo rapidly strategized, then he could grab the first one to get near enough and make fast work of him . . . then the next one . . . and well . . . that might work.

No time like the present . . .

He grabbed the first attacker by the leg and swung him hard around before letting go to bounce him off a nearby boulder and down onto the sand of the beach below. But then from out of nowhere something struck him hard in the head. He saw then that his earlier assessment of the zombie species was perhaps a bit premature. They should at least be equated, he was now forlornly realizing, not with the stupid animals, but perhaps with the smarter ones who could use rocks as weapons.

Because here came another projectile of that sort, one of the smaller stones that the zombies must have been finding scattered among the boulders. This one struck Udo in the head too. Apparently they were good shots as well.

The pain, Udo easily shook off, but then his vision started suddenly blurring. Even more seriously, his consciousness seemed to be waning as well. His solid rocky perch seemed to be starting to slowly pitch and sway beneath him.

Oh God . . . oh God, Udo thought with sincere fear finding its way into his fuzzy mind, especially when next he looked up from the almost entirely supine position his groggy state now left him in to see one of the undead standing over him with a watermelon-sized rock held aloft and most likely aimed for the same target they all seemed to like. His noggin.

In a last ditch effort, all Udo could think of to do now was roll said target from side to side, move his arms repeatedly into defensive positions near the same area while at the same time trying to watch for when the zombie might drop the rock on him.

Then the strangest thing happened.

But it couldn't be, he was almost bemusedly thinking in his now even groggier state of mind.

Maybe he was hallucinating.

Although he then remembered too, hadn't he just seen a giant snake? So what was so weird about a giant crab? Or at least a giant pincher-like appendage, which he had to admit was all he'd really seen as the big and rock hard looking grabber had come quickly from somewhere, placed itself around the neck of the zombie about to brain him and with a mighty snip and snap it was now his attacker's brain that was rendered unusable as its container . . . namely the zombie's head . . . toppled and fell between the rocks. Luckily then too the other rock, the one the now headless zombie had held aloft, slipped from his grasp and took the place of his absent skull. Then, the now-even-stranger looking, lving dead creature fell to the boulders below.

All of which helped Udo regain at least some of his spunk. But then, just as he rose up on an elbow to take a look at whatever creature that pincher had belonged to, at least some of it flowed right out again. Spunk, that is.

Mostly because these, "surprises," the Lord kept delivering in rapid order were more than a little unnerving. At least Udo could only assume they came from Him. For was *he not* the fountain of all life? Or something like that? That was in the bible, wasn't it?

But one look at this newest creature had Udo wondering if maybe that shouldn't be, fountain of all really weird life too. As he'd previously noticed, this thing did indeed have crab-like pinchers at the ends of its two foremost . . . legs? Or actually, Udo was realizing with further examination as he watched the thing now starting to tear into the other zombies, but actually they were more likely modeled after a scorpion's, since also the beast's body was like that of a scorpion too. And the head was like some giant . . . tiger . . . or a lion maybe? But . . . hairless and scaly?

Whatever, Udo left it with again and mostly just wished he didn't have to be around when the thing got finished tearing the dead guys' limb from limb. Which it was literally doing so at a rapid rate. Body parts were flying all over the place. So would he be next? Oh well, he figured. At least it would be better than ending up as cannibal chow.

Either way, he could tell he wouldn't have to wait long to find out. The scorpion, monster, lion thing was quick. The zombies it hadn't gotten with its pinchers, soon fell prey to the scorpion-like tail. The beast even just then rapidly swung the deadly tail around to jab its sharp point with a hollow thud down through the top of the remaining zombie's skull. The living dead guy danced like he'd been electrocuted then fell dead.

The spookiest thing of all, though, was the screeching, howling growl and possibly a personal call of victory it emanated. All the zombies were definitely vanquished and the creature just stood among their remains. After its cry it snorted like a horse at the air.

Udo forced a quiet breath. *Maybe it will just go away.* Sure, he'd still be trapped there, but he'd be alive. He'd—

Uh oh. Now the creature seemed to be noticing Udo, looking his way with its strange . . . oh my gosh . . . it had snake-like eyes that seemed to look right through him. *Super creepy.*

With renewed energy, renewed through fresh fear, Udo tried once more to free his leg but with the same result. He still kept trying though. The creature was coming his way and so quickly it was already almost on him.

Oh God, just get it over with. The way the thing walked so stiffly on its crazy legs with the front two held up, pinchers at the ready and tail held high: all very scorpion-like. So of course Udo was terrified. Besides which too, the thing was at least as big as a Toyota . . . SUV!

"Kitty?" Udo tried with purposeful temerity as the creature pulled up just short of him. The strangest of all cats then just looked at him, sort of puzzled for a moment, before next coming even closer until it was right over him. It bent down and gave Udo one of its snorting sniffs, then reared back and let out a screaming roar once more.

Underneath the air rattling blast, Udo swore he could feel the resultant vibrations right before bits of blood soaked flesh and whatever all else the thing had eaten rained down on top of him in cold little flecks. An odor like barbecued death followed.

Udo started breathing again as next the creature turned around and with its pinchers wedged beneath the boulder, pried it up and then pushed at the huge rock until it toppled off and down from the jetty. The last thing Udo remembered was feeling new levels of pain and then watched the blackness come and get him. It took him kindly away across the ocean, seemingly across all time as well it seemed, before also very kindly winking out.

CHAPTER XV

AFTER SHAKES

"At least the potty holes still aren't full. I can tell by the sound of how long it takes to hit the bottom when you dump it out," Joannie Henkman proudly proclaimed.

"You are just so frickin' smart," her brother jabbed back. He always had to empty the bucket for her out the window anyway. For safety and all that. But there was always his little sister waiting nearby, back against the wall, listening intently while also cutely pinching her little nose. She was too much.

That was the only cute thing about the whole "emptying the potty," process that had happened so far. Much more memorable was a greatly less cute occurrence that had happened a day or two earlier after Griner had used the commode. As the holdup man was bringing the spout back in from the window, something else came with it: a half-dead hand grabbing hard along the spout's rim, pulling with all its might.

Obviously the hand was attached, most likely, to one of those half-dead zombie things coming to visit again. But that potty spout was good as gold to them, so no way was Griner letting go. The zombie didn't seem to want to let go either. A real tug-of-war was starting up.

Then another zombie arm shot in through the other half of the small window. It looked a little bigger than the first one and grabbed even harder. But worse yet, this time it didn't grab the spout, it grabbed instead onto Griner's lower forearm just above his wrist.

"Hey . . . hey," he shouted, the second 'hey' coming out more forcefully and louder than the first. The zombies—as the cellar trapped survivors were learning---were pretty darn strong. So with two against one, right away they were starting to win the tug-of-war. Which of course too meant Griner's arm was being pulled closer and closer to the window. He couldn't help but think then about what he'd read in that zombie book. That if they bit you . . .

And even though he knew that was fiction, still the sight of his arm alarmingly close to where the dead monsters might be able to get at it strengthened him mightily and immediately. He twisted and pulled, harder and harder, but he still couldn't break free. Then after that burst of power he'd received had burned off, the power of the zombies won out once more and his arm continued to move steadily up the window's way.

Out of nowhere, and quicker than Griner could see, a machete came sweeping down and through, abruptly ending the tug of war. The old con fell back, bringing the spout and the lower arms of two zombies with him. He blinked and noticed for the first time Jason just off to the side, still in a stance of semi-readiness. The machete in his right fist was already halfway to a new striking position once again. A small, nervous smile graced the young man's lips and a faraway, crazed look filled his eyes.

"Good job, kid," Griner growled, then looked to his arm. He shook the dead appendages free and tossed the spout aside. He looked back at the boy and had to laugh. Jason seemed to return to himself and joined him. After a little more laughing the young man slipped the machete back in its sheath hanging from his belt.

The machete was another item Udo had wisely stored in their basement. Jason had kind of just been wearing it for fun ever since he'd found it tucked away in the corner by the gun locker. He'd almost even forgotten it was there. Until just then with Griner, who he secretly thought of as his new father, about to be taken by them zombie things. Without thinking he'd quite literally . . . swung into action.

And since the machete was unused and very sharp . . . and with his adrenaline flowing like it was, the resultant severing was almost inevitable.

Understandably, ever since then, Jason always wore the machete when emptying out the pot. Griner, on his trips to pottyville, as Jason liked to jokingly call the whole stinky process, would always have one of the guns nearby. And poor Ivy, well she was a different story.

When her, 'just-a-few-days,' supply of booze ran out, the DTs came running in. Then Ivy'd been running to the commode ever since. Mostly just to throw up. It got so bad they eventually set her up with a bucket by her cot.

At first, that seemed to be the worst of it. But then came the shakes and how she was 'freaking out' . . . as Jason liked to put it. She was seeing snakes and screaming about spiders crawling all over her too. Joannie had cried a lot at first, but in between taking turns holding and comforting Ivy, Jason and Griner had also explained to the little girl what was happening to her mommy. Then Joannie handled it much better, and even helped out.

After about 36 hours, Ivy's mental state returned to almost normal. Finally as well, she was able to keep water down and since then she'd been sleeping for the past twelve hours, much to the relief of the others.

Everything else in the homemade shelter seemed to be going okay . . . or as well as one could expect in a zombie apocalypse as Griner was still sardonically calling it all. From the book of the same name he was still reading. But really, it was. Going all right, that is.

There hadn't been any more visits from the reaching dead. Everyone was pitching in, rationing the food and water. And sure it was getting pretty smelly. They were *all* getting pretty smelly. But they believed they could probably make it another week or two, they'd all decided at one of their impromptu discussions that Griner usually led. Then they also decided he and Jason should seriously go to work at getting the hatch at the top of the stairs open. At that time they would then try and make it in the outside world . . . *very carefully.*

Griner was surprisingly happy with the way things were going, all in all. His arm was healing well and hardly hurt anymore. And he hadn't mentioned it to anyone, but he even sort of pictured himself the head of their hastily thrown together little family. He'd already taken over the role of surrogate father for Jason. Ever since meeting him in that scared straight session he'd liked the kid. Then finding out about his dad having died and seeing the kid's fighsty nature and propensity for lawlessness—he was like the son Griner'd never had.

And little Joannie was such a sweetheart, but quite the little soldier too. She was always surprising Griner with her intelligence and bravery. Life in this bunker could have been nearly unbearable if she had ended up being a sniveling crybaby like so many other children her age would have been in such a situation. But not her. How could he not like her as well?

Then there was Ivy, or how he really thought of her, Jason's mom. The most surprising thing of everything that had happened—although calling the arrival of zombies and other killer monsters into their world *not* surprising didn't really work—but other than that, it was most . . . refreshing? Yet also disturbing? But also okay. That he was finding Jason's mom rather attractive.

Her full head of brunette hair, cut the way high school girls used to wear it in his day. Her petite but full hipped physique somehow accented in her jeans.

Her sneakers and sweatshirt. And then in the middle of it all her stern, librarian looks, were---in a good way . . . well . . .

Even now, as Jason and Joannie turned in, instead of turning in himself he pulled a chair over to Ivy's cot and started in just watching her sleep.

"You turnin' in, Grinds?" Jason asked across from his cot.

"Soon enough. Just wanna keep an eye on your mom in case she throws up again or something. You know . . . make sure she doesn't choke on it."

The former holdup man reached over and cut the light down coming from the camp lantern on the box nearby to a dim, romantic glow. That is, if anything in a smelly, bomb shelter basement in a world lost to zombies could be romantic. Somehow though, it was.

"All right, dude. Good night," Jason added back.

"Good night, kid . . ."

"Good night, Mr. Griner," Joannie chimed in.

"Good night, sweetheart."

For Joannie, Griner had used his best, never-been-a-father-before, fatherly tone. It was almost not growling. The little girl's sweet voice had drawn his gaze away from Jason's mom for just a moment, but then seeming to notice Ivy's pretty lips moving ever so slightly he looked quickly back. "Good night, darling," he whispered very quietly her way, trying to sound like the husband he'd never been either. He wanted to kiss her too but decided he better wait.

He kept thinking about it though, and plenty more as he watched her a while longer. It was so quiet in the basement, and quiet outside too. Very, very quiet. Quiet enough to get him thinking maybe it might be time. Time to try and leave already.

Rebecca was starting to wonder if maybe she was dead too. They should have never listened to that big, muscle bound, freaky looking statue dude. Hadn't he said just steer for the sunset?

So they had, day-after-day after day, rowing until their hands bled. But nothing. Nothing but ocean, dark green to dark blue. With nothing else to watch, she'd noticed that. How the water changed color like that with the position of the sun. It would be black at night and then silver in the morning. Then dark green to dark blue. Then find the sunset and steer into it. Day after day-after-day.

But there was nothing. Nothing else anywhere. It seemed like forever since they'd seen anything. A few giant balls of trash had gone by. One with plastic six-pack loops reaching out from its edges. Damn thing was as big as a whale too. Then Rebecca saw fish caught in some of the loops. Some dead and rotting too. *No wonder God is killing us,* she heard herself think before even making the thought. Or that was it felt like anyway, which was really weird.

Apparently though, the Big Kahuna wasn't ready to kill her and her shipmates quite yet. Rain had come. The generous downpour had lasted a good half hour, not only treating the boat bound survivors to a catch-the-rain-in-your-mouth party, but then also left more than a few inches of dirty but drinkable water in the bottom of the boat. In the hot sun it had dried up, however, in just a couple days. Then poor Rebecca had even gotten a splinter in her tongue while licking at the wood. Now in the middle of the parchment-like texture her mouth felt like there was also a tiny staple of pain. She'd eventually pulled it—hopefully all of it—out and the pain eased but still . . . and anyway, that was the least of her problems now. Because then they'd all become too weak to row anymore, so they were just drifting . . . drifting and drifting . . . drifting and drifting.

But then maybe because she was a woman and much smaller than the men, she'd lasted just a little longer. Although now all she could still barely do was see. She couldn't get up, but she was able to move her head just enough to get a glimpse of Derrick and Justin, and boy were they were out of it. Like her, they too lay on the boat's rounded wooden bottom, but unlike her, their eyes were closed and neither moved a muscle. Hopefully, they were still breathing, but she honestly couldn't tell.

Considering their situation even further—and she hated to think about it this way—but being so near death must have been making her selfish, because she could tell she mostly hoped that Derrick was still alive.

Which in many ways was totally understandable. She'd only just met Justin, while she and Derrick had a history as boyfriend and girlfriend. Their relationship had fallen apart, though, or at best slowed down, because of her refusing to have premarital sex. But maybe there was still a chance for them. Yeah . . . *if we can survive the end of the world,* which Rebecca also knew was an implausible consideration given their current state of affairs. *Survive . . . yeah right . . .*

She kept looking at him, though, enjoying her view of Derrick and his hair. She loved how he'd let his afro grow out. And his skin too, so dark and so beautiful. Like dark and hard wood. Which she like to think of him like that too, his wiry but well-muscled body firm under her touch. She tried to say his name but couldn't; she no longer had the strength to do that either.

Thinking she'd caught a glimpse of something passing overhead, she used all the strength she could find and rolled over. She could see nothing now, though. Just the sun so big and white and hot. She swore she could actually even see the waves of heat pouring down from the burning star, radiating and iridescent and beautiful.

Then she figured that it was all her imagination especially when next it looked like some large, winged creatures came down, which must have been what first caught her eye. A black silhouette then joined by another and both of them then flitting back and forth across the colorfully refracted light everywhere else.

Seeing more of them, but still only in outline, now Rebecca could tell they seemed to be big, muscular men with long hair and, of course, the wings. *What is it with the big, muscular men these days?* She half humorously thought and then swore she could feel the boat lifting and rising into the air. Surely she was imagining it all, she thought once more and then everything went black. Finally, it cooled off.

As they started off, mounted for now on just an old blanket they'd found in the house, Kellen kept her fingers in a loose grip in the shiny black and slick, but very thick and strong, long hairs of Shadow's mane. Aaron was seated right in front of her where he could put his little hands in Shadow's mane too.

Shadow had no problem with the load. Aaron was small and Kellen, though she was tall and fairly strong, probably weighed about a buck and a quarter soaking wet. So Shadow easily kept a steady, smooth—smooth for a horse, that is—and strong gait up the trail cutting through the back half of the Andrew's property.

The acreage there, which had been sloping green fields before, was now pretty mountainous, Kellen and Aaron were learning with wide eyed wonder. It was nice however, they both realized in their own way, how their path wound through the rocky and rising terrain. It was almost as if it had been cut there by trailblazers over the years—which it hadn't of course--*or maybe laid out by Disney engineers,* Kellen couldn't help but also think—which was equally unbelievable—but she wasn't counting anything out. With the way things were going . . .

Like also, who ordered the full moon so bright that out here in the hills and valleys now it was almost like daytime? Finally the young cowgirl even reached across with one hand to pinch hard on her forearm for like the third time today just to make sure she wasn't dreaming.

But no, she wasn't asleep and dreaming. This crazy world all broken up with zombies coming out through the cracks and mountains where valleys used to be was all too real. Although maybe at least somebody—and it was sort of looking like it was maybe the same somebody who'd made it all happen—but at least somebody seemed to be helping her out. As crazy as that sounded too.

The help came this time as now up the trail she could see what appeared to be part of their stables that had busted off from back at the ranch proper and landed directly ahead some how. Making mountains could get messy, was all Kellen could think and pulled Shadow over toward the prize which was impaled on a jutting section of a very large rocky outcropping dead ahead.

She could tell it was a part of their stables because of the paint, which remained from the recent repainting last spring. Knowing that, she also hoped—

"We stopping, Kellen?" little Aaron asked.

"Yeah, honey. We're stopping."

Kellen had to smile as she got down off Shadow. It was so funny how kids were always asking questions about things that were already happening. "You stay up there for now though okay?" She put a hand on Aaron's little leg. Then she checked and slightly adjusted their load of the two, water bottle-filled backpacks, which were held across the horse's hind quarters by their own straps that she'd rearranged and tied together, creating the new saddle-bag-like configuration.

"Okay," Aaron answered. Kellen felt comfortable leaving the boy on horseback knowing Shadow was smart enough to carry him to safety if trouble erupted. For herself, after getting her ground legs back she adjusted the rifle across her back so it could be quickly deployed if necessary. She slipped the lariat off her shoulder and with a more discerning eye looked over the large rock formation on which the piece of the stables was impaled.

For sure, this was going to take some climbing, she could tell. Again. Luckily, just as she had done well on the rope in gym class, the next year when Smith's Sporting Goods had brought in their portable rock climbing wall to the gym she'd done well on that thing too. In fact, ever since then she'd even been hoping to try her hand at some real rock climbing. No time like the present, she figured and pulled her deerskin riding gloves from one of the bags.

She wasn't wearing them to ride with since Shadows mane was more manageable with bare hands and fingers, but she'd grabbed them up back at the house with her rope, kind of just out of reflex. She pulled them on tight.

Next she led Shadow and his precious cargo, the ever-questioning little Aaron, across the trail and up onto a rise. She positioned them just far enough away in case any rocks fell in Kellen's upcoming climb or, heaven forbid, in case she fell.

With that done, she returned to the stony formation and slowly scanned it from base to pinnacle. For sure the remnant up there was a part of their stable. From this close she could really tell. In just the full moonlight the colors were actually rather muted, but now for sure she could tell. The paint looked fresh and pretty much red, just like they'd used last spring. Looking around and remembering how far they'd come she knew too they were about the right distance away from the house for these to be their stables. But where the rest of it was, who knew.

Another question she had to ask herself, as she looked over the hard climb ahead, was whether or not the presence of part of the stables up there also indicated the presence of what she hoped might be inside of it. Namely, some tack: a saddle, a better blanket than the one they'd gotten from the remnants of the house, and hopefully a bit with reins. And since as far as she could tell there didn't seem to be any of those zombie things hot on their trail, the not-so-experienced rock climber figured it was worth a try.

Plotting her climb, and then just getting right to it, she saw that along the back side of the tall tower of rocks was where she could step up once, which she did, then again, and then there, *yeah there!* Now she was about five feet closer and only about seven or eight feet still short.

And look at that, she then also saw. A strong ridge of flanking rock curled up the side of this main piece, almost the rest of the way. The narrow but useable shelf looked like it could provide a several inch wide foothold all the way up as well. Now, if she could just rope onto something up there . . .

Yeah! There off to the side, by the section of stable wall was a sharp spire of rock shooting up and off at an angle. If she could just lasso the big point of it . . .

She got her grip right along the part of the lasso she needed and started swinging it round and round over her head. Luckily, there was a good hand hold for her to use as well right in front of her in a crack along the rock face.

With her recent practice from the bottom of her bedroom she got it on the first fling. The rope cinched up tight, catching well as it slid down, catching and holding on a large tooth of ancillary rocks erupting out of the upside down cone of stone.

She gave two hard tugs to set the cinch. Now, all she had to do was shimmy up the remainder of the ridge, which she started in doing, firm hand grip over firm hand grip, step by step. Then in just a minute or so she was almost high enough to touch . . .

Yeah, there. And there too. If she could just squeeze over in between the spire and the main group of rocks . . . *all right.* She made it! Now she was wedged nicely in and didn't even have to hold on. It was like a treehouse high in the rocks, which now she just had to reach up into and feel around a little. But first . . .

With some rough flips of the lariat's lead she freed it from the spire, looped it into a good roll and draped it over her shoulder again. If she needed it to get down she'd toss it over the spire again, but she could tell she probably wouldn't. So for now . . .

She reached up and touched the lower ends of some of the broken boards making up part of the stable wall. Then she gave the whole construct a slight shove. *Man. It was really stable.* She'd kind of been hoping she could knock the whole thing down with a push or two and then pick out any tack that had come down with it. But no chance of that, she could tell now.

So it was back to her original plan, but definitely continuing with that. She knew there was a pretty good chance that a saddle and hopefully a bridle too would be in there because, in the stables, and in front of each stall, before the quake, freshly cleaned and oiled tack hung on big wooden holders awaiting each horse's next ride. And from what she could tell, this piece of the stable did have the telltale port-style windows—two of them in this piece—that only adorned the front wall. *So just maybe . . .*

She got a little higher and reached up inside the wall. She could feel . . . well . . . nothing. But then something brushed her hand. *Yeah, over there to the right. Okay. Okay. There.* She had it. Felt like a rein. Yeah. Probably. It had that smooth, worn feeling. Now to just get it down.

She tugged hard, but . . . no . . . here . . . whip it . . . yeah. Off it came and fell down around her arm and hand like a coat falling from a hangar. She held it up and looked it over. It was a halter with the reins attached. A nice big set up without a bit. She liked it better without a bit anyway, and knew when the horse was older and well trained, she didn't need a bit anyway. *Shadow will do fine with this. Awesome,* she figured and tossed the rig down behind her to the ground. It *thwapped* hard not far from Aaron and the horse. Shadow voiced a slight protest and pawed hard at the dirt trail.

"Kellen," Aaron called out in fear.

"It's okay, Kiddo. Shadow," she called back, both to the boy and the horse. "It's okay!" That time she said it with authority. Because that was the last thing she needed. To spook the horse. "Aaron? Are you okay?" She couldn't see him without turning around, and that was a little precarious at the moment.

"Are you coming down now, Kellen?"

"Just a minute, Hon. Let me look a little more," and with the word 'more' she stretched up into the stable wall area again and felt around. What she was hoping was that one of the saddle stands had gotten knocked up in there too, and if she could get a grip on either a piece of a broken stand or a stirrup or—

Nothing there though. Maybe over here on these rocks, she was thinking as she felt along the smooth hard and even warm surfaces where some of the rocks up inside the recently constructed shelter leveled off. Nothing though. But wait. There was something. Kind of thick but . . .

She pulled whatever it was quickly out, kind of curious about what—

Oh my God!

It was a snake!

Not a particularly large one, but just the same. Although, at least it wasn't a rattler. She'd seen a few of those on the ranch and the coloring of this one, a dark brown with what looked like yellow bands around it, told that her right off this wasn't. But still without even thinking she just flung it away.

Who could blame her? But just as the snake landed, and ironically not too far from the reins and harness she'd already dropped, of course it caused an even greater reaction in the stallion this time. Especially when the viper then quickly crawled away.

"Nooo, oh shi—" Kellen yelled, at least managing not to cuss, cutting it off before the t like that. The Andrews had always frowned on crude language, especially in front of little Aaron.

Not that the boy would have heard this time anyway. Shadow had taken off up the trail and also dumped little Aaron before he did it. After a loud neighing came the sound of a receding gallop, and now the kid was bawling like a stuck pig, but still, from the sounds of it at least, right where he'd been.

Kellen got down off the rocks so fast she wasn't even sure how she did it. In fact, the last five feet or so she'd just sort of fallen, landing hard on her boot heels before then further falling and smacking down hard where a guy would have kept his wallet.

"Oooff . . ." and then, " . . ahhhh," came forced from her lips. The oof when she got her wind knocked out, the ahhh when the pain in her tailbone reached her brain.

She scrambled to her feet as quickly as she could and staggered over to the still bawling little boy. At least he was in one piece, Kellen could tell. In fact, he appeared to be sitting up rather comfortably with his back against a large boulder but still crying his eyes out.

"Aaron. Are you hurt? Did you break anything?" She held the boy by the shoulders and lightly shook him to get his attention. He stopped down to a sniffle and looked at Kellen with watery eyes.

"Shadow. Shadow's gone!" he bawled back, which was a good sign as far as Kellen could figure. If he'd been hurt, he would have been yelling about that first.

"So you're okay? Can you get up?"

"Yeah. I guess so. My bum bum hurts though . . ."

"Mine too . . ." Kellen had to smile as she helped the boy up. "Which way did Shadow go, Hon?"

"Up. Up there." Aaron pointed up the trail where it wound higher into more of the new mountains.

"Come on. We gotta catch up. He won't go too far. He's too smart . . . knows we need him. He just got scared. Come on," she said again as she came back from picking up the bridle and reins. She took the boy's hand and they started up the trail.

"He's got all the water too . . ."

"I know. Don't worry. We'll find him," she reassured the boy, and was partly reassuring herself too. At least she still had the gun and the rope. But she also knew they better find Shadow. And the water.

And quick.

CHAPTER XVI

TILL DEATH AND THEN SOME

It seemed like tomorrow to Udo, as he came to, but who could tell for sure. No more calendars. No more clocks. It could have been longer, should have been longer, should have been like six months. Because somehow now his leg was completely healed. That can't happen overnight. Well . . . normally.

Somehow too, he suddenly realized, he'd been taken down off the jetty and laid into a lounger-style hole dug out in the sand, just like he used to do it in his surfing days. Back then, after his first set, he'd find a good spot on the beach and dig a seat down into the sand about armpit deep as you were sitting in it. Then you could hang out there perfectly comfortably, resting your arms there on each side and resting your legs too up high on the sand in front of the hole. Any extra sand made in the digging could then be piled up behind as a headrest. Many a time he'd napped like that, back before all this, but with the same Southern California sun basking him, just as it was now.

But who, or as he then realized, *what* had dug out his seat this time? *Yeah*, Udo knew. Because there it still was. The big scorpion lion monster had dug it. Somehow.

Don't ask, Udo knew.

Anyway, there was kitty, just lounging itself about twenty feet in front of Udo's spot, which of itself rested in a cozy, also dugout-like section on the shady side of the jetty.

Out from there it looked like kitty had been a little busy. Several half eaten corpses and the bare bones of a few others littered the area. "Kitty," Udo called out affectionately. It had saved his life after all. Then he was also thinking of calling the creature over for a good petting, but as the thing fixed him with its cold-as-death stare, he decided maybe not.

It was good to have a pet though, Udo was starting to think, as he got up. He looked over his leg and it was amazing. Not a mark. The freakishly all white, well-muscled limb looked to be brand new.

Udo tested his leg out too with some squat jumps, getting his usual six feet or so of air. He ran and jumped and flew a little in a tight circle before landing and running some more. Satisfied, he turned and returned to where he'd come to. But kitty was already gone, or almost, just cresting where the beach did the same before opening up to the aforementioned parking lot.

Udo waved at the big beast, and would have said thank you too. But he knew it wasn't necessary. The creature howlingly growled at him one more time before scuttling off out of sight.

Figuring he better get busy then, because who knew how long he'd been knocked out, Udo got back up on top of the jetty. He noticed a fairly strong head wind blowing back his hair, so he figured what the heck. He thrust out his arms and really just let it happen. He lifted off.

Just a ways up into the air, he let the wind turn him while also angling his frame for more lift. He'd seen birds do this, and just as it happened for them, he too, just by holding this position, was taken higher and higher as he turned and turned the whole time. *Up drafting*, that was what he had heard it called before, and, as mentioned, he'd seen birds do it, but to be doing it himself . . .

"Wheeee," he couldn't help but scream as up and up he flew. High enough finally, or so he figured, he leveled off. After blinking out some tears from the wind, he sighted the coastline below and coursed hard along it. Then he saw it, the other line he was looking for, a broader and black one cutting out into the water: Sandy Point Pier.

From there he knew he could get his bearings and hopefully make his way to his old house. That was the plan anyway. Sort of like he'd tried to do with the old bell tower in the first simulation the Lord had put him through. But hopefully this would work out better. And hopefully then too, there would still be something left, both of his house, and his family.

On a lighter note, Udo was also thinking probably it would be fun to check out good old Sandy Point Pier one more time too. Just for kicks or whatever. He had so many memories there after all. While at the same time too, he'd be recharging his batteries the rest of the way. He was still feeling a little worn down.

So once he was over the pier he looped and swooped lower. At about fifty feet, he gradually let himself get vertical before gently setting down. Or as gently as he could, still learning like he was.

Almost always when he landed--and he'd only flown a few times---but always when he landed he still had to use quite a bit of space to slow and stop. As his feet touched he'd start running and running, slowing as soon as he could to a jog, then stopping with a hard walk: clomp, clomp, and clomp. But this time in doing that, he came precariously close to stepping right off into a huge gap in the pier's walkway.

"Whoa," he even said and had to pinwheel his arms to help apply the brakes with his toes. He came to a screeching halt that left him half bent over the hole in the pier before quickly straightening up.

"Whewww," Udo followed the whoa with and looked down through the car sized hole. Yeah. Just like the smell had told him. There was a dead body. Or no, make that two or three of them, whom he could then see, bloated and bluish gray, floating and bobbing ever so slightly in the dark waters beneath the pier. So much for nostalgia.

Although thinking about it then, about those dark waters, Udo remembered a time when on a bet Eric Sievers had swam all the way across under the pier when they were just grade school kids. They had ditched school that day about twenty years prior and Eric Sievers never turned down a bet.

Which had all been really cool, except when Eric came out on the other side he was so exhausted—most likely from the fear inherent in traversing the hidden, mysterious waters—that he then couldn't swim all the way back in to shore. Of course then the lifeguard had to go out and get him and they'd all gotten busted then.

"What a rip," they'd all forlornly agreed outside the principal's office, except for Sievers, who'd been taken home straight from the pier. When he got home his parent's had totally flipped, Udo also remembered. German people could really cuss . . . and his dad tanned his hide.

Back in the present, Udo smiled and shook his head. He looked at the hole one more time, then realized the quick solution to the roadblock. He quickly and easily leapt the ten feet or so across. He kept forgetting about his new powers.

He turned then to head further up into the carnival area when another thought crossed his mind. He looked back again to the hole. No way could one of those zombie things . . . well . . . they seemed like they even had a hard time just walking very well, let alone jumping. So . . .

But the hole really only cut off one half of the pier walkway. The boardwalk, as the locals called it, was actually like a four lane highway of wooden planking, and about the same size as the asphalt variety. It had two lanes going out to the carnival and two coming back to the beach. Both sides were also separated by a gap of at least five feet, with chest high fencing bordering the gap on both sides so no tourists would unexpectedly fall into the drink.

But the recent cataclysmic events—which the Lord had thoroughly explained to Udo while he was readying for his return—had rendered the left hand side of the wooden highway entirely impassable. A hundred foot section on that side had apparently not only been ripped out but now lay both on its side and sideways, half-submerged like a ship wrecked at sea.

So no zombies would be able to get up that side. Now if Udo just finished off the break on this side, he'd have a zombie free zone.

Udo looked about, and then he saw it. One of the nearby, old fashioned lampposts, which lined the pier all along its outer edge, had been knocked over. Unlike several of the other's, this one's cement pillar body hadn't dragged it down into the deep.

The very strong and perfect being got over to it, found he was able to heft it, and brought it back. He used it then—and more specifically the end with the big concrete base—like an oversized post hole digger to knock the remaining section of the pier down into the water, completing the cutting off on this side too. *That should hold them,* he could tell. Now only something that could fly, or jump pretty far like he could, would be able to make it out to the carnival portion of the pier.

That done, Udo inspected his new piece of equipment. He noticed with all the use he'd put it to the lamp post had cracked about halfway up. So he finished the job, breaking the top half, the part with the lamp, all the way off. This left him with the bottom half, including at its end the hammerhead-like block of concrete mounted on the approximately five foot long, four inch wide, shaft of steel. He stepped back into a clear area, swung it a few times like one of those weighted bats they used to use in the on-deck circle when he was a boy playing baseball, then, just as he also did as a child, he let it rest on his shoulder. Now he was armed. Just in case Mr. Snakey Snake showed up again.

Better yet, he carried his big weapon with him into the carnival area of the pier, smashing it down onto the ticket turnstile, which was not exactly operational anyway. He wanted to test the big bludgeoner out by using it some more. After smashing the metal turnstile he inspected the big cement head for cracking. It still looked good, while the turnstile was completely flattened. All right, he'd keep it around, he figured and rested it over his shoulder again before continuing on into the carnival proper.

It was wonderful, Udo noticed, how the carnival was pretty much intact. He especially loved the beautifully painted and carved mural, archway sign that curved over the entrance. Its sun bright seascape featured dolphin and surfer alike riding a big perfect wave with bikini clad girls sunning in the sand. The words, "Sandy Point Pier," seemed to artfully spew from the smiling faced sun crowning it all.

He continued in under the historic sign and was equally and pleasantly surprised to see that the inner, circular promenade area was fairly pristine as well. Although too, just as he remembered seeing before from the beach when he was first rejuvenated, the whole thing sat slightly at an angle now. But at least here from up close it wasn't quite as noticeable. Although the Ferris wheel, the Tilt-a-Whirl, Bumper Cars, and a couple other rides he couldn't immediately remember or recognize all rested somewhat lower than normal off to his right.

Then to the left the mini-midway with its several contest booths, all of them empty though now with others shattered or caved in on themselves, Snow Cone City, Ice Cream Corner, Frank's Far Out Furters, Barbecue Bonanza and other less memorable and now sign less eateries still called out their names in faded fashion, like ghosts long dead.

In the middle, and cracked right down the middle itself was the Castle of the King, a faux but enormous sandcastle replica, cement wall surrounded and fountain bound, flowing throughout with water pumped through some of its windows, across a balustrade or two, filling it's moat. On hot days kids could even swim there if the waves were too much for their size.

Udo could almost see them now, splashing and playing, even his own kids, Joannie and Jason who'd been there too in their younger days. He shook his head, though, and they were gone. Then after a sigh he took in the rest of action taking place in the Castle of the King: a great battle scene with knights saving more than one fair maiden from fire breathing dragons flying overhead.

And when it was lighted up at night . . . ohhhh, Udo remembered . . . that was when it was really cool. But now, as mentioned, cracked wide open in the middle and half demolished. Its lights would probably never come on again; its fountains never again to flow. *Bummer* was all Udo could think. *Super bummer.*

And bummer too because the whole place was dead and quiet and still now. Come to think of it, Udo also realized then, not even the ever present call of seagulls could be heard. *End of the world all right.* Or how had the Lord explained it to him, Udo tried to remember. *Something about maybe, maybe not. Or something like that.* The slate had certainly been wiped clean though. And long overdue too, Jesus had also said. There would be a remnant, though, and another chance, thanks to him. *Hadn't the Lord said that too?*

"Thanks to me?" Udo had squeaked out like a schoolboy, squinting up at his Headmaster, or really Jesus of course.

"Chances sometimes only come when asked for," the Lord had further elucidated. Of course, Udo felt good about that. *He* had asked. It never hurts to ask. Ask and ye shall receive. *But what about once he rescued his family? Or didn't. Would it all end then?*

Ahhh man, Udo concluded with. All this heavy thinking was really making him tired again. He was thinking maybe he shouldn't be tired again already, but for some reason he really was. Sort of like when he had a big lunch, and the afternoon was nice and warm, and he couldn't keep his eyes open if he had to. For some reason he felt like that.

So he sat down hard on one of the big benches that ringed all the way around the fountain castle. He'd taken more than one nap on these babies. Off season and many a week night the carnival was hardly crowded at all, and since he knew Mr. Aronstein, the head of security, he could sleep there for a while if he wanted to, if him and his friends had drank too much or whatever. Rather than go home drunk, they could sleep off their buzz there, then brave their parents' relentless questioning later.

At least he didn't have to worry about that now. For some reason all of a sudden, he didn't feel the need to worry about anything. He was just so tired. He saw a nearby piece of old banner just up the bench, grabbed it and made a pillow with it.

As he lay back, he could have sworn he almost heard the sounds of days gone by refilling the wonderful old place. Then, as he closed his eyes he could see it too, and there in the crowd, *was that . . . them?*

Udo settled for just opening his eyes at first. He figured for sure he was still sleeping, and dreaming, and it felt so good that, 'let's just go with that for now,' he was thinking.

All right?

Please?

But then he heard it again.

"Daddy?" It was her voice too, so he sat up right away. "You fell asleep, daddy." She was right there too, his little Joannie, sitting right next to him. So Udo figured he *had* to still be dreaming.

He blinked his eyes and looked at her hard. She sure looked real. Taking the next step in the verification process he slowly and ever so gently touched her sweet little arm. She felt real too.

"What's wrong, daddy? You're . . . you're crying."

Udo felt his cheek. He looked at the bit of tear on his fingertip. His cheek had felt different too, he then realized. Well, different in that it felt *normal*. As mentioned, he'd noticed early on in his perfected form, at least here on Earth, that his skin was quite hard actually and smoother too. But oddly now its suppleness had returned.

He didn't care though. His daughter was here. His beautiful and sweet little girl was sitting next to him in her darling summer dress, the blue and white one with the aqua toned highlights she loved so much. Udo remembered that dress, just like he remembered too, that Joannie loved to wear it on beach outings when swimming wasn't on the docket, like trips to the pier and the carnival.

So what is going on? Udo continued to wonder. He'd already looked down to the rest of his body a couple times. Sure looked like he was back to normal now too. Totally. Gone was the skin tight, wet suit like outfit he'd had on before. A Hawaiian shirt and casual shorts above sandals, just like the old days, was what he had on now.

In fact, he was then thinking too, that he really must have traveled back in time. Joanie looked to be all of five or six. Not the eight years old she was when he'd died. *What was going on? Had everything just been a nightmare? His dying and then all the weird stuff that had happened since? You couldn't have a three year nightmare, could you?*

He just let it go though then and smiled. Whatever was going on, he didn't want to screw it up. It felt too good to be with his daughter again, but buying into it all the way emotionally, he then had to fight back more tears, tears of incredible joy. He even giggled too and reached down to pinch his little girl's cheek. It was a game they used to play. He'd pinch her cheek, and she'd say, "Hey, Daddy," and then punch him back.

He'd started the game to sort of in a way teach her to fight back whenever someone touched her against her will. But then it was just fun too, and this time he did it to both feel how real she was, and then to also feel her punch him back. To see how real he was too.

Wow, he had to then think. *This all really is real! It isn't just a dream.* And had he just not noticed it before, because his concentration on Joannie had been so intense? Had he not noticed how the rest of the carnival was up and running now too? Because it sure was, and as he looked around some more it looked like everything was just as he remembered it from the old days.

The midway coursed with a large crowd. The rides twirled and sang, both with the sounds of their mechanized motion and with the screams of glee coming from their riders. The well-worn pipe and chime music swelled up all around. Kids with Cotton Candy and stuffed animals just won strolled along the wide way while tourist moms and dads, camera toting and shopping bag adorned, accompanied and somewhat directed them.

"I want to ride the Tilt-a-Whirl, Daddy. Can we ride that now?" Joannie asked, bringing them back to the here and now.

"I don't know if you're big enough for that, honey. Want to try the Ferris wheel?" Udo carried on with his daughter, all the while looking around some more, then wondering out loud, "Where's your mom, honey? And Jason?"

"Oh. You know him, Daddy. He just took off. Don't you remember? You told him to meet us at Frank's for dinner at six o'clock. Don't you remember? And here comes Mommy. She just went to the restrooms. There she is, Daddy."

And yeah. There she was, and it was her from a few years back too, beautiful with her long hair like silk in the sun, and her summer dress a matching version of Joanie's. His heart wanted to stop in his chest. His soul rose hard in his throat. *Oh Lord, let it be like this again . . . and forever,* he prayed and waited for her to come into his arms.

CHAPTER XVII

TEAM DEATH INFECT

Mike was glad to be of service again, and especially on an important mission like he was now. At least the master had said this was an important mission. It was kind of hard to tell, especially since it was just him and the woman and the little girl. He wasn't supposed to understand though, the master had explained. Just in case. Other beings might read his mind if he knew. Then the mission might be ruined. So Mike was also glad he didn't know any more than that. Just that this was a very special mission, and that was good enough.

Either way, special mission or not, here they were again, riding one of the silver discs, him and the woman and the little girl. And, at first, their ride seemed to be taking them on a familiar route. Familiar to Mike at least. And like his other friends had, the woman and the little girl looked mostly just confused and agitated as they rode.

Mike was enjoying it though; especially when they seemed to be approaching a dead end, but then suddenly the disc turned left, and the dirt and rocks there got invisibly blasted away somehow, partially by the river of lava burning and chewing into them but also by some unseen power blowing into the stuff too. *Man, wasn't that exciting!* For the whole last leg of the trip they constantly seemed to be heading into dirt and boulders that only feet in front of them would then be blasted away at the last second. *Talk about a thrill ride!*

Then they got there, though, and like before, the river ended up welling into a cavern, and just up to the left, Mike could see light breaking through, his signal of where to lead his new charges.

Just like before too, he had to assist these helpless ones up and out, then down a short slide on a four foot high slab of concrete. Because actually, their exit point erupted right up out of the middle of the extra-wide sidewalk fronting the beach, or the boardwalk as Mike remembered the locals called it, even though it wasn't made out of boards. But either way their escape hole blew up there in a jutting, upside down V of the concrete itself.

Then, per instructions, he started off with his two new friends closely in tow, and up only a short ways started taking them onto the wide, though somewhat slanted, this time wooden walkway, or truly a boardwalk, on the pier.

There were two sides to choose from, like two sides of a street, Mike was thinking, but he could see right off that the left side wasn't going to work. A whole and very long section on that side was completely collapsed and mostly sunk into the water. So they took the one on the right.

He watched his charges carefully as they went. He had strict instructions about that too. They mustn't be lost, not by any means; the master had bellowed and let him feel great pain as a reminder.

Uh oh, Mike suddenly thought and had to stop the woman and the child with a hard growl. There was a large gap in the walkway coming up, too large to get across very easily. So Mike got ahead and coming up on the hole noticed that on its far edge there was a piece of the walkway still intact, a piece just wide enough to scoot across on. But they'd have to be careful.

Mike went first and made it easy enough. Luckily the strip of usable walk was right next to a fence that ran along the gap between the two halves of the pier and Mike had held on to it as he went, just in case. He then turned to watch as the woman came up to the strip. She looked at it and then away and down to the water visible in the gap below. She then looked up at him and rolled her jaw to let out a croaking whine. Her arms, which she always held in close to her body, became animated in drum beating motions while she stared hard at the strip and took a running start for it.

Mike stopped her with another even louder growl. He grabbed hard on the portion of fence nearest him and shook its thickly wired construction until it rattled loudly. He growled again and twice made the motion of grabbing onto it. The woman looked at him blankly. He finally growled once more and pressed his body against the fence while grabbing it one more time.

A quieter and higher pitched growl got both of theirs attention then as the little girl pushed her way past the woman and somewhat awkwardly but safely grappled with the fence. She next scooted her way across the boardwalk remnant too, just like Mike had.

The woman finally followed then, going more slowly. Halfway across she lost her footing with one leg that for a scary second dangled over the opening. But but then her grip on the fence tightened and she pulled herself across the rest of the way.

The remainder of their journey was much easier. The hardest part was keeping the woman and the girl from getting too distracted as they entered the carnival. They were like dumb animals sometimes, Mike realized with chagrin. Just like his other friends had been. All it took was something shiny and moving and they were enchanted, at least for a little bit. And even though the carnival was even deader than they were, there were still remnants of decoration intact.

Which did, however, make it even easier to get them into the "Mansion of Madness" once they reached it at the back of the Midway. It's crazy façade of mirrors and monsters with giant, googly eyes and crazy clowns and kids running away from them and flying monkeys and an open balcony on the second story where a life-size ghost chased a life-size werewolf who was all the while chasing a life-size little girl in red—all of it was still intact and like candy to the zombie's hungry eyes.

Mike wasn't interested in all that, though. He also didn't have the patience to let the woman and the little girl stand there and gawk at the mansion all day. So he hurried them along and brought them inside, just as he'd been instructed to do.

At first, it was very dark inside, and Mike, just like his charges, wasn't sure where to go. His instructions had ended here. But then the building came to life and an obviously mechanical but also somehow lifelike figure, looking like a devil dressed in a tuxedo ran out on a track, gave them a stiff and squeaky curtsy, and started slowly up one of the three hallways that left their entry area in different directions.

They followed the mechanical devil, especially when it stopped once more and repeated the curtsy. Then it rounded a turn and entered into a dark room where luckily the mechanical man was spotlighted. As if knowing that it had brought all three zombies with it, seeming to even look at them while they still waited outside the door, the eerie machine turned once more and waved, then fell through a hole suddenly opening in the floor.

"Please . . . please . . . come right in . . . it's time to have fun," a voice said from somewhere in the darkness at the top of the room.

Mike wasn't sure at first. It all seemed kind of scary, but then he realized that their master, the real devil, *liked* scary. And since it was him who brought them here . . . of course it was scary.

Mike laughed and laughed at that one, then noticed how his two subordinates were just looking scared and confused again. He stopped laughing and replaced it with several growls, at the same time motioning for the two to get through the damn door.

He followed them in. He noticed first how the hole in the floor had closed and turned into a large, all black disc. The spotlight had grown in size too and now showed most of the floor, but the walls and ceiling were still lost in darkness.

Mike next noticed how coming from the disc ran a black stripe painted in the floor that started thin and got thicker and thicker as it spiraled out around and around. Mike tested the floor's sturdiness as he walked toward the disc, and satisfied with its safety; he called—just another growl really—back to the shadows for the woman and the girl, motioning as well for them to come out.

Eventually, the two did come, very slowly, looking about into the darkness still shrouding everything else beyond the floor's edge. Mike growled again at them for more encouragement and they picked up their pace, but it didn't matter. Suddenly the whole room exploded in bright light and the floor started spinning. Also revealed were mirror after mirror after mirror completely enclosing and bordering the floor about eight feet high.

Worse yet, especially for the zombies, all of whom now looked frightened, was that the circular wall of mirrors spun faster and faster and now too the floor was starting to spin in the opposite direction.

The woman and the girl began to wail and screech, then fell first to their knees before completely collapsing. Mike fared somewhat better since he'd made it onto the center disc which wasn't spinning at all. Then from there, his fear soon changed to wonder, watching the mirrors and the lights and the swirl of the floor going round and round was really something to see. After a little while of that he next noticed how his charges had fallen to the floor. Then he noticed two very strange looking beings coming toward them from the mirrors. And there was something about them. Something really scary. Mike was even thinking if he didn't get out of there, surely he would die.

Again.

Luckily, the hole in the floor opened up again and instead he fell.

"Oh . . . my . . . God. You have got to be kidding me," said the one that looked like, and indeed had been in his previous existence, an interior designer. And even though now he was a zombie too, as layer after layer of too much makeup might belie, he still possessed all his wit and intelligence, unlike the other walking around dead things, as he commonly referred to them.

This most wonderful gift he'd been given was earned really, earned because long before he left the living, he had already surrendered himself to the Dark Lord, enabling the King of the Dead to make all the necessary adjustments beforehand. He was indeed a special one, a zombie of no ordinary design or appearance.

Which one could easily see, starting at the top where his blond hair lay stiffly slicked but sweeping over his cute little head like a blade dangerously tickling his ear, something obviously first designed and done only by the finest Hollywood coiffures. Below that, and under all the aforementioned makeup, his slightly too large lips and eyes were oddly combined with a small, pointy, upturned and obviously surgically altered nose. All to which he almost constantly daubed his puff applicator, whenever his also frequent checks with his little makeup mirror showed even the slightest hint of the grayish green starting to show.

He did have his image to think of after all, or so he liked to think, but really maybe not. It was just that coming over into his undead existence with the wit and intelligence also came his deeply ingrained vanity. So even though the bright lights had obviously long ago gone out, he somehow still thought the cameras hadn't.

All of which stemming from the fact that also in the world of the living, he had been a *star*. The star of a wildly successful television show highlighting modern and flamboyant interior design. As such, he had enjoyed a miraculously successful yet sinful life, and then in death his master had come to him and made him an offer he couldn't refuse. Literally.

"How can I refuse you, my lord," the designer had almost panted back at Satan, sitting on his throne mostly lost in the shadows across the large and dank, also mostly dark room. Death had left the interior designer there, maybe fifty feet across from his majesty and properly displayed. The forever cute one hung naked in chains a foot off the ground, his arms and legs pulled taught and held out like the limbs of a letter X.

But the designer wouldn't have had it any other way. As far as he was concerned, this was way better than heaven.

"Yes, my pet, my favorite pet of all, gay or straight," the father of perversion practically cooed from the shadows. "That's exactly why I've kept you around and helped you succeed as greatly as you have. I know you love me and would do anything for me ... and you have such unique and needful talents."

For now, and such a time as this, of course the devil had donned human form, at least from the horns down, and even those tastefully trimmed to sexy little spikes. As he descended from his throne the red satin robe, which was most likely all he had on, opened up to reveal just enough of his muscular physique to make one think that. Above that he now wore an incredibly handsome face, adorned again by a jet black goatee and shortly chic hairstyle, complete with a few stray strands wandering across his cruel but perfectly tan and dominating brow.

The designer liked very much what he saw. It was the familiar form his master had taken more than a few times, which would then make it irresistible for him not to let his master take him. Then with each taking the designer would always have to give the promise of more service to him, but at least then from him who could give so much in return would come greater and greater reward: success, fame and fortune.

But always still there was the same question.

"How much longer, master," the designer would eventually ask once they were done. "How much longer will you . . . keep me around?"

Always, of course, a very important question. But then this last time, when the designer had died—or should have at least—in the great earthquake that took everything out from under him and then instead of dead he found himself there, chained up in his master's chamber, well, then the question definitely took on new and even more extreme import. But the answer this last time had started out the same as it always did.

"Nothing is written in stone," Satan would always start off with. "Except the Ten Commandments, and look what's become of them." Then the devil would laugh quietly at his little joke. "Don't worry my little pet. That is a question that cannot be answered. Not yet."

And to soften the blow then, daddy the devil would hold his human toy lovingly close to his strong, bare chest. Which every time the unbelievable power so near always won the designer deeper and deeper down until he didn't care if there could be no promise for the future.

But then this last time his master added, "Although, I have to admit, it may end soon for both of us, my little puppet." Then he tousled the designer's hair before playfully pushing him away to swing in his chains. Then the great being got far enough away to pontificate proudly.

"Or not. But isn't that the way it's always been? In truth it's always been like—" Satan mentally searched for the best analogy. He did so love to make things dramatic. "Like waiting at the station for a train that has no schedule. And its . . . it's a train . . . a train that is packed with explosives. Explosives set to go off on arrival . . . and the resulting explosion will destroy the whole station! Will destroy everything!"

The sexy devil had worked himself into such a state of distress; he was kneeling on the floor with his hands held out in front of him. "Everything! All the many marvelous kingdoms I have built entirely with my own hands!"

Well, someone's been holding something in for a little too long, the designer was thinking, but knew better than to say anything. Especially when his master then started back toward him, a look of incredible grief molding his features into a mask of anguish, very unusual for the usually cool and confident lover of his.

"But now I can hear it coming," the dejected prince of evil forlornly and tearfully admitted into the top of the designer's head while softly but strongly cradling it as well. All of which was quite disconcerting for the designer, but even more disconcerting to then feel the dark lord's tears falling on him, and then to also watch them run red like blood down his own bare skin.

But then it was oh so wonderful, oh so wonderful to hear him next say, "But maybe, just maybe, we can knock that damn train off its track. Or better yet, leave ... leave the station!" The devil seemed to catch that word out of the air, his hand flexing hard. "Leave the station before it gets here. That is what I need your help with this time."

And still those words, his master's words, played in the designer's mind somewhere in the background while at the same time he carried on his current conversation with the technician.

"You know I never kid, Mr. Valentine," the technician reminded the designer, even though he knew his work partner's statement had been entirely rhetorical. "And don't be dismayed. Our master almost had him, this current target of ours, this so perfect creation. Our master almost had him in his giant jaws in one of the conduits. I believe A-13 or 14, not far from here."

It would have been humorous to note then, were anyone watching the two, that the technician's mousy manner was remarkably mirrored by his appearance. His head sported an overly large and scantily haired cranium above a small, no nonsense face. And either his eyes were very large or, and more likely on second thought, his thickly lensed glasses perched on a small, also mousy nose made them that way. He scanned his computerized clipboard with them before continuing.

"Yes . . . A-13 . . . exactly 1.7 miles to our north. But, as I said, he got away, this perfect specimen and servant of you-know-who . . ." With those words the technician had curled half his upper lip, "and hence, we have been called in."

The super geek slipped the computer board inside his stiff, white lab coat, upper left chest area. He must have had a large pocket for the thing there.

"Well, personally I'm just happy as a hamster to be here and can't wait to get started," the designer chimed in with and clasped his hands together. "And I mean . . . with such an important mission . . . I mean we've got to get him . . . am I right? He's the key, apparently. And I think we can do it," the dapperly attired young man added enthusiastically while placing a hand on his coworker's shoulder.

The technician looked at the hand, and then purposefully lifted it away. "That's what our Intel says."

With purpose, the nerdy fellow brusquely stepped over and looked out through the wall-sized, two way mirror before them. The huge panoramic view it sported was of the midway of Sandy Point Pier, and in particular, of the carnival within.

In fact as well, it soon became apparent the view the two servants of Satan enjoyed was of the Castle of the King directly across. Their observation or control room, obviously, had been magically constructed and was now housed, barely noticeably, in the second-story of the façade of the aforementioned Mansion of Madness.

The technician, who had indeed wielded the magic—borrowed from his master, of course, and of the black variety---then harnessed the same power by touching his computer tablet's screen to next cause a bar-type stool to suddenly form just behind him. A matching one formed just as magically next to it as well. The designer, after visually marveling at its sudden appearance, took the second one for his seat.

The technician's fingertips continued to deftly dance across his pad's screen and next materializing along the wall were some see–through mirrors. Then panel after panel of control mechanisms arranged in a circular console materialized, set and arranged in bank after bank, right at the most easily accessible height for manipulation. Almost in their laps.

"Will this suit your needs?" the technician inquired, turning to his cohort.

"Oh yes. Yay . . . yay," the designer enthused and held his arms up like a cheerleader holding pom poms. And even though he had none, he cutely gave them a little shake. A quiet pop left them both staring at his obviously, and at least disjointed, if not broken, wrist.

"It's a good thing you can't feel pain. Here." The technician calmly took the designer's wrist in his hands and quickly popped it back into place. "We'll need to get back to the master's labs soon after we finish here for another . . . revitalization. Can you use your fingers?"

"I think so," the designer replied warily and moved his fingers in a typing motion. "A little stiff. But what's a girl to do?" He giggled.

"Yes. We must proceed." The technician rolled his eyes, then quickly glanced at his pad again. "Subject Alpha has just arr—"

Interrupting the technician was a violently loud crashing and smashing sound emanating somewhere just behind their observation and control room. The designer turned to the technician, his eyes wide like saucers.

"That's probably him," the more scientific of the two assured his startled partner, and sure enough around the corner here came Udo.

The designer all but fell out his chair. Udo's perfect physique in the skin tight wet suit was almost more than he could handle. And plus then too the way the muscle man was carrying his new weapon, the big concrete slab adorned light pole like a bat over his shoulder, well, *super macho* was a term lightly traipsing across the décorator's enflamed libido.

"Oh my goodness. Well, now I get it," was all he could say. The two of them watched as Udo ambled over to one of the benches ringing around the Castle of the King. Then the perfect being sat.

"We are close now," the technician reported. Both men were quiet for a moment.

"Isn't it just amazing," the designer next mused, "that it would all come down to one man? I mean, just think of it. Last I heard—before all this of course—there were almost 8 billion people on the planet. And now what . . . just this one?"

"Nooo," the technician scoffed. "Our last calculations show possibly dozens . . . if not more, of the living variety, that is. But their number dwindling as our master tightens his net."

"Oh . . . really? Well . . . but still . . . you know what I mean. Isn't it odd how it's all come down to just a few? *Everything* depends on the actions of just a few!" Both times the designer had said the word 'few' in a very high tone.

"Just like in the beginning," the technician sagely countered. "Only then it was just two, as you may remember. The scene of our lord's greatest victory."

"Oh . . . yeah," the designer froze with, and then a look of sudden realization expanded his features. Then his mouth melted into a sneer. "Well . . . that's symbolic right? Adam and Eve and all that. I mean really . . ."

"Does our master seem symbolic to you?"

"Oh."

"Yeah."

Then the designer went into gossip mode and bent to his partner's ear. "But this one. This one . . . I know what's going on. The master tells me things. Whispers sweet nothings into my ear . . ."

"I'll bet he does," the scientific one snidely countered with this time.

"And, I hear . . . well . . ." The designer bent even closer and whispered something other than a sweet nothing into his partner's ear.

The technician looked down and shook his head. "I would advise you not to worry your pretty little head about such things. Nothing is written in stone. Just do your job," and the ever serious one looked back up. ". . . which needs to commence at this moment."

The designer had frozen with *the nothing is written in stone line*. He knew damn well where he'd heard that before. There was no getting away from him. "Oh . . . you are just no fun," he gave up with and both men adjusted their postures before inputting data into the instrument panels that like the glass walls had stopped rotating around them.

"This ought to do it," the technician uttered and with the push of a button a barely visible, gaseous cloud seeped up from the decking just behind Udo. He was still sitting upright on the bench, lost in thought and staring with glassy eyes at various areas of the old, dead carnival. "That'll put him out in just a minute. Then you can go to work on this rat trap. Bring it back to life. Meanwhile, I'll get to work on these two."

With those words the technician's stool rode around the perimeter of the room as if on a rail. Then the rear portions of the glass wall filled with the image of the girl and the woman that Mike had lead into the spinning room of mirrors.

The room was still, though, now, as were the two dead-looking dead ones collapsed on the floor. The two female zombies started to move again however, as the technician started punching keys on the panel on his side of the room.

"How far back am I to go?" the designer asked, fervently inputting data on his side of the circular bank of panels.

"Exactly three years and thirteen days. Time of day stays the same."

Only moments after Udo wadded up the old banner, lay down on the bench and set the makeshift pillow under his head, the surroundings started undergoing an incredible transformation. Molecule by molecule, inch by inch, the aged, wrecked and altogether worn out materials of Sandy Point Beach Pier and the adjoining carnival unwarped, unrusted, unbroke and aged in a backward fashion, from old to new.

All the while as well, translucent, ghostlike forms of all the people who had been there over the past three years and thirteen days came and went in fast motion. It was quite a chaotic scene that slowly but surely gained both more order and more substance.

On his side, the technician had been hard at work transforming the two female zombies into the spitting images of Ivy and Joannie Henkman. They were aged appropriately, as well as anatomically accurate. As a door then opened into muted sunlight, little Joannie made her way out of the Mansion of Madness and around to sit down next to Udo. The technician's stool, and his eyes, tracked her every move.

Once she was in place, the pseudo Ivy Henkman took her spot just across the promenade on the edge of the crowd now no longer translucent in the least. Then, since it was quite entirely beyond the technician's ability to pretend or jest in any manner, the designer was the one to say it.

"Annnd . . . action!"

The moments Udo waited for his wife to cross the promenade seemed to stretch out forever, but that was fine with him. The anticipation was absolutely delicious. And like a fine wine . . . all the better when sipped slowly and savored. Although actually he wasn't thinking in such artistic terms. He just really wanted to see her again, to touch her, speak to her, hear her voice, and hold her.

"Ivy," he said barely louder than a whisper and more like a question. "Ivy . . ." This time he said it a little more loudly and even started her way. At least he tried to, but little Joannie tugged very hard on his hand to keep him in place. *Why would she do that?* He stopped and waited and then tried again but not with great force. He just wanted to—

"Wait daddy . . . don't leave me," Joanie whined up at him this time, while still holding him back again too. And with an amazing amount of strength as well, Udo was noticing. It wasn't like her to do that and she was never *that* strong.

But whatever, Udo let it go with. Here was his love coming toward him now. "Honey. Omi-gosh. You should have seen this dream I had. Just napping here and—"

But something was wrong. She had slowed down as she got nearer. And she had the strangest look on her face.

"Honey? You okay?" he tried at her and then noticed . . . *what? Now she's limping?* And she looked like she was trying to talk, but all he could hear was a low and horrible moan . . . like . . . like those things . . . what things?

Like memories of a bad dream he started to see the zombies in his mind and he knew it hadn't been a dream. This . . . this! This was some kind of dream. Or like a giant hallucination. That wasn't his wife! It was one of those creatures!

With the realization, Udo watched the woman coming toward him die and decompose right before his eyes. Her flesh grayed and sagged, then turned greenish and opened up darkly bloody over deeper layers of connective tissue, muscle and then bone. And worse yet, she was getting closer and closer.

Next Udo couldn't help but notice that all the people all around them were gone now as well. The pier and the carnival almost instantly returned to how they had been before . . . decayed, broken and altogether in a shambles. And if that zombie woman still approaching wasn't his wife then who was—

He looked down quickly at the girl still holding his hand, but not quickly enough. Because yes, just like Udo suspected she was gripping his hand, that hand, his left, with both of her own and holding on white knuckle tight.

Or wait, Udo then realized, *those really were her knuckles!* The actual bones and ligaments were showing through the skin gone there now.

She slowly looked up at him and now he could see in her face too that she was a zombie child, not his cute little Joannie. The face of this thing was green and half gone.

But just as he finally did the math, so to speak, or realized what was going on and realized too how much danger he was in, as mentioned, it was too late. The little dead girl had taken just a second to smile—and not just a toothy grin but a lipless one too that also showed generous segments of her gum less jaws—and then with astonishing quickness, ferocity and strength she bit down hard as a hyena onto Udo's wrist.

"Arghhhhh," he yelled and immediately flung the half-wasted waif high and hard and far away across the carnival. Her body could then be heard crashing through several layers of old wood and boards.

Remembering then too that the zombie woman was near, he turned back her way. She was already on him, though, so Udo naturally reacted with a backhand to knock her away. Only problem was, although maybe not a problem after all, was that his backhand was a little more . . . forceful than the normal human beings. As a result the zombie's head got clean knocked off. Really clean.

Then not so clean after that as the dripping noggin rolled quite a ways across the boardwalk flooring before clinking and clunking down through the pier's under structure after falling through a hole. What remained of her, the body, fell like a sack and the dark red blood of the finally dead again gurgled from her newly opened neck hole.

Udo grabbed at his just bitten wrist and stared at it. The skin, as thick and slick as it was, had just barely been broken. Droplets of his blood, clean and red like rubies welled in small puddles along three even smaller wounds. The girl's jagged and half-shattered teeth must have been pretty damn sharp.

Udo continued to just stare at his wound, the pearlescent crimson color of the blood contrasting so beautifully against his alabaster skin. He stared and stared, almost as if he could also see that inside the blood the diseased particles swam about, while others earlier deployed had advanced further along, coursing deeply into his circulatory system. The mini-monsters maliciously made their way up and down his bloodstream, wreaking havoc, destroying and then rebuilding again, albeit in a fashion much less efficient than originally intended. Soon his transformation would be complete, or almost anyway.

CHAPTER XVIII

HOW TO MAKE A PERFECT MONSTER

Satan's zombie disease had been designed to work very quickly. It needed to because of the circumstances surrounding its existence and usage. Outside of laboratory conditions, dead tissue has a very short window of time for successful revitalization. And even then, once the lethal little particles reached the cellular level and started to work, it was a constant battle between living and dying tissue. This is why a zombie's outer appearance always belies a high degree of decay and decrepitude. Yet, inside that dilapidated shell, the will and passions of life and the desire to still live keep them going. They are quite aptly and frequently called, the living dead.

Udo, however, was destined to be a different story. Prior to his infection, and unlike all previous victims of the disease, he had already been reanimated once, and by science far superior to anything Satan could come up with. He was, in fact, the possessor of a body and mind created specifically by the Lord to be perfect and eternal. And though he could be killed, in this world at least, Satan's zombification concoction was finding him a bit more of a match than its usual victims.

"Yes . . . this should prove quite interesting," came from the syrupy sly yet rough and powerful voice of the dark lord. He had materialized just behind the technician and the designer in their observation booth. All three were very interestedly watching Udo as he suffered the first effects of his infection.

Through the enhanced capabilities of the booth's viewing window, the perfect being looked larger than life, though far from lively. He stood slumped and visibly shaken in the middle of the carnival area. He hadn't moved since he'd flung the little zombie girl high and far away then slapped off the head of her *faux* mother.

Satan, on the other hand, appeared as he always did for the designer. From the neck up at least. The rest of his body wore a crisply pressed and snappy silk suit, burgundy in color and complete with white handkerchief neatly folded and chest pocket displayed. White gloves tightly fit his hands.

"Wow . . . nice threads," the designer had to comment.

"I would say mind your work, but you are pretty much done here," the dark lord countered and with a dismissive wave of the hand sent the designer flying skyward.

"Hey . . . ahhh," the pretty man thing yelled as he broke through the ceiling and flew high into the blue above.

"Medical," the devil next said into his collar, obviously speaking into a communication device nestled there. "Expect Valentine on arrival at Area 13. Patch him up. Store him. His services will hopefully be needed in the future." He paused a moment before continuing. "I am currently with Subject Alpha. Are you ready for him?" Waiting and with a finger to his ear, he seemed to hear the appropriate response. Suffice it to say that an evil grin if ever there were one then curled his lips.

"As we expected, my lord, he is fighting the infection quite effectively," the technician reported while also very studiously watching both his notepad and several of the monitors in the instrument panel right above his lap. "His heart rate is 220. Blood pressure is 280 over 160 and climbing. Of course no human—"

"Oh . . . but he is much more than human. And you can spare me the details. You have served me well and have nothing further to prove. Just continue to monitor and record. I will review our findings later. Just stay at your post while I prepare for his transportation."

"But his bodily systems! In response to the attack they are growing even stronger. Truly he is infected but what was once mighty, we may have made even mightier!"

"The better to serve me," the dark lord said through his smile before levitating out through the hole still there in the ceiling. The technician stole just a moment from his surveillance of Subject Alpha to glance up to watch his master morph into something shadowy and black that floated higher above the booth, then through the ceiling, before finally floating across and down into the carnival area where he could then watch it on the viewing screen. The smoky form continued floating until it settled near and then seeped beneath the boards not far from Udo's feet.

At first Udo hadn't realized that he'd become infected. He was too busy being really angry that the wonderful thing he'd just experienced: the heartbreaking reunion with his little girl and his wife, was all a trick. Seething, both inside and audibly on the outside too, his breath hissing through his teeth, he roughly grabbed up his new hammer weapon, thinking and feeling just one word . . . *SMASH!*

But then as the disease hit, he suddenly felt very tired and could only lean on the hammer's handle, grasping it with both hands. The disease was winning the initial battle within him. He might have even returned to the bench to sleep some more but then he could feel his body fighting back and not letting him sleep, or even rest.

Starting in his chest and radiating outward was a slight warming sensation, and even worse, he could literally feel his blood boiling. Or maybe not boiling, but more like bubbling. Yes, bubbling like soda pop in his veins.

Which, understandably, was quite irritating. He wanted to rip his skin off and let it all out. He wanted to see if it really was carbonated like it felt. After a moment, however, that all stopped and or subsided enough for him to tolerate a new phenomenon taking its place.

Now his muscles seemed to be flexing on their own. Even weirder, then they looked to even be growing. Finally, as a third effect resulting from those first two, Udo was suddenly consumed with an intense desire to really use them. His new muscles, that is.

All of this fitting in rather nicely with the bad mood he was already in. Before he could stop himself, Udo was swinging his hammer like a madman, smashing everything around. He leapt out and up and wherever he landed it was the same thing.

Smash!

Smash!!

Smash, smash, smash!!!

Before long, all of the carnival's various buildings, starting with the smaller ones fell like kindling to his savage attacks. He swung and swung the mighty mallet and more than that also leapt from rooftop to rooftop, sometimes a hundred feet at a time. His power *had* definitely increased since the infection started. His perfect physique was incredibly pumped up to nearly twice its normal size, yet also was able to move with even faster superhuman speed.

Before long, most of the old carnival, or the remainder surviving the earthquake, was not surviving the Udoquake. The whole carnival and the two big display buildings beyond lay in rubble. Most of the supporting walkways as well. Udo had punctuated the surroundings repeatedly with his hammer blows. From a short distance away, the casual observer might have thought Sandy Point Pier was on the brink of total collapse and surely soon to go under. It was a good thing the sea was calm that day, a passerby might have also thought. *A strong wave could just sweep the whole thing away!*

But not yet. There was still one last building to destroy. Well, one real building and one that was decorative only but very large: the Castle of the King. Udo had also left the Mansion of Madness alone. They were the structures which most heavily triggered feelings of nostalgia for him.

In fact, the whole time he'd been rampaging it had been with a heavy heart. *All the memories.* Udo felt he was destroying them as well. And even though his body and his half-crazed mind drove him on madly to destroy—*just destroy it all*, the voices told him—those two buildings he'd managed to avoid. Until now.

Now he just stared at them and seethed some more. He held out the great hammer before him while his whole body swelled with power. He breathed deeply and rapidly.

The Lord had warned him that a zombie bite might quite likely turn him into a crazed monster. Udo could feel exactly that happening. And even worse, the chemically created psychosis was now being augmented by the aforementioned voices screaming into his head. Only now instead of telling him to destroy, they were taunting him, seemingly trying to push him to the brink. His perfect heart was running like a steam engine.

"You idiot! You'll never be able to rescue your family now!" the first one piped in. "You can't even see straight!"

"Your little girl will be eaten alive by those zombie things!"

"Just because you were so easily tricked."

"And, where was *He* all this time. The Lord. The mighty all-powerful one. He could have prevented this!"

"That's right! That's right," Udo screamed out loud, the anger making him take aim at the biggest and easiest target around. "God! Why can't you just take them up? You can do that! But no, you just—" but then words escaped him and he could only scream out, "Aaahh," in finality, and he leapt high and far for the Castle of the King.

He landed hard atop the remaining portions of the large, cartoonesque structure on a tall fake turret. He started in with the hammer again then, beating the heck out of the one remaining flying dragon attached to the turret.

After he'd knocked it into several pieces that dropped and smashed on the boardwalk below, he was looking around for his next target when something caught his eye, something quite out of place. Across the way, high in the second story of the Mansion of Madness, he saw just a wink of light. Just enough of a wink to make him look longer and more carefully.

He continued looking, looking then even more closely until he noticed how a section of the wall seemed more freshly painted over. Finally, as he concentrated harder and focused his abnormally acute vision there, the disease somehow enhancing his vision even more, until it seemed he could see right through the wall. Or no, he could tell then, the strangely painted portion was actually masking a two way mirror. Which, because of the setting sun's angle, he could see through it now.

Mostly what he could see, or that which was most important to Udo, was that inside there was a man, a strange looking, bookish little fellow sitting at a bank of controls and staring right back at him through thick lensed glasses, which magnified his eyes. The man also looked like he was studying Udo, breaking his stare at him to also input data into a computer bank he sat in front of.

"Oh those bastards," Udo cursed quietly, realizing what was going on. The giant snake. And now this. God had mentioned the enemy, Satan, and how he liked to use different forms and disguises. And this mousy looking guy may or may not be Satan, and may or may not be some guy working for him, but either way he sure looked like the one who must have been behind the whole zombie charade. The sonuva—

The last part of that lovely phrase Udo screamed as he sprang for the Mansion, his hammer held high. He'd decided to smash into the little guy's room and then try to take him alive so he could then pull him apart, limb from limb as the saying goes. The little geek would pay.

Halfway there though, and in mid-air, the strangest thing happened. What had to be the world's biggest eel busted up through the boardwalk just below Udo. The shiny black and gray sea thing had to be as wide as a bus, Udo was figuring, his current view right above it allowing him to see that much. But then he soon realized too the thing was long enough to zip up the thirty feet or so Udo was in the air to snatch him whole into its equally enormous mouth.

From there all he felt was tight, wet darkness all around him. Then with at least a little mental clarity remaining, Udo could also tell by the jostling redirection the big beast was taking, that it had zipped right back down into the water before leveling off and moving on through the ocean.

In the quiet on the pier that followed, the second story of the Mansion of Madness began to quiver and quake. Within another moment it all started crumbling as erupting out of the old ride came a large silver disc hovering on its own.

The disc continued to hover slowly while also then moving forward nearly silently along the remaining length of the pier. Once there it tilted upward and the quiet hum coming from it steadily grew to a high-pitched whine. In the blink of an eye—*no, really*—the craft then zipped up into the sky and vanished. Apparently the technician was in a hurry to get back to base and continue his studies of Subject Alpha.

CHAPTER XIX

BACK TO BASICS

So this was how Jonah felt, Udo was thinking, this was how the old prophet felt, hanging around in the belly of the big fish. Although, as Udo well knew, especially after replaying the image of the giant eel and its mouth reaching up toward him and its crazy looking eyes staring up at him too, that really he was, more accurately, in the belly of an eel. But *eel . . . whale . . . whatever. Either way it sure was gross.*

Like how right off—and this probably just like Jonah may have had to also do—Udo had to lift his head out of the warm mucky stuff he lay in and turn it to the side to breathe. Worse yet, as one might imagine, something smelled really bad. About that time, he passed out.

In what seemed like only moments later, he came to, but now suspended in chains. Their brightly silver embrace wrapped tightly all around him as well, as far as he could tell, from head to toe. One thing he knew, he sure couldn't move, except to wiggle his toes, and all he could see of himself by dipping his chin to his chest were the incredibly large, broad and thick, shiny silver links pulling taught across him there.

All of which he wanted to verify but couldn't. There sure as heck didn't seem to be any mirrors around, and in fact as he slowly spun about he could see only darkness near. *But then—*

What was that? Something even darker than the darkness and rather large seemed to fly closely by. It sounded like a bat, a really big one, but—

There went another one! And was that laughing he could hear too? *Very deep voiced laughter?* Then also a light thudding followed by a pitter patter like bare feet trotting. The footsteps slowed until they seemed to come to a stop. And all that just below him somewhere in the equally dark nothingness where now he could just barely make out a circular floor of some sort. The floor was a slightly lighter shade of black a good ten feet beneath him.

As Udo continued to spin he kept watching below until he saw one. One of the things that had been flying around but now was down there.

Assistance came then in the form of a newly arising but still dim light, provided by a ring of low flames licking up over the edge of the round platform the beings were walking on.

Yeah. Now I can see them.

The one in front of him at the moment looked like a big man with big, black wings and arms too, rather muscular ones at that. *And what was that?* Looked like a long sharp pole or something the dark being seemed to be carrying. *Oh . . . wait . . . oh . . . the pole had three sharp tines coming off its head, like a pitch fork.*

"Ahhh," was all Udo could wail then, not knowing that the other winged and dark being below also had a pitchfork and must have occupied the opposite section of the platform and was in fact right behind him. Udo felt him, though. Or more accurately felt the million or so volts from his pitchfork course into him as its tines bit between the links of chain at his lower back.

Even worse though, as the edge of that pain started subsiding, the demon (for that was what they had to be, Udo could only surmise, seeing too now the spiked ear tips sticking up on each side of their hairless heads) the one in front of him did the same thing. This time, though, Udo got to watch the searing shock of electricity-like energy pulsing in blue bolts up the long shafted instrument. Udo took this one too with another screaming yell.

Slowly slipping away then he took a moment to reflect on the fact that later he would most likely remember the sensation he'd just felt as one in which he could tell his teeth were dancing on their tiptoes in pools of shocking jolts, mega volt jolts that would then course down through his jawbone and throughout the rest of his skeleton, literally rattling his bones.

Then he collapsed in complete exhaustion—though still hanging and chained up like he was he could only still lightly sway there like meat on a hook. His head lolled and his eyes were closed—but still he could hear and process what someone, somewhere near was saying.

"What!" the first voice blurted out loud and angrily.

"It would appear—" a more timid and analytical voice started in with before the other one cut him off.

"I know," he yelled even more loudly this time. "I was using the term rhetorically!"

"It is still impossible to tell what the long term effects will be, however," the other one that sounded timid said but obviously was brave enough after all.

"He is progressively weakening. The disease is winning. In fact, he's half dead," the first voice came back with, very angry now. "That last reading my good servants took showed disease levels at twice that which any human can withstand. Which I suppose I should be happy about. I designed a wonderful disease! It can even kill God's own perfect ones. Oh boy! Except that now the most powerful being on the planet is totally worthless to me. Get rid of him!"

"If we could continue to monitor . . . the effects may be interesting and useful!"

"Listen," the authoritative one said more quietly now but with anger still edging his words. "We almost have enough souls anyway. Just a few more. Especially the—" he cut himself off then. "Care. Superhuman care must be taken with them. They we cannot lose. But this one we have lost."

By then all the anger was gone from his tone and he sounded very sad instead. Soon the fight returned. "Oh, I wanted him though. Just to spit in that bastard's eye. To make it a 'slam dunk' as the humans like to say. Because you never know, he just may have another trick up his sleeve. I can just feel it. Something even to do with this one. But now that we have at least ruined him we can let the almighty have back that which is His. That was always the deal anyway . . . right!"

Then Udo felt himself falling. He fell and fell, but at least the chains were gone now, so he moved his arms and legs to try and brace for a landing.

But soon he realized he had been falling more than a moment or two. Must have fallen pretty far. It might not matter how he landed. The fall was probably going to kill him anyway.

Oh thank God, thank God, thank God, he mentally intoned as he wetly realized he'd fallen into water. Down, down and down deeper he went, feeling disoriented but better. His worn and sore body felt rejuvenated by the coolness of the water. He looked up and there! A dim light was showing at the surface. And yes and of coure, He was floating that way too. *All right ...*

Then he realized the strangest thing; he didn't seem to feel the need to breathe. But with renewed energy he swam up anyway, just to get the heck out of there, and hopefully out of the hands of the enemy too.

On the surface Udo floated and looked around and saw, but after he saw what he did he didn't want to see anymore. It was the most horrible sight he'd ever seen.

Low flames again burned up from the bases of the rocky walls surrounding the mostly circular and cavernous enclosure, dramatically highlighting the fact that probably hundreds of zombies were all milling around in it. The entire structure was about the size of a small arena, Udo was thinking. *Yeah . . . like the one the college basketball team played in. About that big.*

He further noted then the way the rocky ceiling glowed red as well. As if all the stones in it were burning coals. All of which he'd been taking in instead of looking at the people hanging from up there too. That was the horror of all horrors he'd been trying not to look at most of all.

Even worse though was how he could tell by their screams and the way they were flailing their arms about that they were still alive. Unlike all the others in the room, they were *living* humans, a few dozen or so who hung from their heels by hooks stuck through their flesh and probably bones too.

But then even worse was how the zombies below were ripping into them, tearing an arm off of one, heads off of others, then even guts spilled out of others too. The zombies feasted and feasted and feasted. They practically bathed in the red shower falling from above.

Udo looked away, and then made his way over to edge of the lake or pond or whatever it was that he was in. It was kind of like a pool, he was even thinking, feeling the pool-like edge, a foot wide concrete lip that ran all along it.

He waited there, considering his options. It wasn't like he didn't want to mix in, but the crowd just wasn't his type. And of course escape was his first and greatest desire, but all he could see were zombies milling about everywhere. If there was a way to escape, it would probably be somewhere out there, on the other side of them all.

So just as he remembered doing in his previous life, Udo got out of the pool by putting his hands on the edge and pushing up, then next a foot on the edge and puh again and—

Whoa . . .

He'd barely been able to make it. What happened to all his strength? Oh . . . yeah . . . that's what those guys had been talking about while he was all chained up up there. About what the zombie disease was doing to him. But did that also mean—

Oh no.

Oh God.

He looked down at his hands and arms and was shocked at what he saw. He was thinking maybe some shrinkage or discoloration, but it was horrible to see how his skin was missing in patches, and what was there was a ghastly grayish green. From the looks of it, now *he* was a zombie too.

Which also explained why as he milled in with the masses of the other undead they acted as if he wasn't even there. Now, he was just another hungry reveler at the zombie party to end all zombie parties.

"That's it! Feast my friends! Eat . . . eat your fill and then go out and find more food. Victory is almost ours. Then we will all be together forever . . . yes . . . yes. When you've had enough, find your ride. You remember how. The silver sleds will take you out. That's right. And on water now because the lava is not needed anymore. So no more burning. Our pathway has been cleared. Victory is ours. So let's go. Let's go. Still more hunting to do . . ."

Udo had made his way to a slight high ground and looking back could see the body of water he'd been in was fed by streams coursing in from the cavern walls. On them, round blobs of shiny silver floated in and then floated back out again as zombies in teams of two or three mounted them while they waited by the edge of the pool he'd just been in.

While he watched them go, a strange feeling started welling in his mind, and even in his body too. It was like the words he'd heard were almost hypnotic, or like dreams you have when you're sick. Surreal, absurd but real. And in their wake was a desire inside his mindof something he now wanted to do more than anything else.

He staggered through the crowd, which was all he could really do now, stagger and sway. His infection was growing worse and worse by the moment. But it was something about the words too—both a phrase and a feeling trying to take root in his consciousness. It seemed to just keep floating down and dripping into his ears, filling all of his mind with new desires and ideas. Before he knew it, Udo was really hungry, hungry for the flesh and organs falling down and lying all around in puddles of blood and other bodily fluids. All he had to do was drop to his knees and start slurping it up.

So he did.

He ate and ate and felt the blood and meat filling him, filling him so much, but he couldn't stop. And like will happen when one eats too much, soon Udo could barely even think straight. Cutting in through the fog, from either his own mind in its newly infected state, or possibly through the powers of someone, or *something*, else, Udo could see himself from above. As if he'd left his body and was seeing someone else down there doing the horrible things he was now doing.

Oh God, what have I become? Oh God . . . He couldn't remember exactly how this had happened. How he'd been tricked and infected and now taken over and turned into this monster. All he knew was how awful a thing he was.

His memories flooded back to him of Jesus and heaven and his family. But now they were like fading things. Lost in all the blood everywhere else. In his mind. On his mind. And on his hands and his face too. He could feel its warm slipperiness.

No! Nooo, he wanted to scream. No blood on them! Not on them! They were too beautiful for that, so wonderful, his boy, his little girl and his wife too. Wait . . . wait he wanted to yell too. Because they were leaving and he could see them. His family was leaving. Jesus too! Jesus was leaving and taking His love with Him. He couldn't feel it anymore! Nooo!

Udo *tried* to yell it all out then too. He lifted his bloody face to the ceiling of the hell dome and screamed with all his might, but the words didn't form too well. Instead, a giant shrieking growl erupted from his lungs, which even scared the other zombies milling around nearby. They staggered back from their newest, and quite likely strongest brother.

Next Udo raised and shook his clinched fists, meat filled and dripping toward the still glowing red ceiling. With all the effort he could muster, he finally formed at least the crude syllables of what he wanted to say.

"I keeel youuu . . ." he roared up into the air and stopped all the other zombies dead in their tracks, no pun intended.

Almost in response, the voice came back down again. "My friends . . . we seem to have acquired an enemy in our midst. There is an enemy among us. We need to destroy him. *You* need to destroy him. Get him my friends. He is God sent and of the good. He is not like us. He is not like us at all. Destroy him! Tear him apart! Tear him limb from limb, and then tear those pieces to pieces too. I will shine a light on him for you."

Udo winced under the brightness suddenly shooting down on him from above. He tried to get away but the light followed him like a shadow. Looking up, he could see the seemingly disembodied spot it emanated from.

Looking around next, he could see that the other zombies seemed to all be coming for him now. There were so many. Udo was glad, though. He couldn't wait. He would take them all on. He just wanted to kill. And kill. And kill.

He'd show them how to make pieces.

CHAPTER XX

COME FLY WITH ME

Officer Hernandez was wishing at the moment that he smoked since he was outside and all. He remembered how they always said it felt great to smoke after sex. And maybe too because, as he honestly had to consider these days . . . the chances were he probably wouldn't be living too much longer anyway. So why not? Light one up. Savor the afterglow.

He didn't have any butts though.

How about that butt on Dr. Ichikawa, he couldn't help but connect that thought up with then. Although he felt bad right after he did. Because as far as he could tell, he was already in love with her. Hopefully . . . well . . . hopefully she felt the same way.

Either way, at least now he wasn't a twenty-nine-year-old virgin anymore. The guys at the station were always riding him about that. Too bad now there weren't any guys anymore that he could brag to about it all . . . or a station either. But still at least he wasn't a virgin anymore. And that felt good.

He wondered too what his mom would have thought, since she wasn't around anymore either. Just today he'd flown over the board and care facility her advanced diabetes had left her in, and it was completely gone now too. *Pobrecita mama'* then he crossed himself and said a quick prayer.

Knowing her, though, he had to realize, she probably would have insisted on marriage, being such a strong Catholic like she was. Which at least because of that he could think for sure she probably went to heaven. Which made things at least a little easier to take.

John was thinking maybe he should marry her anyway. Dr. Ichikawa, that is, errr . . . Janet. He was supposed to call her Janet now. But he was thinking too that maybe he should marry her more than just because he loved her. To make sure he'd get into heaven too. He wasn't as strong a Catholic as his mom had been, but he still believed in all that stuff: Jesus and heaven and everything.

But oh yeah, the officer realized then too. Good luck finding a priest these days. And anyway, of course it all depended on whether Janet would even want to marry him anyway.

The young police officer finished off the rest of his water bottle and looked out into the night. He looked deep and in detail at the areas just beyond the double chain link fence guarding the Highpoint Park helicopter fueling station. Very quiet. No activity that he could see.

That was another bonus about the station he thought of as he tossed the empty plastic bottle into a nearby trash can. Several cases of bottled water were stacked up in one corner inside the place. Then even better was the old single bed that Sid used to use.

Sid Meckels was an older fellow, retired firefighter in fact, who used to work the station, but only seasonally as a volunteer. He manned the place mostly during the fire season when all the helicopters fighting the brushfires would come and go like clockwork. Someone had to be there to quickly fill their tanks.

And even though the killer quake had come in season, where the old codger was now was anybody's guess. He wasn't here. Officer Hernandez had visually scoured the place when they'd landed. Poor old Sid must have been caught out, for some reason, and wherever he was now, most likely he was dead.

But back in the day, and during peak seasons of brushfire activity, Sid would sometimes stay at the station for weeks. Depending of course, on how long it took to put the fires down or if they continued coming one after another after another. So, the bottled water was kept on hand and also can after can of chili, various soups, cases of crackers, canned fruit, cookies, powdered cheese, and powdered milk. There was also a portable TV with nothing on it to watch anymore and a police band radio with nothing on it to hear anymore either.

And the bed, which finishing the list with then, Officer John Hernandez couldn't help but think of the old twin size rattrap with a mixture of embarrassment, instant nostalgia(it was the first place he made love)and passion.

But the point being, John knew that if they had to they could hold out here probably for weeks. As long as no zombies showed up. And if they did, the double chain link fence with razor wire topping it should slow them down. Hopefully long enough for him and the future Mrs. . . . err well . . . the good "Dr." to get to the chopper and escape. He had the bird fueled up and packed with weapons and supplies already. All they would have to do is get on board, start her up and off they'd go. One thing was for sure: zombies couldn't fly.

But where would they go?

The Dr. had suggested a cabin in the mountains she knew of in Big Bear. She'd stayed there with friends last ski season. But it was a fairly well populated area, John knew, and probably now populated with zombies to boot. If it was even there anymore.

Then he thought of it . . . *we can fly to the islands.* There were several of them off the coast and most of them within the helicopter's 200 mile travel range. Catalina would have been a good choice, but it too had a pretty hefty population *so . . . more zombies?*

Maybe it wasn't such a good idea. *We'll fly over and see,* he and the doctor had concluded when they'd been checking and charting out a course earlier in the evening. *We'll take a good look, a real good look, and if we see any of the undead, then on to one of the other islands.* There were about a half dozen in all within their range. And a couple even housed Navy bases on them. Others were only lightly inhabited.

The map they'd found in a stack of them Sid had on hand too. Then, just as the attractive young doctor had traced a straight line from their current position to Catalina, while at the same time he was measuring the mileage, they had bumped heads. Which then led to shared and slightly embarrassed laughter, but in the aftermath thereof they looked deeply into each other's eyes at close proximity and well, finally after much posturing . . .

A kiss.

And well . . . then . . . as they say, nature took its course.

Officer Hernandez then shook all that—especially the memories of her beautiful nakedness in the half-light—out of his head. Back to business, he was thinking and walked out to the inner fence. He wanted to *make sure* the whole area was still zombie-free before he turned in.

All right.

Quiet here.

No sign of movement or anything here either.

He moved down the fence line another twenty feet and waited a minute or so. *Still nothing.* Just the darkness of the woodsy park area, treetops and patches of grassy field highlighted by the full moon above.

Then he went on and over to inspect the next side with more of the same. But this was where the highway cut by about a half mile out, and it *used* to do so under tall banks of lights while flowing with lights itself as well from all the cars on it. Now, however, the once great byway was all dark and busted up and flat out disappeared into the side of a new mountain.

Anyway, nothing happening there either.

Then he went around back behind the station where the community of Highpoint used to be, but it was all a shambles now too. Although at least it was lighted up . . . lighted up with sporadic fires still burning, burning down and through the shambles. *Ashes to ashes*, he couldn't help but think.

But all was quiet there too, except for the occasional snap, crackle or pop from the stuff still burning. No movement though, which was what he really meant by quiet. No zombie activity observable, Officer Hernandez concluded, and half-humorously realized that's how he would have written it in a report.

Just one more side then, the far one with a giant canyon there, eerie and completely dark. Not even the full moon could light that thing up. And no doubt neither could zombies traverse it.

So all of it quiet, at least for now. Maybe he could head on in and get some sleep. That is unless Mrs. Hernandez . . . err, Dr. Ichikawa . . . err Janet. *Yeah . . . unless Janet is in the mood for a little more looove.*

He'd talk to Jesus about all this fornicating later. Oh yeah, his mom had taught him all about the evils of fornication that time when he'd been caught necking with Melissa Dominguez at Our Lady's Junior High. Then she spanked half his butt off too.

So eventually John knew he'd have to ask the Lord for forgiveness and then repent, which was another good reason to find a priest. *But where the hell—oops . . . err, heck . . . where the heck was he gonna find one of those?*

He headed back in.

It was so good to be real again. To touch and feel. To eat and taste. To see and hear and ride hard and strike and kill. It had been horrible buried in stone like that, but at least their spirits were free to roam and to catch on to one of the pitiful humans. It was a way to sort of live for a little while before destroying them and as many other humans as they could while they visited. All of it also done to keep the human's precious little souls from ascending to the Almighty. It was a part of the General's plan all along. Keep as many souls here as he can.

So then their first task upon returning to the surface was the retrieval of all those lost and wandering souls also set free in the great cataclysm. And they had tasted so good. The power in them felt good once inside too. Then they'd fly home to the General and turn them over to him. Then out to hunt for more, more delicious souls, so easy to find. There was so many!

It was a good time to be a demon.

But even better was what the General had in store for them now: *A great adventure*. With the great power of all those souls, the General could take them anywhere. Then they could find new worlds to take. Get to other worlds out there, out in space. Start over. Get away from Him. Him who meant to trap them here. The damn almighty.

The General had designed a ship, though. A great ship using the souls as fuel to travel to the stars.

The demon threw back his big black head to laugh. He looked up at the glowing heavenly bodies out tonight. Imagine that. Just a few days ago he was encased in solid rock deep in the earth and never anywhere to go. And now, he'd soon get to go to the stars. Those very same stars he was looking at now and then too to other worlds the General had talked about. Worlds their wings could never carry them to, but with the power of the eternal fueling their ships, they could go anywhere. They could bend space and time, the General had also said, but the demon wasn't sure what that meant. It sounded like fun, though, and he had to think the almighty had not thought of that one. The big demon laughed some more.

They were still a few souls shy though, the General had also said. After all their work the take had not been adequate yet, which was fine with the demon. So far it had been happy hunting. The humans weren't too hard to catch. Pretty slow and dimwitted really. Pretty much as to be expected, having dealt with them in the spiritual realm as much as they had.

The demon then fondly remembered a group of them, a group of the humans that he and Dagon and Malphus rode up on, about thirty of them hiding in one of their grocery stores. And even though they had their puny human weapons—the projectiles from which could not even pierce their skin—they were eventually and easily rounded up. The undead ones, so many as they were, those who did all the dirty work handling the disgusting humans, eventually overpowered them and killed them all. Out of which, except for those needed for food, more of the undead were made as well. As per the General's plan.

They really just went along, the demon begrudgingly admitted, only to oversee the undead and to make sure no souls got away. Then too in case any humans could be taken alive; the demons would have to harness them properly and take them back to one of the mountains. The undead could not do this. So they had to. It wasn't battle, glorious battle like he remembered from before, but it was something. It was a needed occupation. Part of the whole process of getting away from the almighty before he could imprison them again.

The first and truly hardest part of which, the demon came back to the present with, was the finding of the surviving humans. But the General was so smart and could see through the eyes of all his undead servants and the animals too. Sooner or later they would see and get them all. It would just take some time.

Which this time meant coming down this mountain and across the sloping park area ahead. Then onward to the fenced-in, smaller than average building where the flying machine was landed now next to it. That was how they found these two. The flying machine had been seen. Seen by many of the undead. The General knew about this place anyway, this place where the flying machine could get its fuel. He knew because he knew about everything the humans used to do. So now he knew the places they were most likely to be.

Like here.

Where he'd been sent and now it was the demon's job to bring them in. *Soon enough*, he was thinking. *Soon enough.*

The zombies arrived early for breakfast. Good thing they weren't looking for anything professionally prepared. As far as they were concerned, today's special was the human burger, preferably blood rare. And as another trite old joke might have put it, with a side of thighs.

The owners of which, Officer Hernandez and Dr. Ichikawa, had overslept. Most likely due to their state of near exhaustion, arrived at by means perhaps not too biblical—although the two had promised to wed after the second . . . no third . . . third time—but as they both still slept deeply at the only slightly post-dawn hour, neither had yet arose.

Of course they then both did, simultaneously and urgently as one of the undead marauders banged a hand hard against the station's thick metal door.

"WHAM!" Both the officer and the doctor sprang upright, creaking and nearly cracking the metal springs barely holding up their single mattress love nest.

Then since he was on the outside half and, voted or not, was the one most likely to kill, again, almost faster than the naked eye could see, which he was by the way, naked that is, Officer Hernandez got up, grabbed the shotgun and looked hard at the door. He noticed first off that it was still bolted fast, but said bolt shook and rattled with each new thumping. Which were coming all too frequently now.

"Get dressed, Honey," John said over at Janet, which he was doing himself, stepping into his dark blue nylon jumpsuit and pulling it up and around himself.

"Omigod. It's them, isn't it? Those . . . those . . . monsters. Omi-god, omigod," the doctor kept repeating, but at least getting up, but also then just turning in tight circles and repeating more of the same phrase. After about a half-dozen or so of said cirlcles, she grabbed up her clothes but then could only stare at her new lover, obvious dismay pulling at her features.

"Yes. I believe it is those . . . monsters. But we can do this. Focus! I know you can do that. Focus and take it one thing at a time. Code blue! Code blue! Does that help?" the police officer tried on her.

"Yeah," she had to admit, laughed a little and hurriedly started pulling her clothes on. "You know, one time—"

"Sorry to cut you off, dear, but let's get going. We'll reminisce later. We're gonna have to go out the top through the trap door I showed you in the back. Everything we need is in the chopper. Just get your shoes on," he told her because she had everything else on, mostly just the light green scrubs she'd been wearing before. The lab jacket she could do without, late summer like it was.

"Your boots aren't even laced up," she said while tying up her white sneakers.

"Don't worry. They won't fall off. Come on. That door's pretty stout. But they'll get through it soon. All we gotta do is get to the chopper before they do. After we get on the roof, we'll jump into the dumpster. It's got a bunch of boxes and stuff. Should be no sweat. I checked it yesterday. It's all lined up. Ready?"

They both turned hard toward the door as something big knocked into it with a slam and the metal bent inward and buckled.

"Come on!"

"Yeah . . . yeah," Dr. Ichikawa said, started in a run right behind the police officer, then held up. "The maps!"

"Grab 'em," Officer Hernandez said over the sights of the shot-gun. He had a bead on the front door just in case, and kept it there too while off to the side his eyes also followed her quick skip and a step over to the card table across the room. She wrapped the maps up tube shaped and stuffed them under her arm.

She got back to him and he told her to just keep going, get on the roof while he watched the door. She hesitated, then disappeared around a half-wall bisecting the room just as another loud bang rocked the door, this time almost bending it in half. That made just enough of a hole for one of the zombies to get one arm and his head in. The police officer fired and the thing's head busted open. Blood showered out. Even better though was how then the dead—and really dead this time—creature plugged the hole up. The officer made a quick retreat.

He got up the emergency ladder in the back room with practiced alacrity, and up on the roof he scanned and just as quickly found his sweetheart in the right spot, standing at the edge just above where the dumpster waited below.

"Honey? Johnny? We got a problem," she shouted back at him.

He quickly got over and saw what she meant. The zombies were already back there, about a half dozen of them loosely milling around the dumpster. They were definitely between them and the chopper. They roiled about just as uselessly as the long but neatly coiled fuel hoses near them. The chopper waited just on the other side of the tanks.

"What the hell!" Officer John Hernandez had to say, looking back across the roof to the front area of the station, not knowing at the same time he was answering his own question. Because what he was looking at was something exactly from that very place he'd just mentioned.

Hell.

The demon rode tall on an all-black horse, just like him, and a horse larger than any perhaps ever seen, also just like him. Both rider and horse shared one other characteristic that no doubt would be the most striking on first observation. That being that from their mouths, fire licked out in lazy wisps.

"The rest of you get back there too," the big black hell man then yelled with an incredibly deep voice. He seemed to be controlling the zombies, riding herd behind the stragglers in this bunch coming up now to the front of the station over the flattened fence.

At least he's still out front, Officer Hernandez let it all go with as he turned back to concentrate on figuring a path to the helicopter. He couldn't get the image of the big demon creature out of his mind, though. He kept seeing its face and head that were that of a man, albeit one rather large and very cruel looking and whose flesh seemed to resemble black leather.

And then what at first had appeared to be parts of a helmet of some sort were actually the thing's ears, so large they each covered that side of its head and ran up to sharp points about a foot high. They looked very hard and sturdy. They were jet black and shone like metal.

Also metallic was what looked like light armor of a grayish blue color covering strategic areas of their muscular frames. The evil being prodded its zombie cattle along with a long, silver weapon or tool.

And then . . .

What?

How was he doing that?

Officer Hernandez stopped down. He seemed and felt frozen in time. He'd tried not to let it, had felt it happening at the last second, but by then it was too late and somehow the demon had captured his mind.

He was still looking down below, first at the zombies milling between them and the helicopter, and too at Janet yelling at him now, calling out his name, shouting what's wrong? "What's wrong?" But he couldn't even hear her.

All he could do was slowly turn back toward the demon, where the image he had of the creature in his mind merged with the reality he was seeing just then. The combination was overwhelming. He held on.

It got worse, though, as then the big hell being extended one of its long, clawed hands toward him with a bent index finger beckoning him over. Worse yet, was how then John even felt himself helplessly obeying. He—

Suddenly out of nowhere a streak flashed by in the sky, something the officer couldn't see any the details of, so he continued to track the flying . . . man? Yeah. Only a little bigger maybe. Something obviously at least big enough to hit the demon hard and knock him not only off his big horse, but then also hurl them both some fifty feet and more where they tumbled and tumbled. All the way down the sloping hillside fronting the station the two big beings rolled.

At least that broke the spell Officer Hernandez was under. He stopped halfway across the roof where his hypnotic state had lead him and put his hands on his knees. He let his mind clear for just a moment because he knew a moment was all he had. He could hear Janet crying uncontrollably and immediately got back over to her.

"Oh my God. What is wrong with you? You can't just flake out. Not now!" she screamed at him.

"I know. Or I don't know. That demon thing . . . over there . . ." he still somewhat groggily pointed over to the front area of the station. Janet followed his finger but of course now the demon was gone. She turned back to her new lover, the man with the shotgun, the helicopter pilot who would have to fly her to safety now.

Again. She had to take action or they didn't stand a chance. "Come on John. Get your shi_ together." On top of that she slapped him.

At least he looked back at her now, shock both clearing and widening his eyes.

"I had to do that to one of the doctors this one time during a code. He froze up. You have to do something sometimes. You have to do something. He thanked me for it later," and she tried a smile.

He managed one back. "I'll thank you when I get the chance," the officer much more clearly and sharply said. "Right now we gotta get the heck outta here."

He swung the shotgun around. He thought of something and slipped a shell out of the clip holding six on the side of the gun's breech. He shoved the red plastic tube up in the thing to take the place of the one he'd just fired. He stepped up to the edge of the roof again. "Look!"

Janet got over with him and took a look too. "What are they doing?"

"That big demon thing I seen. I think he was controlling them. And since that other thing came flying down and has him halfway down the hill now, it's like they don't know how to act."

Just as John had been describing, the zombies really did seem to have lost direction. The ones that had been out front were for the most part heading away from the station now, maybe to help out their leader who now seemed to be under assault. The ones out back seemed even more disorganized than before. Obviously, this was their chance to make a break for it, Janet and John both figured at the same time. They looked at each other with eyes wide and ready.

"Okay . . . here's the deal," John started with. "I'll jump down into the dumpster. Give me ten seconds or so, and then you follow. I'll blast any zombies nearby and then we make a dash for the chopper."

"All right."

"And see that two by four down there in the dumpster? It looks about six feet long. I'll give that to you after I help you climb out. If any of those bastards get close to you . . . shove them away with that, or club them if you can, and just keep headin' for the helicopter. All right?" John had used extra strength to say those words. He felt bad about not training Janet on the weapons yet and she seemed deathly afraid of his 9mm. They were scheduled for training this morning.

Oooops.

He tried one more time and she screamed and shook her hands real hard. He holstered his nine. Better off to keep it, in case he emptied the shotgun.

"Board, board, board," Dr. Ichikawa almost chanted, looking at the thing too down in the dumpster. The zombies had thinned out anyway, John could tell. They just might pull this off.

"Oh boy . . ." was all Janet could say, looking down and rolling on the balls of her feet. The gritty sandiness of the station's roof crunched beneath her work-all-day-and-night sneakers.

"I only see about four or five left . . . and I got eight shells . . . so no sweat. Right?" John tried.

"Whatever you say," Janet concurred as enthusiastically as she could. She put one sneakered foot on the edge of the roof and got ready.

John slung the shotgun back over his shoulder, sat on the edge and pushed himself out far enough to fall into the dumpster almost dead center. He stumbled a little, but righted himself easily and made room for her. "Okay. Come on!"

"That's a good idea," Janet realized out loud, sat herself too and pushed out from the edge. She fell . . .

Udo was thinking about counting all the heads but decided what the heck. There were so many it didn't matter. A good days work for sure. A few dozen or so, enough to make a ring about fifty feet in diameter. He looked at them surrounding him in the wide circle all around and smiled. None of them smiled back however. In fact, most of them sported expressions of varying degrees of shock and surprise, if not downright terror. And, being too that most of them came from zombies, many had missing parts and patches of skin gone showing skull segments in various stages of decomposition. Some even fed maggots at the moment. A sad looking lot if ever there was one.

Thinking of that, Udo gingerly felt around on his own face. As far as he could tell everything still seemed to be in place. *Oh,* he realized then too and wiped some of the blood from his chin.

What a mess, he summed it all up with, looking around some more. *It was quite a struggle here in the Devil's mountain.* He thought of those words like they were on a theatre sign somewhere. "Struggle to the Death in Devil's Mountain." He smiled, and continued to do so, fondly remembering it all and at least partially replaying some of it in his mind while he continued with his busy work, getting ready for the ritual.

At first it had seemed like it could go either way, Udo remembered. Some of the tougher, braver zombies, maybe ten or so, were actually following the orders of the big voice coming down from above. They were making their stumbling way over, seemingly to confront him. But once he lit into them, remembering all his moves from before, and though he wasn't as strong or as quick as he had been, he was still stronger and quicker than any of these half-dead guys.

Besides which too, now he didn't have to worry about getting bit. He already had the disease! And also because he had it, he couldn't be killed . . . again . . . or whatever . . . unless someone caved in his skull . . . or took his head . . . or ripped his heart out. Which from the looks of it, none of these other zombies seemed to realize. Because they weren't even getting close. It kind of really wasn't even fair anymore.

So after he was done with them, the rest of the horde present, who had just watched him make mincemeat of all their friends, and could see too the scattered limbs and heads and even hearts—Udo had just ripped them out and dropped them at his feet as the battle raged on—well, needless to say all the rest of the zombies couldn't get out of the cavern fast enough. They were at least smart enough to figure out their living dead lives were definitely in jeopardy.

Seemingly in response, the voice overhead started up again and tried to help as best it could. "Go to the loading area, my children. The discs are all there now. Just jump on board and let them carry you to safety."

All of which they were exactly doing while Udo was catching his wind, as it were, surveying the scene. All were in retreat now. A half body pulled its way onto the last silver blob out. He and three others standing rode the disc straight out on a medium sized river exiting at the base of the mountain's inner wall.

All right. That was that. It was quiet again now. No groaning and moaning and growling. No blood curdling screams from the people, the poor people hanging by their heels.

Udo scanned the ceiling. Against the backdrop of all the large red coals composing it, he could see the torn in two bodies still hanging there, or really just their trunks, drip, drip, dripping. At least he'd been able to salvage some of *their* heads too. They were easy to see, relatively normal in color, albeit bloody, compared to the average zombie head.

Udo had to round them all up anyway. But would God take their souls like he did the zombie ones in the ritual? Who knew, Udo had to leave it all with then. He'd just do the best he could. Round up all the heads, eat as many of the hearts as he could find, say the prayers and lift up holy hands to the Lord.

The rest would be up to Him. That much Udo had learned for sure. *So just do it,* he decided, remembering that phrase too from the commercials in his day.

He was just about ready when-

Something big and black suddenly came flying down, then the pat, pat, pat of its thick soles settling on the cavern's stone floor could be heard.

Udo remembered that sound. It sounded the same as it had when he'd been above in that chamber and all chained up. Then yes, he could see it now too, tall and dark in the shadows across the way, the big wings still out but the thing tucking them in now. Then a flash of winking silver came too, the tri-tipped spear they sported, the one that felt like a million volts shocking into him all at once.

Oh yes. It was one of the demons from up above.

Of course his partner came down next and in an almost identical fashion. Almost immediately they also identically began twirling and thrusting their tri-tipped spears, practicing various maneuvers with the things while still approaching. Basically, both of the big, dark beings were about the same distance from Udo, twenty to thirty yards each across the smooth floor but closing.

Udo eyed his surroundings, thinking maybe if he made a break for it, he could run pretty fast after all. So if he could just get to one of those exits . . .

But then, almost as if whoever was running this place could read his mind, the exits closed off with what looked like thick, metal doors sliding down across them.

So no choice then. "Let's dance," Udo said, mostly to himself, and started turning in place too, eyeing first one attacker, and then the other.

He noticed as he did that the one who landed second was the furthest from him. He saw too that the stone floor between them was wet and slippery with scattered blood puddles here and there. Especially near the demon, who as Udo fixed him with his gaze, stopped advancing and did the same.

Udo broke for him in a run.

As he did, he quickly refreshed his memory, going all the way back to his high school days. In particular, baseball practice when coach Bagwell would make them drill over and over again on how to break up a double play. Then, just like riding a horse—most likely because he had done it so many times—it worked perfectly. He slid well and far.

It was obvious the demon had never practiced nor played baseball in his unholy career. And because of that the creature initiated the best maneuver it thought it could for a rapid frontal assault. A rapid frontal thrust of its trusty pitchfork.

But considering the above average speed, even as a zombie, that Udo could obtain, and too that the floor really was rather slippery, needless to say the perfect zombie sent the demon sprawling you-know-what over teakettle.

Better yet the hell being's weapon clanged and then skittered across the floor. Meanwhile Udo, as he was also trained to do, popped right up and turned to assess the new developments.

First, he noticed that the other demon from across the way was closing faster now, running in a long legged, heavy jog. Udo knew he'd have to move fast. Again. So quickly he next scanned over to the other demon, the one he'd just taken out, and saw that it was just now getting to its feet too. But there. There! There was the creature's big weapon laying a good fifteen feet away.

Udo made a break for it.

On his way to the special spear he noticed the demon on one knee now, shaking his head. He must have hit hard on the even harder floor, Udo could only figure. Udo knew he could get to the spear first for sure.

Just as he was almost to it, something hit him like a bull in the side, knocking Udo off his feet. Not only that, it also sent him about ten yards in the same direction where he then staggered once again to his feet. Protruding now from his side was the tri-tipped spear of the other demon who obviously had thrown the damn thing—quite proficiently—from across the way.

Udo slowly spun with the spear in him. If he could just get a grip on the thing and give it a good pull, he was thinking. The spear had hurt like heck, but he darn well knew he couldn't be killed. Not like that anyway. *This stupid spear,* he thought angrily, finally got a good grip on the thing's shaft and yanked.

The pain of all that hadn't shocked him this time, though. Maybe he was too dead now. His pain receptors dead now too. But at least, at least now he had a weapon. At the moment, though, he only seemed to be able to use it as a cane, or like a staff an old wizard might lean on in a head wind. But really Udo was getting *his own* wind while trying to regain some strength as well. They couldn't kill him but they had sure set him back just a little. The demons seemed to think they had him on the ropes too and self-assuredly ambled over.

"Hey. Where's your boss? I think you're going to need his help pretty soon,"

Udo teased them and got ready for action. He used all his strength to hold the spear at the ready, then even managed a twirl and thrust himself. He seemed to be getting at least a little better.

"We don't need him to take your puny little half-human life," the one that Udo had knocked down angrily answered. His voice was very deep and scary sounding. Too bad Udo didn't scare too much anymore after all he'd been through. "And you can't kill us anyway, you fool."

Udo got ready to reply, but then a voice from above cut him off. "He can try . . ."

It wasn't the same voice as before, though. All three combatants looked to the ceiling somewhat inquisitively. Then Udo recognized the voice as that of his Lord and a smile spread his lips. The demons looked at each other in sudden consternation and shared whispers, agitated ones at that.

So that was it, Udo realized. Since this was his Lord talking down from up there now. The voice before, the one controlling all the zombies and these demons too . . . that had to be . . . him.

"Looks like there's a new sheriff in town," Udo quipped at his adversaries, not sure how accurate his assessment of the situation was, but thinking probably it at least meant that Satan had either left this death mountain on his own or had been chased away by the Lord.

"Correct on both counts my boy," the voice came down again, but this time only into Udo's head. The demons were still squabbling among themselves anyway, and since he apparently had the big guy's ear, Udo had to ask Him something.

"I still gotta fight these guys?" he let out mentally too, remembering from before how to communicate with the Lord that way. "You can't just zap them with lightning or something?"

"Uhm . . . I don't know if you noticed, but you're inside a mountain. And a metal one at that."

"You know what I mean."

"Yeah. Okay. I know. I'm sorry. And yeah. You gotta fight these guys, which I know you want to do anyway; which is why I chose you. You're a real fighter, my boy. So fight hard! And fight well. As I know you will. Remember you are fighting for your family. They are still alive."

"They are?" Udo sort of asked up at the ceiling, but wasn't surprised when he got no response. He could tell now most the time when the Lord was done talking to him, and it was usually like that. Just all of a sudden and He was gone. But usually He gave you just enough before He left. Like now letting him know that his family was still alive. That was all Udo needed to know.

Which told him also that possibly the only thing between him and his family were these demons. They would have to be destroyed.

So Udo started in doing his own dance now with the trident, feeling at least partly reinvigorated, using his superior mental capabilities as well to immediately design and implement several fighting moves that he both showed off and practiced while the demons still seemed to be arguing with each other.

"And I don't know if you noticed," he continued to jeer at his adversaries, "But I've got just as much weaponry as you guys do now." He showed off a couple more fancy moves with the trident.

The demons weren't impressed. They'd finished their own infighting with one of them summing it all up succinctly with, "If we don't kill him, Lucifer will kill us!" Thus agreed, they slowly separated and began moving in for the aforementioned kill.

A most troublesome development occurred then, however, as the demon Udo had taken the trident from somehow and from somewhere on the left side of its body pulled out a sword. The big black creature swished and swirled its broad silver blade very adeptly in more ostentatious movements.

Also rather mysteriously—these demons were a very tricky lot, Udo was learning—somehow the other demon, using his partner's swordplay as a distraction, had with great speed hurled his trident right at Udo's head. The semi-perfect being moved just in time and just enough and the killing fork hurled close by his neck, nicking him on the way.

"Holy—" Udo hissed and felt quickly for the wound. Yeah. Blood. But luckily just a little. Except not so lucky now because then that demon pulled out a sword too.

You're fighting for your family . . .

You're fighting for your family . . .

You're fighting for your family, he kept telling himself, suddenly finding the need for encouragement. The closer and closer these demon guys got, the bigger and badder they looked. And so did their swords. *Maybe if it was just one . . . but two?*

You're fighting for your family . . .

Then like a bolt from the blue, as the saying goes, which later Udo would realize it sort of really was, several good-sized boulders fell from the ceiling. Even though none of them directly landed on the demons, they did land nearby and the hell servants had no choice but to dance out of the way.

All parties concerned—or in other words, all present—looked up. A large hole now graced the big dome-like cavern's ceiling, and as the demons looked at each other, seeing what the other might do considering this new development, Udo took advantage of the situation to hurl his tri-tipped spear as hard as he could at the demon he'd knocked off his feet earlier, hoping he might still be a little dazed and slow.

It worked. The spear took him hard in the chest and knocked the demon reeling back until he fell into the lake in the middle of the cavern where Udo had first plunged.

That should hold that guy for a bit, but now, could it work again? He started in a hard run for the other demon, then started his slide. This time, however, the target simply flapped his large wings a few times and lifted up several feet until Udo slid by harmlessly beneath.

Quickly realizing what had happened Udo started to pop up again, but it was too late. The demon was already on him. He forced Udo onto his back and straddled his shoulders. Man, these guys are strong, was all Udo could think. And he might have added that man, they were fast too, because in the next instant the hell creature had his sword at Udo's throat. Then all he could think was, *I'm going to die. He's going to chop off my head, and I'm going to die.*

He couldn't move a muscle. The demon felt like twenty tons on top of him.

"Foolish half-human," the demon croaked down at him, and just as Udo felt the sword's blade starting to bite, one of the most hideous, yet at the same time beautiful sounds he'd ever heard played in his ears once more. The shrieking, howling growl of the half lion, half scorpion thing he called kitty had found him again.

Or almost.

This time the thing was falling down straight toward them from the hole in the dome overhead. The demon had no choice but to very rapidly roll off of Udo and get as far away as he could. Udo might have done the same, but it was too late. The creature landed right on top of him.

And probably because the fall wasn't really all that far, forty, fifty feet or so at the most. Or maybe too because the creature's legs were so strong and stiff like they were. But either way the thing landed and made absolutely no contact with Udo's still supine form and then just stood over him with its horribly ugly face just inches away from Udo's.

"Kitty," Udo said again this time, the affection in his voice kept low and loving. He couldn't help but smile. The creature then might have even licked its old friend's face, but instead it did the only thing it seemed to be able to do verbally. It screamingly roared once more.

Udo took it and still couldn't help but smile, even with the noise and the force of the beast's hot, smelly breath so intense he thought his hair might catch on fire, or, as he almost did then, might retch up some of the meat he'd just ingested. Luckily, neither occurred.

The loving reunion was cut short, however, as suddenly with a loud clang, the demon's initial strike at the creature glanced off its thick back covered in the armor-like plating the thing had there. So of course then the creature turned on its attacker and sent its next howling growl in the demon's direction.

The demon, while starting a slow retreat looked at his sword, then looked back a little more frantically toward the water. His partner had survived the spear hit from Udo and was now pulling himself up and out at the edge of the indoor lake. He ran his partner's way and just as he came up on him shouted down as he took to flight right over his head.

"Fly or die," he shouted down at his friend, which said friend found even easier to understand when a couple more of the lion/scorpion creatures came dropping down through the hole in the roof as well. The still ground bound demon took in this most ominous development, shook off the effects of the spear wound in his side, and wobbly lifted off with his huge leathery wings.

He zigged and zagged but then seemed to have just enough energy left to follow his partner up through the hole and away into the wild blue, and in this case literally, yonder.

Udo struggled to his feet. The three kitties were already busy doing what they did best, eating zombies. There were plenty of parts scattered about after all. But at least, and watching them now, Udo knew for sure who his feline/arachnid friends worked for. One of them was even at the same time using its snout and pinchers to scoot around the heads and hearts into separate piles, which the other two were going to great lengths not to eat. Udo rested and watched.

Upon completion of their chores, and apparently their mealtime as well, the three helpful critters scuttled over to the lakeside and waited. Soon one of the discs floated up, and they cutely and amazingly efficiently boarded. They floated off, no doubt in search of more zombies.

"Yes," the voice said down from above again. "And what a better way to do so then to use their own highway, such as it is."

"So that's you, huh?" Udo couldn't help but comment, actually very happy to hear from the Lord again, but too tired to show it.

"Oh yes, my boy. The eternal battle rages on. And . . . you looked like you could use a hand."

"Yes. Thank you."

"And I hope you've worked up an appetite. You've got several hearts to ingest over there."

"Oh yeah. Okay. Actually, I am kind of hungry. And the funny thing is, now that I'm half-zombie that sort of dish is particularly appealing."

"Funny how things seem to work out like that, or as I believe my writers put it, 'He makes all things come together for my good.'"

"Hey! That's right!" Udo remembered all of a sudden too. "And by the way, what'd you do with what's-his-name? You know. That tricky little devil."

"He took off the moment I showed up . . . as usual. He has other facilities like this anyway. But we'll shut this one down, and eventually the rest, when you're done with your duties here. Which by the way—"

"Okay . . . okay," Udo gave in, knowing what he had to do. He slowly got to his feet. "Are you always in a hurry?"

I know, my boy. I know it seems that way. But remember what I said about your family? The clock, as always on your home planet, is ticking."

"Oh! Yeah," Udo heartily remembered, because with all the action that had been going on he forgot about them for a bit.

But needless to say, and with a lighter mood, the Lord's strangest servant then got right back to work. The hearts went well with several swigs from the water in the lake nearby, and soon the circle of heads, as previously mentioned, was completed.

Udo next knelt in the center of the circle and prayed. Then right after amen, he rose up his arms and face to the Lord and through the hole in the roof came down the rainbow-like light that signaled successful completion of the ritual. The incredible happiness and joy happened inside of Udo then too as soul after soul after soul slipped out and up the kaleidoscope expressway, on their way to judgment before the Lord.

This time though too, perhaps as a reminder that he still could, Udo was lifted up through the hole as well, a living, or make that a half-living caboose on the end of the spiritual train headed heavenward. He got unhooked however once the train got quite high and some distance from the devil's mountain. Then Udo got another reminder that he also could still fly, but only after he'd already fallen about halfway to the ground. He leveled off and soared onward and outward across the new land below.

So it was settled then. Officer John killed first one . . . then another . . . then the third zombie within range of the dumpster. All were good, clean head shots.

He quickly shouldered the shotgun and climbed out.

"Come on, honey," he tersely said back at Janet and held out his arms. She hurried over and started lifting herself out of the dumpster, struggled momentarily, so he grabbed up under her arms and helped her make it the rest of the way.

"John," she screamed right away as she landed and looked hard over his shoulder. He turned but was too late. Another zombie just coming up lunged hard for him and knocked the shotgun rattling away across the ground.

Then it was a wrestling match and John, as he should have, concentrated his efforts at keeping the rather large zombie's rather large and ever snapping mouth away from all areas of his body. They rolled and grappled until, unfortunately, the zombie ended up on top and was pressing ever so closely to John's face. He, meanwhile, tried with all his strength to keep the mad thing at arm's length, one hand hard against its throat and the other just below it, pushing against its upper chest.

John was slowly but surely losing the battle until the sudden thunderclap of the shotgun and what must have been its forceful emission knocked the zombie aside. The spent ex-police officer had just enough left to roll to the side and from there blinked and tried to figure out what was going on.

"But--" John could only say, looking up at his new girlfriend still holding the shotgun at the ready.

"It wasn't that bad after all," Janet said smiling, but then winced and rolled her right shoulder. "Kinda hurt though too."

John was ready to laud her with all kinds of praise, but then remembered that would have to wait. Another zombie was coming up behind her. "Look out," he said weakly and gave a nod the zombie's way. Janet spun, took aim, but . . . click.

"You gotta pump in another round," John yelled.

"Huh," Janet yelled back and awkwardly tried to manipulate gun's pump. Then all she could do was scream, drop the gun and stagger back.

"John," she called out as she did.

"Go! Get to the chopper. I'll get the gun and—"

He never got to finish his sentence, though, because as he reached for the shotgun two more zombies rushed him from behind, knocking him to the ground once more. The refueling station's asphalt lot was quickly becoming his intimate friend. And worse yet, now three zombies had him surrounded and were closing in. But it was okay. He was about to make a new friend in Udo.

Of course it had been him that had landed in the demon's lap like a man-sized meteorite. Then before the hell creature could recover its diabolical wits,

Udo quickly struck with the demon sword that the Lord had let him keep for his fearless duty in his recent rumble in the devil's mountain. He took the demon's head with great haste.

Then the weirdest thing happened as the demon, headless now and no doubt expired, and that big horse he'd knocked it off of, both caught on fire and burned and burned. The horse continued to do so as it ran off across the hills, then simply disappeared in a great billow of black smoke, apparently and entirely burnt up.

Udo watched all that with some amazement, but getting used to all the weird stuff going on these days and knowing time was of the essence, he turned back and started up the hill he'd just tumbled down.

He hurried because he could have sworn as he was flying in—and what a trip that had been, getting his bearings, north south east and west at least with the sun rising and the ocean visible from the top of the metal mountain so he'd just headed south then noticed Highpoint Park still intact somehow and headed for it—but then he saw all the zombies and then the demon. He nosedived right for him.

But in all that, catching a glimpse too of what looked like maybe some normal humans up at the fueling station that Udo already knew about. One time on a family outing to the park a helicopter had landed there and the kids had ran up the grassy hill to get a closer look.

Which of course struck Udo as funny, or more accurately, ironic, because now here he was running up the same grassy hill to the station again, albeit a little faster than his kids ever did.

Yes, there they are . . . the humans, Udo could see and closed on them fast.

"Oh my God," was Janet's reaction. She had only gotten halfway to the chopper before turning back with the board John had earlier told her to use.

Her words, uttered upon spying Udo's approach, were understandable considering the demigod's current condition. His physique had returned to nearly perfect shape with his systems overcoming the disease like they had, but his previous skin tone of almost alabaster was still tinged with grayish green, especially toward the extremities. Add to that the tattered condition of his wetsuit-like outfit and how half of him was spattered with blood, and it was no wonder when Janet added, "What in the—"

Especially, too when suddenly one of the zombie's grabbed her from behind and she fought him off for a few seconds but couldn't get the board around quick enough and almost got bit. But then even more suddenly the zombie didn't have anything to bite with anymore. Now Janet's biggest problem was getting out of the way of the blood spurting up fountain-like from where the zombie's head used to be.

Her next big challenge was trying not to get any throw up on her shoes. Especially after Udo made just as quick, albeit rather messy, work of the other two zombies nearby as well.

"Johnny? Are you okay," Janet asked, coming over to her man, putting a hand around his waist, both to comfort him and hold herself up too.

In her other hand she held the shotgun, which she'd stopped to pick up, just in case. Although from the looks of things all one had to be careful about now was tripping over a head.

Which oddly enough, the E.R. Doc then noticed, the crazy statue-like being, who wonderfully at least seemed to be on their side, seemed to be fervently collecting. *Really!?* Janet wanted to scream. *The heads? He's collecting the heads? At least though,* she then also noticed, *he's sheathed that sword he was doing so much damage with.*

Officer Hernandez had just been watching him too. "I'm getting' better by the minute," he finally answered.

He'd been groggy as a dog ever since that demon had put the whammy on him. But his head was clearing quickly now. He was mostly glad to see that they at least seemed to be safe for the moment. But then here came that action hero guy with the sword. "Uh oh," he let quietly slip. Janet brought the shotgun up to her chest.

"Hi," Udo said, sounding like an old friend at a barbecue and Janet and John couldn't help but relax at least a little. "Don't worry. I am on your side. I won't hurt you. Do you need any more help?"

The two almost newlyweds just looked back at Udo, not completely slack jawed but close. Finally, John stuttered to life. "Nuh, no. I mean . . . you've helped a lot already. We should . . . we should be okay for now. Too bad we don't have cell phones anymore. Do you? I mean, it would be great if we had any more trouble and then we could just give you a call . . . but . . . well?"

Udo looked at him confused for a second, then remembered what a cell phone was and laughed.

"What . . . or who . . . who are you?" Janet had to ask.

"My name is Udo. I used to live here. I was . . ." Udo hesitated a moment, wondering how much he should tell these people. He didn't want to freak them out, but if they hadn't already freaked out, chances were they probably wouldn't now. "I lived and died here. Now the Lord has sent me back. I am . . . somewhat at least . . . I've taken some damage here . . . but I am what people are like in heaven. We have perfect bodies and increased abilities there."

"I'll say," Janet couldn't help but somewhat suggestively intone while giving Udo the once over. She was new to this relationship stuff. Med school, internship, first year rotation. She hadn't had time for anything but the extremely rare romp in the hay up until now.

John, meanwhile, had mentally come around enough to be a little bit perturbed by her actions, but not too much. He'd have a word with her later, if they lived that long.

"We're going to try the islands offshore," he addressed Udo with instead. "I'm sure you know what's going on here . . . Odo? Is it?"

"Udo. And yes, for the most part. From what I can tell, there's been a worldwide earthquake. The Lord mentioned it to me before I left. I am really just here to help my family. Or so I thought at first. I've been . . . sidetracked, however. A lot. He's got me killing a lot of zombies now too. Then I get to use a special ritual to send their souls back to him. Which if you stick around you can watch."

"No . . . no. That's okay. We should probably get going. You never know . . ."

"These days? Yes," Udo told them and looked up, then remembered something else. "And you're right . . . about the island. That will be your best bet."

"Yeah, we figured . . . once we find the right one. Hey, would you like to come with us. I can take a passenger," John offered. Then remembered, *oh yeah, was he flying before?* Or *just falling horizontally*, which was actually what it had kind of looked like.

"No. That's okay," Udo answered anyway. "I have more work to do." Then Udo thought of something else. "But my family! Maybe you've seen them. A woman . . . forties . . . boy . . . thirteen . . . no . . . fifteen by now . . . girl . . . ten. They lived over on Griffith way. You ever fly over there?"

The street name struck a chord with John. *Was that? Why yes.* He remembered it now. *But-*

He'd caught himself before blurting out to their new friend because he remembered too that there had been some robbery suspects there, and then the quake had practically demolished the place. He didn't want to tell that to a guy with a sword. And besides, that information wouldn't really help him anyway.

"No," John answered. "I've only seen a few . . . people. The doctor here . . . one of her fellow employees . . . that's been about it. But who knows? And like you said . . . the Lord told you?" John had framed his last statement as a question, realizing how crazy it sounded, and when the being didn't immediately answer he just kept on, thinking maybe they should put some distance between themselves and this guy. "They might still be there. I'd check Griffith way. Good a place as any. But you better hurry. Like you were saying . . . these days . . ." John kept backing away. Udo watched him going.

"Yeah . . . you're right," Udo agreed. "Good luck. I'll try to check up on you later."

"Oh, thanks," John said and took Janet's arm to steer her toward the helicopter. He hurried her along some more. "Weird how happy that guy was in the middle of all this . . . well . . . just weird, that's all.

"Weird is an understatement. But man, was he in some shape."

"Yeah . . . well . . ." John still didn't want to go there yet. How she'd been ogling the guy. "But how about his coloring. Was that some kind of disease or something? Was he sick, or what?"

"I'm not even sure he's human," Janet answered and looked to where the strange being was still collecting the heads. Then she turned back to John. "But are you all right, John?" she asked her man and put an arm around him.

"Oh sure. I can fly that bird in my sleep." He let a half-smile lift his lips and put his arm around her too.

"Not just that. All of a sudden you got real tense when we were talking to that guy. Not that I blame you, but are you really okay?"

"Well," John started with and then while he helped Janet on board and checked their supplies, he explained it to her. He knew if he wanted a relationship to work, he had to open up more. Then they both shared their questions about Udo and what he might be and what the heck he was up to with all those heads while they lifted off.

Finally it was another new and strange thing for them to see as from above they turned wide for the coast and both could have sworn they saw a rainbow shooting straight up into the sky back where the station had been. Would wonders never cease . . .

CHAPTER XXI

ON THE TRAIL

They'd only been walking a ways, maybe a mile or so, but it looked like the little boy's legs and feet were already giving out on him. Kellen could tell by the way he was shuffling his feet and the frequent sighs he let out too.

"Your dog's barking at ya, little fella?" she asked Aaron, remembering the phrase from somewhere in her memory. Maybe it was from that time when her dad and she had gotten stuck driving out in the desert. They'd had to walk several miles to find a ride.

Aaron ran at her all of a sudden and hugged her legs hard again. "There's dogs! Where? Don't let them get me, Kellen!"

"No . . . no. Aaron," she reassured the boy. "It's just a saying! It's okay. There's no dogs here. It's just a saying . . ."

Of course, though, she *had* to pick the boy up then. He'd practically crawled halfway up her body already anyway. He was shaking as well and hid his sniffling face in her shoulder. Poor kid, Kellen couldn't help but think. Maybe they should find a place to rest, get some sleep. It was probably two or three in the morning anyway. She was hoping to catch up to Shadow though first and then rest. But he could be anywhere. The poor horse was probably spooked, hungry, hurt, who knew what all. *Good old Shadow, where are ya, boy?*

She took a quick look around while still holding Aaron at her hip. At least now he'd lifted his head and managed to quell his sniffles. He looked up into the night sky.

"Look at the big moon," he said in awe.

"Yeah. Thank God for that," Kellen concurred, half sighing. The mostly full moon had risen higher and made it up over the mountains to help light their path better. The best break they'd had so far.

"They said in Sunday School it was Jesus who made the moon. They said too He made it all, the stars and everything. How'd he do all that, Kellen?"

"I don't know, kid. He's God, I guess. You know . . . God can do anything. At least the Bible says so." Kellen had looked away to roll her eyes while saying all that. She wasn't sure she believed in God so much right now.

"Jesus loves me this I know . . . Cuz the Bible tells me so," the little boy sang, his voice understandably a little shaky. "I can't member the rest. They taught us in Bible school that much though."

Kellen just held the boy a little longer, remembering that song too, but not really feeling like singing either at the moment. "Come on," she finally said and put him down. "We'll take a rest if we find a good spot . . . a safe spot . . . over this here next rise. Or if we find Shadow we can rest on him and let him do the walkin'." She managed a small laugh then, trying to keep it light for Aaron.

They started up the trail again. It still ran easy, easy to see and easy to hike, a couple feet wide and winding up and down through the gently rising and falling, mountainous terrain.

"What's a rise?" Aaron asked after thinking about it for a minute.

"Up there. See how the trail leads up from here a ways then cuts in between those real big rocks and then you can't see it anymore?"

"Yeah."

"Well, that's a rise."

"Oh . . . okay."

On the other side of that rise, as the two shortly found out, the trail started down a gentle decline, winding its way into a sudden valley filled like a bowl with a couple acres of how the land used to look before the earthquake had mountainized everything. Southern California countryside spread before them, sporadically décorated by boulder outcroppings coming up through wild grass with thick brush or low trees sprouting up here and there as well. The colors were muted, of course, in the moonlight, but all of it easily discernable.

Better yet was what Kellen then heard as she started scouting out a good spot for them to rest.

"Shadow," she said quietly and in reflex, having heard the horse's strong and deep neigh. She looked too, quickly and in the same direction and could see there, down to the left in the valley below, just before a large group of boulders and not far from what appeared to be a small lake or pond, the big horse, dark like the night sky and silhouetted against the lighter, surrounding terrain.

But something else was going on down there too. Shadow kept neighing, and looking harder Kellen could just make out other forms moving around the big horse.

"Come on," she ordered at the boy and towed him in behind her as she started quickly down the trail toward the action.

After just a bit she could tell what was going on, and it wasn't good. There were zombies. Four, no five of them, and all of them going after Shadow, and oh—

Good shot, boy, Kellen mentally cheered. Shadow had reared up on his hind legs and caved in the nearest zombie's head with a quick flick of his right forearm and hoof. Then as the now entirely dead attacker fell, the big horse burst through the bunch but held up not far off and turned back.

Why didn't he just run off? Kellen asked herself, and then saw her answer. One of the zombies had turned back to what Shadow was staying and fighting for. Another horse was lying nearby, luckily, gratefully and most likely dead. The smaller horse lay on its side and was still. Its body looked opened and bleeding with even muscle and bone exposed in more than one area of its anatomy.

"Oh God," Kellen uttered and quickly brought her rifle around. She was what . . . thirty . . . maybe forty yards away? She could make that shot.

Still walking toward them, she let fly and cocked in another. At least she had gotten one of the zombie's attention she could see, but it looked like her shot had hit him in the neck. A fresh spurt of blood shot out from there as the zombie turned her way.

"That's it. Step right up," she yelled.

She squeezed off a second shot and watched the same zombie go down again, this time for good. Two down—one for her, one for Shadow—and three to go.

She quickly slung the gun back around behind her and grabbed up the boy. She rapidly scanned about for a good spot, and then hurried over to a large but low-topped boulder about the size and height of an old sedan. She took the boy over and set him standing atop it. "Stay near the middle. I don't think those creepy things can climb too well."

"Don't go . . ." Aaron whined.

"You'll be okay. Just stay in the middle. I gotta go get Shadow."

As she started off, Kellen scanned the surroundings of Aaron's boulder crib. It should do. It really would be difficult for any of those zombies to get on top of it. Especially since there were no smaller stepping stones nearby. And plus too, Aaron was stuck there as well. He couldn't climb down off the five to six foot tall boulder. It'd do for now. She didn't have time for anything better anyway.

Heading back down, she could see that now the three remaining zombies had turned again to the dead horse. Shadow was having none of that though and galloped hard through the group. The already wobbly creatures scattered and fell like bowling pins.

"Shadow," Kellen called out, then remembering it, whistled his call, a short, high-pitched tone followed by a longer, low one. The horse turned her way. Unfortunately, so did the zombies, and even more unfortunate, they were only about twenty yards away now.

The closest one, as it was heading right for her, should have been an easy shot. But their damn, uncoordinated walking style had its head bobbing up and down, up and down. Then she realized though that she just had to time it. Down it would dip, and then bob back up. *Down . . . then—*

She squeezed off her shot.

Yes.

Now there were just two left. But they were too close too. Kellen retreated quickly, running in fact over to the horse. Shadow reared up and neighed wildly.

"Whoa . . . whoa," Kellen tried, approaching from the side as she knew she should, all the while talking too, saying the things she always did to the horse.

Shadow calmed, seeming to recognize her and her words. He turned towards her, pawed twice at the ground and nosed at her the way he always did when she approached.

Getting lost in the moment, Kellen lovingly came closer and reached around under his muzzle, stroked the far side of it and coaxed him her way even closer. Looking into his eyes then, she could see the sudden widening and also in the big blackness there the reflection of the two dead killers coming up right behind her.

She gasped and turned quickly and managed a couple steps, but then fell backward. On her butt and her back she kept scooting away, but they were almost standing over her now. They were—

For the next several weeks, and maybe even for the rest of her life Kellen would replay the moment, or two moments, actually, that then occurred. But she would never be able to slow it down enough to see the amazingly precise kicks that the big black horse had delivered, one right after the other. The first of which knocked one of the zombie's heads clean off like a football from a kicking tee.

Then, before that one's body hit the ground, the next invisible flash of black leg sent the final attacker pin wheeling several yards away, where he then lay still, obviously suffering a killing blow to the head as well.

Kellen had to tell herself to breathe, and then she did. Shadow had come around behind her and amazingly enough was standing almost silently, snorting now and again, but apparently quite relaxed, a veteran warhorse already somehow. They both grew suddenly alert, though, as the sound of little Aaron crying his lungs out came down through the valley.

"Come on, Shadow," Kellen called out, already running up for the boy. The horse, knowing little Aaron's voice too, followed quickly behind at a gallop.

Aaron was only scared, though. There were no new attackers. Kellen coaxed him over to the edge of the boulder and lifted the little boy down. The three returned along the trail into the valley, not stopping until they reached where the fallen horse lay.

At first, Kellen wondered *which, or whose, horse it might be?* It was hard to tell. She looked like a sorrel mare, *poor thing*, with its mostly white tail and mane mostly red now. *Was it Gypsy?* Gypsy was such a sweet horse; she sure hoped it wasn't her.

Then she saw the saddle. Which meant of course it wasn't Gypsy after all. It couldn't be. It couldn't be any of their horses. Their horses were all stabled for the night when the quake hit. The hands had all gone home too. So where had this horse come from?

Oh well. That didn't matter, Kellen knew. But the saddle . . . that mattered. And it looked like a big saddle too. Plenty of room for both her and Aaron and big enough to fit Shadow. And yes, she could see them too. *Saddle bags*. But they would need cleaning, if she got the chance. And getting all the gear off the poor thing would be quite a job too. But she knew she could do it. *Awesome*.

Aaron was already busy gathering up the water bottles that had been scattered about, no doubt strewn that way as Shadow commenced battle. The boy even seemed to be having fun with his new task.

"Here's one. And here's one. And oh . . . here's another one," he happily narrated while he worked.

"Good job, kiddo," Kellen cheered. She had to admit, the boy was a pretty amazing little guy at times. Kids . . .

Her mood quickly hardened, though, as she then turned to commence with her much grimmer task. She worked quickly, being very adept with horse tack and gear. Frequently she had helped the stable workers after school and on the weekends too. She loved working with the horses.

But this was something else. Her face was locked in a grimace while she worked and her concentration was almost super human, forced that way by the gory surroundings. From the displayed entrails of the dead horse she was working on to the decapitated zombie just on the periphery of her vision, it was everywhere. She tried not to look at it, but then accidentally and-

Gross!

As she continued to work, however, as step one easily lead to step two, then three, four, five and six, then things started falling into place. She could feel a strange sense of victory lifting her spirits. Mostly because now she knew they were going to make it. She just knew it. *Somehow. Somehow they were going to make it.*

How could they fail after all, now that they had good, strong tack carrying them on Shadow the zombie killer and her the .22 caliber crack shot and Aaron the wonder boy with Spaceman Spike.

She had a chuckle over all that, then grimaced again. A piece of horse guts was clinging to a strand of her hair. She fished it out and flung it away.

CHAPTER XXII

WHAT ARE YOU GONNA DO?

"Thank God we are getting the heck outta here," Ivy half-said and half-sighed, waiting on the basement stairs, all packed up. It was cute too, because just behind her was little Joannie looking like a miniaturized version of her mother, all packed up as well, and her also with a similar look of determined exasperation. Since her hands were full, with a short puff of air the little girl blew a wayward strand of hair away from her slightly sweaty forehead. It had been itchingly bothering her.

Other than full hands, packed up for the women entailed each of them handling a piece of luggage: Joannie with the overnighter and Ivy with the weekender from the old set Udo had also stashed away down in the basement. Each of them also sported backpacks filled to bursting. Add to that the .22 rifles—luckily a junior version for Joannie which Udo had even taken her out to shoot before, adult size for Ivy—and the ladies hands certainly were, as mentioned, full.

But at least Joannie's backpack was of the smaller variety, though still she bowed ever so slightly under its bulk already slung across her back. Ivy, being the wiser and less energetic of the two, sat on the stairs, her larger and even bulkier backpack resting its weight on the stair step directly above the one she sat upon.

Meanwhile, Jason and Griner were at the top of the stairs checking their weapons. They'd been working in shifts from that same spot for the past couple days,, burrowing holes in the wooden, hatch-style door with the big hunting knife Udo had also very fortuitously left for them in the basement.

Then, once the holes were large enough, the metal pole that had been used to support the tarpaulin walls of their corner commode was used to push up at the debris just above and blocking the hatch closed.

It had taken a lot of work, a lot of holes, and a lot of careful placement and angling of the pole. Along with that a lot of muscle had been used pushing up on the pole. But after all that, and with both Jason and Griner able to do said pushing at the same time when needed, soon they'd gotten most of the heavier debris pushed up and aside. The two men were then able to shove the hatch all the way open. As of yet, however, they hadn't ventured out.

"All right. Now remember," Griner instructed down at the ladies as he got ready to fling the hatch open again, this time for their big journey. They had just finished their meeting on the whole topic but the old con just wanted to make sure. "You guys wait here while we first scout out the house . . . or what's left of it . . . then scout out the rest of the area too . . . and then we'll come back for ya . . . okay?"

"Rodger dodger," Ivy cracked and rolled her eyes.

"Mom, get serious, okay?" Jason tried.

"Well . . . we haven't seen any of those things in almost a week."

"I hope they've all eaten each other," Joannie said with feeling. "But if not, I know how to use this thing!" She held her little .22 up, and everyone laughed, even her eventually.

"We're all gonna give it too 'em, honey," Griner growled down. "But only if we have to. If we can't hide or get away, like we discussed."

"Oh yes . . . I know. Only if we have to. And aim for the head," Joannie enthusiastically recited, and brought her little gun up as if practicing just that.

"Joannie Henkman, zombie hunter," Jason put in and chuckled. Joannie wanted to sass back, but her mother stopped her.

"Okay, you two." She looked hard at each of them, then to Griner. "Any day now," she added and waved her hand like a whisk broom at them.

And even though it was night, not day, because they'd decided to only travel at night if possible, the men took Ivy's sarcastic remark and gesture as their cue and emerged from their basement shelter.

Before going any further and also as already discussed in their meeting too, Jason slowly and quietly lowered the basement hatch closed. Then, both he and Griner carefully placed enough debris back onto it to hide it. Griner had also already scouted the immediate vicinity and found it clear.

He'd also noted, as Jason soon would too as they continued, that at least the Henkman residence had *half* survived the quake. Literally half, because like some sort of cosmic joke the two-story home had practically been sheered in half, or appeared to have been at least. From the looks of it too, the other half, or possibly even two-thirds, had collapsed. But at least some of it had survived, including one of the upstairs bedrooms along with the stairway leading up to it.

The stairs were still amazingly sturdy as well, and the two soon came to the second story landing safely. The same one in fact that Ivy had come to that fateful night when the police had surrounded the home and the quake had then buried them in the basement.

This time, however, it was Jason and Griner who took turns looking out the medium sized window, pushing aside its frayed curtain. Amazingly it still hung intact.

"Looks real quiet," Griner said, his voice little more than a whisper. They'd agreed to just whisper once outside the basement. That is, until they could tell for sure it was safe. The ex-con was also careful as he passed the binoculars quietly over to Jason, with the added touch of signaling the kid to remember to keep quiet. He raised his index finger vertically across the middle of his lips. Griner was learning that with both kids. You had to repeat the important things, twice to Jason and three times to Joannie.

While Jason took his look at the neighborhood, helped by the moon in an almost full state, Griner turned back. Though he'd noticed it before, the startling view out the back of their adhoc lookout still shocked him. It was almost like all of a sudden he was flying. From this vantage point there was nothing but air after just a few more feet of flooring.

Weirder yet was how the air after that was so dark and thick. Smoke hung in it, most likely from the frequent structure fires he could see too scattered here and there, a mile or more away though, thank God. They burned sporadically throughoutSandy Point Beach, the town, or what remained. Low hills now erupted there too, not too high though, it luckily looked like as well.

"Used to be I could see the ocean from my bedroom window," Jason said through a sigh as he turned around now too. "Which was right over there!" He pointed emphatically directly across from them where only the new hillsides were in view now.

"Yeah, well . . . hopefully the ocean's still there. Behind them hills," Griner growled.

'Four point seven miles," Jason said as if he'd just read it out of a book. "That's how far we are, or were, from the ocean . . . before . . ."

"Well. That's plenty of room to put a hill on. Then slope it right down to the shining sea. And that's the way were headed anyway. You can move a mountain, but an ocean, that's a bit more difficult, I'll bet."

"Hey yeah . . ." Jason enthused a little too much and Griner shushed him.

"Come on," he then whispered hard at the young man. "Let's go get the ladies. Looks safe enough to me. At least to start with."

"Yeah. I don't see any of them creepy things." Now Jason was scanning the wasteland side of things too. He quickly brought the binoculars down though, and looked a little angry. "That sucks though man . . . I had a full baggy of good weed I'd just bought stashed in my dresser. Now look . . . gone." The young man held out his hand like one of the models on, "The Price is Right."

"Just as well. You get stoned now you'll wake up half eaten."

"Munchies for some monster."

Griner ended Jason's reverie. "Let's go." He got up and started back down the stairs.

"Yeah but," Jason started to whine some more but knew not to push it and fell in quickly behind Griner. He was planning on sticking close to the old man from here on out.

"Well, Geronimo, is the coast clear?" Ivy greeted them with as they came back down through the hatch.

"Geronimo?" Griner had to question, ducking in.

"Wasn't he that guy who could see a long ways? The lookout guy," Ivy tried to explain her joke with.

"What?"

"Can't see the ocean at all anymore," Jason put in, crestfallen.

"It's just a saying," she told her son. "But really, you can't?"

"That earthquake really did a number. There are new hills and mountains all over, even between here and the ocean," Griner had to tell her.

"But we have to make it to the beach," Joannie whined. "My dream!"

The little girl had dreamed that they could make it to safety by boat to an island paradise. And whether the others believed her dream or not, they'd all agreed that the beach and hopefully a boat was probably their best chance.

"Don't worry, honey. The oceans gotta still be there," Ivy consoled her child. "We'll just have to climb to get to it."

"Geronimo?" Griner questioned again.

"I don't know, Clay," she somewhat apologized to her new man then turned and took his hand too. "You know me. Just being a wise-acre."

"Clay?" Jason couldn't help but crack wise with himself. They'd all found out that was Griner's first name just recently, which Jason didn't mind, but he just *had* to give his mom a hard time because she was calling him that. *And holding his hand!* They were getting a little too friendly these days for his tastes.

Griner took a moment to squeeze her hand back, look her in the eyes, wink, and then give her the hand back. "That's all right, Miss Ivy," he cracked back at her, keeping it light, noticing that Jason was a little perturbed.

They'd talked about this the other night when they'd found a moment alone and things had gotten pretty heated. Griner hadn't kissed anybody like that in a long time, and neither had she. But then they also decided to cool it off for now. Keep it light. If they could survive and settle someplace new . . . well, maybe then. But for now to get romantically involved would be crazy . . . probably distracting . . . and possibly fatal. But still she liked to think of him as her man.

So the man then got back to business. "Everybody ready? Locked and loaded?"

"Yep."

"Uh huh," the two women answered, which were really the only ones he'd been questioning. He'd gone over everything with Jason already three times. The boy had his 9 mm and the flashlight in his pocket that if needed he would power on and hold crossed under his right in the classic law enforcement position, which Griner had drilled him on, which, as much as the wannabe criminal hated doing anything like a cop does, but he knew it was best for now.

So off they went, the Henkman family reformed, creeping out at least somewhat prepared into the apocalyptic night, still alive at least, which was more than most of the rest of the Human Race could say these days.

High and low, high and low, he looked and looked, looked and looked. And since even some of the fauna had survived, he looked through their eyes too. He could do that, occupy a consciousness and see things just as it did, even with animals.

Just like with his ever faithful ravens, so bold and big. Of course they had survived, taking to wing with the first precursor vibrations and then safely aloft to watch it all shake, shift and reform beneath them. Then all of it was over in a highly tumultuous minute or two and afterwards sooner or later plenty of dead flesh to feast on and keep going. Just keep going, their consciousness always seemed to be screaming.

He loved that, Satan did, the blood thirsty and heartless emergency to survive always on an animal's mind. If only that bothersome God fellow just hadn't created the humans as well.

My, what big eyes you have, he made himself think of then to lighten the mood. All work and no play and all that, and because too through the raven's eyes the view really was quite big as they flew and flew, and as mentioned, looked high and low, high and low.

Seven more souls, seven more souls, or eight were even better. You can never have too much fuel. But seven would do in a pinch. Get him and his minions very, very far away, far away from this world and its God.

And sure, God could get to the other worlds too most likely, but would he bother? And besides, He always seemed to admire initiative. So maybe He would let his once upon a time good servant go and leave him be. *Please just finally leave me be. Was that too much to ask?*

Oh well. It was worth a shot. He loved that saying the humans had. Worth a shot. Take your best shot. And he, the arch enemy would, as usual, take his best shot. He loved the shooting, the action. He loved the humans too, loved to hate them and make them suffer before destroying them, that is. But now there were hardly any left, no one left to play with. *So why not leave for that reason too?*

Either way it was a done deal, or hopefully would be. He was ready. His ship was ready. Just seven more souls . . . seven more souls . . .

The dark lord was doing all this ruminating while watching the many monitors he had in a control room not all that dissimilar to the one Jesus had entertained Udo in front of not so long ago. It just wasn't quite as relaxing or plush or lowly lighted as the Lord's had been. There was no sofa, just him in his big desk chair on wheels before his own big bank of TV screens.

He pushed back from it all then, looking for the moment like a fairly normal humanoid, having again assumed the dashing form he'd taken for his friends, the designer and the technician. The Devil as playboy, as it were. Although then as he turned, for a moment at least, one had to shockingly notice the dozens of eyeballs that filled his face. And weirder yet, was how each mucoid orb was supported and or suspended on thin tendrils that had allowed, during his more intense observational duties, to spread his visual capabilities. The individual and oh-so-many eyes could then extend snake-like across and all the way down the long wall of TV screens, multiplying somehow as they went, and as mentioned, looking and looking, looking and looking.

Enough of that for now, though. He'd seen enough to know that there were at least that many souls still out there. And his teams were, 'on it,' as the humans also liked to say. That was too bad about what happened with those two and their helicopter. That *damn* perfect creature the Lord had created. He was obviously protected. No matter what he did, he couldn't catch or kill that bastard. Even the zombie disease—the greatest one he'd created yet—even that hadn't stopped him.

But more than that, now the perfect being was killing off his zombies as well, and a little too effectively, the dark one fumed. And then on top of that, sending their souls up to old smarty-pants . . . the ultimate insult.

He wanted to explode.

So not even that had worked out all that well. How many souls had that cost him? God always had to get His fingers in the pie, steal some of his thunder, in this case, steal some of his souls he'd worked so hard to steal.

Even Satan had to laugh at the irony of that one though then. But he would still get his. He'd still get his.

And then he'd be off and away from here, him and his servants and their beautiful ship. *His* beautiful ship, he sweetly thought of the teardrop shaped craft as he ran a clawed hand along its sleek skin.

It was fairly large, five stories tall and about fifty yards long, fitting almost perfectly in this one of the many mountains he'd made, this one constructed above the underground hangar of the air force base where the humans had made the ship for him.

He'd known about the secret hangar and the ship they were building in it from before, when in the spirit he had roamed here so often, playing with the minds of many of the military personnel and the scientists, the engineers stationed in its surrounding installation, the Air Force Base, as the humans called them.

The name of the base escaped him at the moment, and he never really cared anyway. The humans had quite a penchant for naming their cities and their companies, their streets and their just about everything else—in this case their military installations—for people and ideas that they wanted memorialized. It was as if by doing so they might somehow stave off the second death that was coming for all of it, and them, sooner or later anyway, the death that also brought the never remembering of it all too. Memorialized . . . that was such a meaningless word.

So *Air Force Base Whoever* was how he thought of it, and probably the whoever being someone he had known before they had named the airbase after him, someone who had known a lot about air travel and all the latest equipment they had developed to do it with, including *his* ship, this ship they had built for him.

He had brought them all here anyway, their best scientists, their best engineers, and the alien technology for interstellar travel already here in the crashed ship the extraterrestrials had flown here. He just needed to tweak it a little, adapt it for the soul drive so now it could really go places.

But all of it, the hangar and the ship, was somewhat damaged in the quake. So it was restored, yes restored, and definitely ready to go now.

Maybe in another century or two—if they'd been allowed to have them, these secrets he knew—the humans might have caught up to him. Maybe by then they would have come up with something rudimentarily similar, which maybe too was another good reason for the Lord to do what he did. He had noticed how the almighty had always kept the humans on a short leash like he had. The Moon . . . and then some probes to Mars. Seriously! No wonder they had never gotten anywhere. He, the capitol H He, He must not have wanted them to.

Which of course was one of the first realizations that made him, the small h him, the perpetual enemy, Lucifer to his army of the other fallen, think that maybe there was a way out somewhere out there. Since He didn't want his precious children getting too far out there and possibly running away. Was that why?

Maybe somewhere out in space, the crystalline mind of the Father of Lies further theorized, probably at the very edge of it all, maybe out there . . . maybe there's a place where, or a way to . . . escape it all? To escape *Him*?

Soon enough he would be finding out. Soon enough he was going to take his shot. Just seven more souls . . . seven more souls.

Just for such a time as this, the master had said, such a time when the surviving humans were few and far between. For now they would have to go without the human flesh while they hunted the few that remained, which of course made them hunt all the harder. High and low . . . high and low, Mike the chubby zombie and the many hunted high and low.

Last time in the mountain, the master had some cows and sheep and some big pigs strung up there and though the feast was not quite as fun, they were still very hungry and the fresh, raw meat filled them up. But it wasn't like eating a human. That was especially good for some reason. So the hunt continued harder than ever.

And now too the master's greatest warriors lead them on their hunts. They couldn't touch the humans, not directly. That was forbidden, the master had told Mike, because he was wondering about that. Then, sometimes you are too smart for your own good, the master added, and Mike got the hint. He stopped wondering altogether, at least around the master.

Another thing he had figured out was how those of his kind that still remained were the smartest ones, the survivors. It was sad when his friends had died that time on the beach, but now he knew why. And he knew why he was still here. He was smarter than them.

After that assignment on the pier, he'd dropped down through that hole and the silver disc had carried him back to the mountain. Then he was given a rest period. He slept and slept in one of the areas filled with all the mattresses there in the mountain too. Then he went back to work and the big warrior had led them out to that place in the big park where the people with the flying machine were. That was another word he couldn't think of. What they called those flying things. He could almost think of it but . . . oh well.

But then when things started going bad, unlike the others, because he was smart, he hid in the tall grass. While the crazy statue man went around killing everyone again, killing all the others like him—he laid in hiding.

Then the living humans got away in their flying machine and while he still watched—this time because he wanted to, not because the master told him to—the statue man did his thing again with all the heads that made the rainbow go up into the sky.

Mike had still waited in hiding then because the statue man was still there. And he seemed to notice—just like Mike had—that while all the other heads had disintegrated in what looked like pure energy going up into the rainbow, the head of the master's great warrior the statue man had also brought over was still there.

It was different then though, after the rainbow left. The statue man picked it up and looked at it inside and out, all of which Mike could see well because his spot in the tall grass was not far from the outer reaches of the asphalt. Where the rainbow had come.

But the warrior's head was silvery in color now, silvery black, and evidently hardened too. The statue man knocked on it like it was a hollowed out shell, which it was. And then the weirdest thing of all was when next the muscular creature slipped the skull right over his own head like a helmet!

And it must have fit him. It must have let him see out from the thing even too. In the next moment, after looking around with the thing on now, the statue man started walking very purposefully toward him, toward Mike still hiding in the tall grass.

So of course Mike was very scared then and got right up to hopefully get away. Not that it would have helped him at all. He knew what the statue man could do.

All of the sudden, there he was, coming down from above like he had jumped or even flown just the short distance to catch up to Mike and now was dropping down right in front of him.

At first Mike just wanted to say—although he couldn't—but he *wanted* to say *what a cool mask that warrior's head had turned into,* because really it had. It looked pretty much like it had as one of the warriors except silvery now and you could tell the eyes were just solid shells too but see through and all black.

Then the statue man spoke, and Mike could hear his words coming out through the mask's mouth, which had frozen in a pained smile with the warrior's big teeth and fangs showing through too. But before speaking, the statue man had grabbed Mike up hard under his shoulders.

"You tell your master," Mike heard him say, and his words sounded very angry. "You tell him if he hurts my family. I will keeel him!" The last part of which Mike heard as he was falling away, including the crazy laugh the statue man added on at the end, because after having his say, the statue man had then thrown Mike back, way back, like maybe a mile it felt to him, and then he landed hard but then luckily in more of the tall grass and the soft soil beneath the big field of it all.

Then he'd picked himself up again and started back to the mountain. After a long hike and this time all alone, he made it to one of the streams and a silver disc. He rode it back and made his way very tiredly to one of the mattresses for rest. Honestly, he hadn't even considered passing along the statue man's message to his master. *Are you kidding me?*

CHAPTER XXIII

KEEP PUSHING

Kellen kept pushing on, riding most the night and then into the first few, coolest hours of the morning. They had to get there, to the coast. She'd had that same dream three nights in a row, the one with Jack and Irene on their cruise ship, then the tsunami. Get to the island. Get to the island. Well . . . hopefully the island was off the west coast, which it probably was. If the dream meant anything.

Yeah . . . if the dream meant anything. But having it three nights in a row like that, didn't it have to mean something? And even if it didn't, where else could they go? So to the coast, which Kellen knew was west of course. Or that-away, confirmed by both the setting sun and the tiny compass embedded in Spaceman Spike's starship.

Kellen had heard too of an Island out there called Catalina. *Was that it? Or were there other ones too?* She wished she had been more into geography in school, but truth to tell, she hated it. But still anyway, that really was probably their only shot.

"Hey, kiddo. Look at that big patch of shade up ahead!" Kellen tried to put some enthusiasm in her words, but at this point it wasn't easy. They'd ridden all night again, and now it was eight or nine in the morning. And even with the added enthusiasm, the boy hadn't looked up anyway; he was asleep in the saddle, literally.

Kellen was almost ready to join him but unlike little Aaron, no one was holding her up with a big arm across her midsection. If she dozed off they'd both wake up when they fell out of the saddle and landed on their heads. *Nahhh.* Better idea: *get into that grassy, shady spot up ahead, break out the bedrolls and sleep as long as the daylight let them.*

Supplies were still okay. Plenty of water bottles were left along with a couple of boxes of power bars. And they'd even had to leave half the apples they'd gotten from that one tree. Still lots of those were left. A little sour, but they were edible.

So they just took some rest for now. They'd earned it after all. They'd really covered some ground so far. In three days, she was thinking, and maybe hoping too,maybe they'd almost made it there. Although she couldn't smell any ocean yet. They'd only had about eighty to ninety miles to go after all. But that was freeway miles from when they'd gone on vacation to Sandy Pants Beach back years ago. That was what they called it, joking around, of course.

"Every time I go there, that's what I get. Sand in my pants," Mr. Andrews would say and they'd all laugh, no matter how many times they'd heard it. And then Aaron would goof around saying it over and over again, "Sandy Pants, Sandy Pants, Sandy Pants."

Kellen had to smile remembering all that, but then had to force back tears seeing Jack and Irene in her mind again too. Luckily, she had plenty to do, getting herself and Aaron down off of Shadow in one piece, getting out the blankets, setting up a new little campsite for them.

She tucked the boy into his little bedroll bed. He hadn't stirred but just a little when she first laid him all the way down. "Night night, Mommy," he said, his words slurred with sleep. Kellen just smiled and made sure his head was squared away on the little extra bit of folded blanket that was his pillow.

She had a power bar for herself then, some swigs of water, got some apples and with her pocket knife quartered them and fed them to Shadow. "That's a boy, our big strong Shadow. You're a lifesaver, boy. You know that? Yes you do . . . yesss . . ."

She tied him up to the thick, half trunk that was the first branching off of the tree giving them their shade. It was nice too that thick tufts of wild grass, some dry, some green surrounded the trunk's base. Shadow right away started rooting around in there for dessert. He'd had a good long draw in a creek they'd crossed a few miles back and would be fine on that end for now Kellen knew.

One last thing then: every time they bedded down she'd try to find some high ground to scout out as much of the surrounding terrain as she could. Sure Shadow always stood guard, sleeping but also stirring then with the scent of anything . . . well . . . pungent in the area. And one thing zombies were was pungent. But then too, just to help herself sleep, she always took a look.

Which this time entailed hiking up a couple hundred foot slope off to the right of the little valley their trail had lead them down into. It quickly turned into a hill, one of many that soon after gave way to mountains.

Atop the hill she slipped her rifle from her shoulder and held it at her hip, right hand through the lever. Not much sign of anything . . . *but hey . . . wow . . .* she'd never seen a mountain like that before. Although it almost wasn't big enough to be a real mountain. The crazy thing was actually closer to the size of that Matterhorn one they had at Disneyland. And it kind of just sat out in the middle all by itself, like it'd been placed there. *And what? It looked like it was made out of . . . metal.*

Oh well. They'd try and steer clear of that, that was for sure. Just in case. It looked like the trail headed away from it anyway. But just when you think you've seen it all . . .

Then she saw something else that she hadn't seen for a while and brought the gun up. She sighted on first the one, and then the other. They'd landed in the top branches of the shade tree they were camping out under.

A pair of ravens. Or crows as they called them on the ranch. She didn't shoot either one though. She didn't want to wake the boy after all, and she was also sure as heck she wasn't hard up enough to eat a damn crow.

They took off pretty soon anyway as she started back down. She was tired as all get out and couldn't wait to lie down and probably sleep the whole day away. *Yeah . . . that sounded pretty good.*

"It's not here! The Island! It should be pretty close by now, but look!" Janet offered the binocs to John, but he declined their aid.

Instead, he scanned around *au naturel* as best he could, at the same time taking the chopper in a panoramic, sweeping circle. "Are you sure this is where it should be?"

"Pretty much. We headed out straight due west from that point on the coast we found on the map. At least the earthquake couldn't have made a new point. Not one that big. Ya think?" Her question being mostly rhetorical as it was, the lady doctor didn't wait for John's opinion. Instead she just kept busily working with the map, ruler and compass, and did some more figuring. Then she intently eyed the fuel gauge. "We've also used almost half a tank. Maybe we should head back."

"I think I see something. Due south. Was just a speck at first, but it's getting bigger already. I'll keep heading for it. If it's nothing we'll cut in for the coast from there. Like your map shows, as we head that way we're already getting closer to the coast. And we had a seven knot headwind all the way out. Believe me, we'll be fine."

Janet scanned her map again. "Okay. That could be one of these here." She looked down then. Her knuckles showed white on the hand that tightly gripped the ruler. She looked over at John, at first caught off guard by how handsome he looked in his ray bans and the jumpsuit under his dark Hispanic features. At least she'd gotten that done before the end. Finally fallen in love . . . err well . . . infatuation maybe, she wasn't sure . . . but at least that . . . before—

She made herself stop thinking about that though, the bad that could happen, without realizing that the question she had to ask was all about that too. But she had to ask it. "What then, honey?" She put a hand on his leg too. It seemed the natural thing to do seated right next to each other like they were in the pilot and co-pilot seats of the helicopter. Behind them a small passenger area opened up, partially taken up with supplies.

He put his hand on hers. He liked to hear her call him honey, so he returned the favor. "We'll keep looking then, hon. we'll keep looking as long as we can. I'm hoping to find some more survivors, maybe a colony or something, anything but zombies. Right about now I'll just settle for some fuel. Another one of the pilots told me that there were naval installations out here on a couple of these islands. If they haven't disappeared too, they might have some . . ."

His last sentence had gotten drawn out like that because suddenly his attention was taken away from word formation to analyze what he was looking at. It was definitely an island, and from the looks of it with a whole lot of something on it. He glanced over at Janet, seeing that he didn't have to tell her to take a look with the binoculars.

"I'm seeing buildings, big metal gray and brown ones . . . and . . . and there's a big flag . . . a U.S. flag!"

"Okay," John said, at first a little excited but then coming back down as he thought of something. "I just hope it hasn't become the United States of Zombies. Or in this case a zombie navy. That sounds like a navy base."

Officer John allowed himself a small laugh after that, but she didn't. Then the two rode silent, grim faced, their hands tightly intertwined until John had to get his back to start a low sweep of the island installation. Janet got the binoculars ready too, and they headed in.

The skiff carrying Rebecca, Derrick and Justin sat wedged safely and slightly sideways, but at least all the way out of the water on a sand bar. Above and all around it was a nice day, blue and clear and almost perfect in temperature. There was a little bit of humidity in the air, though. Clouds were backing up for some reason not too far off behind the shipwrecked trio. Just beyond the skiff, after a few hundred feet of startling blue water that stretched out flatly, undulating and rippling with currents and tides and small waves, a very large island mounded up.

At first the majestic creation sported only the gradual incline of spotless sandy beach that stretched out as far as the eye could see to both the left and the right. But then the real beauty started as great banks of trees, tropical in nature and verdantly thick, looking like a leafy, green curtain, unsuccessfully hid the rolling hillsides behind it.

Even more impressive were the high and rocky mountains rising up behind that, great stone foreheads over craggy eyes that stared back out to the ocean and beyond. For the *piece du resistance,* waterfalls big and small sliced nicely through and over the foreheads, their combined landings on the rocks below and in lake after lake a roaring and wet symphony, just enough background sound behind it all. *God's* greatest designer had no doubt been at work on this one.

Inside the skiff, the three thirty-something's seemingly slept, which was miraculous enough, considering what they had been through, virtually lost at sea for almost a week with no food and just one short storm's worth of water.

But then here came another one, another storm. The one just mentioned as clouding up that now had become more defined and condensed in shape while darkening too.

After another short span of time, while traveling right over them, the little but powerful bank of clouds dumped its liquid contents in a steady, shower-like stream with mechanical precision, filling the skiff with several new inches of rain water.

It was almost as if somewhere in the middle of the confined yet tumultuous meteorological formation a water angel rode, manning a special spigot in assistance to the rescue of the three boat bound survivors. But one who then must have flown fast and far away unnoticeably as within moments the formation entirely evaporated and traces of both it and any possible inhabitants were nowhere to be seen.

Not that anyone was watching. Least of all the three aforementioned survivors who just then started coming to, Rebecca jolting bolt upright while Derrick and Justin more groggily rejoined the land of the living. Derrick moaned and in a prehensile but somewhat spasmodic fashion made the first movements his hand had been able to in several days. He weakly gripped for something not there as if looking for some type of handhold.

"Derrick . . . Derrick," Rebecca excitedly called out and scooted over to cradle the young black man's head while his eyes batted to life. She had to leave that lovely task, however, noticing that Justin was blowing bubbles in the puddle filling the lowest sections of the hull. "Oh my—"

She rolled Justin over, then got up over him and tugged him into a seated position. He gasped to life.

"Where . . . where?" came from Derrick as he lifted his own head this time.

"Honey," Rebecca almost shouted with somewhat forced happiness as she came back over. "Are you okay, babe?" She squatted next to him, lightly rubbing his now extra dark and lean shoulder. Lying out in a small boat for six days without food will do that to a person. He still had some muscles left there though too, and they balled and jumped tight under his skin as he rose up on his elbows.

"Are we back together," he said over his shoulder at her, looking genuinely confused. "I . . . I . . ."

"Oh. You don't remember?" She looked into his eyes and could tell that was the case. But she didn't exactly want to enlighten him. He had dumped her just before the quake hit. As men sometimes do in such a case, he had taken her to an expensive seaside eatery for said dumping. Then right after he dumped her, the quake dumped them both.

"I remember an earthquake . . . a really big one . . . we were at lunch . . . at the Shores . . . then sand was everywhere . . . digging up and up and finally out . . . then the zombies . . . I mean, real zombies. But that had to be a dream . . . a nightmare. Wasn't it?"

Rebecca looked hard to the side. Tears tried to come. She was torn. She had loved . . . and still loved him. But he—

She thought about turning, turning and telling him, and was about to when the overwhelming beauty all around her caught her eye.

The water is sooooo blue and clear.

And just look at that island!

And the . . . the weather was perfect!

Then she heard the voice. "A new beginning . . . a new beginning . . ." Or was it just the wind?

"Maybe that's what it all was, honey. Just a nightmare." She took his hand in both of hers. "Or maybe we can just think of it all that way. Maybe—"

"I don't remember much either," Justin weakly let out. "Or yeah . . . I remember being at a party on the beach then all the sand gave way beneath me . . . digging out too . . . then you guys and your boat . . . yeah, this boat . . . yeah." He grabbed hard at the side and lifted himself up. "Zombies though? Nahhh," the muscularly built, long brown haired surfer type scoffed and with a weave to his otherwise smooth movements all but lunged in a dive off the edge of the sand bar then came up quickly in the waist high surf.

He flipped his hair back, whipping an arc of water far and back and high behind him too. The pearlescent drops caught the light like diamonds before returning home with a splash.

"Ah yeah," Justin cheered through a wide smile. "Hey. Ya think they got a surf shop here? You guys bring any coin? Maybe we won't need any. I kinda get that feeling!" He kept on, talking to himself mostly as he headed off for the island, striding long through the water that very gradually was getting shallower and shallower. He looked from side to side. "Not much surf though . . ."

"Okay, honey, up and at 'em," Rebecca told Derrick as she helped him to his feet. Of the three he was the shakiest. "Come on, watch your step. Up and over."

The once-upon-a-time nurse had a new patient for the moment, and better yet, one she happened to be in love with.

"Thanks, Rebecca," he said back at her as they continued through the water. "Thanks for all your help. I'll be better once we find something to eat . . . and drink . . ."

"We'll be all right. We'll make it together, babe. You'll see . . ."

"I'd have to be crazy to leave a girl like you. Ya think?" he said at her and managed a small smile.

"Yeah, as a matter of fact, I *do* think . . ." She held him closer and laid her head on his shoulder.

"Not like I have much of a choice now anyway . . ."

"Hey!" She jumped back and splashed him. He fell to his knees but the water level by now was only inches high.

"Help! Help!" he weakly cried, feigning distress, well, sort of, and she returned to his side. Soon they were crossing the sand, picking up their pace when Justin turned back to wave at them from the top of the beach.

"You guys come on! Come on! You have got to see this," he shouted and turned and ran.

CHAPTER XXIV

SOUL SEARCHING

Udo was thinking he'd better head back to the beach and the pier. He knew at least a remnant of that old thing would probably still be there. *Didn't he leave some of it still standing on his last visit? Yes.* He remembered. And enough for him to find it again now. So he had at least one dependable landmark.

And finding it would be no problem. Just keep heading down the coast. Then once there, like he'd figured last time before everything went sideways, he should be able to find his way back to good old Griffith Way, the street his home was on.

Hopefully.

Still.

In fact, there was the pier now, right down below, sticking out like a black finger into the ocean. Or that's what it looked like from up high where he was now. He was flying really well, hadn't crashed in a long time. He could swoop and glide and even dive if he had to, like when he'd taken out that demon back at the helicopter fueling station. He had to be careful doing that though. Diving, that is. He'd only done it that time because it looked like those people were in real trouble.

Then luckily there'd been that field and hill for him *and* the demon to land in and then roll and roll and roll down. Otherwise forget about it. It was real hard to change direction in a dive like that very fast. And also very dangerous. Even more dangerous than flying up so high like he was now.

Because, as one might easily surmise, the worst thing he had to watch out for was a serious head injury. That could kill him; just like it could the zombies. Except maybe with this new demon head helmet he had he might stand a better chance. The Lord had really blessed him with this thing, Udo knew, leaving it there like that after the last soul releasing ritual.

It was nice too how some of the flesh melted down like it did so his neck was covered when he wore it too. In case someone tried to cut his head off. Plus the thing was harder than anything he'd ever felt before, and he was betting it could stop any blade. Or those spear things the demons threw. Not that he wanted to find out, but just in case, that was comforting to know. Or at least believe.

But even better was how when he looked through the eyeholes certain colors would come on, highlighting things he would never have seen otherwise. In particular, zombies and anywhere they'd recently been would light up in red glowing outlines. That was how when he'd first gotten the thing he'd been able to see that chubby zombie hiding in the weeds like he was. He could totally see right through the tall, dry grass and him lying there, but all lighted up with a reddish glow.

Then as the zombie walked away, Udo could see his footprints glowing in red too for a bit until they disappeared for some reason.

Even better of course, and what could come in particularly handy as he looked for his family, was how human outlines and footprints would glow in *blue* when viewed through the eyeholes. Udo knew he could find them now. Only hopefully not dead yet, or anything like that.

He set down on the sand not far from the entrance to the pier, knowing most likely there was neither zombie nor human nearby. He'd done a panoramic sweep from above and seen nothing colorful or glowing. In fact it was kind of weird, he was thinking, how he hadn't seen anything interesting all along the coast either. Not the happening place it once had been was all Udo could figure. *What a difference a week makes. Were there even any survivors left, living or living dead?*

But something told Udo he hadn't finished off all the zombies yet either. Or the demons. And he had to believe the baddest of the bad guys was still around.

Yeah. Him.

Either way, there was only one thing to do: keep searching. Searching and searching for any or all of them, any survivors, but for his family first. *Family first*, that was easy to remember. He quietly chanted it even as he started in a loose jog up the beach's gentle incline then remembered fondly back to that first day when he'd been running near here, across this same sand and found himself unexpectedly airborne. What a rube, he almost said and then laughed out loud.

This time he got airborne again, but stayed relatively low, cruising slowly at about a hundred feet, high enough to get a good view. As he went, he constantly scanned around. He figured as he traversed the few miles between here and his old home that his family *could* be anywhere, and he'd just have to keep his eyes open for any telltale blue. He remembered when the Lord had first told him they were still alive that first time a week or so ago now; He had said they were still okay and laying low.

Laying low.

Interesting choice of words. Did that mean they were down in the basement survival shelter he'd built? Hopefully. And hopefully too they'd still be there. He just had to get there to find out, so Udo continued on slowly, scanning and scanning.

In fact, Udo also remembered then, thinking about the shelter, it had been another message from the Lord that had led to the building of the thing. It had been 'a word', as the people in the Christian community called it, from the Lord that he had received in a home Bible study group that had led to the creation of the shelter those several years ago. An apocalyptic word. Which by word they meant a message from Him. From God, or Jesus, if you will.

He and Ivy had joined the group through church, really just feeling sort of stuck in their Christian experience, their Christian 'walk' as it was also called. So they'd joined a home church group dedicated to the development of the *spiritual gifts*, as they were called too. Prophesy and healing and all that stuff, was how he and Ivy thought of it, not really sure which gift they may or may not have. But they wanted more, "More from the Lord," as they so enthusiastically put it back then. So they tried that whole scene out.

And at first, to them at least, it was a pretty wild scene. More than they had been prepared for, with most the people either speaking in tongues, manifesting the Holy Spirit as they called it—which could include any number of unnatural motions and or utterances uninhibitedly displayed—while others too had broken off in small groups to pray and heal the one in the center of their own subgroups, while others sat alone just deeply praying, trying to receive the afore mentioned 'word' from the Lord, or visions too. Whatever might come would be received.

Noticing those of the latter category, and suspecting that singly praying like that would be the easiest first step to take, while also simply getting used to the intimidating but interesting environment, he and Ivy lowered their heads to pray along.

Later Ivy would admit she was only praying for a quick exit. It was really Udo's idea to join the group. So he prayed in earnest, asking the Holy Spirit to use him as it might, show him a purpose he could fulfill, a greater purpose, a more important and meaningful way to serve the Lord and help others.

Then it came.

And came.

And came.

Image after image exploded in his mind in hyper realistic color and sound. Quick cut scenes: the world ripping itself apart at the seams, his house collapsing but all of them, him and his family—or so he thought at the time it was them—diving into the basement to try and survive.

Udo came up blinking. That was horrible! But so clear and even cinematic! But it couldn't be-

So he tried to let it go.

But it wouldn't let him go.

And when they left the home group, after a few more visits but never to return—Ivy refused and he didn't want to go alone—it was okay because he had a lot of work to do anyway, stocking the basement up with supplies: canned food, water, survival implements . . . equipping it too with cots and bags, a commode tarped off in the corner, weapons and anything else he could think of. *Oh yeah. Redesign those little windows too. Waste disposal. Had to have that.*

So hopefully they had ended up down there, Udo finished his reverie with. Although then too, like Udo was also thinking, if they weren't there anymore, if they'd decided to make a break for it, hopefully they'd headed for the beach. Now if he could just find them and tell them about the island. Or help them get there, which they may have already, because ever since he'd gotten that other 'word' from the Lord to tell those people with the boat to go into the sunset and then to the island, he'd also been praying and praying someone in his family would get the message too. So . . .

And besides, Udo knew too the other way to the East was totally impassable; that is for humans anyway. He'd flown over that way and for at least as far as he could fly, there was no way. What resembled a volcanic rift valley, at least to Udo's untrained eye, at the bottom of which a steaming river flowed in a line as far as he could see, completely bordered off the coastal area after only twenty, maybe thirty miles inland. It cut off Sandy Point Beach and the surrounding areas from the rest of California, almost like God had planned it that way. Or maybe . . . yeah maybe the other guy had, the bad guy, hoping to keep his prey contained.

Either way it helped Udo narrow his search. His family would *have to* head for the beach. Sooner or later. So now just to back track and keep his demon mask enhanced eyes peeled.

Which he was still doing, continuing his search, but walking now, *not sure, not exactly sure . . . oh okay . . . what do you know!* There was the big plastic ice cream cone from the frosty freeze that had always been on the corner of Mission and Sandy Point Beach Parkway. The rest of the building was rubble, but there was the old light up cone knocked down from the roof now but there on the ground and on its side.

A landmark at least. So he knew up Mission now for a couple miles, which was going to be tough to follow all chewed up like it was, but he was noticing you could follow the streets by the big spikes of curb popping up along their borders every now and then. Especially, on the main thoroughfares like this. They had the really big, strong curbs.

Then in a couple miles he should hit Harbor, and if he could see it take a right and stay on it until it passed under the highway. Then Griffith way a left not far from there and hopefully home.

Sure, he could do it, and with one last look at the old frosty cone, he headed off. Boy were those cones good, he remembered too. He always got a large one, and chocolate dipped. *Man oh man. They were so delicious.* But now no more. He'd have to check up in heaven if he could get one up there. Bet he could, Udo was thinking too, if he ever made it back up there. But first to find his former home, and the search continued . . .

It might have been sad or pitiable for him to watch, if the king of evil were prone to such emotions, but of course he wasn't. Instead he was excited and filled with pride as he watched the souls he and his minions had captured and trapped. The little things of light coursed up and down and all around in the giant, test tube-like chamber he'd made to house them in, forever trying to get somewhere but finding no way to do so.

The seamless and entirely unbreakable chamber, about the size of a four-story-tall closet, was encircled midway up its length by the narrow catwalk upon which the Devil now walked, attired in his snappy black spacesuit he'd tried on, preparing for the big day, liftoff day, rapidly approaching.

Looking up, Satan also then saw that at the top of the soul-drive chamber an incredibly bright light shone. As planned, this would be the light that the souls would repeatedly try to, 'go into,' as they believed they were supposed to, like they were doing just then.

However, at the height of their quest in a special section at the top of the chamber, receptor pods dangling down sapped them of the spiritual energy they had built up getting there. Then they almost lifelessly drifted back down until they could recharge and try again. The energy harnessed by the pods would then power the ship's warp drive capable engines. At present, said energy was filling booster batteries to be employed at liftoff for that extra burst of energy needed to clear the Earth's gravitational force. From then on the little immortal bits would continue on in their quest, interminably. Or that was the plan anyway.

Simply put, that was the *Soul Drive*, and about all the detail Satan wanted to think about it in at the moment. He tried not to think too much about it, or his ship and the trip they'd all be taking soon, just in case the almighty was listening in like he often did.

Although then too, and to finish his thoughts off, he further recounted from there all that remained was directional guidance, passenger stasis and structural maintenance of the ship. All of which was being programmed into the ship's completely computerized and robotic operational systems. Then it would just be off and away, next stop somewhere on the other side of the universe.

At which point, he and his second in command would automatically be aroused from stasis to assume manual control of both the ship and planetary scanning equipment. Then to find a new home or, as also recently realized, a way out of this universe entirely, and then a new home there.

Satan had to smile at that one, liking the sound of it all. He smiled too because he could feel the pull of the power of those souls as he ran his hand along the glass. Then smiling as well because his most recent intelligence reports informed him that there were two, living human children about to be captured. Each were in different locations, but teams were close to both.

The souls of children were the most powerful of all. They would be all he would need to complete his energy needs. But, after thinking on it he decided maybe this was something he better do himself. So leaving the soul drive chamber across the catwalk and outside a self-sealing and thick, metallic door, he continued on.

He continued from there up a long hallway on each side of which innumerable hatch-like doors rose in row after row after row: behind the doors the many stasis chambers for all the occupants making the journey waited for them, primed and ready to go. Just pile in you big demons, slip the stasis suit on, and nighty night. Papa Satan would take care of his babies.

At the end of all that he exited the ship but still stood on a small plank which automatically extended out away from the ship's gleaming hull. The plank stopped extending before then morphing into a seat at the end of a stout pole. Satan let himself softly fall into the seat. His new place of repose then somehow began moving along the ship's hull, giving him another of the many inspection tours he'd made over the last few weeks.

Although really now he was only marveling at his creation; the inspections were completed. He rode this chair, though, more accurately, so he could once again notice close up how the ship wasn't even really a color. It seemed instead to be the complete absence of color encased in metal. In a gleaming fashion, the hull then reflected everything around it, including himself gawking at it with a huge grin. He loved that.

But seriously, the material of the ship's hull had painstakingly been developed by both him and his engineers and scientists pushing the boundaries of known science. Opposite of resistance, the hull would actually increase their speed, flowing effortlessly through and absorbing the energy of the dark matter most of their journey would be taking them through.

Ahhh, enough of all that, Satan concluded then. He always got sidetracked near the ship like this, taking in its wonderful, and if he did say so himself, *brilliant design. But where was he? What had he been thinking about-*

Oh yes, the children, and in remembering them he then transformed into his natural state, the large and winged one who really couldn't fit in the chair he'd been riding in so he hovered out and away from the ship. He flapped his large wings then and started up, flying for the large aperture the metal mountain's peak had become as, at his signal his engineers tested its ability to open for tomorrow's lift off. For now though only he lifted off and coursed high into the sky above.

"Well, I don't know, honey. I mean, why risk it? Let's just get the gas and go."

"They might have some really cool weapons around. Heck, maybe even a cafeteria and a kitchen with lots of food, emergency generators. This place could be a gold mine."

John and Janet had found the Naval Station's refueling dock located on the far northern end of the approximately twenty-mile long, strip-shaped island. And other than the base that blossomed inland from the dock for about a mile or two, the rest of the island was uninhabited and wild land running all the way to the other end.

So they'd landed on the seemingly almost all steel constructed docking area that housed not only all needed fuel apparatus for the naval vehicles— and now hopefully their chopper too—but also included the military helicopter landing pad where they'd set down.

After Janet spotted the island, John had taken the chopper low for several sweeps of the place. They had seen no observable activity of any kind across the wild lands, but at the base there did appear to be dead bodies strewn about here and there and some were in groups. Birds worked on them, walking and pecking, tearing and eating, but nothing else appeared to be living or moving as far as they could see.

They *could* see, however, that the complex of gray and light brown buildings included some made of metal, with others on the outskirts resembling apartment buildings. These were probably housing for the enlisted inhabitants, and other assorted smaller edifices for whatever else they might need. Who knew what might wait in there, but since the helipad and attached dock and fuel dispensers were clear at the far end of the island and set off quite distant from any other structures, John went ahead and set her down there.

"All right. Full tank," John called out and completed the fueling process. He returned the nozzle to its metal holder and capped the helicopter's tank, then continued. "Honey, we take it slow and careful. We make sure we always have an out. And with me and the shotgun and the nines, you and the twin .380s, I think we'll be okay. You remember how sweet those babies were, doncha?"

"Yeah," Janet answered and brought her hands up to each of the automatic pistols hanging in the double shoulder holster rig she had on now. On the way over, at John's behest and with detailed instructions on how to use them during their flight, Janet had jumped into the back of the chopper and gotten fully strapped. Then out through the chopper's side opening she'd fired round after round. She was thoroughly over her fear of guns now. But fear of zombies . . . well, she grimaced just thinking about running into more of them and John noticed her discomfort.

"Look, honey," he kept trying. "The place is totally quiet. And we're gonna go in . . . and get right back out. In and out. And hey! I just thought of something. Maybe on those boats. Come on. Come on!" He started over to the center portion of the dock, angling toward the cutout sections along the seaward edge that held each of the several amphibious attack boats the Navy had stored there.

"Okay. But any sign of trouble," Janet put in while catching up with him. He turned back, halfway to the boats already.

"And we'll skedaddle back here, get in the chopper, and we're off." John made a flying away motion with his hands to help. Janet was already coming anyway.

"All right. I just hope you can skedaddle real fast," she told him and punched him playfully in the arm.

"I can with a bunch of zombies on my tail."

They laughed and Janet took John's hand as they headed for the boats. "I didn't fall in love just to get killed and eaten you know."

"Me neither, Hon. Me neither." They clasped hands and continued on.

Inside the first boat they came to, Janet kept watch while John got down into it to look around. She had to admit, it really did look pretty safe from where she was now. The only way any zombies could get to them would have to be across the long and flat decking of the dock. There was no way anything could sneak up on them out here. So she just stood there, one foot up on the prow of the boat, looking out across, her hands on her hips.

Every now and then she'd bring her hands up to her guns again but knew better than to pull them out. John had trained her not to. That way she wouldn't start shooting too soon. Which she wasn't supposed to do until she knew she could put one in their head, which in target practice had turned out to be about ten to fifteen yards, or two car lengths was a good way to think of it too, John had told her. At two car lengths, she was lethal.

"Payday!" John shouted then from down in the boat. After a few moments, he raised up with a military style, automatic rifle in each hand. "And check out these clip vests too," he added before going back down in, then came back up with a rifle in each hand and a clip vest draped over each arm.

Adding to that there was his shotgun slung across his back now and the two nine millimeter pistols in his own double shoulder holster rig, and saying he was loaded for bear wouldn't have quite covered it. He was loaded for zombie.

He got back out onto the dock with all of it, and then took the time needed to help Janet get her own clip vest on, while also checking her out on the proper loading and firing of the military rifle. Now they were both loaded for zombie.

And that was about good enough, they both finally agreed. Something about the place was giving them the creeps, they'd also agreed. *So we'll head back to the chopper, continue looking for other islands, even if only to return here for more fuel if we have to. But for now . . .*

Then they heard it.

A man, or it could have been a woman? But it was most likely was a man, and for sure it was a human at least, screaming bloody murder.

"Oh my God," Janet, out of reflex really, uttered with a gasp.

"Not again," John said with both a sigh and more than a little anxiety. "Looks like we'll get a chance to try out our new weapons, dear."

"Can't we just go?"

"That was someone still alive. You know we can't just-"

"But they're obviously . . ."

"Exactly."

". . . getting killed."

"But there may be others . . ."

"Johnnn . . ."

"What if I had just left you there when you were stuck on that rooftop?"

Janet didn't have an answer for that one. Instead, she just watched as John held his rifle up and pulled back on the clearing rod. After a sigh, she did the same.

"We'd better set it to semi too," John added and showed her how, swiveling a small switch on the rifle's side. "That way you won't waste all your ammo right off. Which means each time you want to shoot-"

"I have to squeeze the trigger completely and release. Yeah, yeah, we went over all this."

Another scream ended the lesson. John started across the dock, this time back toward the navy base in a semi run. Janet fell in behind. John looked over his shoulder and let her catch up. "It sounded nearby. Over there."

Over there was what must have been the base's chapel, marked by a small cross on the door. The small, neatly square building was set off and surrounded by an equally neat and similarly small, green grass lawn.

"No," Janet could only utter, a new level of dread and disgust painting the word. One more scream, drawn out particularly long, pretty much pinpointed the source as exactly that. The chapel.

"Come on. I'll take one side of that front door, you take the other," John ordered low-voiced, adhoc combat commander that he'd suddenly become. Then he hustled over to the door, this time not looking back. He knew that Janet could hold her own, physically at least. Their first night together he couldn't help but remark concerning the near perfection of her small but well-muscled physique. She in turn had informed him that her greatest getaway, and or avocation, was training for and competing in triathlons. He might have to worry about keeping up with her instead, he'd had to remind himself ever since. Except in the use of weapons, of course. Although she was also picking that up quickly too, as smart as she was.

All of which only explained why John wasn't the least bit surprised as almost simultaneously Janet slammed her back against the wall just to the left of the Chapel's classroom style door as he slammed his back against the wall just to the right. Then he exchanged a wide-eyed look with her while also carefully and quietly trying the door's knob.

As he felt it turn easily and all the way, before opening the door, he came across it to get close to her. He felt safe in doing that because now right next to the door like they were, they could hear much more accurately what was going on inside.

Another scream had come, this one blood curdling close, and then also to be heard was the all too familiar moaning, groaning and growling of zombies. Evidently, a group of them had cornered someone inside and was maybe already taking bites.

"Drop back over there. Behind that flagpole and those rocks," John whispered and nodded back across the grass and a walkway to their right where three large decorative boulders surrounded a tall stout flagpole, somewhat miraculously still flying the flag. "I'll try to draw the zombies out and take an opposite position on this other side. On my way out I'll shout out how many there are. Wait! Wait until they all come out, and then we'll open up on them. And remember—"

"I know. Head shots," Janet added and kissed him quick on the cheek before hustling over to the boulders and taking a knee behind the biggest of them. John waited until she was settled, still able to see her rifle's muzzle peaking up over the light brown, curving crown of the big rock. He slowly slid the door open and then just as slowly turned into the room.

It was a plain, small room on the inside too. Probably generic, John had to guess. One small chapel, the unit's name may have read on a Government order form somewhere. Complete with a Virgin Mary statue in one corner up front, St. Something or other right next to the door, and a big dramatically lighted cross up front too. The religious symbol hung dead center in the room's front and at an angle up high behind the glass pulpit set there too.

What wouldn't have been on the order form, or in any way documented at all, would be the man hanging on said cross, apparently freshly crucified there, and from the waist up at least he wore the attire of a priest. Nor would one find, at least on any order form written in earthly form, mention of the three zombies eating his feet.

The priest screamed again and after John quickly scanned the room to see there were no other threats present, he brought the automatic rifle up, sighting alternately on each of the three zombies, and finally on the priest's head too. The small scope atop the rifle made it so easy.

No, he thought then and knew he had to stick to plan. There might be more zombies somewhere outside and his shots might bring them running. Because, sadly enough, as John had also noticed, all the zombies present were former members of the armed forces of the United States of America, Naval branch. And *weren't they in a place where there were possibly lots more of the same?* Well, at least that made the next part of his job a little easier.

"Hey, you stupid swabbies. Army rules!" he yelled and the khaki-clad zombies stopped their feasting and turned. The priest had already passed out, and now that the feeders had moved aside, John could see the mangled bloody stubs where his feet should have been at the end of his otherwise naked, lower extremities. At least though, he did have boxer shorts on.

Hell, John mentally cursed and also made a note to be sure and come back if he could to help the priest. If everything went as planned, that is.

So far, it was. The zombies were halfway to him already, one each going around and coming up the outside aisles of the folding chairs filling the chapel's floor for the most part. The third, a particularly large fellow, was clearing his own path right up through the middle, knocking the chairs out of his way without even seeming to notice their presence.

Their attention was obviously and very successfully diverted his way, so no doubt, John knew, they would follow him out. Out he went.

"Three. They're Navy guys. But they're still zombies. Take 'em out. Then we gotta head back in. The screamer's still alive . . . I think." John had yelled all that across to Janet while he took his position on the opposite end of the grass lawn. Now they had the doorway of the chapel triangulated and in their sights at about twenty to thirty yards. Turkey shoot, John was thinking.

Omigod, omigod, omigod, was going through Janet's mind until she took a deep breath, then, *headshot . . . headshot . . . headshot,* took its place.

Bap . . . bap, bap . . . bap, bap, bap, the rifles took turns barking from each corner of the base of the kill triangle. The zombies only got a few steps onto the grass before the spray of bullets slowed them down. The big one's head fragmented in red spray as rounds from both sides impacted into it at the same time. All three fell quick and then didn't move.

"Good shootin', girl," John almost sang as he came over to Janet just getting out from behind the boulder.

She held the gun pointed up toward the sky as she'd been trained to do when not shooting, and a big, "whew," was all she had to say.

"All right," John added, coming even closer. "Now. Like I said, there's a survivor in there. At least I think he's still alive. So I wanna go get him. But let's be honest, there may be more zombies, and the sound of our gunfire might bring them running."

He paused to take a breath. Janet couldn't help but fill in the pause. "Let's just go then. Even if that guy isn't dead, he probably soon will be. Or he'll turn into one of them. Let's—"

"I'm sorry, honey. I can't. I'm Catholic, remember? And this guy . . . well . . . you'll see." John started back into the chapel. "Just stay here and watch the door. And keep an eye on that walkway that leads into the base. You've got the perfect angle to watch it, and if any more come they'll have to come that way. Start shooting the second you see anybody, and I'll get out here."

Janet watched him disappear back into the chapel, wanting to argue more, but she hadn't really had the chance. "Ohhhh," she could only utter in exasperation and one more time, lock and load.

She turned and looked hard up the walkway John had mentioned. At least there was still no one coming, living or dead. And John was right; it really was the only throughway connecting this part of the base with everything else. She hunkered down behind the boulder again, resting the rifle across the top of it.

Inside the chapel, John scanned the room rapidly once more with his rifle at the ready, then made his way quickly up to the hanging priest. He felt hard at his jugular then slapped him lightly in the face.

"Hey . . . hey . . . can you hear me?" he tried. The priest's eyelids fluttered and a barely audible moan escaped his lips. He didn't have time for this, John was thinking, and quickly scanned the priest's body.

"What the—" he couldn't help but say. Both of the holy man's legs had tight tourniquets applied above each knee.

"Demon," the priest croaked down.

"What? Hey. I'm gonna get you out of here, all right?" John spit the words out while also checking how.

The priest's wrists were only bound to the cross at least, not nailed. John quickly slipped the combat knife from its upside down scabbard that the clip vest also housed near his heart. The strong and sharp, Navy issue blade went right through the bindings that looked to be just thin rope. The priest's body rocked against the cross but stayed suspended by more of the rope running under his armpits and across his chest.

"Satan . . . torture . . . laughing . . . coming back . . . coming back . . . for more," the priest also managed through dry lips.

"Don't worry. We'll be long gone," John told him then got close under the priest's torso. Luckily the guy was pretty small, and for just a moment he couldn't help but wonder too what the heck the guy had been talking about. *A demon and Satan? Watching? Surely he was hallucinating. But then who had tied those tourniquets? Zombies wouldn't do that. Maybe more of those big, black things like they'd seen at Highpoint Park. Were they--?*

Either way, they had to get outta there. So blindly then, because he was wedged right up under the still suspended priest so he could catch him over his shoulder when right after cutting . . . *the . . . rope . . . first on this side . . . there . . .* and now if he could just reach over . . . *right there!* And then perfect, the little guy fell down to drape right over his shoulder. Together they turned and went.

Just as they got to the door, "Bap . . . bap," Janet's rifle popped outside.

"Oh shi_, John cussed, and then felt bad about it, what with the priest draped over his shoulder and all. But that was the least of his concerns.

He barreled out through the door, looked quick along the front of the chapel to the corner around which any advancing zombies would have to pass, but so far they weren't. Scanning just a little to the left he could see Janet standing behind the boulder firing away some more, so he knew, however, someone was coming.

He hustled out to almost exactly the same spot he'd taken before and set the priest down. By the time he'd then got his own gun up, the zombies were there. One . . . two . . . three . . . four . . .

Again, the two mowed down the dead invaders, the last of which fell not far from John and the recently rescued priest. Janet ran over with one of the .380 caliber pistols in her right hand, her rifle slung across her back now. "Oh my God, John," she said with a gasp.

Then the doctor in her kicked into gear and she all but fell on the poor little priest. "He's still got a pulse. Thready though. Probably lost a lot of blood. Those wounds are horrible. Did you place those tourniquets? Good idea. We need to get—" Then she remembered where she was.

John was still in high gear too. He swooped down and had the priest cradled in his arms in one smooth motion. "We *need* to get him on the bird and get the heck outta here, doc . . . I mean, honey. Okay?"

"Yeah . . . yeah . . . of course," Janet agreed and then quickly fell in as her love, and if she'd had a chance to think about it, her hero, ran just ahead of her. She couldn't help but notice the priest's bloody red stumps bouncing up and down with every running step John took as well. Luckily, her new patient was passed out.

"When you set him in the back, sit him up John! I need to try and get him to drink and get some of those antibiotic pills we have into him. That's our only chance," she shouted, coming up next to him. She noticed too how he kept looking back over his shoulder toward the chapel. She looked too and could see nothing coming, but still he kept checking. "What are you looking for, John?"

"Demon," he told her point blank, knowing she wouldn't probably even process the answer.

"What?"

He was right. "Nothing," he told her and checked back one last time, remembering exactly what the last demon he'd seen looked like, but, thank heavens, there wasn't one there now. He turned quickly back to loading the wounded priest into the chopper.

It had to be the greatest honor a zombie could possibly receive, Mike was thinking, loaded into a harness atop one of the master's great warriors who was flying high in the sky carrying him to his next mission. And how much more of an honor because there flew the master too right next to them. Mike was smiling so broadly the skin in his cheeks was splitting. Literally.

Then they were there and coming down into the strange place unlike any Mike had ever seen before. It was amazing how clean it was, and the buildings looked very strong, which maybe was why they weren't as screwed up as everything else was after the big earthquake. In fact as he looked at more of it, the plain square buildings and neat grass and not much else, it reminded him of that place he'd been in before that they called prison. They even had the tall fences too, but not the sharp cutting wire on it like the prison had. He couldn't think of the word for that wire either, but . . .

Once they landed he just stayed in the harness at first because they had much to do. So the warrior, with Mike still riding, walked fast to a building at the end of the place that had a cross on it. As they approached the building and then even entered it, Mike was feeling kind of sick. But that passed, and even more so was replaced by hunger as Mike soon saw a still living human they had on another cross at the front of the room they were in now. He was hoping he might get to eat some of him, but the master told him no, he would feed later on some meat they had in the other buildings, as long as he learned his lessons well that the warrior would soon be showing him.

That all started after they left, and Mike was sorry and felt empty somehow to leave the master but was glad that the master was having fun with the man hanging there who was screaming and screaming while the master was laughing and laughing.

He soon couldn't worry about any of that anymore though when the warrior took him over to a boat in the water. The boat was still tied to the part of this place that stuck out over the water like a pier but only smaller. He remembered the word pier from being on the one before in his other mission, but now he couldn't remember the word for the smaller one to which they tied boats.

But that didn't matter to Mike. He was just too excited to be trained for this new mission. The master had told him that neither he himself nor any of his warriors could make this trip in the boat. Only he and the other zombies could do it . . . or try to do it. It would be hard to find this special place they were supposed to go to, a place somewhere in the middle of all the water that was called another word he couldn't think of, another place just like where he was now.

But his job was to take this boat, with as many of the other zombies as they could fit into it, to the other place like this one somewhere in the water and then, once there, to find everyone and eat them. That would be wonderful.

Although how they would find this place, Mike sure didn't know. But the master would talk to him in his head like he could and help him. He had promised. And him and all his many servants were looking for this place all the time and should find it soon anyway.

So then the master's warrior showed him how to take in all the lines—he called them lines, the ropes tied to the boat, holding it close—how to take them in and then make the boat go, first backwards, then turning, then ahead and looking . . . looking. He would probably remember it all. If not, the master would help him.

The warrior took off then, and Mike watched him rise up into the air. He could fly so good on his big, black wings. Then the master joined him soon, and off they went.

Mike stayed in the boat and practiced, not really doing it all, but going through the motions, as he remembered hearing it called. Practice. Practice makes . . . practice makes . . . makes something.

Then he heard the flying machine up above again and hid down in the boat. He hid because he knew humans were on the flying machine, humans with guns. He knew that because it was the same one from before. Did it follow him? He wasn't sure, but he wasn't taking any chances. He hid down in the boat, but stayed up just enough to peek over the edge.

And there! There were those same people coming out of the flying machine landed now. And they still had guns too. And what if that statue man showed up again, Mike realized. He'd better hide better. Good thing the boat had deep places he could get into and wait until they passed. *Yeah.* They would never find him down here. And just in case, he could put some of these things over him too. There, it was completely dark now. They would never find him now.

CHAPTER XXV

TAKEN

He was so hungry. Hungry all the time. All they had to eat ever since the earthquake—he thinks that was what it was called, earthquake, or quakeringer, or something like that. But ever since then and when the house fell in, he and Kellen had to leave on Shadow to find help, and all they had to eat were the pow pow bars, which were okay. After a while though, even they didn't taste all that good anymore. In fact, they even didn't taste like anything anymore.

Then there were the apples too, but they weren't all that good either. Not like the ones mom always brought home from the store. These ones they got in a tree by the trail and they were tiny and hard. But he ate those anyways. Just because there wasn't anything else except the pow pow bars, and just like them now the apples didn't taste like anything anymore either.

But now, just now, he'd woken up so early—which meant early in the afternoon because these days they slept at daytime—but he'd woken up early because he could smell bacon cooking. *Bacon!* The smell had even come into his dreams, and then he was even eating bacon in his dreams too. It was so real it had woken him up and now he could really smell it. *Bacon!* He loved bacon. It was probably his very favorite thing in the whole world to eat. *But who would be cooking bacon?* They sure didn't have any.

Aaron sat up on the blanket and looked all around. He could still smell the bacon cooking, and now his mouth was all watery inside from it too. It reminded him of when his mom would cook it for breakfast. *Ummm.* He had to find it. He was sooo hungry that his stomach growled.

Looking over, he could see Kellen was still sleeping, but he thought maybe he should wake her up. Maybe—

No! A big voice said in his head.

But, he said back, only just in his head, just like the voice had. Then the voice said some more.

Don't you remember that time when you and your dad surprised your mom with breakfast in bed? Remember how happy she was? Why not do that for Kellen now too?

"Okay," Aaron even answered out loud this time and checked quickly over at Kellen again. She was still asleep.

The little boy sniffed the air. Man oh man, he thought to himself. The smell was getting even stronger. He got up and walked to where it seemed to be coming from. Over to and then up the trail, he continued on and the smell kept getting stronger and stronger. He kept going.

He hadn't walked too much further, just up over the next rise, as Kellen had taught him they were called, before the smell sent him into a small canyon off to the right. Once there he listened hard, thinking he could hear the crackle crackling of the bacon cooking too. Oh yeah, he knew then. *That way. Maybe over behind those big rocks. Because wasn't that smoke there too?*

"Well there he is," the man cooking the bacon said, looking over at the little boy from the small clearing behind the boulders. He looked like a real cowboy, Aaron was thinking. And there was the bacon, sizzling in a black frying pan over a little campfire. A good collection of it rested on a paper towel atop a much smaller boulder, like a little table nearby.

It looked so delicious, crispy and shiny. Aaron couldn't take his eyes off the bacon as he kept walking toward the cowboy. "Can I . . . can I have a piece?"

"Well sure, partner," the cowboy told him. "Help yourself."

It was so crunchy and tasty too. First one piece, then two, three and four. Aaron ate them all very fast because it was so good. "I'm . . . I'm sorry. But I'm so hungry and bacon's my favorite?"

"That's all right, partner. But hold off on these." The cowboy plopped a fresh group of sizzling strips on the paper towel atop the little boulder table. "We need to make you a real breakfast. And since we're on the trail, we have to eat it in a sandwich."

Aaron's eyes were glowing like on Christmas morning as he looked down to the pan where the cowboy now was cooking a couple eggs and what looked like two halves of a big biscuit.

"All righty then," the cowboy drawled out after a minute—that really could have been more time than that but Aaron's sense of time was lost in all the scrumptious smells—while with strong, tan hands the trail driver deftly used a little tin spatula to put the sandwich together.

"Uh . . . uh . . . uhhh," Aaron whined and reached for the sandwich.

"Slow down there, partner. You'll burn your mouth. Let it cool just a little. We've got plenty of time after all."

Aaron didn't want to wait, but then when the cowboy explained it to him like that . . . his words were like magic. He didn't care about anything anymore. He felt very safe all of a sudden. And when the cowboy let him have the sandwich, it was so delicious. Then he heard it.

"Shadow!" Aaron cried out with joy because there was the big horse too, coming up and nuzzling the cowboy who pet him back. "You know our horse?"

"Oh yeah . . . we're old friends." The cowboy stroked the horse's muzzle a little more, fed him a little something too, then mounted up into the saddle almost effortlessly. Aaron watched him and wolfed down the rest of his sandwich.

"Can I have another one?"

"Not now, partner. We gotta get back on the trail."

The cowboy stuck his arm out to lift him up and Aaron let him. He did it so smooth it felt like magic, just like everything else was starting to feel like magic too. The little boy was so happy. It was like the whole world had become one of those cowboy movies he liked so much. And just like Kellen had, the cowboy let Aaron ride in front too. *Oh boy . . . was that sandwich good . . .*

As they were riding up the next rise it seemed to lead right into the setting sun. Better yet, then the cowboy man so big and strong behind him started singing and whistling a song just like those movies always had in them too. Aaron just relaxed and enjoyed the ride. *This was so good . . .*

Part of the reason he was doing this himself was because he would miss this place, this planet Earth as they'd decided to call it. He had seen so much of it, and so much of it was so beautiful, as long as there weren't any humans around. So here he was again, the dark lord low over the land like the black of night. He took human form then again though, so he could more thoroughly enjoy the aforementioned beauty.

Like this gorgeous little valley, with the way the hills held it in their stony hands and those hands attached to mountain-shaped and enormously strong arms. So much beauty. So much grandeur. And then the valley inside the little bowl they held, or more accurately like a terrarium, as they called them, glass encased, artificially constructed environments the humans would make.

But this was God's terrarium, this little valley. Yes. God's, not theirs. He could tell by the unmistakable, pseudo chaotic symmetry that marked all of the creator's work. The pond was at the lowest point, then up from that was some of the smoothest, finest sand imaginable along its shore, untouched except by the tiny paws of the so cute foxes and squirrels and the very ferocious and most efficient killers on the planet, the mountain lions. God, how he loved them.

Then the beauty really started as the pond's shore gave gradual birth to fine grasses and the little baby boulders like tiny children spawned by the larger rocks. Then more of them bigger and bigger adorning the rising hillsides bearded too by patches of wild grass, crawling even right up to the bushels of scrub brush sprouting here and there as well.

Also to enjoy were the small trees and the bigger ones, but the most prized tree of them all not far from the pond, using its water to grow wide and bonnet-like and bigger than anything else in the small valley. It was a spreading old Oak. Just look at that. What a lovely fire it might make someday.

Satan drank it all in, or tried to, until his vision caught then on the two humans sleeping on the blankets beneath the tree. Like he was saying, they ruined everything. Like pigs in a pretty garden. Soon he would be free of them though, he reminded himself to mitigate his rage at their intrusion, to avoid descending on them like a pack of wild dogs, or no, like a mountain lion. He would show them just how efficiently *he* could kill.

But no. No, no, no, no! He needed the little child. Needed his precious little soul that was so small but powerful because it was so pure. Oh yes, pure as the driven snow, as the humans liked to say.

Which then was the other part of the reason he was getting this one himself. It was too valuable to risk. He couldn't risk a semi-mindless zombie or an overly powerful fellow fallen one breaking the package, accidentally or on purpose. He knew how intoxicating the powerful little gem would be. He would even have to watch himself, make sure the little one got all the way to storage, unharmed and undiluted.

And the young woman with him? She had special value too, as a virgin like she was. But she was a teenager. Semi pure by now for sure. He would have to let his minions handle her. To take them both at once would be risky. One never knew, just never knew what might happen. And the little one was most important anyway. Get him and go. Get him and go home, the dark lord quipped and had to smile.

And where was this horse his scans had told him about? He was a potentially dangerous player. Had to keep tabs on that noble beast. Not hiding about though, another near perimeter scan told him. *No? Oh well.* A horse's soul was of very little value to him anyway. Not worth a more vigorous search.

So now.

He scanned the girl.

She was sleeping, and all he needed was just a little push, a nice dream to draw her in deeper. *Yes.* Now she was deeply asleep.

He morphed once more into his classic, and more practical for this job, form before lifting aloft quietly with the soft flap or two of his wide wings. He glided down to just as softly land next to the boy.

The little tike didn't stir though. He too was sleeping deeply already and likewise pushed there by his truly. *Oh those humans and their dreams. So convenient and helpful.*

But then, oh the power, the power of the purity he could feel radiating from the boy. His long-clawed fingers quivered with excitement as they slid ever so smoothly under the little being and lifted him to his hard, black breast.

The leader of the fallen then lifted aloft again, soaring high in less than a second, high and gone far away over the hills and the mountains.

Kellen came to with a start and sat bolt upright. That'll happen when one of the best dreams you've ever had suddenly turns into a nightmare. Sweating, she took a breath and blinked her way back to reality.

In her dream, she'd been at one of their family backyard barbecues, and everyone was there as usual, which was fun enough, but then when they sat down to eat, and the ribs and chicken and the sweet white corn on the cob was dripping with butter and salted and peppered just right, she didn't ever want to wake up.

She ate and ate and finished off with a big piece of hot apple pie capped with a half-melted scoop of vanilla ice cream. But then the bad stuff started happening.

She could see Aaron across the yard from her and for some reason just walking off all by himself. That was kind of scary, but when she saw too that he was walking toward the edge of a giant and dark canyon somehow now on the edge of the Andrew's ranch, the scary got turned into raw fear.

But that's right, she remembered then as reality started seeping into the dream. Everything was changed now, ever since the earthquake. Oh yeah, the earthquake. So maybe the canyon had come from that.

Not that it mattered, because now Aaron was almost to its edge. "Aaron," Kellen yelled and yelled and then started running to get him too, but in that horrible way dreams could do, it was like she was running in quicksand.

She tried yelling some more, this time yelling at anyone who would listen, "Someone please! Please! Aaron's heading for the edge!"

But no one would listen either. It was like she wasn't even there anymore. Everyone just kept partying, eating and drinking and laughing.

While she watched then—because there was nothing else she could do really—and just as Aaron was about to step into oblivion, a huge, dark and evil looking, winged creature swooped him up and flew away with him. Then crawling up out of the canyon came zombies. By the dozens they just kept coming and coming, and still there was nothing Kellen could do. She could only watch and struggle to do something, but the dream wouldn't let her. Even then when the undead marauders tore into her loved ones, piece by bloody piece.

Soon all she could see was blood all over the place and body parts flying around. All she could hear was people screaming and the zombie's moaning and groaning and growling and the shuffle of their feet shuffling and scuffling across the ground. They kept coming. They just kept coming. She closed her eyes and could still hear them coming. Were they coming for her now too? The sound kept getting louder and louder, sounding so real, so real and right there until finally it woke her up and she came to, as mentioned, with a start and sitting bolt upright.

After blinking her way back into reality, as also mentioned, she immediately wished she hadn't. Or at least wished the reality she blinked her way back into was a different one. Because there were the zombies again, only this time for real.

"Aaron," she called out reflexively and started searching frantically for the boy right off. There was his blanket right where she'd put him to bed, but he wasn't there. And where was Shadow? The horse was nowhere around either.

There wasn't much time to worry about any of that, though. The zombies— and at least in real life there were only about six or seven of them that she could see—were getting nearer, coming down off the trail into the little valley where her and the boy had slept most the day away. "Aaron," she tried again, more loudly this time. "Shadow," she tried too, and then gave the little whistle she knew to call him with as well.

Nothing, though.

She started scrambling back away from their campsite, glancing around one more time, even more frantically now, looking for the boy. Then she thought of something else too. *My gun! Where?*

There.

The Marlin .22 was leaning against the trunk of the tree they'd slept under. *That's right.* She'd leaned it against there just before sacking out. She had to get there before the zombies did. *Could she?* It was only few yards away. Four or five steps and a grab. Here goes nothing, was her last thought as she jumped up and took off in a dash for it.

She made it too. She grabbed at the rifle just as the first of the zombies was entering the shade of the tree. Now if she could just—

Thwokkk!

She hadn't even gotten her hand all the way around the forestock when a bone jarring impact not only made her let go, but also made her fall back onto her butt. A medium-long, all silver metal, trident, or pitchfork-like weapon had somehow flown from somewhere hard and fast, pinning her rifle right where it was, tight against the tree trunk.

Since there was no time to try and pull it free—the zombies were only a few yards away now—Kellen could only scramble to her feet and back away. She would have also just turned and ran, but as she did, more zombies were coming up from the other direction now too. She looked hard to each side in rapid order and could see now they had her entirely surrounded.

So maybe . . . what? Up? They couldn't climb trees, could they? She, on the other hand, sure could.

The Andrew's ranch had a big old Oak a lot like this tree that she'd climbed maybe a dozen times in the first few years she'd moved there. They were easy to get up into, depending on how low their trunks sent secondary trunks up off the original. And sometimes too, like this one did, they'd shoot thick and stout branches off vertically only six feet or so high. In fact, as she looked up she could see one right over her head so she jumped straight up, got her arms around it and then a leg and swung herself up onto it.

Up on the limb was a good start, but more zombies were there now, rocking and shaking her quite fragile and not so safe . . . haven. Luckily adjacent and higher braches ran nearby and she quickly got up onto the most accessible one for her, but at least too it was further out of reach for them.

Not content, however, she climbed higher and higher. She wanted to get as far away from them as she could. But then what?

Finally, and as high as she could get, four-fifths of the way to the top, she found an uneasy but strong enough seat that afforded actually quite a nice view of their little valley. The zombies, who now seemed to number ten to fifteen or so, all milled moronically around the tree's trunk. None even attempted to ascend, as they all seemed completely at a loss for any ideas of what to do next.

"Holy—" Kellen let slip, keeping it quiet at least, not wanting to agitate the *unholy* gathering below. She hoped too, that if she just stayed still and silent they might go away.

Her sudden utterance, however, that had put all that in jeopardy had been entirely unavoidable. Because just then, coming under her already somewhat shocked gaze, Kellen had for the first—and for her part she hoped the last time in her life . . . seen a demon.

What was even worse than that, was that the big, mostly black and high horned creature was gazing right back at her. With big yellow eyes. Big and bright enough to be seen even from way up where she was.

The creature's steely stare never left her as he slowly rode up on his own hell horse, even bigger than Shadow and somehow even blacker, except for the noticeable flames it snorted from flaring nostrils. The big being dismounted and withdrew his weapon from the tree trunk, then walked back with the horse, almost to their original position.

He then seemed to be—which with great alarm Kellen soon realized— preparing to launch his great weapon again, straight at her!

He suddenly stopped then, however, and went to his knees quivering in pain. Even more strangely, an extremely large crow alighted on his shoulder and seemed to either be pecking weevils *out* of the creature's ear or whispering sweet nothings *into* it. Take your pick, Kellen resigned herself too, watching it all and mostly just glad the trident spear thing wasn't hurdling her way.

In only another moment, the crow rose aloft, and with nothing else to do, Kellen watched it circle above the tree before deftly coming in close to her through the oak's upper limbs and landed just as smoothly on a small branch directly in line with her vision. The evil and bloated looking bird stared at her from only a foot or two away and blinked.

Well, this was something new. She'd never been this close to a crow before. Which had to mean . . . what? Hadn't this supposed bird just been sitting on the shoulder of that strange . . . monster thing down there? And now was staring into her eyes like . . . like . . . a person would. What the—

Man . . . does that bird have the blackest eyes. Black like the deepest darkness she could ever imagine even but kind of shiny black too, like that sticky black tar stuff she'd seen them using for the roof that one time. She remembered they had a whole bucket of the stuff and she'd taken a tiny rock and thrown it in. The pebble sunk and sunk until it disappeared. *That stuff was so thick . . . and sticky . . . and deep . . . and black.*

Kellen shook her head. Why was she thinking about that dam tar now! Why-

Then she looked the crow in the eyes again and felt her mind slipping away, slipping down into that same black darkness, just like the stuff that had been in that bucket, so thick and so sticky it felt like there was no escape. Deeper and deeper she felt herself slipping and soon she could hear laughing, evil laughing and soon too she could see who was doing it, sitting on a throne of human bones but beautiful somehow, beautiful and seductive, and he was taking her hand.

No.

The thought and the word had quietly came from somewhere deep down inside her too.

The boy still needs you, came the next thought. But the one on the throne of bones was too strong, she could tell. It was the Devil. It was Satan, and he was taking her . . . taking her . . .

Oh Jesus, she thought out as a last resort. I'm so sorry for not saving the boy, so sorry for not being stronger, so sorry for everything. Oh Jesus, she pleaded.

The sound of the crow's screaming caw brought her out of it with a sudden shock, also suddenly reminding her that she was still high up in the upper braches of a tree. It was almost too late. She rocked and wobbled on the branch and almost fell off, but at the last second, sent an arm out blindly and somehow her hand found another branch to hold on to. She steadied herself and started breathing again.

She looked and looked throughout the surrounding branches and foliage for the bird but could see no sign of the black thing. *Good.* She never wanted to see a crow again.

She heard the big horse's snort below. It was especially deep and loud, of course, coming from such a huge specimen. She looked down there then too and could see that now the beast, and it's equally ungodly rider, were heading out. Following mindlessly behind were all the zombies, mostly just moaning and groaning and shuffling along again now.

Once they were gone, Kellen carefully and on somewhat shaky legs climbed down out of the tree. She struggled back to the blankets, found a water bottle, and drained half its contents. She then laid sideways, suspended on one elbow. First, tears came hard and slow, but those that followed flowed with a force all their own. Kellen could only try to keep her head above their ever rising tide, sobbing and gulping for air until finally the tears came no more.

CHAPTER XXVI

HOMECOMING

"I don't know why, but for some reason I was just thinking about a big, chocolate-dipped cone from Frosty Freeze," little Joannie Henkman marveled, truly not knowing why, but it was true. Right there like a picture in a magazine, but in her head. And then even worse, she could see herself taking a big lick, feeling the creamy coolness on her tongue. The experience was so real it had roused her just as she was starting to get to sleep.

Her and her bedroll were tucked down into a corner of the now abandoned building they'd decided to lie low in for the day, their first, full-fledged sleeping session since leaving the night before. The building was a multistoried unit put together in the old days, all-brick and block shaped. It had housed a shoe store on this lower level, with four apartments filling in the second and third stories. Since the quake the upper stories had mostly collapsed down onto the shoe store, or maybe more accurately they'd slid down on top of the front half of the store. This included the lovely display windows on each side of the double glass door entrance, which lay mostly in rubble, sealing off any access to the building from the front other than the door sized and relatively short tunnel through the rubble.

Which was perfect for them, Griner had suggested and eventually in the ad hoc meeting they'd held inside, they'd all agreed. Heck, the old con had told them too, we can probably block the little tunnel off and then the only other access into the otherwise stout structure was a single rear door, all metal and double locking from the inside. Perfect.

"Well maybe we can just stop there and get a big tasty cone tomorrow," Jason said to his sister from his own nearby bedding down spot in the old building. They both shared a small area in the deepest recess the building afforded, a rear corner of what in fact used to be the shoe store's back room storage area. You know, where the salesman would go to get the same thing in a ten and a half or whatever.

But then everyone—meaning the Griner / Henkman gang—went to work back there, picking out the finest in footwear of course, shifting around the toppled shelves of shoeboxes and then building them back up as walls to make a room-like environ for the kids, where they were now bedded down.

"Grinds said we'll try to head right up Mission tonight, then in a couple miles we'll hit Sandy Point Parkway, and the Frosty Freeze was always right on the corner there." Jason was kind of joking but also trying to help his little sister feel better. He sort of wished he could get one too, though. He had to admit those cones were awesome.

"I wish," Joannie put in, knowing full well the whole world—or at least all of everywhere she could think of—was literally and completely broken and useless. Which then made her also wonder, "Jason?"

"Huh," he responded but kind of wanted to tell her to shut up and go to sleep. It was so nice and dark and cool back in their little hideout, even though outside was a bright and somewhat warm day. And he was awfully tired. But instead, he bit his tongue and let her ask her stupid question.

"Do you think we'll ever get to taste ice cream again?"

Jason gave a little laugh. It was probably because they hadn't seen any more zombies or any of them other monsters for almost a week that now had his goofy little sister worrying about ice cream. Which, actually was kind of a good thing. And then he remembered, like Griner and his mom had told him to do, he made himself think carefully about what to say to a poor little kid caught up in a zombie apocalypse, as Griner usually and quietly called it all these days.

"Well, I don't know for sure," he started in carefully with. "Hard to say what's going to happen, you know." Then his old smart aleck self came out. "But you tell me, psychic lady. You're the one who keeps seeing this island we're supposed to go to. Are there any Frosty Freezes on it?"

"Jason . . ." the little girl started to whine.

"Oh, come on Joannie Macaroni. I don't mean it like that. I mean, you really are a psychic, I think. I believe you! I really do." He had recovered quite nicely there, he was thinking. She'd bought it too.

"Well, no then. I mean, if you really care about it at all. No. There won't be any ice cream at all at first. Can't you tell! We're going to have to start all over again. But it'll be better this time. He's leaving. He's—"

"Omigosh! What is all this yelling about?" Ivy Henkman interrupted with, sticking her head around one of the shoebox rack walls.

"I'm sorry, Mom. I guess I got kind of excited. I—"

"*I guess,*" Jason put in. "And who's leaving! You said, '*He's* leaving.' And you said it'll be better this time. What's *that* all about?"

"I don't know." Poor Joannie shook her little head, then looked confused. "I said what? I don't know. When you asked about the island, my head just started filling with pictures and ideas. Sometimes I don't even know what I'm saying!"

"Well, I *do* know that both of you better try and get some sleep. We've got a lot more work to do when you get up. We've gotta pack everything back up and hopefully make it to the beach before tomorrow morning. So get some rest, okay you two?"

"Yes, ma'am . . ."

"Sure, Mom. Good night. Or good morning . . . or whatever."

"Just get some rest," Ivy Henkman left it all with and turned to go, waiting for just a second to make sure.

Nothing.

Okay.

Hopefully they would sleep now.

Her and Clay were set up to bed down in another shelved off area they'd constructed not far from the back door. When they were ready to sack out, and shortly they would be, they were planning on putting in the tunnel a rig of two of the shelving units that when assembled together created a head high battlement that wouldn't let anyone pass through. They figured they could rig it into the walls of the tunnel which were comprised mostly of bricks and big beams of wood. Hopefully they could both wedge the wire walls into the stuff, then use bricks to hold them that way. At the same time the whole structure, being made of empty shelves as it was, and mostly wire, allowed for the firing through of any and all weapons that could be brought to bear on intruders trying to get past and in.

Yeah. They were on it.

Which was why then too as Ivy returned to Clay, who was just then putting the finishing touches on the battlement, having assembled it completely and set it in place across the tunnel's mouth, she came up comfortably behind him and put her hands on his stooped and toiling shoulders from behind.

"That looks great, Clay," she said too, gently squeezing the hard muscles he had there.

"I think it'll do. And together with the broken glass . . . and I'll tell ya, I am surely sleeping light these days . . . but I think we'll be forewarned, as they say. Although I haven't seen anything the least bit threatening out there yet."

"I wasn't talking about all that," Ivy cooed in his ear as he stood back from his construction. At the same time, she playfully grasped then squeezed the nearest half of his buttocks.

"Feeling a little frisky are we?" he countered with as he straightened up, took her in his free arm, hugged her hard and kissed the top of her head.

"Frisky isn't the word for it." She maneuvered her way to a frontal position and looked up at him with big eyes. The look said more than words could have.

"Look. You know what we agreed on. As painful as it is . . ." Griner tried to hold her back, but definitely not wholeheartedly.

"Yes, well, I was thinking. What if we get . . . well, you know. This could be our last night . . . or day together, you know?"

He looked back at her eyes deeply with his own. "You've got a point. But we'll have to be quiet. And I don't know if you noticed, but our bedding is not exactly luxurious. And these old bones . . ."

"There's only one particular *bone* I'm interested in . . ."

"You are so bad," he chided her after a small laugh. He playfully but firmly turned her around and slapped her on her own buttocks. He pointed her at the same time toward their bedding down spot just across the room. The carefully stacked up collection of broken and flattened out cardboard boxes, old blankets and balled up jackets for pillows looked somehow romantic in the dimly lighted brick walled corner aglow from the little battery powered lantern. "Go fluff our pillows while I spread out the glass and seal the door. Then we can continue this conversation, safely tucked in, as it were."

"I'll be waiting with baited breath," she said suggestively, then turned and wiggled her way off. She was a little out of practice, though, at being sexy and they shared a quiet laugh. "I'm trying, Clay . . ."

"Well . . . keep trying."

Ivy picked up a piece of cardboard box nearby and playfully threw it at him. He mockingly ducked for cover, then gave her a good smile and turned to go. His smile died quick. He wasn't too sure about this. *Oh sure it would feel good, physically, but . . . but what? Why was he having such a conscience all of a sudden? Just do it. Enjoy it.*

He'd been having these feelings lately, good feelings. Or maybe he should say feelings about being good, like as a father and the head of this new family he'd suddenly found himself living with. Or maybe he should say, *surviving* with. He just wanted to do things right for some crazy reason. Even get married . . .

What? Like you even could find a church these days, his conscience, the bad half started in on him.

Well, you never know. There might be a reverend out there somewhere. And that's all you need right? Or a justice of the peace . . . a priest, the good half of his conscience countered.

Right. Like that's going to happen. She's right! You could also die real soon too. Come on, one last time. What's it been, almost six months since you had that hooker right after you got out of Chino last time?

Well, and that's another thing too. You need to tell her more about your past. You've never been an angel, that's for sure.

She knows that! And did you feel that butt!

Griner shook his head hard and made himself blink several times too. He could drive himself nuts like this! He rubbed his forehead.

Back at the mouth of the entrance tunnel, he set his sawed off against the wall. He grabbed up one of the two, medium sized boxes sitting there just outside the entrance filled to the rim with pieces of broken glass. He'd had the kids gather it all up from the coffee shop across the parking lot from where they were now. That place had been walled in by almost all glass, which in the quake had all been shattered.

He dumped the shards in a ten-foot wide or so diameter out from the door. Not that it would stop any zombies or whatever else might come, but it should make just enough racket to alert them inside, or at least him. Then he could get everyone else up and hopefully they could all get to safety. And everyone was going to sleep with weapons nearby too.

As he was bending down to get the second box of broken glass, he couldn't help but notice a couple crows over by the crumpled and shattered coffee shop. It was weird how they just seemed to be silently watching him. He found a piece of the glass not too sharp on one side, got his index finger on that side and slung it like a skipping stone at the big, black birds.

"You sonsabitches won't be having me for dinner," he growled at them. Though the quickly shooting piece of glass didn't find its mark, it did scare them enough to force them into taking flight. They cawed like mad and lifted up and up on strong wing strokes before coursing higher and higher away across the white and blue, sunshine filled sky.

Udo could smell them first. Well, it'd been almost a week since any of them had been able to shower. *So go figure.* Although it wasn't just that. His heightened senses were coming back online now too, as more and more he was slowly but surely overcoming the zombie disease.

It wasn't just the stink he smelled anyway. He'd also stocked up the basement shelter with a couple four packs of stick deodorant, one for the men and one for women. His brand too, at least the one for the men. He couldn't miss that odor. It was a pretty distinctive smell, the one the sailor guy on TV wore. And for the ladies he'd gotten the one the fairy queen on the unicorn wore. That was Ivy's favorite. He'd recognize that smell anywhere too. *Ivy . . . hey, Ivy!*

He broke in a run up Harbor Boulevard, leaping from shattered ruin to shattered ruin. Then as he approached the Pacific Coast Highway overpass, he made one big leap up onto the half of it still there like some giant's broken and jagged diving board remnant. Bummer though, that there wasn't a big swimming pool for him to dive into below, he couldn't help but half-humorously think.

He had found something even better, however, looking ahead up Harbor. His sight was getting way better too, possibly helped along by the demon head mask, which certainly then aided in his spotting them among the rubble about a half mile ahead. He could see their blue-lighted outlines scrambling around the corner of a half-demolished, old brick building.

Oh! He could barely contain his excitement. *Look at little Joannie with the junior .22* he'd gotten for her and then they spent all that wonderful bonding time shooting bottles and cans. But who was that rather rough looking man with the bushy red moustache bringing up the rear. And Ivy was with him, but hopefully not *with* him, he somewhat anxiously added to his thought train.

Well, he had to find out now. He wanted to see them anyway, help them too, and help them get to the coast, then to the island. He could just fly right over there, he was thinking, and just about as he was going to do so, he suddenly felt very tired. Well, maybe he would just walk. *Why risk an accident now*, now that he was so close.

Besides, the overpass, or at least the near edge of it that ran sidewalk size down to ground level, was easy enough to walk on, a little steep, but manageable. *All right. Down and down a little more. How beautiful a day it is too. The sun is so warm and high. He could even smell the ocean. He could—*

"Udo," a familiar voice called out just as he easily climbed over the white metal and now very twisted railing where the overpass reached street level.

Where, he thought at first, rather than *who* and looked around. "Oh," he said then as he saw him. Wasn't it *him*? It looked like just some guy sitting on an amazingly preserved little park bench in an equally amazingly preserved little piece of park, which Udo knew they'd had around this area back in the day. Those small plots of perfect grass right by the road, especially down by the beach, where people could stop and sit on the little bench and watch the sunset. *But had there been one right there? Did it really matter?* Because even if there hadn't been one, He could have made one, just like that, of course, since he was Jesus and all.

"Sit . . . sit, my boy," the Lord said and patted the spot on the bench right next to him.

Actually, and as to be expected Udo knew, Jesus was dressed rather nicely in an outfit the rich might have worn to a yacht party. That is, before the marina was ruined and all the yachts were flipped and sunk by a tsunami. You know, topsiders, khaki slacks, a nice pastel polo and a sweater over the shoulders just in case.

Udo sat and the bench shook first then sagged under his bulk. The Lord smiled, slapped his hand hard on Udo's even harder thigh, and then continued. "You hungry? Can I get you something? A nice, fresh fish sandwich?"

No. That's okay. Those hearts really stick with ya," Udo said back, really meaning it, because they really did, all that strong muscle tissue took a while to digest. And besides, he also knew probably that there were more coming soon. He turned to look at Jesus.

"Here . . . here. This is creeping me out." The Lord reached over and carefully lifted the demon head helmet off of Udo. "I'm glad you got it though. Do you like?"

"Oh yeah. It's great. It helps. You know . . . amazing though too. "

"Good . . . good. And it has helped you find your family, I see."

"Yes, and they look well," Udo said and just vacantly stared at whatever was in front of him. He hadn't figured it out yet, why he was suddenly so happy and relaxed, but then he did. It was always this way around . . . Him. "Are they?"

"Yes. They are fine." The Lord looked down and seemed to shift from light to a more serious mood. "I am helping you to feel okay right now, my boy, and I mean extra okay, because I have something very hard to tell you."

"Uh oh," Udo could only vacantly say, noticing too for the first time the giant cross that the wreckage this part of town had become seemed to have erected in the middle of itself somehow. Pieces of building, metal, concrete and hunks of wood had all been magically drawn together then twisted and rose high in an almost perfect cross shape, maybe a couple hundred feet high or so, like God himself had pulled it up out of the ruins.

"Kind of like a signature, I guess. Dad did it for me. I just wanted to come see it. And like I said, talk to you a little bit."

Even through the immeasurable joy, Udo felt the sadness seeping through the cracks. He measured his words carefully. "I can take it. I know your position requires you to make very difficult decisions, like this whole operation. Like it's happened before this too." He looked down. "I'm yours and just very grateful for all you've given me, this whole chance. I just saw them, as you said, and all I ask now is that I guard them and help them make it. That's all."

The Lord sat up out of his relaxed posture, leaned forward and brought his hands together. "I know you've gotten the message about the island. That's good. And the job you've done so far has been wonderful. Just a little longer my good and faithful servant." He put his hand on Udo's shoulder this time. "You can see them, and will very shortly, but for the most part, they can't see you. We are breaking a lot of my father's rules, you and I, just by your being here.

"That's the real reason behind this helmet I've made for you. So you can at least be near them, to help them, to fight for them, and they won't know who you are." The Lord looked at the helmet, into its eyes, then wrinkled up his features and set it to the side on the bench. "One can see you though, and she will see you first, and soon. She already sees into our realm as it is. Your daughter."

"Joannie," Udo could only say and let a tear run down his hard cheek. It would be worth it just to see her, at least. *And the others? They couldn't know it was him? So really he couldn't be with them, talk to them in a personal way?* That was a big price to pay, but worth it. Just as long as they'd be safe.

"Okay. That's good enough for me. I better get over there. Make sure—" Udo had made a move for the helmet, but a touch from the Lord on his arm stopped him midmotion.

"For now, just rest. It's not time yet. Soon. But for now, just rest . . . just rest . . ."

Udo sat back and saw the big cross again. The Lord's words tripped lightly into his mind and made his eyelids heavy. The cross got blurry and dark, and then everything else did too.

This was a very strange little boy, the Devil could only assume. He just sat there, no crying, no screaming, no wanting his mommy, though of course she was very dead, which the boy may or may not have known, but still, he'd been so looking forward to all that. Maybe even some pants-wetting too. *Dammit!*

The mind scans weren't very revealing either. *He wasn't autistic was he? Maybe he was in some kind of shock. Had they ever scanned for that before?* He would have had one of his technicians take a look, but there wasn't really time for that. The window of opportunity for the other child was going to open soon and could close any time after that. *These damn humans were so unpredictable. Just like this little boy. Dear, dear*, Satan let it all go with and shook his head.

He'd transformed already, back into the playboy look, then even pushed his little horns down, just in case. He took off the silk smoking jacket and slipped on a lab coat. Then he looked in the mirror. The jet-black goatee and mustache magically disappeared then too. He added some wire rim glasses, then even aged about twenty years until some gray peppered his hair, just in case.

Not that this kid was going to spook anyway. He'd tried every hideous form imaginable already, just to get a reaction. *Nothing.* It was too bad really. If he were sticking around, he could use this kid, as long as he was trainable. Probably make a real good serial killer.

All that didn't matter now, however. Looking like a kindly middle-aged physician, the father of murder exited the small room on the other side of this other, identical small room separated by the two-way mirror through which he had been watching the little boy.

He entered the second room, stood before the boy, smiled and extended a hand. Aaron blankly looked up at him, managed a small smile of his own, then stood and took his hand. They exited the room.

Then, maybe even more amazingly, even the huge spaceship parked inside the big hangar at the end of the hallway didn't elicit much of a reaction from the boy either. Perhaps it might have, had the boy known about the soul separation chamber that waited for him inside.

Joannie was having more and more trouble telling the difference between her dreams and reality. Something was happening to her. That was for sure. Besides the very real dreams that sometimes came true, there was other stuff too. Even before the earthquake, her bed used to shake late at night sometimes. Not like earthquake shaking, so it wasn't to portend that event or anything like that, she knew. She had looked up that word, portend, when she'd found it in a book about her dreams coming true. But the bed shaking was faster, almost like vibrating, and only happened once in a while. Of course she hadn't been sleeping on a bed lately, so . . .

But was this one of those dreams? She couldn't tell for sure. It seemed so real. But like in a dream too she could tell that she wasn't totally in control. She tried but couldn't do exactly what she wanted to. Like when she first got up—which was one of the things that was weird about these dreams, often in them she'd be waking up in her real bedroom or in the basement too, but later the strangest things happened, and then she knew it was a dream.

Well in this dream, or whatever it was, she wanted right away to go wake up Jason, but she just couldn't. That was very dreamlike. And then like in a dream too, there was something else there with her, some power or something, making her do things she knew she shouldn't do. Like going off on her own.

Should I bring supplies, she thought then in one of those moments that made her wonder if she was really dreaming. Because could you do that in a dream? But then something that really seemed dreamlike happened. *No, you won't need any of that stuff anymore. Do you have your shoes though?* A voice from somewhere enquired.

Oh yes. We sleep with our shoes on these days.

Well, that's good then. Shall we go?

Oh I guess, Joannie thought and was turning to go, but then the voice stopped her.

Not that way, this way.

Joannie stopped in her tracks and put her hands on her hips. This seemed more and more real. *But voices out of nowhere?*

Now exactly who am I talking to here? And why can't I see you? The little girl mentally projected.

Your daddy told me you were smart.

You know my daddy?

Yes, we're very good friends. And you are a very good girl.

Well, when? When did you know my daddy. He's dead.

Do you believe in heaven, Joannie?

She was going to answer, was thinking about it anyway, when the very dark wall in front of her, that she knew was the very back of the building, suddenly lighted up with the outline of a little archway.

The thin line of light grew in both width and intensity until a section of the brickwork within slowly swung open like a little door. Again, and dreamlike, she slowly walked—or was she moved as if on wheels, she even had to question—over to the opening.

It was so very bright she had to bring her arm up to partially shield what she was trying to see out there. Soon, though, her eyes grew accustomed to it, and she could make out first green grass, then a blue sky behind it all and in the middle the outline of someone standing there. She looked and looked and in a moment could tell who it was.

"Daddy . . . daddy," she yelled out in joy and broke in a run for him. She noticed too how nice he looked in an all-white but beach style, casual outfit.

"Baby," he said with joy all his own and went to one knee to more easily take her in the big bear hug that then followed. If the hug wasn't a world record breaker for length of time, then it was close. After it, father and daughter took turns wiping each other's tears away.

Eventually they stood and turned and hand in hand walked across the grass toward their obvious destination, a beautiful white and wooden dock, sitting seaside, that somehow they were already so close too.

There tied to it was an equally nice, older style all wooden but highly polished speedboat. The two, both Udo and Joannie, had seen one at the marina one time and since then had always wanted one. Now they had it.

On their way there and as they boarded, Udo and Joannie talked and talked, Udo explaining that it was so wonderful to see her, but for now it could only be for a little bit. He told her also that she was the only one able to do so, able to see him because she was special. This was, of course, much more than a dream.

Joannie took her turn then, asking if they were going to heaven. Her father explained to her that no . . . but all this was being made possible by Jesus, and she must always believe in him and obey his commandments. That way later, much later, she could go home to heaven and be with her daddy again. Right now though, they were going someplace else.

Quiet and content in that knowledge, the little girl sat back in the boat's comfy little passenger seat and looked over at her daddy. He was so tan and handsome as he took the boat out. The first wisps of wind blew back his long hair that she'd always loved so much, golden and brown. It was the happiest moment of her life up to that point.

So nice. The ocean's water was so pretty too in its dark blue and the little spray it threw off and up around the boat kissed her lightly on the cheek as they picked up speed.

Udo turned the boat toward the sun already low on the horizon. Luckily its yellow light was nicely subdued by the boat's tinted windshield. Joannie squinted through it, not caring where they were going. She just hoped it would take forever to get there.

Sure it was a hard decision, leaving Janet and the priest back on the island and coming back, risking it all just to look for more survivors. But that was what he was, Officer John Hernandez. He was a police officer, and this was why he'd become a cop in the first place, to help people and save lives. No matter where, no matter when.

That was the true essence of all the men and women he'd ever worked with in law enforcement. That was what it was all about on the gut level. Oh sure, more than a few would get corrupted and either through perceived need, or just plain old greed would sell out that ideal. Especially after realizing that almost everyone in power, the ones who formed and maintained the power structure all police officers really answered to . . . it had been corrupted too. But not Officer John Hernandez.

This would be his own statement, his stand against all that. All the corrupt cops, hell, all the corrupt people probably too . . . they were all probably dead. But not him. The last cop on Earth was going to do something right . . . something good.

Plus, it was all pretty doable. He knew Janet—and hopefully the priest too who as he left them was still bravely battling death---would be okay. There was just something about that island. *Man, what a place!*

Then too it hadn't taken all that much gas to get here from the zombie navy island---as he called it---where he'd filled up the last time. From there to the new Island--which they still couldn't find on any of the maps---then to Highpoint Park Station again for another tank topper, then to here and still plenty left.

So here he was, The Eye in the Sky, as he liked to think of himself back in the day. And then he'd even play that old song, the hit from the eighties of the same name. He'd had a CD player put in the chopper as soon as administration Ok'd it.

Yeah, and then the young officer saw the CD again. *There it was, under a small tangle of lines and a couple spent clips.* He slipped it in the CD player one more time and took the bird in low for a scan of wherever he was.

All of a sudden Udo was just sitting on the bench again. The only difference from before was that Jesus was gone now. Also it was several hours later. Udo could tell by the light and the cooling of the air. It was that transition time now with late afternoon giving way to early evening.

So what, had he just fallen asleep there and dreamed it all? No, he realized, that would have been too simple an explanation, especially since he'd been sitting there with Jesus before. Things were never that simple with Him around.

And besides too, that had been way too real for a dream. He could still see little Joannie and feel her little hand in his. *To hug her like that . . .* he could still feel that too.

Hadn't the Lord said she would get to be with him one more time? *Yes. So . . . yes.* Udo was sure it had been real.

Then the boat ride in that wooden runabout he'd fallen in love with. Heck, they both had, both him and little Joannie had gone gaga for that baby when they saw it at the marina that time. And how wonderful it was then to safely deliver her to the island.

But really . . . had he? He had to wonder. It couldn't be that easy, after all the fighting . . . the demons . . . the zombies . . . and those other things too. And—

Then it hit him.

There was only one way to find out. *And besides, what about the rest of them? How horrible it would be if Joannie were stuck growing up without her mom.* He just *had* to go check and help out there too. Hopefully they all could still get there. Get to the island.

Udo got up and started in a slow run, but then leapt from one large mound of rubble to another. He remembered from before that it was a half knocked down, brick building right along Harbor here. *Wasn't that the shoe store? Yeah,* he remembered that place. *Super Shoes.* He and his family hadn't shopped there, stuck on a budget like they were. It was one of those trendy, higher-priced places. But he still remembered it. Yes, there it was, he saw now again.

He slowed to a walk and carefully approached. He'd already picked up their scent again and so now knew they had to still be there. Just like before, only now from ground level he could see again that the front half of the building was little more than a slanting pile of bricks with broken boards poking out like quills on a dead porcupine.

Pretty smart, pretty smart, he realized. There was probably only one entrance around back. That's the way it was with these old buildings. Although then too couldn't he see a gap in the rubble? Either way, Udo decided to just make a quick trip around the building for now. Make sure the perimeter was secure, then maybe go in.

Cutting down the little alleyway between the old building and the newer but similarly destructed one next to it, the ex-zombie—ever since his dream visit with Joannie he seemed fine—suddenly stopped. There hidden in the shadows was a light golden outline, most likely only visible through the demon head mask's eyes Udo had naturally donned once more. It was a small arc, maybe four foot tall at its highest point, somehow cut right into the brick, but with the also brick door of the thing shut now.

That just isn't normal, Udo couldn't help but think, for some reason the phrase his daughter always used coming to his mind. "That's *not normal,* daddy," she used to say. It had apparently become a favorite phrase of all the popular young ladies back then.

But then that thought caught in his mind. *Did that mean maybe she had something to do with this? Yes . . .* and *use this door,* Udo sort of heard then, although too it kind of felt like just an idea of his. Either way he knew better than to ignore it. He went over and then knelt down before the arch.

A light push was all it took to help the doorway silently swing open. As quietly as he could—which with his perfected skills mostly returned now was whisper quiet—he crawled and then crept up into the relatively dark room.

He stood silently there for the moment, all the while also slowly scanning 360 degrees. The helmet mask's enhanced visual capabilities not only helped him see but also outlined the sleeping figure of first Jason in a foremost position, then further back in the corner someone even smaller. *It was—huh? It couldn't be!*

He moved in closer, quietly. He mustn't let them see him, or if he did he would have to leave quickly. But if he were quiet . . . ah yes . . . his boy, Jason. *Man, is he really growing up, much stronger and bigger. And with the gun right there with him,* his boy was becoming a man.

And of course he wanted to wake him and hug him too and tell him about Jesus and to be good. Be a good boy, or I'll whip you. He couldn't give up being his dad and suddenly felt so sorry for not being able to be there for him anymore. He—

A stirring over where the other smaller one slept caught his attention. He scooted over there, having to check anyway, because he hadn't thought . . . but there she was . . . little Joannie still here. He leaned in closer. He—

Uh oh. All of a sudden Joannie opened her eyes, looked right at him, then just as quickly and without a reaction shut them again. He dropped quickly back into the shadows.

What the—

That was her but—

And he had to be a sight with the demon head on. But nothing. Maybe she thought she was dreaming and—

Another sound then grabbed his attention like fingernails on a chalkboard. *Ivy? But . . . she wasn't supposed to be doing that!*

No way. No. NOOOoo . . .

All thoughts of being quiet left Udo's mind in a flood, a flood that also carried away reason, understanding and almost all ability to maintain self-control. He flung himself around the corner, and there they were, and sure, they were trying to be quiet, but Udo had that damn super hearing again now, *that damn super hearing.*

Hey! Why did he, that scraggly guy with the red mustache, why did he have to be saying her name like that. "Ivy . . . Ivy . . . Ivy." Of course, leaving no doubt who that other blue outline was underneath him. Which Udo had at first hoped wasn't Ivy, because luckily at least all of it was somewhat obscured in the thick shadows.

But when she said her 'oh baby' and then made that noise she always used to make, kind of like a cat but kind of growling too, and then . . .

"Ahh," Udo finally just yelled, ran over and grabbed the guy off of her before throwing him across the room. He landed hard and looked stunned, so Udo turned back toward Ivy.

"How . . . how could you?" he now only half-yelled, half-whined. Then with all his muscles flexing spasmodically he just stood and looked at her.

The look of stunned fright on her face started Udo's return to sanity. Then as her features started to thaw and she almost incoherently and very quietly said his name, if he hadn't had an extra durable heart, surely it would have burst right then, right there.

Which also of course continued his return to normalcy, sort of, this time happening from his own subtle brand of fear, fear of failing his Lord. *They can't know who you are . . . they can't know who you are . . .*

The words screamed in Udo's mind and he ran back to the man who had been with her. *Who had been with her!* These words also screamed in his mind, and as the man was just then getting up, at first Udo only helped him continue to do so, grabbing him under the shoulders.

But he did more than just help him then as he lifted him up and up, switching to do it with just his left hand under his chin, freeing up his right. Then he could hear the man's heart, *badda, badda, badda*, and Udo's ideas swung back to what he knew best, his current assignment, eating such things. He readied his right hand for extraction.

The gun's loud report had only barely registered in Udo's ears as the mule kick that came with it slammed into his still luckily helmeted head. The bright flash of light that then came too—not as big as the one that killed him the first time, also luckily—got swallowed up in the big blackness that took him away from everything after that.

Ivy couldn't believe it. *Finally. Finally.* Why hadn't she done it sooner, she couldn't help but consider, just lying there with Clay after was so wonderful. *Why hadn't she . . .?*

At first, as she darn well knew, she hadn't been able to let Udo go. But then all the booze and drugs had finally killed him off in her heart, but it had killed her heart too. So she drank more and more booze and did just enough with what little the government gave her to keep the kids off the street. Give them a chance.

But now this! Wasn't it so ironic? Here in what was looking more and more like the end of the world, she was finding a new beginning. Off the booze and with no drugs around and this man—not the perfect man—but somehow they'd fallen in love and most likely the new beginning wouldn't last too long, but for now . . .

Just one more time.

And he could! A second time! Oh how wonderful that he could a second time. Of course, Udo had too. Hadn't he? Who cares? This right now just felt so good. *Oh Clay.* Then she couldn't help it and made that same sound she used to.

But then—

Oh my—

Would the horror show never stop! What the hell kind of monster now! Omigod, look at that thing! And it just picked up Clay and threw him like a rag doll. Clay!

Great. Now, it was coming back. God it was strong! And like a human, but that skin. It looked like a living . . . a living statue. And that head . . . hideous . . . but it was like a . . . a . . . helmet. Oh yes. You could hear when it spoke it was a helmet. But . . . what?

No.

It couldn't be . . .

"Udo?" She could barely say it and then only like a question. Which that then froze the thing in its tracks. *So did that mean?* But Udo wasn't *that* big. And he was dead . . . ashes even.

Then, oh God, it was going after Clay again. Clay! She had to get over there. But put some clothes on first of course. The kids would be up with this racket. The kids—

Kaboom!

The sound of the gunshot was extra loud in the little all brick shelter and Ivy almost jumped out of her skin *and* the jeans and t-shirt she'd just jumped into. It was so loud even the air had to clear of it before her mind could think and see again.

Clay was up on one knee and at least still moving and in one piece. And there across from him lay the . . . statue thing very still.

Across the other way stood Jason in just pants and shoes and his pistol still held head high and steady. He lowered it and spoke.

"What the hell is that thing? I know I got it in the head, but I think it just ricocheted off. It don't look like no zombie."

"I don't know," was all Ivy wanted to say for now. First she had to check on Clay. "You okay, baby?"

Griner ran a shaky arm across his sweat-beaded forehead. What the hell, was all he could think. One minute I'm closing in on ecstasy, and the next thing I know some crazy Hercules statue like thing with a metal head is getting ready to—

"I'm okay . . . I'm okay," he let it all go with. *No use getting everybody riled up. But,* "We better get packed up. Is that thing dead?"

"Hey, Grinds," Jason said over and snickered. "You better get some clothes on."

"Holy shi—" the old con cussed almost and ran back into their adhoc bedroom. Even in the midst of all the madness, Ivy and her son had to laugh at that scene. Then they moved in on the strange creature lying face down right before them.

"Did I kill it?"

"I don't know. You go get your sister up . . . start packing. I don't think," she started to add, thinking out loud really, almost ready to say she didn't think this creature . . . man . . . thing . . . she didn't think it would hurt them. *What if . . .* then she noticed Jason still standing there. "Go! Get your sister up. Go!"

The boy hustled off. Ivy looked down at the strange being, reached out and touched his shoulder and then his back where the muscles bunched up over his shoulder blades. She quickly withdrew her hand. It certainly felt dead, cold, and hard. This couldn't be her Udo. He didn't have muscles like that.

And it certainly was some kind of helmet the thing had on too. And yeah, there was a pretty big dent in the back of it where Jason's shot must have hit. No blood though. So he was maybe not *dead. Maybe—*

In the quiet that had come over the place, except for the subdued shuffling and scuffling sounds of everyone getting ready to go, Ivy next heard a different kind of shuffling and scuffling. *It sounded like something . . . several something's were walking through Clay's broken glass burglar alarm outside the entrance.*

She got up quickly and hustled into the bedroom. "Clay . . . something's coming . . ."

"Where? Out front? Shi_," he said all at once, knowing that was where it had to be. He stepped up the pace of his preparation, moving now right into weapons check. Ivy followed suit.

In another minute the Griner/Henkman gang massed for planning in center sector, brick house headquarters. Udo was absent from their meeting, however.

"Hey, where'd that thing—" Jason was the first to ask. That froze them all for a moment.

"I don't know. But we don't have time . . ." Griner managed to get out then also managed to breathe again.

"Jason. Where's your sister?" Ivy shot out almost like bullets.

"She's . . . she's not here?" Jason had to ask, also all the while looking fervently about. "The little brat . . . she was supposed to be right behind me . . . she's out of it, Mom. She wouldn't even talk to me. She's probably still in our room. I—"

"Come on, kid. You and me up front. We'll hold 'em off," Griner started in, his turn to issue orders. "Ivy, you go get Joannie. She is probably in some sort of shock or something. *Who can blame her?* Get her out here and set her up behind this wall. Then join the fight if you can . . . okay, honey?"

He gave her a quick hug and peck on the forehead. They were both shaking. "We can do this," he added, just as much for himself as the others. "Come on, kid," to Jason then. "You locked and loaded?"

"Just spent the one on that other . . . thing. So I still got eleven plus the other clip. Right here." He slapped his back pocket.

"Alright. I got the scattergun. Extra shells. Hopefully Ivy can get some with the .22. Either way, here we go. And remember, only head shots," Griner reminded the kid, pumped in a round, held the shotgun to his shoulder. He flashed a wide-eyed glance at the kid and waited.

"Okay," Jason answered and got a good two-hand grip. "Ready."

They rounded the separation wall into their entrance's anteroom. The thirty by thirty foot area would make a good kill box, Clay had figured. It was part of the plan, clearing a path in the tunnel of fallen bricks to get there where then the invades would run into a wall of bullets. So, 'kill room,' all right. Just hopefully they wouldn't get killed there too.

But then, *whoa*. Or maybe more like . . . *whoa!*

Not because there was at least four or five moaners trying to break through the shoe display rack barricade they'd wedged across the entryway. They'd expected that. But then there was Udo, holding the barricade hard in place at the end of his extended, big, rock hard and mostly white arm. And he was laughing. Until after his chuckle he spoke over at the two much more normal humans looking at him.

"I have to take their heads and their hearts. It's what I do. You can stay and watch if you want. But it might be better if you went out the back way. There's a small door in the wall at the very back, past Jason's . . . err, I mean, the boy's bed."

"Hey! How'd you know my name?"

"You . . . you got this?" Griner could only ask with a stammer.

"Yes, be ready though. Out back. There might be more there. And take good care of them. And her. Or I'll be back . . ."

"Hey. Your voice sounds familiar," Jason tried this time. But the being was just too strange looking for him to make the connection, especially when it then turned to look right at him and the yellow eyes in the metal, demonic helmet mask glowed dimly.

"Take care of your mother and your sister. And be good," Udo, the dad, told him.

All the while, he still rather mightily and easily held the barricade in place. But the press of zombies on its other side was bending the thing and it was obvious they would most likely soon break through. "I would recommend that you go while you still can," Udo sagely advised.

Jason stared at Udo as if in a trance. Griner grabbed him hard by the arm. "He's right. Let's go, kid."

As they went, Jason lingered one last look and noticed for the first time that the zombie killer held a hammer. It was the same one they'd used to help build the barricade. *He was going to go after all them with a hammer?* For a second he doubted he'd ever see that thing again, until he heard it laugh once more, then the onslaught of moaners coming in followed by what sounded like a giant blender set to chop, filled with zombies.

"Clay, there's a little—"

"—door." He finished Ivy's sentence for her.

". . . back here," she added in conclusion. "What? You knew?"

"He told us. The visitor. You were right. He is on our side, from the looks of it. There's a bunch of zombies coming through the front door and he's holding them off."

"With a hammer," Jason put in. They all just looked at each other. "And he's winning, from the sounds of it."

"How's the kid?" Griner next asked.

"She's right—" Ivy cut herself off, though, as looking around she could see no sign of Joannie. Then she yelled out her name. "We found that door just a second ago. I told her not to . . . but she must have. At least she had her pack on and her rifle. I've got her little suitcase."

"Come on. We better join her," Griner suggested, and they all fell in, all packed up and crawling then even through the little doorway Joannie must have left open on her way out.

Unlike Udo had feared, there were no zombies out back. In fact, it was eerily quiet in the little bit of alley and somewhat dark already with just the half-light of the late day left.

"Joannie," Ivy called out again, seeing the little girl rounding the corner at the end of the alley, probably heading back to Harbor Boulevard. "I don't know what's wrong with her."

"Uh oh," Jason put in, finding the girl's little rifle half-way up the alley and picking it up. They all took turns yelling her name then and hustled to follow her.

Out in the shambles of what was left of Sandy Point Beach, city proper; at first none of them could spot the little girl. But then once they did, they wished they hadn't. Somehow she'd gotten a good thirty to forty yards ahead and was still making her way steadily across what looked like a parking lot chewed up by artillery fire.

Even worse, the most hideous creature they'd seen yet, a huge, dark and demoniacal looking thing—in fact Satan in his half humanoid, half dragon version, though none of them knew that—seemed to be waiting for their little girl. This was the, twenty foot tall, rock hard but really a leather-like skin, form the Devil had been trapped in the earth with before bursting up and out. Maybe his truest, physical form, his battle body. Just in case. He extended a long and strong, black scaled arm and hand for Joannie, only yards away now.

And even though none of them knew this was Satan, they certainly got a taste of his power, when try as they might, none of them could gain a step on the horrid event about to take place. In a world full of strange scenes, at least in that little corner of the old USA, one of another type was just then created as Jason, Griner and Ivy all started moving in super slow motion, that type of extra slowed, slow motion usually reserved for nature documentaries where a frog's tongue can even be seen spearing and slurping up an unsuspecting fly.

Now all three of the gallant pursuers looked like they were in some sort of strange Tai Chi class devoted entirely to the exercise of running and climbing over obstacles. The upturned chunks of asphalt between them and Joannie might as well have been mountains.

Griner, who was in the lead, eventually got the idea to stop and level his shotgun at the big beasty thing's head, which he did, albeit from a bit too far of a distance, and also all of it accomplished over a lengthy—relatively speaking—span of time, due to his slow motion movements.

All of which only allowed the creature to take the few remaining steps it needed to get close to Joannie, surround her and himself with his huge thick wings, which also then easily deflected Griner's assault. Then, before any of the others could do another incredibly slow thing, both the demon king and Joannie were airborne and then long gone.

Witnessing this sucked all the air, hope and at least momentarily, volition from the three would-be rescuers. But at least with the slow motion state removed, they collapsed at normal speed, as if it mattered.

Ivy began sobbing uncontrollably. Griner looked to the patch of sky his recently, though not officially, adopted daughter had just disappeared into with her captor and yelled a string of expletives. Jason seemed about to do the same but then thought better of it and went instead to his mother, partly to console her, but mostly to inform her that her grieving would have to wait. More zombies were headed their way.

Officer John knew the most likely place to find any more survivors this late in the game would be wherever the greatest concentration of people had been in the first place. Made sense. And then too, he'd also figured, in those places where the destruction had been the least catastrophic.

But then too, he also had to remember he only had so much travel range, considering fuel needs. Luckily, the Highpoint Park Station had plenty of fuel still, but starting his searches from there he made sure to use conservative estimates to allow plenty of lateral travel leeway for thorough searching.

Using those parameters, he'd made it as far north as the Grapevine, off of which all the grapes had definitely fallen, and the vine too dropped into the giant burning and smoking abyss that now stretched from the point of San Clemente to other points even further north than he could venture. *What was the point after all he had to ask himself, no pun intended?* The sky up that way was a solid black mist of probably toxic fumes emanating from the endless fires that had become the landscape up there too. He couldn't risk getting downed by bad air.

On his way back south from there, he'd also then made a panoramic sweep of greater Los Angeles County and could see no signs of life anywhere. Unless he wanted to call groups of zombies dying of starvation, life. And most of them dying like that, John could tell, because they were trapped in little pockets of unnavigable—that is in walking or climbing mode—terrain with nowhere else to go and nothing left to eat.

Strange too were these small—relatively speaking at least—silver mountains that he'd seen, three of them so far, the first of which exploded as he drew near for closer examination. That had been a close call, but then he'd risked getting close to another one because he'd noticed the rivers flowing into it that carried car sized, circular blobs of silver that believe it or not carried groups of zombies.

Having been unable to learn anything else than that, he circled and pulled quickly away. Just in time too because then that one also exploded. He saw the bright flash and then the thick plume of smoke these explosions created and circled back after to see the pile of molten metal the thing had become.

Interesting.

So he was extra careful with the third one, which was further south and a little larger than the others. It too had the small rivers flowing into it but showed no other signs of activity. No need to get too close, he was thinking of course, but Officer Hernandez made a mental note to check back later.

He was then ready to head back for more fuel when he decided a sweep over also nearby Sandy Point Beach might be worth his while, especially when he saw the giant cross.

"What the—" he let quietly slip in the otherwise unoccupied cockpit of the chopper and swooped in for a closer look. On the way, he almost hit Satan ascending with Joannie wrapped up tight in one of his big hands. Had he not been transporting his precious soul package, the destroyer probably would have pulverized the helicopter with a dismissive backhand . . . or fried it with a fresh blast of his fiery breath.

Seeing that, of course, at first John couldn't believe his eyes and momentarily lost touch with reality. *Zombies? Okay. I got that,* he was thinking. As crazy as that was, he'd at least gotten his head around all that by now finally.

Then the other demon thing, the one at the battle of Highpoint Park. And the statue guy, well, he was working on processing them. *But now on top of that an even bigger, black flying demon thing kidnapping a little girl? What?*

John pulled up hard to keep from nose diving into the wreckage of everything below and leveled off. He took a tight turn around the cross to get a closer look there too. Wow, he could only think. Something incredibly powerful had to have pulled and twisted and mashed and molded all the-

Hey! Survivors! And they weren't under attack. Although wait . . . wait . . . yeah. There. A group of five or no . . . six . . . make that seven . . . seven zombies headed their way. And the survivors hadn't even seen them yet from the looks of it. They were—

Oh no, he then realized.

That must have been their kid.

Maybe he could chase down that demon thing, John thought at the last second and turned the bird back the way the bigger demon thing had flown. There was no sign of it now. He turned back and looked for a place to set down.

At least he could tell the survivors had seen the oncoming zombies by then. And better yet, they were very smartly getting to some high ground in the back of an abandoned pickup truck. And better yet, it was one of those lifted ones. Albeit, only in the back. The front end was severely damage and seemingly without wheels.

So let's see, John was thinking quickly, *where to set down, where to set down?* Not far from the survivors, but behind them. Maybe thirty, thirty-five yards. So no zombies would get to the chopper without going through them.

There was the spot too, the pilot could then tell, a stretch of, believe it or not, grass opened up just off the main roadway just behind what looked like an also neat little park bench. *Would wonders never cease?*

Once down on the patch of grass, he scrambled out of the pilot's seat, grabbed up the U.S. Navy duffel bag of rifle's and ammo, adjusted the ride of his double holstered nines, and took off, low headed, running in the direction of the truck.

Out from under the helicopter's slowing but still whirling prop blades, John could hear the gunfire from the truck for the first time. One thing about these survivors he could tell: they weren't shy. With his trained ear he could hear three different calibers of weapons discharging. They were all in it and probably soon would be low on ammo.

He slowed a little but continued in a bent over run, eyes at first on the truck dead ahead, its front end facing him, smashed, and now John could see it, under a fallen streetlight. As he got closer, the officer scanned around and all looked clear other than the group of zombies, mostly hidden to him at present, advancing on the survivors from the other side. Once up to the truck's crumpled front end he stayed low behind it and studied the situation, listening and watching intently from his rearward vantage point.

He watched the survivors: the shoulders and head of the tallest man who held a center position in the bed of the truck with his back against the rear of the truck's cab, just the head of the younger and only slightly shorter man to his right, and then on this side, the side closest to where John had taken position was the woman, most of her upper body visible as was this side of the truck.

"That's the last one. I'll get him," the man in the center said and started to move over in front of the woman while at the same time bringing his shotgun up to his shoulder. Then John could see they were talking about a zombie coming up this same side of the truck by the woman.

The woman forced her way back in front of the man and brought her own rifle up. "Let me, Clay. I have more ammo. I could use the practice too. And I sort of need to vent right about now."

Before the man could protest, the lady let fly and both by the relatively quiet report of its multiple shots and by the gun's appearance, John could tell it was a .22.

At least she was a good shot, John noticed too with relief. He had drawn out one of his nines just in case, but the three shots from the .22 had impacted the walking dead thing in the head, poofing its matted hair up each time in different spots.

Then the apparently retired mailman—the zombie was wearing the well-known, mostly blue, mail carrier's uniform—met the end of his extended, 'going postal,' moment. Or at least the last week of his life must have seemed like that, killing and eating and instead of serving the U.S. Government serving the real Satan. All of which at the moment looked like wandering loose limbed in a tight circle with blood rivulets trailing down his neck from multiple head wounds until he collapsed, falling still to the ground.

"Hello?" John then tried in the silence that followed. All three in the truck instinctively and very quickly turned and pointed their collective arsenal his way. "Wait . . . wait . . . look." He set his nine down very carefully on the light pole impacted into the truck's hood. "I'm on your side. I'm here to help."

None of the three responded at first, almost as if they couldn't believe their eyes. John slowly stepped back, trained to talk his way out of situations like this . . . sort of.

"I can take off my other gun if you want." He waited, but there was still no response nor even an inch of movement. "I'm the pilot of that helicopter there." He turned slowly and deliberately and nodded back at the bird.

That got some action out of the three, although not a lot. They exchanged quick glances at each other. "Jason. Get down there with him," the man, who John could now tell was most easily identifiable by his bushy red mustache, ordered at the younger one. The boy hopped down out of the truck. "Get that gun off the truck and—"

The sound of more moaners stole his attention for the moment. "Oh Jesus!" he had to mutter then, stealing a couple quick glances back over his shoulder. The woman had already turned completely back around.

"Oh, Clay . . . there's gotta be fifty of them."

"Jason . . ." from the man this time, and the boy froze midstride, also mid-reach for the gun on the trunk's hood. He next flashed a look at John.

"Go ahead. You're gonna need it." John nodded at the nine he'd placed on the hood. Jason snatched up the gun and hurried back to the bed of the truck.

"You sure you want in on this," Griner asked the officer. "I mean you can just—"

"I don't think you understand. There's an island. It's safe. We can all get there."

"Looks like someone else wants to hitch a ride too," Griner begrudgingly had to inform the officer while nodding at the chopper. Another group of maybe ten zombies were headed for it. At the back of their group another one of those big demon things rode on another really big, all black horse.

"Oh God. Listen," John said up at Griner, noticing too that the mustache still had the shotgun right under it, barrel pointed at him. So he kept his arms up while walking over to the duffel bag that he'd purposely left in clear view a few yards behind him. "I got more rifles, AR 15s, in here, and lots of rounds. I wanna give them to you guys. Okay?"

He lifted the bag up and brought it around to the side of the truck, the one where Jason now waited, staring at the bag, his own guns in hand. John unzipped the bag and showed the contents. "I just need one. There are lots of clips in here too. I got my own." He showed his vest a little with a thumb under one armhole. "May I?" He made to reach into the bag.

Griner looked hard at the two closing teams of zombies. "All right. And thank you, I think. Pull your rifle out very carefully and throw the bag by the tailgate."

"Okay. Here you go." The bag clonked loudly in the truck's bed right where ordered. John held his rifle by the horseshoe-like handle across its top. "I'm gonna go try and save the chopper. It's our only hope."

"Yeah, probably," Griner agreed and for the first time took his aim from John. He slung his shotgun across his back and took a knee before the bag. He rifled through the rifles, no pun intended.

"They're all locked and loaded. Clips all have thirty. You know how to load a new one?" John asked the con.

"Oh yeah."

"Okay. I gotta go. Good luck."

"Clay . . . ." Ivy called out.

Griner kept getting out the rifles, scooting them toward the cab. "Jason . . . range?"

"About fifteen cars. And who are those big, black monster things on horses? There's one with this group too . . . at the back."

"Oh God," John let slip. "Whatever you do, don't look at them, the ones on the horses. Don't look at them!"

Griner held out a rifle for Jason who shoved a nine in each of his back pockets. "Just point and shoot. See the sight . . . . see the dot . . . and remember . . . squeeze, don't pull."

"There all set to semi," John added as he started for the chopper.

"I hope you can shoot straight. You're gonna have your hands full," Griner said, and believe it or not, just then put it all together. Because before that the setting sun right behind it had made the helicopter appear all black. But now he could make out the word, "Police," painted on its side. Of course, he then thought of too because of the nylon blue jumpsuit. He had to smile. A cop and a con . . . the last best hope of humanity in a zombie apocalypse? Huh?

Well, whatever, was all he had left to think, or even say, but he didn't take time to. Ivy and Jason already had a couple kills apiece with these bitchin' new rifles, and he had some catching up to do.

Udo had managed to make some *pretty powerful* enemies over the past week or so. That much was pretty obvious. He'd never seen so many ugly, half decayed, crazy-eyed, walking dead cannibals in one place in all his life. He didn't even know there were this many zombies around. Whoever their boss was had obviously rounded up all the troops he could find for this big assault on his family. *What, had they come in buses?*

Maybe there weren't hardly any more people left and this was almost the end. Or maybe for some other reason his family was just really super important. He'd have to ask Jesus about that later, if he ever got the chance. Or maybe time would tell. It didn't matter. He had his job to do and here was lots of business all of a sudden. It was funny, he was just realizing then too, how he would have killed for this much business back in the day when he'd been an appliance repairman. Now they were beating down the door!

Udo laughed high and hard at that one. Then he got serious again, putting extra oomph in his holding of the makeshift shoe-rack barrier. His customers didn't exactly seem happy, but many were even trying to chew their way in now. He hoped he had enough stock on hand.

All he had though, Udo realized sardonically, was one hammer. He looked at it there in his right that was likewise pressed hard against the rack. Luckily, the hammer was a special one, and, *if he could just let everyone get a good look at it . . .*

Seriously though, Udo came back with, knowing the time for tomfoolery was over, and it was *his* hammer. Someone, probably Jason or the red moustache guy, must have brought it out of the basement. It was a good hammer, a strong hammer. Udo knew his work would go well.

He did want to make one modification to the hammer, however. So after using it to smack the hands of the foremost barrier crashers, causing them to pull back for just a moment, he let go of the barricade and stepped back. In that same moment he brought the hammer up, switching holding hands, and used the now much more powerful index finger and thumb of his right hand to straighten out the claw portion of his hammer.

"Nice," he hissed through the momentary quicker breathing the task had brought. He still wasn't a hundred percent.

He tried a couple practice punches with it, imagining the hammer's new spike punching through zombie skull. He stopped his short retreat, re-gripped his new weapon and let the horde come.

His plan was to cut a path right through the middle of them and hopefully draw the pack back out front with him. Because also hopefully, by now the family would have already made it out back through that little door. And what Udo really wanted was to draw this bunch as far away from them as he could, as mentioned, out front.

So he proceeded that way, grabbing the first of the zombies to reach him by the throat with one hand, then with a quick, perforating punch of the hammer with the other, he obviously inflicted enough brain damage to knock that one out of commission. He let it fall and grabbed the next one. *Thwack . . .* and down it went.

Working upstream that way he soon got outside and broke free into the clear. He was also just about to start shouting and waving his arms to bring the rest of the zombies his way when something off to the right caught his eye. Uh oh . . .

It was one of them damn demon things again on horseback. He turned to face it and the thing looked at him and smiled, showing its huge fangs. Its trident spear thing stood firm and tall on its right, held in that hand and no doubt resting on the hell thing's hip. Udo felt the hammer still in his hand and wondered, what, twenty-five, thirty yards? And he was pretty talented these days. He could throw pretty hard too. Maybe just one shot would do it. Maybe . . . but then instead he brought the hammer up and tapped on his hard helmet that had once been a demon's head too. *Clunk . . . clunk . . . clunk.* The demon renewed its smile. Udo took his shot.

As his sight could do these days too, Udo got to follow the hammer as if he were right there with it as it turned end over end over end and then all of a sudden with a different, moister *thunk* and sunk hard in the creature's right shoulder. The thing howled up at the sky, and its weapon fell to the dirt.

The next thing interesting to see and learn was that even a hell horse could be frightened—especially and apparently if it's rider was from hell too and could howl that special way things from there could—and the big, black steed reared up, dumped the demon and ran off quick as a hot wind.

Not wasting any time, Udo meanwhile had leapt, and sort of flied, across and up onto the highest point in the vicinity, the remaining corner of a three story building bordering the far side of the parking lot the whole scene was evolving in.

The demon, understandably addled by recent events, scrambled to his feet before making a reach for his weapon. That was his mistake.

Because Udo, on the other hand, had already jumped the couple hundred feet or so it took to land right next to the triple tipped spear, just prior to the original owner's attention arrived. Then the monstrously large hell being could only look inquisitively at Udo, or more accurately Udo with the demon head helmet on, and then got to watch too as Udo brought the spear up incredibly quickly and thrust it super hard into the demon's midsection.

All of which, of course, turned the momentum of the battle Udo's way. The beast thing doubled over and then grasped the shaft of its own weapon with both hands. The knockout blow then came next as Udo lowered the back portion of the same shaft until it met and then dug into the dirt. Then he tested the tensile strength of its metal by using it as a fulcrum, lifting the demon off its feet, higher and higher until the demon's own weight pressed its body down over the triple tined killing end. With some resistance it momentarily went clear through, even ripping out and then displaying some of the creature's strange, non-human but humanoid internal organs.

The demon then had nothing left to do but fall face first into the dirt. Udo stepped over him and took the spear with him. He more closely examined the bloody trophies still somewhat squiggling on the tines but disappointedly didn't find a heart among them. Oh well, he resigned himself with and might have even then dug down into the now dead demon for its blood pumper, but he had more pressing business.

For some reason, and this he hadn't noticed until now because of the concentration needed to defeat the demon, but now he could tell the zombie horde didn't seem to be the least interested in him anymore. They were filing off back through the little alleyway cutting behind the old shoe store, no doubt heading for his family and that man they had apparently adopted. He could only hope that they'd managed to put some real distance between themselves and these new pursuers.

Well, hoping was all he could do without getting over there to see if he could help. So he did that then, or at first seemed to be, more accurately, trying to, because right after taking off as best he could, he smacked pretty hard into the side of a building remnant, knocking out a crumbling piece or two. At least in all that he also landed in a roofless empty alcove, righted himself and got to flying again over toward the Harbor boulevard environs where they might still be. His family, that is.

Of course, he thought, remembering the big cross the Lord had wrought near there, stretching high above the whole area and realizing too it would be a great place to scan from. So he aimed for it as he soared over, managing to get to it and then landing, rather shakily, almost falling off but able to hang on where the members of the big thing intersected.

With that accomplished, he sighed long and loudly, got his best foothold, then squatted and started in with the aforementioned scanning. *There they were*. He spotted them quickly with the help of his demon head helmet. They were the only few blue outlines in an otherwise sea of red. Ahhh, he thought then too. That was smart, almost perfect in the back of that pickup. As long as they had plenty of ammo, and oh! Look at that! They had what looked like about twenty extra military style rifles spread along the inner edge of the truck bed wall.

It made him so proud to see Jason and Ivy standing so strong and using the rifles so adeptly, dropping the zombies like flies. But where was Joannie? Maybe his trip in the boat really hadn't been a dream. But then hadn't he seen her in the little brick building though too? Well, maybe they had locked her in the cab of the truck or something. Poor kid. She'd seemed really out of it after all. He just hoped she was okay, wherever she was. He'd head down and see for himself pretty soon, once he surveyed the whole field of battle as they used to say. He wanted to see where he could best help. Where—

Oh crap. There was another demon on horseback at the rear of that group of zombies too. Pulling out all the stops was a phrase that came suddenly to mind. The Devil was getting desperate.

And speaking of which, now off to the far western edge of it all, another sea of red was flooding in as well, which at first didn't make sense. But then when the lone blue figure caught his eye and he zoomed in to see who it was, the realization of what was really going on exploded in his mind. *The helicopter! Flying! To the island? Bingo!*

So of course then he was about to spring down in that general direction, to assist in the protection of that most valuable asset, when something else started happening that told him that wouldn't really be necessary.

As Udo spied the phenomena, he was reminded of a scene he'd seen in a movie once, a cowboy movie in which a stampede of cattle was commencing on the far horizon. And just as it had then, at first only a long line of low hanging dust cloud could be seen running from one edge of the screen to the other, or in this case, from one edge of the field of ruin to the other.

But then as the cloud rolled closer, and the accompanying thunderous sound of its source did the same, Udo could start to see the silhouetted forms of the legs and girthy frames and here and there high and strong horns of the cattle making up this stampede.

But wait a minute! Those weren't horns, and of course they weren't cattle either. This time the legs were a little shorter and pointed on the ends, and the girth of the frames ran a little more horizontal than those of a bovine nature. Also, as mentioned no horns were to be seen at all, replaced instead by tall and just as strong but even more dangerous pincher claws of a scorpion sort, maybe four to five foot long apiece.

"Kitty," Udo fondly called out quietly and smiled wide within his helmet. *And Kitty's brought some friends too,* he mentally quipped, a whole lot of friends. *This wouldn't even be a fair fight. A big lawn of zombies was about to get mowed.* The only question to answer was whether or not said mowing would come about quickly enough to save the remaining survivors, his family included.

I'll go help, Udo thought and stood to do so, but then here came that still small voice again.

Their fight . . . let them prove themselves, was all he could make out, but that was enough. His legs, almost with a mind of their own, weakly let him back down to sit and just watch for now.

The pilot seemed to be doing pretty well anyway, Udo could tell, letting his gaze drift that way. An advanced group of only about a half-dozen zombies had made it to the helicopter first, and he seemed to be firing wildly on purpose while retreating to draw them away from the precious flying machine. Which was working well, and then Udo could also tell his plan was to draw them away far enough to then circle back in a run for the helicopter. Then hopefully he could get it started and lift off before the main body of the demon led dead ones reached it *en masse.*

But that all problematic as said, '*masse,*' kept getting closer and closer to the helicopter and unless the pilot could run very, very fast . . . well . . .

But all the while as well, here came Kitty and the other scorpion cats closing just as fast behind the *masse,* so close in fact that the demon had turned and noticing *their* advancing *masse* had unfurled its black wings before alighting straight up out of the saddle.

Udo watched him go, flying north along the coast.

The horse the demon alighted from, unfortunately, was not gifted with the same abilities and disappeared in pieces beneath the advancing zombie eating animal hybrid . . . things, Udo could only think of them as. He loved them though and loved to watch them work. They just kept marching on, overtaking and eating all the zombies like a wave of acid.

Uh oh, he had to think then though, as now the stampede was heading right for the helicopter. The huge group of beasts swelled on its sides, however, and poured around the proportionately smaller craft like a river running passed an island in its midst. They continued on then far enough to consume the rest of the zombies still advancing on the pilot.

He, for his part, just continued to back away, probably able to tell now, just as Udo could, that the wave of creatures had turned to head for the other group of zombies still advancing on the pickup. Which was a good thing, because even though Ivy and Jason and the man with the red mustache were still doing well, Udo could see, the bodies of the zombies close to the truck bed were piling up so high that it appeared soon the attacking ones would be able to walk right up onto them and then into the truck.

Besides, how much ammo could they have left? Udo so wanted to go help, but as he tried, it was the same old thing. The Lord had frozen him there.

Although he could still move his head, which he then swiveled to look in the direction of this new sound, the wop, wop, whirring of the helicopter taking off. *Where was he going?*

Oh. Good. He was flying over the truck now, flying low. Then he pulled up higher and turned a wide circle over the horseriding demon leading this bunch of zombies from the rear. *But what was he doing now? Oh. Was he going to fight the demon?* He was landing close by it. The helicopter was slowly lowering in and—

Oh! Oh wow! That was his plan all along! Just before the helicopter set down its blade whacked hard and sharp into the demon who was obviously riding too high in the saddle to clear under the landing craft. Obviously too, this was a fact unknown to the demon but known to the pilot. Whom of course then left only half of said demon still sitting in the saddle, legs leading up to a bloody and cut level trunk. Which also then negated the demon's ability to control the attack of the zombies, who broke off their assault on the truck and started even more mindlessly rambling before roaming into the countryside all around.

Udo concentrated his vision then on the group in the back of the truck. At first, they looked ecstatic about this new turn of events, but then as they heard the advancing stampede and turned to see its source, they quickly got out of the truck's bed and broke in a run for the helicopter.

That was all Udo remembered seeing then, his family, or most of it, and that other guy, had made it to the copter, which then lifted off and flew into the sunset. But what about my baby? My little girl, his mind screamed just before he fell from the giant cross.

How soon we forget, the still small voice whispered into his mind as he fell and fell and fell.

CHAPTER XXVII

SKY PILOT

Kellen remembered back to how she'd been so worried about the boy's feet as they'd walked and walked those first few miles of their journey. Now she'd chop her own feet off just to get him back. Give her life too, which she was probably going to do anyway, but not for a good reason like that. It was just going to happen, barring any miracle, like maybe a king-size jumbo one. As far as she could tell, she was pretty much toast.

After the demon and the zombies had left, she'd scrambled down out of the tree and at first looked about hectically for Aaron everywhere nearby that she could. Before her tears even dried up, she ran around in a good quarter mile radius calling out over and over while also peering behind every boulder and rustling in every shrub, bush and small tree looking for him. Then she collapsed and cried some more.

After all that, reality started setting in. She wanted to get back on the trail. Maybe Aaron was further ahead somewhere, and after all, it was the only thing left to do anyway. Try to find the boy, and if not that, at least find a way to the coast. Or better yet, maybe both!

She was well rested at least—she'd slept great, a little too great before the zombie alarm clock went off—and now back at it then. She'd been raised that way after all. Cry it all out, or as much as you could, then pick up and carry on. You never knew what might happen. Do your best, and sometimes, good things would happen, her parents had taught her. Aaron might be just around the bend or over the next rise.

No more crying. Time to carry on.

So after scrounging up the remaining supplies that hadn't been trampled by the zombies or the demon and his horse . . . oh yeah . . . horse. Shadow was gone too. *Oh boy.* And she'd said she wasn't going to cry anymore. But at least this time she made herself get up and start going while the sniffles set in again.

After a while her crying died again and she continued on, back on the trail. She also explored, when she could, in more of the small valleys or hillsides off from the trail, looking for the boy, and or the horse. She'd call his name, but only go as far off the trail as she could safely do once darkness of night hemmed in her efforts. *Did it matter anymore anyway,* she forlornly let herself think and just managed to keep going, until the trail dead ended right up against a chasm.

That's right.

A chasm.

As in a deep cleft running through the surface of a planet, and in this case, a *very deep* cleft. But luckily, noticing the new and deeper darkness the empty space above the cleft presented, Kellen slowed and carefully crept up to its edge.

Just a hint of the big boulders and ripped open earth could be seen in the dimly lighted night, but creeping even closer to the edge of it all the young lady could also see that way down at the chasm's bottom a red ribbon river of lava flowed. Then she tried, but could see nothing but utter darkness where the other side might have been.

Kellen stopped a moment and thought. She realized she'd just have to keep going along its edge. Maybe somewhere, some way . . .

But there was no trail anymore either. Not in either direction. So to the left though, she figured. At least that way would be in a southerly direction and most likely to be nearest a beach, if the chasm ever did end. Or some way to cross it ever did happen . . . somewhere . . . some way.

Before long, however, even that way was becoming impassable. After busting through some brush, all she could do to advance any further was climb up onto a rocky ridge that ran along the border of the chasm. She had to be careful though, as dark as it was. Even Spaceman Spike couldn't help anymore. The flashlight's batteries had died last night. She was still keeping him in her backpack though, in case she ever found Aaron again. And anyway, there was more than enough room now in the pack with not many water bottles left.

She climbed up the ridge slowly, hoping to get to its top and then down another side. She could see a little bit of her surroundings, at least, by the dim red glow seeping up out of the chasm now. Enough to tell the big rocks from the little ones, which she knew would afford better, stronger footholds. Then carefully, even on all fours at times, she finally worked her way to the top.

From there and looking out all around she was mostly struck by how dark everything was. She could hardly see a thing. Although then a slightly lighter shade of night now running along the eastern horizon told her the sun was on its way up. Maybe she should wait, she was thinking, until it came all the way up. She also noticed then too that her legs were shaking, so she gingerly sat down on the big flat boulder she found herself standing right in front of. *Ah that was better.* It felt so good just to sit, and the boulder's surface was so cool compared to the heat of her overworked body.

Yes. Much better. This was where she would rest for now. Probably no zombies could climb up here, she figured. Feeling back and around with her hand, she could tell the boulder's flat surface stayed the same for as far as she could reach, *so why not?* She slid out of the backpack and, while leaning back on an elbow, brought it around in front of her.

As mentioned, supplies were low. So let's see . . . two and a half bottles of water left. One broken up and one mostly intact power bar. An apple with a couple soft spots and hopefully no worms. She for sure wouldn't eat that yet as dark as it was. And she decided as well to save the busted up power bar for daylight too. But—oh and there went her stomach growling again—she had to eat something. She undressed the intact power bar, bit and chewed and then drank.

She tried not to think about it, but it was quite obvious she was completely at the end of things, at the end of her supplies so then pretty soon also at the end of her ability to keep going, and from the looks of it at the end of the world too.

Maybe all that stuff about the island in those dreams of hers was a bunch of bunk. *Maybe—hey! What the heck was that! A shooting star?* Well, if it was it was still shooting. *Omigosh. Didn't it figure?* She'd always wanted to see a UFO, and now here it was at the end of everything that she finally was. *Wow. Look at it go!*

First it shot clear across the eastern sky then seemed to come in closer, so close in fact that it no longer just looked like an extra bright star. Now she could see the somewhat tubular shape of the thing and that the body was mostly white with a line of blue light running down through it. *Hey. That looked familiar. But where had she seen . . .*

"Omigosh," she even said out loud this time, but in little more than a whisper, because now the little ship was coming very close. It passed directly overhead like a plane flying low. It made a roar like a jet but only quieter. The sound of it passed like a jet's would too, but then . . .

"Omigod," she even said loudly this time and tried not to freak out too much. Now the thing was coming in for a landing, approaching her slowly, getting larger and larger and lowering in elevation!

But! Oh . . . and now she could see things better because the little ship had some landing lights that had come on. This boulder she was sitting on was really huge and stretched quite a ways back, far enough to make a good landing surface for the UFO, which was about the size of a big car, except tube shaped like she'd seen before and now she could see too that the nose was pointed, and it had these cool looking little wings and the tail section had some too and—

Hey! Wait a minute. No way. It couldn't be!

She rifled through the backpack and felt it in there then whipped it out. She looked at the Spaceman Spike Spaceship flashlight then looked up again at the UFO just landed now with its quiet roar dying out.

No way.

It couldn't be!

The UFO was an exact replica of the Spaceman Spike spaceship, but even sleeker and actually quite beautiful in real life like this. The white, seemingly metallic hull glinted and shone in polished smoothness. The line of blue light running along it midways that also ran out along the wing's edges pulsed in a dimmer state now. The show stopper came next though when a third of the way down from the ship's streamline nose and the window array across it that appeared white too, but white glass, a door flipped up and open and white but black padded stair steps formed and descended to the boulder's surface below.

Kellen of course was standing now and half-heartedly thinking about scrambling as far away as possible back down the rocks. Funny thing was though, her legs seemed frozen in position.

She was glad in a moment, however, that they had been. Because now scampering happily down the steps came a tiny spaceman dressed so cutely in a puffy white little space suit and his helmet off. He was particularly cute because inside the suit was Aaron with a big, big smile and sparkling eyes. Now, whether they had been held before by some great invisible force or not, Kellen could move her legs. Probably nothing could have stopped her anyway. She ran over and scooped the little boy up.

"Where have you been, you little—" She held her tongue through the tears and just hugged him.

"With Spaceman Spike! Well, first there was a cowboy cooking bacon, and we had delicious bacon and egg sandwiches. But then we rode on Shadow until we got to the spaceship. And there was Spaceman Spike! Since then we've been flying all over the place to different planets and everything!"

Kellen held the boy out at arm's length and looked at him. She'd never seen him so happy. He beamed. And just as she was about to question him further, another figure coming out of the ship caught her eye. Well, if it wasn't . . .

He looked just like the toy figure of Spaceman Spike she'd seen Aaron playing with before back at home. He had a puffy, white spacesuit too, just like Aaron's, with the exception that he had his helmet on and it was round and white too with a shining silver faceplate.

Kellen was speechless and could only watch as the life-size toy spaceman walked right up to them. He stood close, and after Kellen set the boy down, the spaceman took Aaron's little hand in his big, gloved one.

"Seee," Aaron said up at her, still beaming. Kellen looked at the spaceman's faceplate as just then with his other gloved hand He pushed a small button on the side of the helmet and the silver plating retracted up.

Probably part of His plan, Kellen then realized, what with their heads up high above the boy like that making it impossible for Aaron to see the face inside the helmet. Because that was no Spaceman Spike. Although how she knew who it was exactly, she couldn't really explain. She just knew.

Which also then explained why she could only shakily go to one knee before him and start quietly sobbing.

"Arise my good and faithful servant," the spaceman then said down at her, and because the voice sounded just like the one that pulling on the string on the back of the Spaceman Spike doll activated, quiet laughter broke through her tears while she did as commanded. She rose. She couldn't look at Him, of course. *It's Jesus, for crying out loud*, her mind just kept telling her over and over, and then she fell into a hug like she'd never felt before.

As the three turned and walked toward the spaceship, Kellen managed to ask, "I heard Aaron mention Shadow, but I don't think he could fit in here." She looked down the length of the ship.

"He'll be waiting for you two at your new home, our next stop on the tour of the universe," He told them, helping them up the steps and into the ship. Kellen could only smile, and though her legs were still shaking a little, she made darn sure to get up those steps.

CHAPTER XXVII

DON'T LET THE DOOR HIT YA

The technician and the designer were in an all-white room in a special section of the soul ship. They were seated on stools again too that were also white and in the center of a circular console surrounding them. Everything was white except for the occasional monitor screen embedded therein giving graphical or other some such colorful readouts. Add to that the facts that both of them also wore white lab coats, and also that the control console completely hid the lower halves of their bodies and, well, if one didn't look closely one might also believe . . . as stranger things were happening these days . . . that both beings were comprised entirely of disembodied heads and hands. The designer's hands then went to work on one of the console's keyboards.

"I don't know. I just don't know," he started off with and brought one of the hands up to his cheek. "I mean, I'll take your word for it. I suppose I have to. In for a penny, in for a pound . . ."

"And if you ask me, you're very fortunate. Just think of it, a whole new world, a whole new type of being to observe and experiment with. Though we don't know exactly what sort of beings will be there, they should be similar . . ." The technician's words dwindled off in wondering as his hands then got busy too, going to work also on the keyboards, dials and switches of the console before him.

The all-white room suddenly filled with holographic images, looking for all intents and purposes like a far corner of the universe complete with planets, moons and then stars too visible on the periphery. In the middle of it all was a sun around which the aforementioned planets orbited, while moons orbited around them.

The two men, albeit reanimated ones, spun slowly on their seats to more fully take in the incredibly detailed and moving diorama all around them. "Reminds me a lot of . . . here," the designer offered.

"That is what's so perfect about it. Readings of a detailed nature were very difficult to obtain related to the incredible distance away this system is. But from all that we could gather, it is very similar to this solar system . . . as you put it . . . here."

The technician then got up from his stool and walked out into space, so to speak, and the designer followed. With a small metallic device in his hand, the technician summoned one of the planets over closer to him. "And this one, just like ours, is the third one from this sun. That's about all we can tell at this time. But as you can see here, once our ship enters the system . . ."

He paused for a moment and pointed across the room with his device and here came a set to scale reproduction of the soul ship into the room, very small of course, but as the technician enlarged it, one could then see inside where in one of its larger rooms a few of the many stasis pods opened up to allow their occupants to arise. "We will be aroused and begin taking new readings to find a good new home for us."

"Oh, aroused, I like the sound of that," the designer quipped before getting serious again. "And you're sure now we have enough fuel to get there?"

"Oh yes," the technician piped up with and activated his device again to show the circular soul chamber within the ship. The colorful swirl of souls pulsed and flowed all around them. "The recent acquisition of these two children's souls puts us over the top. They are so powerful, like little nuclear reactors. The zombie souls were practically mush. But luckily early on, the master and his minions were able to catch many souls of the unsaved. They will make a good base fuel."

"Like you were saying. Could be worse. Could be one of them."

"Hard to say for sure. For all intents and purposes, or at least our findings seem to indicate, they are quite confused and just trying to make their way into the light, in this case our artificial one. Either way, after many, many attempts they then simply go out and virtually disappear . . . as far as we can tell at least. Do they suffer? Possibly. But most likely not."

The designer looked down a moment, and then with features more strained by stress, he had to ask, "So he's aboard already?"

"Yes. They all are, all of . . . *them*. I will initiate automatic systems in just a few minutes. Once we get to our own pods."

"So that's it then?"

"That's it for us. Until we get out . . . there."

"I mean . . . for earth. What's going to happen? Are there any survivors?"

"We think so. A few," the technician said and used his device to turn the diorama before and around them into a bird's eye view of what was left of planet Earth. The view swept over crag and cleft, canyon and river of fire, new mountains, cities in utter destruction then finally the remnants of Sandy Point Beach.

"I can't imagine where," the designer mused. Then the view swept over the giant cross. "Hey. Oh. Does that mean?"

"We think so. As usual, *He's* up to something. We tracked the last of the survivors heading out to sea. But then our equipment went completely haywire. But just as one last jab . . ."

In the diorama, one of the Navy boats could be seen coursing out to sea, and as the view closed in, Mike the zombie and a boatful of U.S. Navy zombies could be seen filling it to the brim. "The master wanted to send this bunch out along the same coordinates we tracked some of the other survivors sailing along. We think their destination is hidden at the other end of a teleportation vortex that hopefully our ship will be drawn toward just as theirs was. We've equipped it to travel that way should they be able to find the vortex.

"Who knows," the technician continued. "As I said, just as a jab, one last attack on Him and his precious children. Plus we are hoping it might act as a diversion from our own escape."

"Why not. Just why not, you know? I mean, who does He think He is?" the designer petulantly asked. "I mean really!"

The technician just shook his head, used the device to bring the room back to its natural whiteness and returned to his console.

"Ohhhh," the designer objected. "I liked that. I was hoping you'd bring me up to speed on how you work that. I—"

While the designer had been speaking, the technician had surreptitiously slipped on a streamline pair of dark goggles. "You may enjoy this then," he said, and the room exploded in an incredible array of flashing and swirling colors.

At first the designer watched with wide eyes and an even wider grin, but soon he started to blink, and his head started to droop. In just another moment he stood stock still with his head on his chest.

The technician stopped the light show and shed his glasses. "Can you hear me, Mr. Valentine?"

"Yes. I can hear you," the designer answered, his head nodding ever so slightly.

"You need to go to your pod now. Do you remember how to get there?"

"Yes, I remember."

"Pod number three-seven-six."

"Yes. Pod three-seven-six."

"Then go now. It is time."

"Yes. It is time."

The technician watched him go out of the corner of his eye while he continued to work. After another minute or two, and with a final accentuated motion of flipping that last switch, the white room went mostly dark except for small, red running lights blinking off and on along the base of the walls.

"Ignition sequence initiated, systems check, all passengers to pods, liftoff in six minutes, forty seven seconds," a voice politely informed him as he walked unhurriedly but efficiently to the door. It whooshed open, and the technician passed from the room.

Outside the ship, a series of metallic lines that had attached to the mostly oval, almost egg shaped craft, snapped back away from it one after another after another. The big metallic mountain that had housed the craft began to crumble from the top down, leaving just blue sky above. The somehow only small pieces—actually this moment of destruction had been planned and the mechanisms to accomplish it incorporated into the hidden hangar's design upon construction a week earlier—crumbled and fell around the big, black-looking egg, and soon it also appeared to be nestled in the silver shale surrounding it.

In just one more moment, it rocked ever so slightly then almost silently started lifting off, straight up and slowly until clear of all surrounding terrain or obstruction. It then increased its speed and angled its ascent into the blue.

On a hillside not too distant and well within good viewing distance, another spaceship, this one much smaller, mostly white and tubular in shape with a line of blue light seaming its side, then took off as well.

CHAPTER XXIX

MOP UP

Zigging and zagging, weaving his way through the air but for the most part moving forward and maintaining altitude, Udo followed the helicopter as best he could. He'd never flown this far before, but now he'd made his way—just like the chopper had—out over the ocean, and as far as Udo could tell—which wasn't very far at all really—they were still headed in a westerly direction.

At least at first he knew they were, when just after clearing the coast they were headed straight into the sun half submerged in the ocean already. Then they'd continued that heading until the green flash—which how cool that was to see, Udo's best view ever of that awesome phenomenon—when the sun winked out below the horizon.

Luckily the helicopter had a little red light winking on and off and he was still able to follow the whirly bird carrying its precious cargo, his family, albeit somewhat modified, hopefully to the island.

Which, of course, Udo was just dying to see. He was almost positive it existed, what with all the little mental messages he'd received about it, and how he's heard from others about it too, and then the all too real dream or whatever it was with him and Joannie and their wonderful boat ride right to it. So he sort of had seen it, and then too his sweet little girl walking so bravely onto it across the blue surf. She was so sure it existed too and that it would be their new safe and happy home. She'd told him all about it on their boat ride.

But had all that really been real? He sure hoped so since then there had been no sign of Joannie after that, and she sure wasn't on the helicopter now. But hadn't he also overheard Ivy and them talking about her while he was in their shelter with them? *So . . .*

Uh oh. Looking up, Udo all of a sudden couldn't see the helicopter anywhere ahead of him anymore. He scanned right, scanned left then even tried flying in both directions too, but no, no way and nowhere. No helicopter.

Then he thought of something else. Maybe if he got some more altitude. Maybe—

Bonk!

What the—

Udo got knocked back all of a sudden, and knocked down, but before he fell too far he managed to regain a horizontal attitude and swooped back up again.

What the heck had that been! It had felt like he'd run into a solid, but soft rubber wall. He'd been slowly absorbed into it and then very quickly flung back, and quite a ways too. *He'd been—*

"Aaaaaagh," Udo even yelled this time as it happened again. Luckily he was able to right himself again as well. *But, what the—*

Udo didn't rush ahead again this time. This time he hung back, and looking very carefully ahead, especially there where the horizon's glow should have been shining through brightly, somehow it was muted and slightly fuzzy. *Some sort of force field? But—*

You can't go, my boy, Udo heard the still small voice in his head say again. *Sorry . . .*

"But . . . but. I just need to know," he said up into the star-filled sky. "Are they okay? Are they—?"

They'll be okay for now, as long as you help them one more time.

Udo was about to ask what He meant by all that when all of a sudden a quiet purring noise caught his ear. The purr grew into a growl, but kind of a gurgling growl, and he looked down and across the water to see its source. A motor boat was coming, steadily heading right for him. It was a bigger boat, bigger than the custom craft he and Joannie had taken earlier, about twice as big. And it was moving pretty good.

Udo swooped down over it and at first couldn't believe what he'd seen.

They can't do that.

Can they?

He swooped by once more and though this time he could, or actually *had* to believe it, he still didn't want to. He was so tired. And he knew now he should have eaten some of those zombie hearts that he could have back after that last battle. He felt like his blood sugar might be kind of low. Could his blood sugar go low?

Yes, but you can do it, the little voice came back with again.

"Hey. Maybe you can just call up a giant fish or something."

"No, my boy. Where's the sport in that? Sure, I could solve any of your problems, or any of my children's problems with the snap of a couple big fingers. But where's the growth in that? Where's the—just get down there!" the voice angrily concluded, this time actually audible, and Udo knew better than to quibble anymore. He floated back a little, descended some too, and dropped in on the boat-load of zombies, more than a little unexpectedly.

Which helped considerably at first, as out-numbered as he was. The fairly wide gunboat had to be packed with at least twenty or so sailors of the armed forces of the living dead. And being such, and many of them trained in self-defense, right away Udo could tell he had his hands full.

The first few nearby didn't even get the chance to turn around. Udo spun the first one's head from behind until it was turned around and facing him. Good thing that sailor wasn't scheduled for inspection today, Udo half-humorously had to think, seeing him now so stiffly still and standing right before him. His uniform was a mess as well. Well, this will end all his problems, Udo then mentally added and went ahead and kept twisting until after just one more twist and then a jerk, off it came. With no time to do much else, he chucked the zombie's head back over his shoulder like a watermelon failing the freshness test and moved on.

He quickly scanned around, knowing whoever noticed him next should be his next subject for attack and saw that in fact a very large black fellow wearing a flak jacket a couple of zombie layers away had fixed him with his crazed, red eyed stare.

On his way there, Udo cleared out one of the other zombies between them with the quick thrust of a knife hand into its chest. While in there he fished around quickly for the familiar feeling of the thing and in the next instant yanked the already expiring entities' heart clean out.

And though he was hungry, Udo had to let that go too. But in the instant he'd hesitated, thinking about eating it, the bar of steel the large colored zombie had been carrying—unbeknownst to our hero of course—came clonking down on his luckily, still helmet covered head. The helmet was hard enough to prevent brain damage, but still not entirely clonk proof. The boat spun quick beneath him and Udo went down dizzy.

The boat still spun, just like everything else did while he lay there. He wanted to get up but he couldn't feel anything. He really couldn't even move, not his arms or legs or anything major at least, but he managed finally to turn his head just enough to realize that he was glad he couldn't feel anything after all. One of the zombies near his leg had pounced on it and was chewing on it like last week's fried chicken. Luckily at least, his skin was real tough like on last week's chicken too, and the dead guy was having trouble just breaking through the leather-like stuff.

Over all though, things were not looking good. And worse yet, more of the crazy cannibals were either falling on him, stomping him, trying to pull him apart, or in any other way destroy him. And he still couldn't move too well. But he was starting to get his feeling back. He could even feel the small puddle of water he was laying in. *The wetness, the wetness just like the water beneath him, a whole ocean full of it—*

Hey! That gave him an idea. If he could just . . .

Still a little weak, he raised his arm and punched the hull of the boat with all his strength. The hard synthetic material made a cracking noise but no visible sign of breakage could be seen. Regaining more strength and then also feeling his attackers increasing their frenzy, Udo decided maybe he better do the same? He beat at the hull with his whole lower forearm and fist like a hammer, over and over and over.

The cracking noises grew, and just as one of the bigger zombies landed right on him—or so it felt, he never did get a look at the guy—an arm sized piece of the hull broke through. Water gushed up almost fountain-like, and the boat rocked and Udo could tell most of the zombies were taken aback by the development. That was one thing good about zombies, he'd noticed. They were easily distracted . . . and disoriented.

But they weren't disoriented enough, and right then Udo decided not to take any chances. *This boat,* though taking on water well and would no doubt sink eventually, *was going down now*! He continued to beat and beat on the breakage he'd made until then—and he hadn't expected such wonderful results—he burst through.

Next thing *he* knew he was flashing back to his old surfing days, like when a really big wave had taken him under. He was going *deep*. About ten . . . fifteen feet. Then he started making his way back up, but at an angle. One that—as far as he could remember—should surface him somewhere behind where the boat had previously been heading. He didn't want to run into the boat's props.

He broke through the surface and gulped in some air. He looked around fast and soon spotted the little red light the boat had on its tail and swam hard for it. After a little bit of that and needing a break anyway, he looked again and could see that it wasn't moving, except maybe down, yeah down. The gun boat was sinking fast.

Udo saw something else then that made him want to turn and hurry off the other way. In the half-moonlight he at first could only make out the heads and flailing arms of a dozen or more undead shipwreck survivors trying to stay afloat. But soon there amongst them came the fins, cutting up out of the water like hand sized blades, but disappearing then just before pulling under a nearby dead guy to munch munch on.

They must have smelled the blood from those ones he'd wounded earlier, Udo could only surmise, maybe that head he'd tossed overboard too. Or maybe too, he more humorously conjectured, Jesus had finally taken his suggestion and called in a big fish, or make that a lot of somewhat smaller but very voracious ones, a mop up crew, now that he'd done all he could do.

Either way, Udo decided to high tail it in the other direction. If he could just find something to stand on maybe he could get airborne and fly back inland. Although what he was supposed to do now, he wasn't quite sure. Just get back to land and then see, he was thinking. Just—

Hey. There was at least one zombie that was pretty smart. The long-haired chubby looking fellow even had a life jacket on and had found himself a two-by-four sized piece of hull to hold on to while also kicking like heck with his legs. Then too he'd also been smart enough to head for the shore, low and dark on the far horizon.

Udo got over to him and joined in, taking a spot next to the undead kick boarder on the open portion of the piece of flotsam. He started kicking too, and before long they were really making some headway.

The chubby, long haired zombie guy regarded him once or twice, Udo noticed, but since his eyeball on this side was dangling down his cheek, he doubted if the poor guy even knew who Udo was; which also might then explain why the zombie didn't get scared or anything and just kept kicking and kicking. Udo did the same, and soon it seemed like they were already halfway there.

Mike was very excited, for a zombie at least. That is, excited about something other than eating somebody. But that was Mike. He was different. As he himself even knew, it was his intelligence that made him different, and that was also what had got him this big job, this last mission, the piloting of the boat with all his fellow servants on board to get to the island where the only survivors were left. And eat them.

Unfortunately, Mike's greatest attribute had also turned out to be his undoing. Well, not that undoing hadn't been what was in the cards for him all along anyway, which was what he'd figured out also with his intelligence. So then he felt like a sucker. He remembered that word from before, sucker. And turkey. Fool. It wasn't good to be any of those things. So he decided he wasn't going to be.

He felt that way mostly because the master was gone. The dark lord had just left them there, left them behind. Being part of the one---plus probably because of his intelligence---Mike had even seen the spaceship in his mind and then let him feel too the master's happiness. Then one phrase had come to him when he thought about these things: a new home.

Mike wanted a new home too. But that wasn't going to happen. The master was going to leave without him, he could also tell. So Mike was going to fix him, or at least get back at him as best he could.

His plan to do that was to screw up this last mission. How, he wasn't sure. They were already on the boat and going, and he knew there were guns in the boat too, but he only knew a little about guns, what he could remember from before. But he couldn't make one work. He was smart for a zombie, but to do complicated things with his hands, like working a gun, would have resulted in him shooting himself in the foot most likely, if he could even do that much.

But he could steer the boat okay. The great warrior of the master had set the glass circle at the front of the boat for him to watch and where to keep the needle inside of it at all times. Mike did exactly that, at first. But all the time he was also trying to think of a way to screw it up. Maybe he would wait, he was thinking, until they were getting close to the island, and then he would just head the other way and keep going. That would probably be best.

But then things got interesting when that helicopter came over. Although it just kept going on and on until he couldn't see it anymore. Then here came that statue man. Oh, Mike realized. He wouldn't have to do anything now probably. The statue man would probably totally screw things up even better. Mike had seen the statue man at work before and here he came, dropping down right out of the sky and into the boat.

And then too, like always, came the fighting and the killing, the removing of the heads from the others, the others like him.

Although then the statue man went down. Someone must have got him good. Maybe he wouldn't win after all. So Mike thought, well, he better do something now, so he grabbed the wheel and turned it all the way hard toward him until the boat just started going round and round and round and round.

Everybody was all screwed up then, but also Mike could tell there was some sort of commotion down in the boat where the statue man had gone down. Many of the others were attacking him. He wondered what he would taste like for a moment but then realized they'll probably never get through his thick skin. Mike had seen him up close that one time, and there was no denying it. He looked very tough, tough to eat, that is.

But then an even stranger thing happened as the water started shooting up right there too! Mike just kept the boat going around in a circle, though, and in a minute it was going a little slower too as the water just kept coming in. Because he was so smart, Mike figured out then that the statue man was sinking the boat and since him and the others couldn't swim, that would about do it. Although, Mike thought then too, maybe he couldn't drown and he would just stay alive, or whatever he was, until he eventually washed up on shore somewhere.

Then the boat really started sinking, and soon they were all in the water. Mike was glad then that the master's great warrior had put the orange floating thing—that he couldn't think of the word for—on over his shirt like he had. The great warrior had thought it was a joke and laughed and laughed, but now when all of the others weren't staying up in the water too good, he was.

Which then Mike wasn't so sure he was glad about after all, because now he could see the fins and could tell the sharks were here. That was a word he could definitely remember. That word and what it meant was burned into his brain. *Shark. They will eat you even faster than a zombie could.*

So of course he just started trying to get away very fast. He couldn't remember how to swim though, just like the others. But then he found a pretty big piece of the boat and just held on and almost automatically started kicking his legs. He kicked and kicked and then one of the sharks came by and came for him, for his head even, but he ducked out of the way and didn't seem to be injured too badly, but he could only see out of one eye now. Then he felt too like he caught his legs on something, but he just kept going, kicking and kicking and then someone else came over and started helping too, someone very strong, and he could tell they started going faster and farther then.

Mike was very glad that this other person was helping, and he tried to look over and see who it was, but with the eye on that side not working he couldn't. So he just kept kicking and kicking and kicking and kicking and kicking and . . .

Watching and waiting, He sat on the beach on a very large piece of driftwood, something right out of the middle of a good-sized tree, fishing. Not a nibble could He get though. He knew there were fish still left in the ocean, lots of them. And there were sharks too, He also knew. Yes indeedy.

After a bit, He reeled in and stood up to look over his line. Oh. No bait. No wonder. He reached down into the pocket of his overalls and came out with a small gold, shiny object. He affixed it to the end of the line then cast out again. The gold shiny lure flew almost impossibly far and trailed a line of colored light as it did. Lost in the tiny, unusually mild surf, the thing could still be traced by the light that had blossomed out rainbow-like, albeit a long thin one. After a few minutes, the long multi-colored arc began flashing red and the Middle Eastern looking man vigorously reeled in once more.

"Ahhhh. It's a fighter," He exclaimed and flipped his long, dark hair back and away from his bearded face. His well-muscled arms and chest—mostly visible because he wore no shirt under the overalls which were also rolled up on each leg almost to his knees—flexed as he worked hard at the line, pulling with all his strength, then letting the pole lurch forward while he reeled and reeled like mad, then pulling hard again until the pole bent almost to breaking.

After another moment, He could see them coming and set the fishing pole in a nearby holder stabbed into the sand. He high stepped it quite a ways out into the surf to help. The two coming in still held hard to their saving shard of gunboat and only just let go of it then to lean hard on very tired arms which were just long enough to keep their heads above water now.

"Ah! You made it! Excellent. Excellent!" Jesus exclaimed. He grabbed at their arms and managed to help them make their tired way onto the sand. As they did, both Udo and the Lord noticed for the first time that the zombie's lower legs were completely gone.

"Oh my goodness," the Lord cried, coming around to attend to the tattered remnants of the living dead survivor's legs. He noticed then to the eyeball hanging on the zombie's tattered cheek. "Ouch!"

Jesus smiled and reached up, placing his hand over the wounded organ. As he pulled it away, the dislodged eyeball was in place again and apparently working fine too. The previously ravaged flesh there had been healed as well.

Zombie Mike blinked and looked around, smiled and even managed a crude laugh, until he saw Udo clearly for the first time and scrambled back away from the zombie killer. The look of fear on his face was extreme.

Udo just shook his head. "Don't worry. I'm too tired to eat."

"And you won't be eating any more hearts anyway. Or ripping off heads. Or getting infected with a god forsaken disease . . . or flying like a crazy pinball into harm's way . . . or getting painfully close to loved ones," the Lord synopsized Udo's recent existence, all the while too coming over to him, still down on His knees. "Only to have them taken away again. And all for me, my good and faithful servant."

By then, the Lord of all creation was crying. Udo would have too, but that was something else he was too tired to do. But with great honor and joy, he continued to watch as his savior began washing his feet with His tears that just kept flowing and flowing while he continued to speak. "As I said once before, it is finished. At least for you, my boy. And you have done so well. Fought so hard. This should help reinvigorate your tired limbs."

The Lord finished massaging his feet, and Udo could feel his strength returning. He sat up. The Lord braced Udo's ankles with a last firm grab on each one, and then got up. After flexing his legs, and satisfied with the results, Udo slowly did the same.

"How are they . . . are they . . . okay?" the now again perfect being struggled to get out, not because of fatigue, but because he was afraid to hear the answer. He knew the Lord knew who he meant.

"Actually, my boy," the Lord started off with and put his hand on Udo's shoulder. "They're even better than okay. You will see, my boy. We'll watch what happens from heaven. Then I hope you can understand why all this was necessary. I really needed you here, in the form you were in. And it had to be your wish and desire to do so."

Udo almost fell over with what Jesus had said, which maybe was why the Lord had placed a hand under his shoulder as He then, believe it or not, had to use it to help the very strong and perfected being stay on his feet.

Udo was okay, physically, but had almost fallen and was still weak because also at the same time a series of images had flashed through his mind with shocking realism: the truck striking and killing him, Ivy and Jason falling into bad behavior, then his meeting with the Lord where he asked him if he could help save them, his deployment back to Earth, the battles and battles. And then what was that, some giant and black, egg shaped space ship flying up through the sky? Which Udo then realized he was back on the beach watching with the Lord as the UFO arced high and fast away across the blue.

Zombie Mike saw the fleeing UFO as well and raised two bony middle fingers, one on each hand, toward it and growled. The Lord and Udo watched him and had to share a little laughter.

"What's that about?" Udo asked.

"His master is leaving without him. Isn't that right, Mike?" The zombie turned quickly to look at Jesus. "Maybe it's time for a new master. Huh?" Jesus held his hand out toward Mike.

The almost permanent scowl on the zombie's face melted into a dumbfounded, wide-eyed stare. "It's okay, Mike. I know who you are. I know what you've done. But you know what? I still love you."

The zombie scuttled over faster than one might have thought possible and wrapped the Lord's legs up tight in a big hug. "There, there. It's okay, my boy. Come on. Let's blow this Popsicle stand. Udo, would you be so kind as to carry our new friend and brother here? I do believe he's decided to come with us."

Udo did just that, once Mike had finished holding onto the Lord's legs. Together then the three started off along the beach as Jesus summed it all up. "Let's go home, boys. Let's go home."

CHAPTER XXX

TURN TURN TURN

"I now pronounce you man and wife. You may kiss the bride," the priest finished with and gently closed the Bible before laying it in his lap. Of course it was more for show than anything, the good book. The vows he had scribbled on the inside cover. But otherwise, he had the ceremony memorized. All the kids on base would use him for their marriages, especially before when he'd been stationed at North Island in San Diego.

But even though he'd done so many before, he couldn't help letting a couple tears fall. He was quite partial to John and Janet after all. They'd only saved his life. He'd even thought they were angels that day when they'd come, the way John had come storming into the chapel and laying waste to those monsters eating on his legs. He was barely conscious at the time of course, but somehow with the arrival of help he had come to just a little more, although even then he saw John as not a man with a rifle but as the archangel Michael with a sword of the Lord, an angel who then took him down from the tree of pain and flew him to safety.

Then it was Janet's turn to be an angel, giving him constant and lifesaving care on the helicopter flight and then here on the island too. He was in and out then, but later he could tell she was a very good doctor, so good in fact that later when she'd amputated his legs it had all went quite well, thanks to the many blessings of this wonderful island the Lord had prepared for them.

That was his theory at least. How else could you explain it all: a secret community and accompanying facilities that apparently had been set up here for some sort of government survival program complete with a medical surgical area inside a sort of mini-hospital?

That had been particularly helpful in his case, of course. But then everything else they needed was here too, just waiting for them. There were fruit trees of all varieties and a green house complex with complete instructions on how to start a survival farm. That lovely couple Derrick and Rebecca were taking that responsibility on, while Kellen the cowgirl, as he affectionately thought of her, and that beautiful horse of her's called Shadow were rounding up the wild cattle on the big island. That's right. Cattle! If that wasn't God . . .

"Father? We've got a half hour while they set up for the reception. Can I take you anywhere?" Ivy asked their spiritual leader, coming up behind his wheelchair.

"Oh . . . no, my dear. You run along. Maybe if someone could just come back when the reception starts. I'm fine right here." With just a quick turn of the government issued wheelchair, the priest was now facing out back along the seaward portion of the small pier the wedding arch had been built across. The ceremony had taken place on the beautiful little beach the pier ran up onto. "I'll just enjoy this lovely view."

"Ahh, but look. The children. Hey," Ivy called out at the kids to come in. Joannie and Aaron were frolicking about in the surf, happy as can be.

The priest quickly held up a hand. "No, no, my dear. Nothing brings me greater pleasure than to watch them. Children are such a blessing. It is so wonderful that they are here."

Ivy agreed, sort of, and sat down nearby on the edge of the little pier. "Father, there's something I want to ask you about. If I could."

"Of course, my child. Although if we need the confidence of my offices or the confessional . . ."

"Oh no, Father. It's not that big a deal."

"Well, all right then," the priest answered, but the topic then brought to mind also the wonderful little church the island had come with, and a captive audience, for certain, all twelve of them. Hmmm, the priest thought then too. Twelve. That's an interesting number. There were exactly twelve of them on the island.

Ivy started talking then, wondering about the whole thing with her husband maybe being that strange, statue being they'd seen near the end there, and she just wanted to ask if he thought God could do something like that, sending him back down here to help them like that.

You never know. The Lord works in mysterious ways, he told her. Just look how things had worked out so perfectly for them, he told her too, and they shared a smile over that.

Not far up the beach, Jason and Griner were fishing and smiling too. It was joyously unbelievable how the fish almost seemed to be fighting to get on their hooks. And it was always like this, which was why even though they only had a short break before the reception, they'd run out to get some fresh fish to fry up later.

Which also too was why Justin had hurried out when he saw the killer set coming in right after the 'I do's.' After all, since he'd found the bitchin' twin fin short board that almost magically had washed up on shore the other morning, he wasn't missing out.

And how appropriate that caught in the leash was a gnawed off lower leg of some poor surfer dude, which otherwise would have been gross and scary, but after what they'd all been through everyone just laughed. They all laughed and laughed at that one.

Then, even better, they'd all decided later to have a ceremonial burial of the leg and made it like a memorial to all the people who'd been killed in the zombie apocalypse. The priest had made a really good speech about it too, and nobody was laughing then, that was for sure. Justin really liked the priest, and though he never thought he'd ever say something like this, he was even getting into all the Jesus and God stuff too. *Like check out this six foot glassy tube coming in. If that wasn't a God thing . . .*

Universal Laboratories had opened up a new room, or perhaps more accurately a new alcove alfresco situated on possibly the same exquisitely carved, all marble patio and parapet, overlooking the same beautiful and lushly vegetated valley below. The valley too was still filled with the same also marble structures of varying size and shape, dwellings, buildings and even amphitheaters, and all of them still connected by pristine walkways and adorned by all manner of gorgeous flower, bush and tree. And yes, the perfect inhabitants there were once again flying around at will.

Jesus was there again too, in the alcove alfresco, dressed the same as he had been before, in the lab coat over dress slacks and shoes. This time, however, his decon suited father was nowhere to be found.

Which was just as well, as he appeared rather busy at the moment, working at a lab table that butted right up to the overlooking parapet's railing, not only to allow Him a great view of the heavenly area below, but also to allow the butterfly he'd just created and freed from one of the test tubes filled with colored light fly into it all directly and easily. The test tubes, as they had been before, were stored on chromium racks arrayed in a seemingly endless cue stretching back into the likewise seemingly endless darkness making up the rest of the room behind Him.

Having watched the butterfly go, a serene smile lighted the Lord's bearded face, lifting up to the immaculately trimmed edges of his facial hair. Then, back to business, he discarded the now empty tube and took up another one. This he did entirely with his left hand while simultaneously with his right he lifted an eyedropper fitted to a narrow mouthed flask of indeterminable size resting on the lab table's black and highly polished top.

It was impossible to tell the exact size of the flask because like the test tubes, it too was filled with light, but an uncolored and extremely bright luminescence, like the emission of a flash bulb but captured and contained. This light, that was so bright as to be squint inducing when looked upon in the amount stored inside the flask, could, however, be comfortably gazed upon when in the miniscule amount housed by the eyedropper. In fact, the single drop dispensed twinkled like a bit of stardust as it fell into the brightly colored tube, and then the immediate transformation took place as either a butterfly emerged with likewise multi-colored wings, or after a small localized explosion, a puff of black smoke wafted up and out.

With the creation of a butterfly, as just witnessed, Jesus watched it make its way down into the valley below. If a small explosion and puff of smoke resulted, he frowned. Either way it was then on to the next one, and as mentioned, there were a lot of tubes to get to.

Suddenly interrupting, a melodic and soothingly muted ringtone bled through the ambient, new age mood music that had been filling the air. The sound's obvious source, a sleek and modern, blue lighted telephone, mechanically erupted up through the lab table. The young man used a momentarily free hand to depress a button on the phone's body.

"Dad. I gotta put ya on speaker. I'm really busy here," Jesus spoke down to the phone.

"I would have come by, but that damn suit. And we've been busy here too. You understand, right?"

"Oh sure. No worries." While he spoke, Jesus continued his work: butterfly, puff of smoke, puff of smoke, puff of smoke.

"Well. We do need to talk, son. Or maybe I should say, I think we need to clear the air about a few things . . . about your recently concluded operation."

"Oh. Yeah . . . yeah. Whatta ya think? Have ya heard? It worked! He's gone. Gone baby gone!"

"Well. That's one of the things I feel we need to clear up. You got so secretive on this one. And, of course, I was too busy with this Multiverse project, as mentioned, to keep tabs on you. Talk about intense stuff! But now my advisors tell me even they got lost trying to keep up with you on this one! You kept it all so hush hush."

"Well, I had to, Dad. You know how powerful he is. He's got ears and eyes everywhere. And I couldn't let him just have those kids! But he probably wouldn't have left without them, which was the point of the whole thing. So I myself, personally, got those kids the heck outta there. All the while too sneaking in a couple clones."

"Clones? Did tech approve that?"

"I didn't have time for the normal channels. And I couldn't risk it, Dad. Like I'm saying. Besides, it worked like a charm. You should see how happy those kids are in their new home. All of the survivors are."

"And our good friend Lucifer has no idea."

"Apparently not. He took the clones right in and then blasted off right on schedule."

"Which is another thing, son. I can't believe you're just going to let him get away!"

Jesus let another butterfly go, discarded the tube, and then turned to a large monitor suddenly visible in the far corner of the room. The smile filling his face now had taken a slightly sinister turn. "You forget, Father, is it not written, vengeance is mine?"

"Oh no you didn't . . ."

With a wave of his hand the Lord seemed to somehow turn on the monitor, which then filled with an image of deep space. There, streaking through the middle of it all went the soul ship, its egg shape stretched into more of an elongated oval. "You gettin' this?" He added up into the air.

"You know I am, son. I'm always 'gettin' everything."

"Watch then. This one's for you, Dad. And for all those poor souls we ever lost to . . . him. It goes like this." A cold steel quality had come to the Lord's words. At the same time he pointed the index finger of his right hand shaped like a little pistol now at the monitor. He let the imaginary hammer his thumb had become fall.

The soul ship suddenly just winked out in the image, but then the diamond of light it had become just as suddenly exploded and filled the screen completely with icy white energy. In response, whatever mechanism was filming the image must have quickly and with quite a range zoomed very far out, very quickly.

From there, the energy could now be seen to be contained in an orb the size of a small planet. The orb slowly but surely started condensing in on itself, causing it to darken in color, first to a shade of gray, then a muted purple and finally a glossy black. Strangest of all, the space that the big ball of light had once occupied now had become a huge, round field of jet black nothingness.

"I suppose that ought to hold him for a while," God said over the phone, cold and quiet.

"Yeah. Like forever. Gotchya!" Jesus pumped a fist at the image on the monitor just before it winked out too.

"And I can see you ran the numbers. Couldn't have picked a better place for a new black hole myself. But how?"

"In the clones. I hid Omega devices in each of the children clones. Wrapped of course in initializing delay emulsion. Just the right amount." Jesus then picked up a tall, cool drink suddenly somehow there on the lab table's top. He took a generous sip.

"I'm thinking of something, son," God on the other end of the speakerphone now said, sounding suddenly thoughtful. "I'm thinking I'm starting to see the genius of your plan now. And omigosh! Just like a chip off the old block!"

Jesus nearly choked on his latest gulp of the tall cool drink, then coughed up a long peel of laughter. The voice from above then continued.

"So, as I recall the last time we spoke on this subject, which, interestingly enough was *seven* days ago. The problem we were trying to address involved the disappointing return we were getting in the category of saved souls."

"Uh huh . . ."

"To wit, it appears you have theorized that the best way to turn those numbers around would be to get rid of the great corrupter, him who now rests, undoubtedly not very peacefully, in the center of a black hole."

"That pretty much was the plan. But I suppose we'll just have to wait and see what the results will be. The new humans—and they will be new without him around to hurt and stunt them—will no doubt thrive on this island I have made for them. And, in several thousand years they also may very well fill up the whole world again and prosper mightily. They will be happy and strong and good. And this time too without him around to lead them away from us . . . the results now, I think, will be drastically different."

"Only time will tell."

"Yes, only time will tell."

"All of that for this."

"It was the only way. They left us no choice."

"And no change in our numbers with this batch just retrieved, I suppose."

"Even worse. We'll be lucky to get ten percent."

"Oh dear, let us pray for better with the next batch."

"Yes. Let us pray."

"Oh, and one other thing, son. A zombie? Really!"

"You should see him now. You know I came for sinners, Dad. Because when they flip, oh glory! Glory, glory, glory!"

Jesus sang and danced then, round and round while a whole host of angels joined him, many of them playing musical instruments very beautifully.

The voice of God was speechless for a moment while on the other end of the phone line, He shook his formless head. Finally, His words filtered down into the alcove alfresco once again but were unheard by the revelers there. "That's my boy," He said quietly and with love. "That's my boy."

Jesus and the angels danced and sang, danced and sang.

###

ABOUT THE AUTHOR

M. Frederic Jennings is on a mission from God. Literally. Supernaturally, the Holy Spirit came crashing into his bedroom one morning as he lay in bed after working his night shift as a nurse at a nearby hospital.

Mark was not a Christian at the time and had only tuned his bedside clock radio to a station playing old-time church music for help getting to sleep. The only problem was, after playing only a song or two, the station next featured a Bible reading segment. While under, "The hearing of the word," as the good book so succinctly puts it, the other worldly visitation by God's spiritual essence took place.

Slowly but surely over the next few years he not only figured out what had happened to him, but also began processing and documenting the incredibly vivid and strange, yet hopefully also meaningful and entertaining visions, characters and story ideas that have come to fill the half dozen or so manuscripts he has completed in that same span of time.

"The Lord will take you into realms others cannot and dare not go," were words of prophecy spoken over Mark in a home Bible study group dedicated to the development of the spiritual gifts. In his latest work, "And the Dead Shall Rise," a Christian zombie apocalypse tale, the new and fresh voiced horror novelist does just that.

Care to come along?

SPECIAL OFFERS

T•SHIRTS, POSTERS, MUGS

Write andthedeadshallrise@donnaink.com to get on M. Frederic Jennings email list for future T-Shirt, Poster, Mugs and "other" merchandise offers. Don't forget to visit his social media:

Facebook: https://www.facebook.com/AuthorM.FredericJennings

LinkedIn: www.linkedin.com/pub/mark-jennings/65/485/5a

Twitter: http://www.twitter.com/AuthorMJennings

WordPress Blog: https://mfredericjennings.wordpress.com

Donnalnk Publications, L.L.C.

Publisher
www.donnaink.com

For bulk orders, special orders, etc.

Special Markets Division
dpInk: Donnalnk Publications, L.L.C.
129 Daisy Hill Road
Carthage, North Carolina 28327
Email: special_markets@donnaink.com

For Promotions:
Promotions Division
dpInk: Donnalnk Publications, L.L.C.
129 Daisy Hill Road
Carthage, North Carolina 28327
Email: promotions@donnaink.com

ZENCON ART OF
ZEN CONSULTANCY

PR & Marketing